Love WITHOUT INFLUENCE

THE BOUVIER FAMILY SAGA

book 2

JADE DOLLSTON

This is a spicy, second-chance romance that is intended for ages 18+. If you don't like steamy love scenes, humor, and a bossy alpha male with a heart of gold, then this book is probably not for you.

⚠**TW: Some scenes of violence, recounting of domestic abuse incident, miscarriage**

CONTENTS

ABOUT LOVE WITHOUT INFLUENCE

Influence (noun): A power affecting a person, thing, or course of events.

Monty

Boy meets Girl.

Boy experiences severe intestinal distress and runs away.

Boy returns and falls in love with Girl despite his... difficulties.

Then Boy's entire world explodes, shattered by outside influences that would have broken a weaker man.

But not me. I took all the pain... the hurt... the betrayal... and became stronger. Harder. My heart is an inanimate stone in my chest now, and that's exactly how I prefer it.

When I'm called back to New York due to circumstances out of my control, I run into her. My only love.

Kassie Ramirez.

But I can't have her, and she wouldn't want me anyway.

I'm not the nice, sensitive boy she once knew. I'm a complicated man with dark needs, the kind sweet Kassie would never accept.

Kassie

Bend so you won't break.

That was my motto for years, and it served me well. It helped me survive when one man broke my heart and another tried to break my spirit. But not anymore.

Now I bend for no one.

Then Monty Bouvier returned.

If he thinks he can waltz back into my life like nothing ever happened, he's got another thing coming.

I'm no longer the shy little "Kasserole" he knew back then.

But when our past hurts are brought to light, we discover that our lives were manipulated by those around us all those years ago.

And I'm prepared to tell all those "influences" to go straight to hell.

PART ONE

THE PAST

CHAPTER 1

"DAMN, I'M HUNGRY," I said, driving through the streets of Queens, New York on a warm June night.

"Pizza?" my friend Joe asked from the front passenger's seat.

I lifted one finger from the steering wheel and pointed at a small Indian diner up ahead on the right. "What about that place?"

"Sounds good. And there's a parking place right in front."

"Must be fate," I said, whipping my silver BMW into the open spot.

As we entered the warm restaurant, the aromas of toasted herbs, coconut, and curry layered and combined as they reached my nose.

"Smells good," Joe murmured as a short Indian girl about our age greeted us at the hostess podium with a smile. "A booth for two, please."

"Right this way," she said, leading us to a booth near the front window. "Kassie will be right with you."

My eyes scanned down the menu. "Everything looks good. Football makes me hungry."

"You played a good game tonight. Two touchdowns and over two hundred yards rushing? You're a fucking beast."

My head snapped up as a sweet voice said, "What can I get the beast and his friend to drink?"

The waitress was standing beside our table in a red dress with a white collar and a frilly white apron. She was a stunner, and my tongue turned into a frozen rock.

"Uhhhhh."

"We'll each have a Coke, please," Joe said, eyeing me with a knowing smirk.

"Coming right up. My name is Kassie, by the way. Let me know if you have any questions about the menu."

"Uh-hunhhh," I hummed like an idiot.

"Well aren't you just the smitten kitten," Joe commented when Kassie departed toward the drink machine behind the counter.

"She's beautiful," I sighed, finally finding my words as my gaze stayed trained on her slender back.

Kassie... I liked that name.

"You should ask her out."

"You think?" Her dark hair was pulled back into a long, low ponytail that swished around her shoulders as she moved.

"Why not?"

"Shh, she's coming back," I hissed.

Kassie approached the table, her big brown eyes flitting from Joe to me. They held me locked in place. Her eyelashes were black and so long they almost touched her eyebrows.

"Here we go. Your drinks and some naan you can snack on." The basket holding the Indian bread was red with a green and white napkin lining it. It smelled warm and fragrant, and my stomach let out a loud bellow.

"Sorry," I said with a nervous laugh, pressing a hand over my belly. "Guess I'm really hungry."

She smiled sweetly, her gaze still on me. "Have you had a chance to look over the menu, or would you like suggestions?" Her voice was a soft, lilting sound that was like music to my ears.

"I'd love for you to suggest something," I told her.

"Well, if you like a milder curry, get the malai kofta. If you like some spice, try the biryani. It's my very favorite, but only order it if you're really brave."

Then she winked at me. *Friggin' winked!*

She was so cute, it made me want to get the spicy dish. The only problem? I didn't exactly like super spicy foods.

Joe spoke up first. "I'll have the malai kofta. I've had that before and liked it."

"Excellent," she said. "And you, sir?"

Kassie was looking expectantly at me, and I scratched the back of my neck. "Exactly how spicy is the, um, bury-whatever?"

She giggled. "The biryani? It's really hot. The Ganjams are a southern Indian family, and their food tends to have more heat than northern Indians."

Great.

"I think you should go for it," Joe added. "Unless you're a pussy."

This asshole...

"The biryani sounds great," I said, closing the menu and handing it to the pretty girl beside our table. Seriously, how bad could it be?

The answer to that question turned out to be *really fucking bad.*

When Kassie brought our food, I took a big whiff of my dish. It was aromatic and smelled delicious. It also singed my nose hairs.

"Go ahead and try a bite. If you don't like it, I can bring you something else."

I scooped some rice and a piece of chicken onto my fork and stuck it in my mouth. The flavor was absolutely fantastic.

After chewing and swallowing, I gave her a big grin. "That's one of the best things I've ever eaten. Thank you for suggesting it."

Kassie beamed, her teeth scraping against her bottom lip, and I had the urge to pull her into the booth beside me and learn every single thing about her.

"I'm so glad you like it. I'll bring you some water in case you need it. The more you eat, the spicier it gets. Eating some naan helps too."

As she walked off, I stuck another bite into my mouth, proud that I'd handled the heat with no problem. Shrugging at Joe, I said, "It's actually not that ba-a-a-a-aaaah." My tongue was suddenly on fire, and I snatched a couple napkins from the holder on the table so swiftly it slid across the table.

I spit the bite of hell chicken into one and swiped at my tongue with the other. "Holy fucking shit," I croaked, slamming my glass against my lips and sucking like my life depended on it.

The cool drink came to an end way too soon, and I grabbed Joe's soda and drained it too.

His shoulders shook, and he finally let out a snorting laugh. "You all right, dude?"

"No, you shithead," I croaked. "I've just eaten Satan's actual flesh, and I am *not fucking okay.*"

He stuck a bite of his dish—which didn't look like it could strip paint off a car—into his stupid, smiling mouth and chewed. "You shoulda gotten this. It's delicious."

"You goaded me, implied I was a pussy in front of Kassie. I couldn't *not* get it."

He shrugged, shoveling more of the food into his mouth. The surface of my tongue had diminished to a low sizzle by the time our pretty waitress returned with our glasses of water.

"Oh," she said, her eyes taking in our empty Cokes, "you guys must have been thirsty."

"We had a football game tonight," I replied. "Must be dehydrated."

"I really like football," she said, her eyes dipping to the dish in front of me.

Fuck! I should probably take another bite since she's standing right here.

Gripping my fork like it was Lucifer's pitchfork, I gathered another bite and ate it. And she smiled at me. I pushed upward with my cheeks, attempting some semblance of a return smile even as the inside of my mouth erupted into a raging inferno. "Mmmm," I hummed, hoping it didn't sound as miserable as it felt.

I forced the food down my throat, and it left a trail of burned flesh down my esophagus and into my stomach. *This is how ulcers are formed. I'll probably require medication for the rest of my life to treat this.*

"I'm so glad you like it. I'll go refill your Cokes." She departed, and I resisted the urge to pour my glass of water directly over my head to relieve what felt like a flu-like fever. Instead, I gulped down the contents in less than two seconds.

"Damn, dude, you sucked that down like a hooker on dollar night."

"Fuck you," I rasped, convinced my vocal cords were now permanently damaged. Pulling another napkin from the container, I forked a large portion of the biryani into it before wadding it into a ball.

Joe smirked at me over his dish of perfectly normal food. "What are you going to do with that?"

In answer, I stuffed the napkin down the front of my sweatpants. "I'll hide it and pretend like I ate it."

"Be careful. Don't want to burn your dick off."

My eyes practically popped out of my head as I yanked the wad from my pants and stuffed it beneath my leg.

"Does my tongue look weird? It feels weird." I stuck it out, and Joe leaned forward to inspect it.

"Ouch, dude. It looks like you have a blister."

"A blister?" I hissed, crossing my eyes to try and see my own tongue.

"Dude, cut it out. You look like an idiot, and your girl is coming this way."

Snagging an ice cube from my glass, I placed it on my tongue in an attempt to relieve the pain. It melted and then fucking evaporated. I guessed that's what happened when the sun resided inside a person's mouth.

"Here ya go," Kassie said, dropping off our drinks and peering into the red basket. "Would you like some more naan?"

Yes! I'd forgotten about the bread. The *non-freaking-spicy* bread.

"That would be super. I'll just get this last piece out of your way." Removing it from the basket, I stuffed half of it inside my mouth. It soothed the flames to a dull roar.

Kassie took the basket away, and as soon as her back was turned, I dipped the other half of the naan into Joe's water glass.

"What the hell, man?" he asked as I laid the sopping bread against my tongue. It served as a kind of bandage, and I closed my eyes in relief.

For the next few minutes, I hid chunks of the savory meat in paper napkins and shoved them beneath my legs. I had just lifted my fork to dispose of another forkful when Kassie looked my way, so I did the only thing I could do and stuck the huge bite inside my reluctant mouth.

I forced a smile at the pretty girl even as sweat beaded on my forehead and upper lip. "Fuck, that's hot," I whined quietly as I swallowed, and the internal inferno process began all over again.

"You're not looking so good, bro," Joe commented, and I shot him a miserable glare.

"Just ask for our ticket when she comes back," I croaked as that last bite made its fiery way through my digestive tract.

Kassie returned with the bread a few minutes later, and thankfully Joe did as I asked.

"Of course, I'll be right back with that."

As she turned away, I stuffed an entire chunk of naan into my mouth, my cheeks puffing out as I chewed. But then she turned back and directed her next question to me.

"Do you want your ticket together or separate?"

Joe's ass remained silent, so I mumbled, "Peparate, peese."

She giggled, and a thrill shot up my spine.

Or maybe that was the paralysis setting in.

"I'll bring you a to-go box for the rest of your food," she said before heading back to the counter.

Joe read the panic on my face and dropped his head back, laughing like a hyena.

"Oo're an ash-hole," I said around my mouthful of bread.

The object of my fascination returned with the checks, a small white box, and—thank fuck—a bag. We handed over our cards, and when she went to run them, I scraped the remnants of my meal into the box before stuffing it and the hidden napkins full of biryani inside the bag.

When she brought our cards back, I scrawled my signature and left Kassie a twenty dollar tip before pushing from the booth with the bag in my left hand.

"Thank you, guys, for coming in tonight," she said. "I hope you enjoyed everything."

"It was great," I lied. "Hey, um, Kassie? I was wondering if you wanted to go out some time."

She tilted her head and smiled sweetly. "Oh, that's really nice, but I don't think so."

Well shit. And I meant that literally because things were beginning to occur below my waist. Things that weren't going to be pretty.

"Um, okay, maybe I'll see you around," I babbled, my words tripping over each other in my haste. "Gotta go now."

I didn't even have time to dwell on the blatant rejection as I hustled my friend out the door.

"Sorry about the crash and burn, man. She just shot you down."

I tossed him my keys before cramming the to-go bag in the nearest trash can. "You drive. Fast."

"Uh-oh," he said, climbing into the driver's seat and cranking the car as I got in the other side. "You feeling some movement?"

"I'm feeling a damn tsunami," I grunted. "Hurry!"

As soon as we arrived at Joe's house, I pinched my butt cheeks together, calling out, "Hey, Mrs. Carson," while I scooted toward the bathroom inside my friend's room.

The meal from hell was attempting to make an immediate exit from my body, and I barely made it to the toilet in time.

I emerged fifteen minutes later with a slight limp and fell facedown onto Joe's bed.

"Have your dad send my dad the plumbing bill," I moaned into the blue-and-green-plaid comforter.

"Dude, couldn't you have lit a candle or something?"

I twisted my head to find him waving a hand in front of his scrunched-up nose.

"If I light a candle, I'm afraid your entire house will blow up," I said wryly. "Can you see if your mom has some Pepto or Mylanta? Maybe a cyanide pill?"

He patted my shoulder with a sympathetic chuckle before leaving the room. Returning a few minutes later, he handed me a small cup of thick, pink liquid, and I rolled onto my back to drink it down.

"Sorry you went through all that for nothing. I can't believe she said no, but there are tons of girls at our school who would love to go out with you."

"Oh, I'm not giving up," I informed him. "I'll go back next week."

Joe's eyebrows lifted in incredulity. "Dude, you're either entirely smitten or insane."

I threw my forearm over my forehead and stared at the ceiling with a smile on my face. "I guess we'll see which one."

Chapter 2

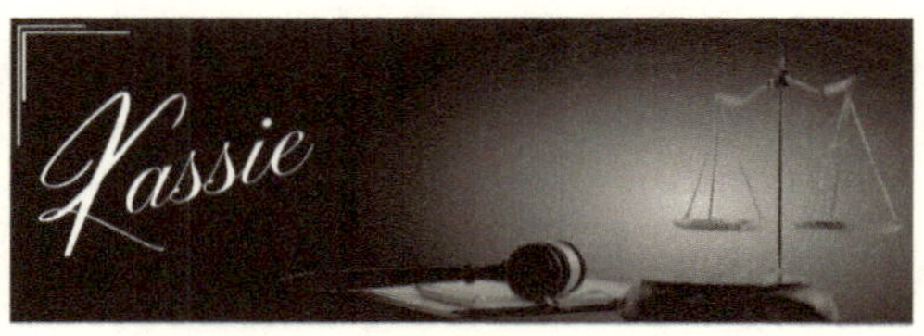

"Those dudes were really hot," Lily said as soon as they left. "I think the tall one liked you."

"He asked me out," I said as I wiped off the counter.

"Seriously?" my friend squealed. "When are you going?"

I shrugged and rolled my eyes in her direction. "I said no."

"Kassiiiiie," she whined.

"You know my parents won't let me date until I'm sixteen."

"Haven't you ever heard of sneaking around?" she whispered, looking around for her snoopy mother. "Be a rebel, Kass!"

"Says the girl who can't stand the sight of blood but is going to be a doctor because that's what her parents want."

"Ouch, you wench. You know I'm working on them." She poured herself a cup of tea. "Hey, I have an idea. Can you go grab a knife and cut yourself, so I'll pass out? Maybe I'll get a concussion and prove to my parents that this med school thing isn't going to work out."

"Lily, no!"

"Come on. I'm not saying you have to sever an artery or anything. Just a nick would be fine. No more than a pint."

I tossed the rag on the bar and wrapped an arm around my best friend. "I'll support your dreams in any way possible... short of drawing blood and giving you brain damage. Keep trying to talk to them so we can go to law school together."

"New customers coming in, ladies," Mrs. Ganjam said as she bustled by. "Less talking and more working."

"Yes, Mama," Lily said, tossing me a wink over her shoulder as she went to greet the newcomers.

"He's baa-ack," Lily sang the next Saturday, breezing into the storeroom where I was doing inventory during a lull.

"Who?" I asked.

"Big tip guy. I just sat him down at the same booth. Go, and I'll handle the other tables."

The handsome guy is here? An unconscious thrill ran down my spine as she yanked me by the arm and shoved me out the door.

"You're awfully strong for a munchkin."

"Don't be a height-ist, you giant."

I laughed as I stopped at the sink to wash my hands. "I'm five-three; that hardly makes me a giant."

"Still four inches taller than me. Would you hurry up?"

"Is he in a rush or something?"

"No, I just want to see what happens." She clapped her hands twice and barked, "Chop, chop! The customer is waiting!"

"You sound like your mom," I muttered as I straightened my apron and adjusted my ponytail. Why was I so anxious? He was just another customer, right?

Okay, a very attractive customer, the exact kind of guy that turned my head. Broad shouldered. Tall. Dark hair.

And those blue eyes? Whewww! Don't even get me started on those puppies.

"Hi, can I get you something to drink?"

The boy whose name I didn't even know looked up at me, and *good grief! Has he gotten hotter since last week?*

"I'll have a Coke please."

"Sure. Is this your first time dining here?" I don't know why I asked that, but I instantly regretted it when the flare in his eyes died out a little. Letting out a little laugh, I playfully tapped his shoulder—which was as hard as a boulder, I might add—and said, "I'm kidding. You were here last week, right?"

His full lips turned up. "Yeah. You're Kassie, right?"

Like a doofus, I tapped my nametag with the end of my pen. "That's what they tell me." *Oh god, shut the hell up, Kass.* "I'll be right back with your drink."

I pivoted away and fast-walked to the soda machine, taking a few deep breaths to calm my mind so I didn't say anything else stupid. When I brought the drink and a basket of naan to him, his eyes followed me all the way across the room.

"Here you go. Would you like the same thing as last time?"

"No!" he practically shouted, and I bit back a grin. He didn't think I'd noticed the redness rising up his neck or the sweat on his face when he was eating the biryani last week, but I did. I had to give him bonus points for eating it though.

The guy ran a hand over his hair, freshly damp from a shower, by the clean scent of soap and shampoo. "Actually, I wanted to try that dish my friend got last time. Mal—uhhh, something."

"Malai kofta?"

He snapped and pointed at me. "Yes, that. He said it was excellent."

Should I mess with him a little bit?

Why, yes. Yes, I think I should.

"Now, that dish isn't as spicy as the one you had, and I know how you like spice. Should I have the chef add some chilis to it?"

My lips pressed together when raw panic filled his eyes. "No, that's okay. I, um, want to try something different this time."

"Okay, if you're sure."

"I am."

When I brought the food to him, I lingered by the table, watching as he took a tentative bite. The relief on his face was evident as he chewed the mild, fragrant chicken.

"Mmm, this is really good," he said, shoveling another bite into his mouth.

"I'm glad you like it. Can I get you anything else?"

He dipped his chin slightly, and his smile was charmingly boyish. "You can sit and keep me company for a minute."

My fingertips fidgeted with the ruffle on my apron as I glanced over my shoulder. "Okay. Mrs. Ganjam isn't here today, so I won't get the look of doom for sitting down."

The guy laughed, and I scooted into the booth across from him, my feet silently thanking him for the break. He picked up a piece of naan and nibbled on the edge of it. "Do you go to school in Queens?"

"Yes, I'm a junior. How about you?"

"I'm a junior too. I attend a private school in Manhattan."

I should have guessed. His brand name watch looked like it cost more than my entire wardrobe. "So you play football, huh?" My mind's eye pictured him in those tight pants, and I had to look away for a few seconds.

"Yes, I'm in a summer league, but I play on my school's team too."

"Do you play any other sports?

"No, I played baseball my freshman year, but I quickly learned I like being a spectator more than a player."

"Which pro baseball team do you like? The Mets or the Yankees?"

"Neither. I like the Cougars."

My mouth dropped open in shock. "From Philly? I'm going to need to revoke your New Yorker card immediately, sir."

He laughed, and I liked the sound. It was deep and as warm as sun-drenched honey. "My dad has always loved the Cougs, and he took me and my siblings to games several times a year."

"How many siblings do you have?"

"Two, a brother and a sister. They're both older than me."

"Ah, the baby of the family."

He chuckled and took another bite. "I am, and they never let me forget it. How about you?"

"I have an older brother who's in the military, so I don't get to see him much anymore. Then I have two little sisters."

His gaze was intent on mine, giving me a hundred percent of his attention as he absently ate his food. "What are their names?"

"My brother is Gavin, and the girls are Luciana and Regina. Luci just turned seven, and Regi is nine and a half."

"Can't forget the half," he commented with a grin that showed perfectly straight white teeth.

"God forbid. What about your brother and sister?"

"My sister's name is Evelyn, but she hates it. Goes by Evie. She's exactly a year older than me, and our brother, Auburn, is six years older than me."

"You and your sister share a birthday?"

He nodded and took a sip of his Coke. "Yep. March twentieth."

"This may be an awkward question since I know your birthday and your siblings' names, but, um, what's *your* name?"

His fork clattered to the plate as his mouth dropped open. Then he squinched his eyes shut and shook his head, muttering, "Shit, I'm such a nimrod." *And totally adorable.* Opening his eyes, he held a hand out, and I let it engulf my smaller one. "I'm Monty Bouvier."

"Kassie Ramirez." Our hands held for longer than strictly necessary, and I can't say I didn't like the feel of his warm palm pressed against mine.

"No wonder you didn't want to go out with me," he said, finally pulling his arm back and letting his fingers drift slowly over mine. "I promise

I usually have better manners. I guess I got distracted because you're so pretty."

The shy dip of his head told me that wasn't a pickup line, and my tongue felt like sludge as his blue eyes twinkled at me. "I-I guess names are pretty important," I stammered, wondering why my hand was tingling.

"You know what else is important?" His voice was low and sexy as hell.

"What?" I breathed.

"Cookies."

A giggle escaped my mouth because that's not at all what I expected him to say. "Cookies?"

"Uh-huh. What's your favorite kind of cookie?"

"Nutter Butters," I said instantly, and he nodded as if that was the right answer.

"Solid choice. You like the wafer ones or the ones shaped like peanuts?"

I blinked. "I guess I've never had the wafer ones."

Monty smacked his palm against the table. "Seriously, Kass? They're fantastic and have a higher peanut-butter-to-cookie ratio."

"I'll look into it," I said, pulling his glass toward me. "Let me go refill your drink."

My heart sank as I walked to the back of the restaurant. Monty was a really nice guy, but I'd recognized his last name immediately. The Bouviers ran a fashion company and were one of the wealthiest families in New York.

There's no way he'd be interested in a poor Latina girl from Queens.

CHAPTER 3

TURNS OUT, I WAS wrong about Monty Bouvier not being interested in me. He showed up at the restaurant the next weekend too.

"I brought you something," he said as soon as I walked to his table with a tall glass of Coca Cola.

"Y-you brought me something?"

He held up a grocery store bag, letting it swing back and forth from his fingers. "I wrapped it myself."

"Aren't you talented?" I teased, taking the sack and peering inside to find a package of Nutter Butters—the wafer kind. "Aww, thank you, Monty. That was really thoughtful of you."

"You can try one now, if you won't get in trouble," he whispered conspiratorially, and I looked over my shoulder.

"Okay, Mrs. Ganjam is in the back."

He opened the red bag and slid the clear tray out to reveal the cookies stacked in neat squares. I broke one off and met his eyes as I bit through the crispy wafer and into the creamy, peanut buttery center.

I couldn't hold in my soft groan as I chewed. "You're right. That's the perfect amount of peanut butter."

His face beamed. "I thought you'd like them, and I should know, since I've known you for two whole weeks. I'm pretty much an expert on you."

"And we know each other's names now. We're practically best friends," I said with a laugh, snapping off another square and biting into it. "You want one?"

"No, these are for you."

"Seriously, I want you to, or else I'll eat the entire package, and my butt will no longer fit in this borough."

His eyes roved up and down my body, but it felt more appreciative than skeevy. "You don't have to worry about that. I think you look perfect."

I was pretty sure I was blushing from my head to my toes. "Thanks, Monty."

As June turned to July, Monty came into the restaurant every weekend, sometimes on Friday nights and sometimes on Saturday. One weekend, he came in both nights.

I began to look forward to seeing him, talking to him, making him smile. So, when I was closing out the register one balmy Saturday night, disappointment coursed through me. Monty hadn't come in last night, and I fully expected to see him tonight.

But he hadn't showed.

I hadn't realized how dependent I'd become on our weekly visits, but I was feeling uncharacteristically gloomy this evening. I missed him.

"You're being stupid," I muttered to myself as I placed the deposit in the money bag for Mrs. Ganjam to place in the safe. "He's not your boyfriend, Kass. He doesn't owe you anything."

"Talking to yourself is the first sign," Lily said, bumping me with her hip as she moved past me.

"The first sign of what?"

"Old age. Next thing you know, you'll be complaining about all those pesky kids and their loud music."

"You make me sound like a *Scooby Doo* villain," I retorted, looking up as the bell over the door rang. My sad little heart swelled with happiness when Monty rushed in, looking disheveled in his athletic shorts and a grimy white T-shirt.

"Hey, sorry," he said, slowing his pace as he approached. "Our game went into overtime."

"Did you win?"

His perfectly plump lips turned down at the corners. "No, we lost."

"That sucks." I peeked over my shoulder to see the cooks cleaning the grill. "I'm sorry, but they've already shut down the kitchen."

His eyes held mine, and I was certain that if the world caught fire in that moment, I wouldn't have been able to move my feet a single inch.

"You know I don't come here for the food, right?" His voice was quiet, somehow intimate, despite the people moving around the restaurant in their nightly closing routine.

"Is it the convenient location?" I asked, my voice sounding higher than usual, and he shook his head as his lips twitched.

"Definitely not the location. My game was almost an hour away. I came here to see you, Kass. That's why I come every week."

Oh. My.

I could admit to myself that I was crushing hard on Monty Bouvier, and I can't say I hadn't hoped he was coming here to see me. Since that first time he asked me out weeks ago, he hadn't made any other advances. But what he just said...

Maybe, just maybe, he was crushing on me too.

"Really?" That was all I could manage because air was swishing through my lungs like a hurricane.

He nodded, flashing a shy little half-smile. "Yeah, I know you said you didn't want to go out with me, but I thought maybe if we got to know each other better, you might change your mind." He chewed nervously on his bottom lip. "Does that sound stalkerish?"

"Totally. Am I weird that I like that?"

"Yep. Complete weirdo."

I smiled like a giddy fool. "I can't believe you're stalking some weirdo girl. Don't you have standards?"

"Apparently not because I'd still like to go out with you."

"Kassie, do you have the deposit for me?" Mrs. Ganjam's voice interrupted our moment, and I pulled my eyes away from Monty's to face my boss, who was standing in the doorway to the kitchen. She was tiny, only an inch taller than her daughter, with a round face and dark hair streaked with a few strands of silver.

"I'm all done," I said, handing over the dark-green money bag.

Her curious eyes flitted between me and Monty, and she lifted one perfectly trimmed eyebrow. "Why don't you go ahead and go, Kassie. Lily can help me finish up."

"Yes, ma'am." My gaze returned to Monty, and I jerked a thumb toward the back of the restaurant. "I need to go change."

"I'll wait here for you, if that's okay."

I nodded, trying not to show how happy that made me.

Going into the storeroom, I threw my red dress in the hamper and changed into denim shorts and a watermelon-colored T-shirt. When I walked back out to the small dining room, Monty was laughing at something Lily said to him.

"What's so funny?"

"Lily was just telling me about you arguing with a customer tonight."

My eyes rolled to the top of my head. "The guy who complained about the taxes?" My friend nodded, giggling at the thought. "He seriously thought I single-handedly came up with the tax rate. I told him if he didn't like it, he needed to take it up with the city and state of New York. It's like he's never been to a restaurant before."

"Our Kassie was throwing out facts and numbers left and right. Completely schooled the guy."

I blushed. "It wasn't all that."

"It was too. You gave him a verbal beat down. That's why you're going to be a brilliant lawyer one day."

Giving her a side hug, I said, "Thanks, Lil. I'll see you next week."

Monty held the restaurant door open for me on the way out and walked to a fancy silver sports car, opening the passenger's side door. My feet stalled on the cracked sidewalk.

"Um, I can't get in the car with you, Monty."

His dark eyebrows pressed together for a second. "Oh, because you don't know me well enough. I get that."

"No, it's not that at all. I'm just not allowed to date or ride in the car with a boy until I'm sixteen." I stared down at my scuffed sneakers. "I'm sorry."

I heard the car door slam closed and then saw his Nikes appear directly in front of my feet. "Kass, look at me." My face lifted of its own accord at his soft but demanding tone. "It's okay. I understand."

"You do?"

"Of course. Is that why you said no the first time I asked you out?"

My lips twisted to the side, and I nodded. "I was embarrassed to tell you. My parents are really strict about stuff like that."

The lower half of his face transformed into a grin. "So it wasn't because you didn't like me?"

With my eyes as wide as dinner plates, I shook my head. "Of course not. Why would you think that?"

He shrugged and graced me with that boyish smile of his. "I don't know. I just thought maybe I wasn't your type or something. Or maybe you had a boyfriend already."

"No, no boyfriend."

Monty shifted his weight from one foot to the other. "Your birthday is next month. If I asked you out for then, would you say yes?"

My lips twitched with the need to smile like a loon. "I would."

His gorgeous face literally radiated when he grinned. "Great. Kassie Ramirez, will you go on a date with me on August third?"

He remembered my birthday.

"I'll think about it." His face dropped, and I laughed, pushing lightly against his shoulder. "Kidding. Of course I will."

"You're kind of mean, you know that?"

"That's what my sisters say when I babysit because I won't give them cookies before dinner."

"So cruel to mistreat your sisters like that." He looked around. "Did you drive, or do your parents come and pick you up after work?"

"I walk. I only live about eight blocks away." I gestured in the direction of our house.

"At this time of night?" he asked, eyes widening in apparent outrage.

"It's fine, I promise. If it's raining or snowing, I can call them, or Mrs. Ganjam will drive me home."

Two tiny lines appeared between his eyebrows. "I don't like to think of you walking home alone. Do you care if I walk with you?"

"I don't mind, but it's not necessary. I do it all the time."

"It would make me feel better." He reached down and looped his index finger around mine. "I know you probably don't want to hold hands because we're not dating yet, but is this okay?"

I wanted to yell that it was more than okay, but I uttered a simple yes as we started to walk down the sidewalk toward my house.

"So tell me about your dreams of becoming a lawyer."

"It's what I've wanted to do since third grade. Our class went on a field trip to the courthouse, and I was fascinated by the attorneys and the judge. The arguments. The objections. I could literally see myself doing that one day. What about you? Are you going into the family business?"

Monty smiled down at me. He was so freaking tall. "I want to be one of the fashion designers at our company. I've always been good at drawing, and I loved going to the office with my dad when I was younger. I think he thought I'd be training for an office job, but all I wanted to do was hang out with the designers and watch them work. Now that I'm older, I intern there during the summer."

"That is so cool. What about your brother? Does he like designing too?"

"He dabbles in it, but he's more interested in the business aspect of *Bouvier*. He'll take over as CEO after our dad retires."

"And Evie?"

He laughed. "My sister wants to work in the marketing department. She has the personality for that kind of work. She's trendy and doesn't take no for an answer."

"Where do you want to go to college?" I asked.

"My brother is at Syracuse, so I may go there. Evie has been accepted to every school she applied to, but I think she's decided to go somewhere down south, either Texas or Florida."

"I have family near Ft. Lauderdale. They come up here every few years, and I get to see my cousins, but I would love to visit them in Florida one day."

"You've never been?"

Nibbling on my bottom lip, I shook my head. "My family doesn't really have the money to go on vacations and stuff," I admitted.

He gave my finger a little squeeze with his and jiggled my hand. "I bet you'll get to go someday. Maybe they'll have a lawyer conference there or something. If you have to go on work trips, you might as well go somewhere fun."

"I hope so. Hey, if I ask you a question, will you be honest with me?"

"Always," he replied without hesitation.

"Did you like the biryani you ordered the first time you came into the restaurant?"

His wry smirk told me the answer. "So we're going there, huh?" When I nodded, he puffed his cheeks and blew out a stream of air. "No, Kass, I hated it. It was way too spicy. Like someone had taken a blow torch to the inside of my mouth."

My shoulders shook with the effort it took to restrain my laughter. "Then why the hell did you eat it?"

His broad shoulders rose and fell. "Because Joe had basically called me out, and I didn't want to look like a wimp in front of the prettiest girl I'd ever seen."

My cheeks heated at his compliment. "That's a pretty good answer, Bouvier. Did you have... digestive issues after eating it?"

"I drank an entire bottle of Pepto Bismol in about four hours, and they almost had to perform an exorcism on Joe's bathroom."

"Stop it!" I said, barking out a laugh as I bumped his shoulder with mine. I realized we'd arrived at my house and found myself a bit disappointed. It seemed like the walk had only taken seconds.

I was normally a little shy around guys, but Monty was different. He was so easy to be with. Like an old friend.

"This is my house." We stopped at the end of the cracked walkway and turned to face each other. "Thank you for walking me home."

"It was entirely my pleasure. Until you brought up the misery of my digestive system, that is."

I laughed for what felt like the millionth time tonight. "I swear, I will never speak of it again."

"See that you don't, Miss Ramirez."

Our gazes clicked together and held there as we stood in contented silence, neither of us feeling the need to fill the space with unnecessary words. Half of Monty's face was in shadow, and the other half was illuminated by the soft blue glow of the moon.

Then I heard the front door open and hastily pulled my hand away from his as I swiveled toward the sound. My father emerged carrying two trash bags, and he halted when he saw me.

"Kassie honey, what are you—" He turned narrowed eyes toward the boy beside me and altered the direction of his question as he set the bags down and strode swiftly down the walkway. "Who is this?"

"This is Monty, Papá. He's a friend of mine from the restaurant."

Dad's eyes narrowed in suspicion. "You work there?"

"No, sir. I'm a customer and a friend of Kassie's. When I saw she was walking home alone, I decided to keep her company."

"She's not allowed to date," my dad practically growled.

Jeez, Papá.

"I totally understand, Mr. Ramirez. She already told me. Like I said, we're friends."

I was impressed with Monty's calm demeanor and matter-of-fact tone in the face of a grown man who was apparently not happy to see him.

My mother broke the tense moment when she called from the small stoop. "Lucas, you forgot to get—well, who is this?"

She dropped the small yellow garbage bag beside the ones my father had abandoned before joining us.

"This is Monty, and he's *not* Kassie's boyfriend," Papá informed her, crossing his arms over his wide chest.

The smile I attempted was more of a grimace, really.

Well, this is going to be fun...

CHAPTER 4

THERE I WAS, WALKING a pretty girl home, and the next thing you know, I'm inside her small brownstone, sitting on the couch with a slice of the most delicious chocolate pie I'd ever eaten.

To be clear, I was inside at the invitation of Kassie's mom, not her dad. The big man didn't appear to be a fan of boys who walked his daughter home, if the scowl on his face was any indication.

At least there's pie.

Kassie was curled up in the corner of the brown plaid couch, and I made sure to take a seat at least a foot away from her. Mrs. Ramirez sat on the other side of me while her husband was in a recliner adjacent.

"So, Monty, do you go to school with Kassie?" the kind woman asked.

"No, ma'am. I live in Manhattan, so I go to school there. I'm a junior."

Kassie's dad's eyes narrowed with each of my statements until I was unsure if he could even see us.

"And what do your parents do?"

"My mother doesn't work, and my dad is in the fashion industry."

Mr. Ramirez spoke up for the first time since we'd been inside. "Like a tailor or something?"

"No, sir. He's... the CEO of *Bouvier*."

Well that got his eyes open. "Your father is Paul Bouvier?"

"Yes, sir."

"And do you plan on going into your family's business?"

"I do. I plan to be a designer."

There was a noticeable tightening of his jaw, so I quickly changed the subject. "This pie is really good, Mrs. Ramirez. Thank you for feeding me. I didn't have time to eat after my game tonight."

"Monty plays football," Kassie added. "He's in a summer league right now."

"Well, isn't that nice? Would you like another slice of pie, Monty?" her mom asked.

I would have loved another piece of the creamy dessert with the fluffiest meringue ever, but I didn't want to appear to be a glutton, so I politely declined. "It's the best pie I've ever eaten, but I think I'm full. Thank you again."

"I'll just take your plate then," she said, and I rose when she did.

"I can take it. Just show me where the kitchen is."

That got me a huge smile from Kassie's mom. *At least one of her parents likes me.*

"Don't worry about my husband," the woman whispered when we entered the sunny-yellow kitchen. "He acts like a big bear, but he's just being an overprotective father."

"I understand. I would be too if I had a daughter."

She took my plate and fork and added them to the ones already in the sink. "I'll take care of that in a few minutes. I was about to do the dinner dishes. And if the subject of baseball comes up, the correct answer is *the Mets*." With a conspiratorial wink, she led me back to the living room.

"Monty, do you play baseball?" Mr. Ramirez asked as soon as I sat back down.

"I love the sport, but I'm a better fan than a player." I gave him my most winning smile, but he didn't appear to be impressed.

"Lucas played in the minor leagues before his knees started giving him trouble," Mrs. Ramirez said, smiling fondly at her husband.

"Were you a catcher?" The man gave a short nod. "Catching can be hard on the knees for sure," I said with a nervous chuckle.

"It is. Do you like the Mets or the Yankees?" he asked, and I swallowed hard, knowing this was a test.

"Actually, my father has always been a fan of Philly, so I've been raised as a Cougars fan." I was concerned that the man was about to glare a hole through my head, so I quickly added, "But of the New York teams, I like the Mets."

His lips twitched, and he almost smiled. Almost.

"Mama, I heard voices." I turned to see two little girls in pink nightgowns standing in the opening to the living room. The taller one's eyes landed on me. "Who are you?"

"I'm Monty, Kassie's friend."

"Oooh, are you her *boyyyyyyyfriend*?"

"No, we're just friends," I assured her, though the thought of it made my heart dance in my chest. "Are you Regina?"

Her mouth dropped open in the cutest little gasp. "How did you know?"

"A little birdy told me."

The smaller girl approached and tapped me on the knee. "Did the little birdy talk about me?"

I pretended to think about it. "Hmmm, is your name Luciana?"

Her brown eyes rounded, and she nodded. "What did she say?" I swear, this kid had the face of a cherub.

"She told me that you're really smart."

The little girl grinned and climbed up into my lap. "I'm the best reader in my class. What else?"

"Oh, let's see... she said your favorite color is pink, and you want to be a princess when you grow up."

"What about me?" Regina asked, settling on the couch between me and Kassie.

Searching my brain for the tidbits Kassie had dropped about her sisters, I said, "I heard you like purple, you can add numbers really fast, and you have a huge wart on your nose."

She raised a tiny hand to cover the lower half of her face and giggled. "Nuh-uh. You're teasing."

I laughed. "Okay, maybe about the wart thing."

"You girls are supposed to be in bed," Mr. Ramirez said, but his attempt at sternness was covered up by affection for his daughters.

"We heard people talking," Regina informed him.

"Well, people live here, and sometimes they talk," he retorted, smiling behind his bushy beard.

Regi turned the puppy dog eyes on him, and the big man melted before my very eyes. "Please, Papá? Just a few more minutes. We want to talk to Monty."

"Ok, mi hija. Just a few, and then you have to get to bed. We have church in the morning."

The little girls began peppering me with rapid-fire questions, everything from my favorite color to the prettiest Disney princess to whether or not I have a dog.

"We can't have a dog because my mother is allergic," I informed them.

"That's so sad," Luci said, tilting her head over onto my shoulder as her eyes went drowsy.

"We can't have a dog," Regi informed me with a wise bob of her head, "because the lord won't allow it."

"The lord won't let you have a dog?" I asked, masking my smile.

"The landlord," Kassie corrected, poking her sister in the belly.

Within minutes, the two little ones were fast asleep; Luci on my lap, and Regi tilted over against her older sister.

"Better get these two back to bed," their father muttered, standing and pulling Regina gently into the crook of one arm.

When he reached for the smaller girl, I stood. "I'll carry her, Mr. Ramirez." He eyed me speculatively—as if assessing whether or not he could trust me to carry the precious cargo—before leading me down a short hallway.

The room was tiny, barely able to house the two twin beds and a short dresser. He placed Regina on the farthest one, covering her with a worn purple blanket before kissing the side of her head with a tenderness I didn't expect from him after the short time I'd known him.

I carefully laid Luciana on the pink bed and covered her like her father had done with his middle daughter. I took a step back, and he filled the space, picking up a tiny stuffed bear and snuggling it beneath Luci's chin. She made a soft noise and wrapped an arm around the toy as he kissed her head too.

The room was silent except for our breathing, and Mr. Ramirez gazed from one bed to the other, his face softened with love.

"They are my entire world," he said quietly.

"They're amazing kids," I replied, meaning every word. I could tell that these two brought joy and energy to any room they were in, and they had already stolen a piece of my heart.

The man swiveled to face me. He should have been too big for this small room, but he looked at home here, like he was a piece of furniture that was necessary for the room to exist.

"I'd always wanted a boy, and I was so excited when my son was born. But then Kassie came along, and... I'm not sure how to describe it. There's something about little girls that brings a light to your life."

"You have a beautiful family, Mr. Ramirez."

"I'm very protective of them, especially my Kassie."

"I understand what you're saying, sir. I have a sister. She's a year older than me, but my brother and I are very protective of her. We would do anything for her."

He regarded me, and I could tell he was processing each word. "Are you interested in dating my daughter?" he asked with point-blank frankness, and I replied in kind.

"I am, when you decide it's okay. I've only been around Kassie a few times when I went to the restaurant, but I was instantly drawn to her. Not just her beauty but the way she treats people. She's kind and sweet, but she can be strong when she needs to be."

He smiled, looking less like a grizzly and more like a teddy bear. "I'm glad you see what I see." His head tilted to the side. "You come from very different worlds, Monty. That concerns me."

"People are people, sir, no matter their backgrounds. I'm just a boy who likes a girl. I don't care where either of us came from; I'd just like the opportunity to get to know her better."

He nodded, contemplating what I'd said. "I have a few friends who have worked for your father. They tell me he's a good man."

"He's the best," I agreed. "I hope I can grow up to be half the man he is. He loves his children just like you do, sir, so I don't think you're as different as you might imagine, despite the, you know, financial stuff. Money doesn't indicate whether a person is good or bad."

His lips curled up just a little. "Point taken. I think I'd be okay with you asking Kassie out, as long as you promise to be respectful."

"Mr. Ramirez, I promise I will treat your daughter like I'd want someone to treat my sister."

"I guess I can't ask for more than that." He gave me a sharp slap between the shoulders. "Just know that I work in construction, and I have access to all kinds of unpleasant tools, Monty."

I swallowed audibly as I followed him out of the room.

Yikes!

CHAPTER 5

"Happy birthday, Kassie."

"Thank you," I replied to the handsome guy standing on my doorstep with a bouquet of daisies. "Come on in. I want to put these in my room."

Burying my nose in the blooms, I retreated to my bedroom where my mother was dropping off a load of my laundry for me to fold later. "What is this?" she asked, her face lighting up.

"Flowers from Monty," I replied happily, setting the clear vase on my dresser and adjusting the yellow bow.

"Such a thoughtful young man. You look very pretty tonight, Kassie. Are you nervous for your first date?"

"No, but I'm excited. I can't believe Papá is actually letting me go on a date."

"He told you that you could when you turned sixteen, mi hija," she said, absently straightening the light-blue pillow on my bed.

"I know. I just figured he would come up with some kind of loophole when the time actually came."

"I believe he's beginning to like your young friend," she whispered, even though my father wasn't home from work yet. "But don't tell him I told you that. He likes to pretend to be intimidating."

Monty had been coming to the restaurant every Friday and Saturday evening and always insisted on walking me home. And each time, my mother would invite him inside, though he had to leave when my parents got ready to go to bed.

"Let me grab my camera. I want to take a picture."

"Or ten," I muttered.

Luckily, Monty was cool with my mom snapping way more than ten pictures, and he posed patiently through it all. When he led me outside to his car, a little shiver went up my spine. I was finally going on a real date with a guy I liked probably more than I should, since we'd only known each other a couple months.

He drove a sporty silver BMW that smelled like his mildly spicy cologne. A lot of guys at my school rocked way too much Axe body spray, to the point of almost gagging me, but whatever Monty wore was softer, more subtle, a scent that caressed instead of assaulted the nose.

"What are you smiling about?" he asked when he climbed in the driver's seat.

"I was just thinking that I like your cologne. It's very nice on the nasal taste buds."

He laughed, and the sound was deep and soothing. "Nasal taste buds?"

"That's the best way I could think of to describe it."

Because you smell yummy!

His face pinkened a little, and I loved that about him. He was very masculine, but there was a soft vulnerability about him sometimes that made him seem more... real.

Monty leaned slightly over the console, and I tried not to stiffen. *Is he going to try to kiss me? Right now?* But he didn't, and I wasn't sure if I was glad or disappointed. Instead, he inhaled when his nose got near my shoulder.

"You always smell good too, Kass. Like strawberries that make my nasal taste buds happy."

"I-it's my shampoo," I said on a breathless stammer. He was so close, and I suddenly decided I wanted him to press his perfect lips to mine. I wanted my first kiss to be with this beautiful boy.

But he reached in the backseat and pulled out a small, square package wrapped in pristine silver paper with a loopy red bow. "This reminded me of you. You can open it now if you want."

"You got me a present?"

He nodded, his mesmerizing blue eyes locked on mine. "It's your birthday. Of course I did."

I was practically shaking with giddiness. "I'll open it now."

He watched with amusement as I meticulously separated the tape from the paper, careful not to tear it. I would be keeping this paper in the treasure box I kept beneath my bed.

When I finally had the gift unwrapped, it revealed a white box with baby-pink writing that read *Bouvier Blush.*

"It's one of our new scents, and when I smelled it, I thought of you."

I imagined him smelling a long line of perfumes and smiling when he got to one that made his thoughts turn to me. My fingers vibrated when I peeled off the clear wrapper and opened the box. The bottle was clear cut-crystal with an ornate B atop the gold lid.

Pulling it off, I took a whiff, and my eyeballs rolled back in my head. The scent managed to be lush and soft at the same time with hints of sweet fruit.

"Do you like it?"

"I love it, but..." I looked down at the gorgeous bottle as rays of fading sunlight bounced off the facets. "Monty, this is too expensive."

"No it's not."

"I think we have very different ideas about what's expensive," I said dryly. It was the first time our financial gap had come up, but now it was staring me right in the face—in the form of a god-only-knows-how-much-per-ounce fragrance.

"Kass, I didn't buy it because of how much it costs. I bought it because it made me happy to pick it out for you. To find something I thought you'd like."

Clutching the bottle with both hands, I relaxed back into the seat. He sounded so damn sincere. "I do like it. Thank you for picking it out for me. I just didn't want you to think I was being prostitute-y for accepting such an extravagant gift."

"Well, if this is a prostitute situation, I'm really getting the short end of the stick over here because I've received no sexual favors whatsoever," he deadpanned.

"Monty!" I swatted his arm and shrieked with laughter at his outlandish teasing.

"Seriously, you're, like, the worst hooker ever, Kass."

"I'm not sure whether to be pleased or insulted by that."

He curled his index finger around mine and grinned impishly. "You know I'm kidding. I'm sure if you ever did decide to go into that line of work, you'd be fantastic."

Sniffing with faux-haughtiness, I said, "Thank you. I appreciate your confidence."

"Try some on," Monty said, twisting our hands until my inner wrist was up. I spritzed some on, and my fingers curled inward when his nose brushed against my sensitive pulse point.

"Mmm, it smells even better on you than it did on the little sample card."

He guided my arm to my own nose, and the light aroma was so perfect. "It makes me feel beautiful," I blurted out.

"That's what perfume is supposed to do, Kass. Make you feel a certain way, whether that's confident, beautiful, sexy, or whatever. And for the record, I think you're beautiful with or without perfume. I just wanted you to feel as pretty as you look."

"You're not normal," I said and then cringed at myself. Apparently, I was just going to blurt out every thought that popped into my head tonight.

"Sorry, that didn't come out right. I just meant that most guys our age don't talk like you do."

Monty laughed. "My dad always tells me I'm the oldest of my siblings, even though I'm the youngest in age." His shoulders lifted and fell in a shrug. "I think every guy has thoughts they're reluctant to speak out loud because people won't think they're cool or masculine."

"I think you're cool." My teeth worried at my bottom lip before I added, "And masculine."

"Good to know," he said with a wink before sliding his palm around and threading his fingers between mine. "You still want pizza?"

"Yep, that sounds great."

"It's your birthday, so you're the boss."

"Heck yeah, I am."

We were seated in a cozy booth in the back of an Italian restaurant, the three short candles on our table lending a warm, romantic glow.

"This is really nice. I'm glad I wore a dress," I whispered. "I was expecting more along the lines of Mario's."

"I wanted something quieter, without kids running in and out of the arcade." Monty shook his head and shuddered. "Plus, the clown on top of that claw machine game creeps me the hell out."

"Don't tell me you're afraid of Mister Doodles."

He tilted his head and batted his eyes at me. "If I said I was, would you hold my hand so I won't be scared anymore?"

"Of course," I cooed, reaching for his upturned hand on the table and folding mine into it. "What kind of prostitute would I be if I—"

My joke was interrupted by a throat clearing beside our table, and I looked up to see our waiter standing there, his wide eyes flitting between me and Monty. "My name is Bobby, and I'll… I-I can come back," he stuttered as we both turned a hundred different shades of red.

"Thanks," my date said easily. "I think Bubbles and I need a few more minutes."

I dipped my head to cover my snort as the poor server scurried off.

"You're really cute when you blush, Bubbles," Monty said.

"Stop calling me Bubbles," I hissed, trying to sound stern but failing as my giggles gave me away.

"What would you like to drink?"

"Hmmm, I think someone named Bubbles would drink something fizzy."

"Have you ever had an Italian soda?"

I managed to pull my eyes from his entrancing face to look at the drinks listed at the bottom of the menu. "No, but that sounds pretty good. I think I'll try the raspberry one."

"I'll have the same." As soon as he turned his head and lifted his finger, Bobby was back at our table.

"Yes, can I help you?"

"We'll both have the raspberry Italian soda."

"Of course. I'll be right back with that." He took a step back before pausing and turning his attention to me. "Bubbles, I'd just like to say that I respect you for what you're doing, and don't ever let anyone judge you for doing what you have to do to survive. I did some things I'm not proud of before I got this job."

"Thank you," I managed to say with a straight face, but as soon as Bobby turned away, I had to cover my mouth with my napkin to muffle the giggles.

"Poor Bobby. The things he must have seen in his young life," Monty said with a chuckle. "What kind of pizza do you like?"

"Umm, what about Hawaiian?"

His forehead creased into a scowl. "Don't tell me you're one of those people."

"Which people? Ones with good taste?"

"You can't put pineapple on a pizza!" he said vehemently.

"Why not?" I demanded.

"Be-because it's a fruit!"

"Tomatoes are fruits, but they put them on margherita pizzas. And there are tomatoes in the sauce."

"Totally different."

"Pineapple goes great with ham. Haven't you ever had pineapple on a baked ham?"

He faltered, his mouth opening and closing. "Yeah, but..."

"So what's the difference?" I hammered away.

His eyes narrowed playfully. "All right, birthday girl. We'll get the Hawaiian pizza, but if it's gross and I starve, my death will be on your hands."

"I'm willing to take that risk," I teased.

Thirty minutes later, Monty was on his third slice of pizza as I smirked across the table at him. He took a sip of his drink and swiped his tongue across his bottom lip.

"Okay, stop looking so smug, Kass. You were right."

Cupping my ear, I leaned forward. "Can you speak up? I didn't quite hear that."

His dark eyebrows lifted. "Are you on the debate team at your school?"

"No, I've thought about it, but I don't know if I would be good at it."

"Trust me, you would," he said wryly. "I've always been firmly anti-pineapple-on-a-pizza, and now I'm a fan because of you. You should look into that when school starts."

"I think I will," I replied, my chest filling with a confidence I hadn't felt before. "It would look great on law school applications."

"Good, then maybe you could put the smack down on someone besides me."

After dinner, Monty and I took a walk around a park, talking and holding hands. It was a beautiful night, only made better by being with a guy I was starting to really care about. A lot.

We arrived at my house fifteen minutes before my eleven o'clock curfew, and Monty took both my hands as we stood on the doorstep to my house.

"I hope you had a good birthday, Kass."

"It was the best. Thank you."

His lips rolled in as he tugged me a half step closer. "I really like you, Kassie."

"I like you too," I said, my voice slightly breathless.

"Would you... do you think maybe you'd like to be my girlfriend? I know this is only our first date, but I know for sure I don't want to see anyone else because I really like you." He scrunched up his nose. "Sorry, I already said that."

"Yes," I told him firmly.

And is he closer than he was a few seconds ago?

"Really?" he asked, like he'd expected a different answer.

"Of course. There's no one I'd rather be with than you."

Yes, he's definitely closer now.

"May I kiss my girlfriend?" he asked, his voice low and delicious, his warm breath gusting against my face.

I nodded, and he slid one hand up my arm, leaving a trail of tingles where his fingers brushed my bare arm. Then his hand was on my cheek and his head was lowering... lowering...

The first brush of his lips was soft, barely there, and I laid my hand against his chest, feeling that his heart rate was quicker than usual. Exactly like mine.

The next kiss was firmer, applying more pressure before he let his tongue trace against the seam of my lips. This was my first kiss, but I knew innately what to do.

My lips parted, and our tongues met, sliding sensuously against each other as he released my hand and lightly gripped my waist. As my arms looped around his neck, the fronts of our bodies connected, his firm and mine softer, and I liked the contrast. He pulled back with a gentle suction and kissed the corner of my mouth.

"Did you just shrink?" he murmured, and I realized my knees were bent, making me shorter than usual.

"I think you melted me."

"I hope that's a good thing," he said, brushing a strand of hair away from my face as I forced my legs to straighten.

"It's a very good thing. I just wish I knew what you saw in me."

His eyes searched my face. "I see everything, Kass. You're obviously gorgeous. You caught my attention the very first time I saw you, but then I got to know you, and found out you're so much more. I see your layers."

"I have layers?" I asked, confused. He had everything—looks, personality, athleticism. And I was just... me.

He nodded, his eyes glimmering a bright blue in the moonlight. "You're kind and sweet, but you're also strong and passionate about things you care about."

"Like pineapple on pizza?"

His lips curved into a smile. "Like pineapple on pizza. You're so smart, Kass, and you always make me laugh. So yes, you have layers. You're like... a casserole."

I laughed. "That's oddly weird and romantic at the same time."

His grin widened. "In fact, that's your new nickname... Kasserole with a K."

I stood on my tiptoes and kissed the strong curve of his jaw. "Well, I guess that's better than Bubbles the Ho."

CHAPTER 6

I STEPPED OUT OF the field house with my hair still wet from my post-game shower to find my dad, Auburn, and Evie waiting for me.

"There's my boy!" Dad crowed, reaching me first and wrapping me in a hug. "I'm so proud of you."

"Thanks, Dad," I said, loving the feel of his warmth on this cool October night.

He released me, and Auburn slapped me on the back and bro-hugged me. "Really good game, Mont. You've gotten even faster than last year."

"Thanks, dude. Are you leaving tonight?"

"Nope, I don't have any plans, so I'm staying through Sunday."

That made me happy. I loved having my older brother around. Every weekend, he drove down from Syracuse to watch my games, but he usually headed back to school directly afterward.

I felt hands on my shoulders and bent at the knees to let Evie hop on my back. "I guess you were pretty good," she said, resting her chin on my shoulder. "I'm hungry."

"Jesus, Eve, you ate nachos and a hot dog during the game," Auburn complained.

"And your point?" she sassed. "Let's go get burgers or something." She did a giddyap motion and pointed toward the gates of the stadium, and we all headed in that direction.

"Actually, I'm going to see Kassie. She's working at the restaurant tonight."

"Great! We'll go with you so we can meet your mystery woman," Evie announced. "Indian food sounds good."

There was no point in arguing with her. Once my sister made up her mind, it was pretty much a done deal, and she'd been bugging me for weeks to meet Kassie.

"Okay, but be nice," I warned. "Dad, are you coming too?"

"No, this old man will head home and let you kids have fun."

As we climbed into Auburn's car, I was half-excited and half-nervous for my siblings to meet the girl who had become so important to me over the past few months. She had completely stolen my heart, and I wanted—*needed*—them all to get along.

Turned out, I shouldn't have worried at all.

As soon as we entered, I zoomed in on Kassie across the restaurant. There was only one other table occupied, and she was just dropping off their food.

Her eyes lifted to mine, and she smiled, giving me a little finger twiddle before noticing that I wasn't alone. She bit into her bottom lip as she made her way across the black-and-white tiled floor toward us.

A flock of butterflies erupted from my stomach as she wended her way through the tables.

A flock of butterflies? That doesn't seem right.

Before she could reach us, she was intercepted by Mrs. Ganjam, who spoke for a moment before giving Kass a gentle shove toward the kitchen area. The butterflies died down at her retreat.

"Evie, what's the name for a bunch of butterflies?" I murmured.

"There are several, but the most common ones are kaleidoscope and swarm, though I prefer kaleidoscope. It sounds prettier. Why do you…" She tilted her face to look at me, and her lips turned up into a shit-eating grin. "Awww, does baby bro get butterflies when he sees his girlfriend?"

I was saved from answering by Mrs. Ganjam approaching the hostess stand. "Hello, Monty," the woman said with a beaming smile. "Come, let me show you to your table."

We followed her to my regular booth near the window, and she patted my arm. "Kassie will be joining you in a minute. I've given her the rest of the evening off since it's her last night with us."

"Thanks, Mrs. G. That's really sweet of you."

Her expression shifted into one of exasperation as she whispered, "I apologize in advance, but the new girl will be waiting on you." With a shake of her head, she walked off, mumbling under her breath.

A blonde woman who appeared to be in her early twenties appeared and spoke in a semi-robotic tone. "Hi, my name is Zima, and I'll be your server. Can I get your drink orders?"

"I'll have a Coke, please," I told her, and Auburn said he'd have the same.

"Sprite for me," Evie said.

"Okay, um, do you want those in glasses?" Zima asked.

We all looked at each other in confusion, and Evie finally asked, "What are our other options?"

"What do you mean?"

"Besides having it in a glass?"

"Oh, uhhh, that's all we have. Glasses, I mean."

Evie pinched her nostrils together but an indelicate snort still managed to escape before I said, "Okay, glasses will be fine. Thank you."

"What the hell?" Auburn wondered in a low voice when she was gone.

I caught sight of Kassie making her way to our table, and I stood. She'd changed out of her work uniform into skinny jeans and a red-and-cream striped sweater.

"You look gorgeous," I murmured, kissing her on the cheek.

"Thanks," she said, turning her attention to my brother and sister who had also stood from the booth.

Evie got to her first, pulling her into a fierce hug and squealing, "Ooooh, you're real! We were starting to think Monty made you up in his head."

"Thanks, Eve-ster," I said flatly. "Kassie, this is my pain in the butt sister, Evie, and this is Auburn."

My brother gave her a less intrusive hug and murmured, "Nice to meet you, Kassie," before we all took our seats, Auburn and Evie sitting across from us.

"Wow," Kass said, her eyes flitting between me and my siblings. "I can definitely see the family resemblance."

All three of us had the signature Bouvier blue eyes, but our sister's hair was a dark caramel color, a few shades lighter than mine and Auburn's.

"But I'm the cutest, right?" Evie asked with a winning grin and an eyebrow wiggle.

"Absolutely," Kassie agreed, laughing at my sister's antics.

"Oooh, I like her, Mont. Can we keep her?"

Placing my arm around my girl's shoulders, I looked down at her. "I think that could be arranged."

Her eyes met mine, and I got lost there for a moment until my sister clapped her hands together in apparent glee. "Oh. Em. Gee! You two are just freaking adorable together!"

"Calm down, sis," Auburn chastised, bopping her lightly on the back of the head before turning to Kassie. "What's good here?"

"Oh hell. Don't let her pick," I groaned. "She tried to kill me the first time I came in here."

Kassie let out a giggle. "I suggested the biryani, which is a bit spicy. You should have seen Monty. He was sweating and sucking down water as fast as I could bring it."

"A bit spicy? I felt like someone had taken a blow torch to my gut."

"I'll have that then," Auburn said with a smirk.

"Not me. I don't have a fire-retardant mouth. How's the butter chicken?" Evie asked.

Kass nodded her approval. "It's superb."

"I'll have that too. I haven't tried it yet," I said.

Zima reappeared with our drinks, mixing up mine and Evie's, which we quickly exchanged across the tiled table. "Do you know what you want to eat?"

We all told her our orders, and she stared blankly at her notepad before writing it down. "M'kay, do you want forks with your meals?"

Auburn spoke up immediately. "No, I prefer to stick my entire head in the bowl and eat like a horse."

Evie's forehead hit the table with a loud thunk as her shoulders shook with silent laughter.

"Zima," Kassie sighed, "I've told you to stop asking that. Everyone gets silverware here. With every meal."

"Okay, it's just... at the last place I worked, we weren't supposed to give out silverware to everyone."

"You worked at Subway," Kass replied wearily.

The poor girl looked confused as she turned and trudged back to the kitchen.

"I swear, I think her mother named her Zima because she drank a lot of it while she was pregnant," Kassie said with a roll of her eyes.

"Actually," Evie said, lifting her head and raising one finger, "Zima didn't exist when she was a fetus. It didn't come out until 1993 as a part of the *clear craze* of the nineties."

"Our sister is full of useless trivia," Auburn commented, bumping Evie with his shoulder.

"She's full of *something*," I muttered.

My brother leaned forward over the table, whispering conspiratorially, "Kassie, do you think you could get me Zima's number?"

I groaned, and Evie shook her head. "Auburn only dates stupid girls because they're the only ones that fall for his shit."

"Hey," he protested, "I could get a smart girl if I wanted to put in the effort." He shrugged, and his lips tipped up at the corners. "But why bother?"

"One day, you're going to meet an intelligent girl, and she's going to own your ass," our sister predicted, rubbing her hands together. "And I can't freaking wait."

"You'll be waiting a long time," Auburn retorted mildly.

When Zima returned, she placed our plates down on the table, and I was impressed that she'd actually gotten the orders correct. She didn't, however, bring forks.

"Silverware," Kassie mouthed to her, and I practically saw the lightbulb go on over the blonde's head. "I swear, training her has been a nightmare," Kass said when the girl went to find the utensils.

"I guess she's not doing too bad for her first day," Evie commented.

"She's been here for three weeks," Kassie informed her with one raised eyebrow.

"Oh, well... damn."

Once we all had forks, we dug in, and I was dismayed when Auburn didn't even break a sweat while eating his dish.

"This is the best biryani I've ever had," he commented, taking another huge bite like it wasn't made by actual demons. "Kassie, why is this your last night working here?"

She scrunched her shoulders happily. "I made my school's debate team, and we have competitions on the weekends."

"That's awesome," Evie exclaimed. "That will really help with law school."

Kass scooted an inch closer to me and laid her hand on my thigh. "Monty is the one who encouraged me to look into it."

Evie waved her fork in a little circle as she swallowed a bit of her chicken. "Did you know the first female lawyer was admitted to the bar in Iowa in 1869? Her name was—"

"Arabella Mansfield," Kassie finished, and my sister's eyebrows shot up. "I wrote a report about her my freshman year."

"Coolness," Evie said, nodding her approval. "Hey, aren't you eating anything?"

"Yeah, I'll share," I offered.

"No, it's okay. I've been snacking all afternoon and evening. Mrs. Ganjam brought cupcakes and all kinds of other treats for my last day."

"What kind of law do you want to practice, Kassie?" Auburn asked, scooping up the remnants of the rice from his bowl. I was annoyed that he still hadn't shown any outward signs that the dish was any spicier than an ice cream cone.

"I want to be a litigator, possibly criminal law."

He set his fork down, mischief crinkling his eyes at the corners. "Excellent. We'll probably be seeking your services in the future for this troublemaker," he said, jerking a thumb at our sister.

"Pshhh, whatever. You know I'm an angel." Evie flashed the fakest sweet smile ever and batted her eyelashes innocently, earning her a round of laughs.

Kassie rested her chin in her hands, her smile turning sad. "I love this. I wish my brother was closer. He's in the Army and stationed in Texas right now."

"Ooh, cool. I think I'm going to college in Texas," Evie informed her. "Our cousins Blaire and Beau are from there, so hopefully, I'll get to see them more often. Well, Blaire anyway. Beau's in the Navy, and I think he's stationed in San Diego, right?" she asked Auburn, and he nodded.

"Kasserole, if you're missing having an older sibling around, I can loan you mine," I offered, shooting a playful look across the table. "In fact, you can have them both."

Zima reappeared beside our table. "Is there anything else you need?"

Auburn sucked on his bottom lip, giving the woman an up and down look that seemed to go on forever. "Your number," he said in a low tone.

She slid the ticket across the table to him. "I already put it on the back." Then she gave him a wink and retreated.

"Smooth," Evie said. "That was equally impressive and disturbing, bro."

Auburn shrugged with all the nonchalance of a guy who could get any woman he wanted. I reached for the ticket, but he waved me away and pulled out his wallet.

My sister smacked a hand on the table. "Kassie, you should come over to our house tomorrow. We can hang out and do makeovers... if you don't mind being around the caveman here," she said tilting her head toward our older brother.

"Don't worry about that," Auburn said with a wicked grin as he stared at the digits on the back of the bill. "I think I have plans."

CHAPTER 7

"Happy New Year, Monty."

"Thanks, Dad. You too. Everything looks great." My eyes flitted around our living room. All the furniture had been removed for the party and replaced with high, round tables and a commercial-grade bar in the corner.

The pervading colors were black and silver, with dots of red adorning everything from the shimmery tablecloths to the elaborate flower arrangements.

"Since it's a special occasion, you and Kassie can have a bit of champagne, and I'll have Geno drive her home."

I nodded before leaning in close. "Did you talk to Mother?"

Dad gave me a comforting pat on the arm. "I did and warned her to be on her best behavior. Where is Kassie anyway?"

"Upstairs getting ready with Evie. Kala and Audrey are working their magic."

"Did she like the dress?"

"She loved it. She was a little apprehensive at first because you know she doesn't like me spending money on her. But when I told her I helped design it especially for her, she fell in love with it."

"It turned out beautifully. You did an outstanding job, son. And your Kassie is the least materialistic girl I know."

My Kassie. I liked the sound of that.

"Thanks, Dad," I said, casting another glance at the stairs. "I wonder what's—" My words froze as I did a double-take.

Holy shit!

Kassie and Evie were descending the stairs, their hands clutched tightly as my girlfriend's eyes searched and found me. Then she broke into a brilliant smile that made my heart swell until I thought it would burst.

I pulled my gaze from her when Evie leaned over and whispered something to her. My sister was stunning in a full-length magenta gown that flared at the waist. Ornate silver buttons ran from the collared top to the bottom hem.

My attention reverted back to Kassie, and my lungs forgot their intended function. The dress I'd designed for her was a one-shouldered, black velvet number with a fitted bodice that hugged her curves so well, it made me salivate. Half-inch rhinestones edged the neckline and the thigh-high split up one leg.

Her thick hair was piled on top of her head in a riot of curls, a few of which hung down and framed her pretty face. The look was understated and undeniably sexy.

I didn't even realize my legs were moving until I was standing directly in front of the two of them, taking each of their hands to help them down the last couple steps.

"Would I sound like a total dork if I said *va va voom?*"

"Yes, but we'll accept it," Evie said, tilting her head so I could kiss her cheek. "You're pretty *va va* yourself, cutie. And doesn't Kassie look like a glam queen?"

"She certainly does," I said, locking eyes with Kass as I bent over her hand and pressed my mouth against her soft skin.

Lips the color of roses parted on a sharp inhale when I sucked lightly. "Thank you," she murmured as I fought the urge to kiss all the way up her arm until I reached that luscious, full mouth of hers.

"You young ladies are a vision," my dad said, walking up and breaking our trance. I linked index fingers with Kassie as Dad brushed a kiss over her cheek. "My dear, that dress is perfect for you."

"Thank you, Paul. It's the most beautiful thing I've ever owned."

"Well, get used to it. I think Monty here is going to be designing many more things for you in the future."

The future. Images popped into my head of Kassie walking down a red-carpeted aisle wearing a white dress I designed for her, and I felt a prickling behind my eyelids.

The vision only solidified the feelings I'd been having the past couple months. I knew for a fact I was head-over-heels in love with Kassie Ramirez. She was my one, and I was practically vibrating with the urge to blurt it out to her, but I held my tongue.

Midnight tonight. The beginning of a new year. That's when I'll tell her.

I felt my dad pat my back as he escorted Evie into the living room. Kassie's hand stroked my lapel, and her eyes sizzled as she looked me up and down.

"You're wearing the hell out of this tuxedo," she said, biting into her bottom lip.

"Thanks. It's a new one. My old one was getting too tight in the shoulders."

Her eyes widened. "You *own* a tuxedo? It's not a rental?" Tilting my head, I lifted an eyebrow, and she giggled. "Oh, duh. Family business. You probably have an entire closet full of formal wear."

"Actually, I have lots of suits but only two tuxes."

Her pretty lips pursed. "Hmph. Is that all? I'm not sure I can date a man with such an abysmal wardrobe."

"Is that so?" I asked, stepping closer and resting one hand on her hip. Kass nodded, and I lowered my head to whisper in her ear. "Then I'll have to up my game. You look absolutely delectable tonight, by the way."

"As in tasty?"

Pulling my head back in surprise, I searched her eyes. "I wouldn't know. I haven't tasted all of you yet."

She rolled her lips inward, and one shoulder lifted in a slight shrug. "Would you like to?"

Those four words combined with her hopeful expression were all it took to turn my dick to stone. Shifting my legs to accommodate for the tightening of my trousers, I narrowed my eyes. Kass wasn't normally this bold.

"You and Evie haven't been hitting the bottle have you?"

She grinned and shook her head. "No, I haven't had anything to drink. I just... you said you wanted to, and I haven't been able to stop thinking about it."

"That makes two of us, Kasserole," I informed her with a half-smile. "Let's go upstairs now."

"Monty, no!" Kass hissed, giving my shoulder a little shove, but she was laughing.

A voice from behind me stalled our sexy banter. "And who is this?"

I plastered on a smile and turned to face the newcomer, wrapping an arm around Kassie's waist. "Mother, hi. This is my girlfriend, Kassie Ramirez. Kass, this is my mother, Chloe Bouvier."

"Very nice to meet you, Mrs. Bouvier."

Mother shook her proffered hand with a fake-ass smile on her face. Auburn and I called it her *public smile.*

"Likewise, I'm sure." Her eyes dragged up and down Kassie's slim form. "Your dress is lovely."

"Thank you. Monty designed it, but I guess you already know that." When my mother's jaw tightened, nervous laughter bubbled from Kassie's throat before she cleared it and schooled her features. "Your dress is stunning, Mrs. Bouvier."

My mother did look impeccable—as always—in a straight black skirt with a matching jacket. The collar was a bright white and hugged the top curve of her shoulders.

"Oh, this?" She waved a perfectly manicured hand. "I don't even remember how long I've had this."

Which was total bullshit. Chloe Bouvier had a new dress made for every occasion, never appearing in the same one twice.

Mother looked over my shoulder, and the corners of her eyes pinched. "What is Evelyn wearing? That color clashes horribly with the red in the flower arrangements." Without another word, she stalked off toward my sister, no doubt to give her a piece of her mind.

"So, that's my mother," I said sardonically, and Kassie nibbled the corner of her lip.

"She seems... nice." Her concerned eyes lifted to mine. "You don't think she heard what we were talking about, do you?"

"You mean about me having my face between your legs?"

Kassie's mouth dropped open and hung there for a moment. "Monty Bouvier!" Her eyes darted around the room, looking for potential eavesdroppers. "I can't believe you said that."

"Have I scandalized you?" I whispered against the shell of her ear.

"Maybe a little," she replied, and I could feel the heat rising onto her cheek.

"But did it excite you?"

Her hand clutched the back of my jacket. "Hmm, maybe a lot."

Hell yes.

The placid notes from the string quartet swirled around us as we danced, and I rested my forehead against Kassie's. "It's about ten minutes before midnight. I wanted to be alone with you for our kiss."

Her head moved up and down and flecks of gold shimmered in her eyes, reflecting the light of the chandelier above us. "Let's go upstairs."

Taking her hand, I led her up to my room and closed the door, effectively shutting out the noise from below. I pulled her into my arms and did what I'd been wanting to do for hours—I kissed my girlfriend.

"Mmm, I don't think it's quite midnight yet," she murmured.

"This is a pre-midnight kiss. For practice." My hands slid down over her hips, appreciating the subtle curves they found. "Come on," I told her, grabbing my letterman jacket and sliding it over her shoulders.

"Well, this is a fancy look," she said, popping a hip and posing for me.

"You're so fucking adorable," I said, leading her out onto the balcony. "I didn't want you to get cold."

Kass snuggled into my side as we looked out over the city. "Thank you for inviting me tonight. It was fun."

"For me too. These parties are usually pretty stuffy, but not with you here with me." I turned us so we were facing each other, and my hands cupped her face. "You're my best friend, Kassie."

Her eyes melted into softness. "You're my best friend too. I feel even closer to you than I do Lily, and I've known her for years. It's like I can tell you all the thoughts and dreams in my head. Is that weird?"

I shook my head, pressing my lips against her curls. "No, baby. We... I think we have something really special together."

Her arms wrapped around my waist, and her voice was barely audible. "I think so too."

My nerves kicked into overdrive, causing my stomach to clench. "But you're so much more than that to me." I laid a kiss on her lips and told her my innermost thoughts. "I'm in love with you, Kassie."

I felt more than heard her soft gasp, and her eyes filled with tears. Then she said the words. The beautiful, anticipated words that filled my heart with something indefinable. Joy would probably be the best descriptor.

"Monty, I'm in love with you too."

As the first fireworks bloomed in the air above us, the love between us bloomed as well. And we kissed, our mouths and souls joining as one. I was overwhelmed, practically dizzy with the swell of emotion inside me.

"I'm never going to forget this moment," I whispered against her lips.

"Every time I see fireworks, I'm going to think of you," she said, darting her sweet tongue out for another taste of my lips.

"I hope so because I plan to be with you for every firework event in the future." My hand slipped up to the back of her hair, and I tilted her head so I could kiss her more deeply. Eager tongues lapped slowly against one another as the booms and crackles above matched the ones taking place in my chest. "Forever, Kassie."

Her hands fisted the jacket of my tux, like she was trying to hold me to her as she returned my promise. "Forever, Monty."

CHAPTER 8

ELEVEN MONTHS HAD PASSED since that night on my balcony, and I loved Kassie Ramirez more with each passing second. She truly was my best friend, the person I could share all my dreams with and never feel an ounce of judgment.

I wasn't one of those guys who was shy or embarrassed about sharing my feelings with her. I told her I loved her every single day, sometimes by text or on the phone, but my favorite times were when we were together.

Her brown eyes sparkled each time I said the words, and I reveled in the fact that I put that gleam in her eyes.

Our physical relationship had progressed as well, our connection growing deeper with each touch, though we hadn't gone all the way yet.

But that was going to change tonight.

I was experiencing a myriad of feelings as we pulled into the parking garage at my apartment. Nerves... excitement... worry.

After parking, I stared at the cinder block wall out the front windshield. "Are you ready?" My voice sounded like someone was strangling me.

Kassie's finger curled around mine. "Monty, look at me." I swiveled my face and looked into her soft, serious eyes. "I'm ready." There was no hesitation. No doubt.

The tension I hadn't been aware I was carrying in my shoulders relaxed, and I lifted her hand to kiss her knuckle. "I'm ready too. I guess I was just feeling a bit nervous."

"Because it's your first time too?"

"Mostly because I'm worried about hurting you."

"It's okay. Everyone's first time hurts."

"Not for the guys. Why is it only the girls that feel pain? It's not fair," I fretted. "I wish I could take the hurt for you."

Kassie removed her seatbelt and kneeled in the seat, leaning over the console to hold my face. "Monty Bouvier, you're absolutely the sweetest person I've ever met, and I know you'd never hurt me on purpose." Her eyes held nothing but truth. "We've been together for over a year, and I'm ready."

"Did you check everything on that ovulation website?" Since Kassie was Catholic, she wasn't supposed to use birth control, so we were using the rhythm method.

She pulled a sheet of paper with a calendar printed on it from her purse. "Yep. I looked it up on one of the computers at the school library. You should have seen me running to the printer after I hit print so no one else would accidentally pick it up. If the track coach would have seen me, she would have signed me up for the sprint relay."

I took the sheet and studied it. "So this here is your last period, and the yellow boxes are the safe days?"

"Yes, and the pink boxes are fertile days."

I noted that today's date was smack dab in the middle of a row of yellow. "Okay, but I'll still pull out just to be safe."

"That would probably be best." She gave me a look of longing that went straight to my crotch. "Can we go inside now?"

"Are you sure no one else is here?" Kassie asked once we were outside my bedroom door.

"I'm positive. Mother is away, Dad is in Milan, and Auburn and Evie are both away at college."

"And Ivy, your housekeeper?"

"At home with her husband. We have the entire apartment to ourselves," I assured her, running my hand down her arm. "Stay right here for a second."

"Why?" she asked as I opened the door to my bedroom and slipped inside before closing it.

"Just preparing," I called through the wood.

"I thought I was going to help with that."

Popping my head out the door, I rolled my eyes. "Not preparing *myself*, silly, because I definitely want you to help with that. I'm making sure my room is okay."

I shut the door again and rushed around the room, lighting the candles I'd set on every flat surface. When the entire space was lit with a warm glow, I opened the door and led Kassie inside.

"Monty, i-it's beautiful," she exclaimed.

"I wanted everything to be perfect for you," I said quietly, my hands in my pockets as she wandered to the bed and examined the rose petals strewn across the covers.

Her face was filled with wonder when she turned to face me. "You did all this?"

Nodding, I crossed to her and rested my hands on her hips. "Is it okay?"

"It's beyond perfect, Monty."

We undressed each other slowly, removing one article of clothing at a time with lots of kissing in between. Our hands roamed, loving touches that elicited soft moans and goosebumps.

Kass was no longer embarrassed about me seeing her body like she was in the beginning. I guessed being told she was the most beautiful thing in the entire world—at least a million times—would do that.

Once we were completely naked, I pulled back the covers before lifting her in my arms and placing her on the cool sheets. Climbing in beside her, I leaned up on my elbow and traced a single finger over every inch of her face.

"I want to remember how you look right now," I told her. "So soft, your cheeks flushed in the candlelight."

"So in love," she added, placing her hand lightly on my cheek.

Lowering my head, I kissed her as her arms wound around my neck. This was the first time we'd been completely naked together, and the feel of her warm, soft body against mine was indescribable. I was hard as a rock against her stomach.

"I love you," I murmured, trailing my lips across her cheek and down her neck. "Anytime you need me to stop, I will."

"I love you too," she whimpered when I nibbled lightly on a spot above her collarbone.

Taking my time, I worked my way down her body, tracing my tongue around her nipples before sucking each of them into my mouth. Kassie's breasts were always so sensitive, and her back lifted from the bed as I feasted on them.

My fingers drew sinuous lines down her torso as my mouth followed, giving extra attention to the spots that always made her skin quiver. A line just above her belly button. The dip of her hip bone. And finally, my favorite spot.

Positioning myself between her thighs, I arranged her legs over my shoulders as I ran my nose through her slit. I'd never imagined I would love the scent of a woman's pussy like this, but I was completely addicted to Kassie's.

Knowing exactly what she liked now, I gave her a long lap from her entrance to her clit before flickering my tongue against the swollen button.

"Monty, yes!" Her small hands dove into my hair, and I smiled against her heated flesh. I fucking loved when she pulled my hair.

I licked and sucked every inch of her sweetness, and my hips grinded into the mattress, seeking some much-needed friction as I devoured Kass. I actually came in my pants the first time I'd gone down on her, but I'd learned to control it better now.

"God yes," she hissed when I slipped my middle finger into her tightness. "More, please." Her hands tugged at my hair, and I worked another finger inside her, curling them forward to find the spot that never failed to drive her wild.

"Come for me, baby." Those words always did it for her, and my sweet girl came around my fingers, clenching them as I increased my suction on her clit.

That's going to feel so fucking amazing around my dick.

I slowed my motions, allowing her to come down from her high, and her fingers massaged tiny circles against my scalp.

"Th-that was so good," she panted as I lifted my head to watch her. Kassie's post-orgasmic look was a thing of beauty, my favorite part of our intimate times.

With parted lips and hazy, hooded eyes, she took my damn breath away. Kissing my way up her body, I hovered over her, my extremely hard cock resting against her stomach.

Her hands slid over my shoulders and pressed until I was lying on top of her, her thighs making the perfect cradle for my hips.

"I'm ready, Monty." Her voice was soft but held no hesitation.

I kissed her forehead and let my lips linger there. "Let me know if it hurts too much, and I'll stop."

"I know you will. I trust you."

I smiled down at her and traced her lips with my fingertip. "Other than *I love you*, those are the best words I've ever heard cross your lips."

Reaching between us, I fisted my length, giving myself a couple long pulls before rubbing my tip up and down through her wetness. And god, she was *so* fucking wet.

My cock found her tight little hole like it knew it belonged there, and I pushed the head into her. I'd never felt anything better in my seventeen years on this planet.

Dammit, man. Don't you dare come before you're even inside her all the way.

"Okay?" I managed to croak out, and she nodded.

As I pushed in another inch, I felt her resistance around my shaft, so I withdrew to the tip before taking more of her. A soft cry told me I was hurting her, and I rested my forehead against hers.

"I'm sorry, baby. So sorry."

"It's all right. Just do it."

Slowly, inch by inch, I entered her, holding her body close as she trembled and whimpered beneath me. Circling my hips, I stretched her until her own hips began moving with me.

Kassie's whimpers turned to soft groans of pure pleasure as her legs wrapped around my waist. "Monty... so good."

A gush of wetness flooded my cock, and I began to move in and out, making love to my beautiful woman. Our bodies fit together like pieces of a puzzle as I tunneled through her tightness, the head of my dick dragging along her slick walls.

Our lips crashed together in a wild kiss of passion as we lost our virginity to each other, and I knew I would never forget this night as long as I lived.

I shifted a little so I could run my hand up and down her side, and the new angle took me deeper. "You're taking me so well, Kass," I groaned as the slick slide of our bodies sped up, escalated.

My hand ended up on her round ass, and I lifted her against me, clearly finding her G-spot because her moans turned deeper, more carnal. Kass arched up into me as her short fingernails dug into my flesh.

I buried my face in the pillow beside her head, trying to control myself while she babbled nonsense in my ear. "Mon... it's... I can't."

She was so goddamn tight around me, fluttering and pulsing as my balls clenched up against my body. My name slipped from her lips as she came all over me, and god help me, I tried to pull out. I really did, but Kassie was wrapped around me like a vine, her arms and legs binding me to her.

Gritting my teeth to hold onto the little bit of control I had left, I tried to slow my pace, but her next words undid me. "I love you, Monty."

She'd said it before, lots of times, but hearing her voice say that while I was deep inside her stripped away all of my restraint.

And I filled her. Kassie's heat surrounded me as I added my own, and our bodies rocked through our orgasms with the most perfect rhythm.

My lips found hers and our tongues played, swirled, danced together until we were both completely sated.

"Are you okay, baby?" I asked, nuzzling her cheek.

Her voice was a soft rasp. "It was better than I could have imagined. Are you sure you've never done that before?"

Lifting my head, I looked down at her with concern. "You know you're my first, Kass."

Her smile was radiant, and I realized she'd been teasing me. "Will I be your last?"

Nodding my head up and down, I brushed my lips against hers. "I promise, you'll be all my lasts."

"And you'll be all mine too." My rapidly beating heart skipped at that. There's nothing I wanted more than to grow old with Kassie.

"I didn't pull out," I admitted, and two lines appeared between her eyebrows.

"I forgot all about that, but we should be okay. The rhythm method is very effective, and we double-checked everything." She smoothed her hands up and down my arms as her cheeks pinkened even more than they already were. "I liked when you came inside me. I felt closer to you than ever."

"Me too. I felt like we were one person." Her face was relaxed with pleasure, and I felt myself hardening, despite coming only a minute before. "I love you, Kasserole."

"I love you too," she replied, her eyes growing sleepy.

Seven weeks later, Kassie missed her period.

CHAPTER 9

I PACED BACK AND forth along the length of Monty's bedroom, shaking my hands erratically.

"What are we gonna do? My periods are like clockwork, Monty." I paused my frantic feet and stared at him. "Clockwork! Do you understand what I'm saying?"

"I understand, sweetheart." He approached me tentatively with a small white bag in his left hand, as if he were afraid I was a ticking time bomb. Which was exactly how I felt.

I started my nervous pacing again until Monty blocked my path and placed a gentle hand on the back of my neck.

"First of all, you're going to go into my bathroom and take this test. We don't know anything for sure. Your cycle could be messed up due to all the stress of senior year."

"You really think so?"

He hesitated slightly. "Yeah, sure."

My eyes narrowed. "That didn't sound very convincing."

"Because I'm not going to blow smoke up your ass, Kassie. There's a possibility you might be pregnant, but let's not worry until we know."

I couldn't be pregnant. I just couldn't. I smashed my palm against my forehead and closed my eyes.

"I can't even imagine telling my parents. That should be really freaking fun. And what about my priest? Lily?" My voice grew to a wail. "Oh god, my teachers at school will know exactly what we've been up to."

Not that there was a lack of pregnant teens at my high school. To the contrary, I could think of five off the top of my head.

But not me. Not Kassie Ramirez. I was a good girl, an honor student with big plans for the future.

Monty pulled my hand away from my face before tilting my chin up. I expected him to say something sweet and conciliatory, but instead he bit out, "Fuck them."

"Wh-what?"

"I said: Fuck. Them. Anyone who judges us for loving each other can go to hell. If someone bothers you about it or says anything negative, I'll burn their house down."

My lips twitched as he did an excellent job of distracting me. "You'll burn my parents' house down?"

Monty's head tilted to the side. "Okay, maybe they get a pass, but that priest has got it coming."

A wry grin twisted my face. "Father David is eighty-seven years old."

"Good, then he's old enough to know better than to shame a beautiful, faithful young lady who is only human." His blue eyes never left mine for a second as his hand brushed sweetly down my cheek. "We had sex, Kassie. It's not like we committed murder."

"I know," I said quietly because he was right.

"I'm not ashamed of making love to you, baby. It didn't feel like what we were doing was dirty. It felt... special to me. Every time."

I could hear a hint of indignation in his tone, and I wrapped my arms around his middle, resting my head against his chest. "I don't ever want you to think I'm ashamed of being with you, Monty. I was taught it's a sin to have sex before marriage, but it doesn't feel wrong when I'm with you. It feels like what people in love are supposed to do."

"Me too, baby." He kissed the top of my head.

"I should probably go take the test now."

"Whenever you're ready. No rush."

"I think I'll feel better once I know one way or the other."

Monty guided me to the bathroom and stood reading the directions with me. They were pretty straightforward: Pee on this stick and wait three minutes for the results. *Three minutes to see if the rest of your life is going to change forever.*

I went into the small room where the toilet was located and pulled down my pants. My hands were trembling so badly, I almost dropped the stick in the toilet. "Shit!" I cursed, catching it before it fell.

The door burst open, and Monty stood there, chest heaving and eyes wide. "What's wrong?"

"Sorry, I almost dropped the stick," I confessed, and to my horror, he kneeled on the fuzzy mat right in front of me. "What are you doing?" My voice was a mere squeak.

He took the stick from me. "I'll help you."

"But... but what if I pee on your fingers?"

"Then I'll wash them," he deadpanned. "Close your eyes and let go, Kass."

I did and felt one of his hands rest gently on my bare thigh. I concentrated on that one and tried to forget about what the other one was doing.

"There you go, baby. All done."

By the time I wiped and pulled my pants up, Monty had taken the stick into the outer part of the bathroom. I didn't even look at the pink and white stick resting on the counter. Instead, I walked straight into his arms.

"Distract me," I begged.

"Okay, let's see. Ummm, oh, I've been wondering about something. Is the sin effect cumulative? I'm not like a religious scholar or anything, but if it's a sin to have sex *and* to use condoms, why don't we just do both at the same time? Then you can ask forgiveness for both."

I looked up at him with an amused smile. "Like a BOGO for confession?"

"What's a… BOGO?"

"A buy one, get one free sale? Like at Payless?" At his look of confusion, I sighed. "You've never been to a Payless shoe store, have you?"

"No, do they carry Bouvier shoes?" For some reason, I found that funny, and Monty held me against him as I was overcome with deep, rolling belly laughs. "From your response, I'm assuming that's a no."

"A big no," I confirmed, swiping tears from beneath my eyes. "Unless you have a line of shoes that's under twenty dollars a pair."

His chuckle was self-deprecating, and I loved that about Monty. While he was the richest person I knew, he wasn't a snob. Sure, he may not be well-versed in discount shoe stores, but I never felt judged because I was.

My shoulders tensed when his phone beeped. "It's time to look," he whispered against the top of my head.

We both turned, holding hands as we gazed down at our future.

Pregnant.

"Oh god," I half-sobbed, closing my eyes and resting my free hand on the counter for balance. My face was flooded with tears, and I let them fall for a while before opening my eyes and looking up at Monty.

He wasn't there.

Because he was on one knee in front of me. "Will you marry me, Kassie?"

My head shook side to side. "I'm not going to force you to marry me, Monty."

He kissed the hand he was holding. "No force necessary, sweetheart. I want to. We've already talked about getting married after college. Now we'll just get married before."

A tornado of thoughts swirled in my head as he continued. "We can do it now or after graduation in a few months, whenever you want."

"My parents aren't going to let me get married at seventeen."

"They're not going to have much choice in the matter. I refuse to live apart from my child. I'm not going to come *visit* my baby like I'm a distant relative, Kass. I'm going to be there every day, every step of the way. For every dirty diaper and middle-of-the-night feeding. For his or her first steps and first words. I'm going to be front and center. So we can either get married and live together, or I'm moving into your parents' house, and I'll sleep on the couch."

His words were soft yet vehement, and I could tell he meant every syllable. "I'm so scared, Mont."

"I know you are, and I am too, but we can do this as long as we're together." His head bowed, forehead resting against the back of my hand for a long moment before he lifted watery eyes to meet mine. "I'm not just asking you to marry me because we're having a baby. I'm asking you because I love you, Kassie Ramirez, so much it hurts. I'll never love anyone as much as I love you." He pressed the sweetest kiss against my belly and cast a chagrined look up at me. "Until our baby is born, and then you have to share me."

"I love you too," I replied, my voice barely recognizable around the emotions that were choking me.

"I want to be with you forever, and I promise I'll be a good husband. I'll always put your needs before mine, and I'll support all your dreams." His lips curved upward. "I'll even take you shopping at that Payless store if that's what you want."

My fears—so prevalent and overwhelming a few short seconds ago—took a backburner to hope. And family. This beautiful, selfless man was going to be my family. He loved with his whole heart, and I knew for a fact that he would make me the happiest woman in the world.

"Yes," I blurted. "I'll marry you, Monty Bouvier."

He paused in stunned silence for a few seconds before rising to his feet and sweeping me in his arms. "I'm so happy, Kasserole." We spun in circles in his bathroom, my feet not touching the ground until I told him to stop because I was getting nauseous.

Then he set me on my feet and took my face in his hands.

"I'll take care of you and our baby. I know it's scary, but I'll make sure we're okay." His hand dropped to my belly as it all sunk in. *We're having a child together.*

"I'll take care of you too," I promised, covering his hand with my own.

Monty's mouth lowered to mine, and we kissed, the saltiness of our tears only making it sweeter.

When we finally broke apart, I watched the boy grow into a man before my very eyes as steely determination swelled his chest.

"First of all, we need to make you an appointment with a doctor. I think there are vitamins and stuff you need to be taking."

"Monty?"

"Yeah, baby?" he asked, guiding me from his room with our fingers linked.

"I won't really make you go to Payless with me. I'm afraid your fancy loafers may literally catch on fire."

His deep laugh filled me with happiness as he wrapped a protective arm around me when we reached the stairs.

I was going to marry the man I loved, we were having a baby together, and it was all going to be okay.

CHAPTER 10

I GUIDED MY CAR through the Manhattan traffic on a cold night in February. When my phone rang, I answered it on speaker phone after glancing down at the display.

"Hello, Evelyn."

"Seriously, little bro? You want to use full names? Because I could start calling you—"

"Never mind, *Evie*," I stressed. "How's Texas?"

"Warmer than it is there, I'm sure."

"Let me guess," I scoffed. "Seventy-two degrees?"

"Seventy-five actually. What is it there?"

I glanced at the dashboard display on my BMW. "Twenty-seven."

"Oooh, bet you wish you were coming to college down here with me instead of in New York."

"Gloating isn't ladylike, dear," I sniffed.

"God, you sound just like Mother. Speaking of the Queen Bitch, have you told the parentals about Kassie yet?"

"I'm on my way to do that right now."

Her voice softened. "I hope it goes okay. Dad will be fine, but Mother will probably get one of her headaches from the undue stress you're causing her." She said that last bit with a pompous flair.

"Yeah, god forbid," I drawled.

"Are you still planning to get married right after graduation?"

"Yes. I wish we could now, but Kassie's parents wanted her to finish high school first. I'm doing everything in my power to stay on their good side."

"Look, bro, I know you don't get your trust fund until you turn eighteen next month, so if you need anything for Kassie or the baby in the meantime, just let me know. You can pay me back later."

"I can't ask you to do that, Evie."

"Of course you can. That's what favorite sisters are for."

"You're my only sister," I deadpanned.

"Whatever," she dismissed. "You could have a thousand sisters, and I'd still be the best."

I fake sighed. "Yeah, I guess you're okay. When is your Spring Break?"

"Not till mid-March, but I'm not coming home."

Disappointment simmered low in my belly. Besides Kassie, Evie was the person I was closest to in the world. Since we shared a birthday, we were practically twins in my eyes.

"Are you going somewhere?"

She squealed with excitement. "Yes, me and five other girls are going to Mexico. It's going to be so much fun!"

"Shit, Evie. I wish you were coming home. It feels like I haven't seen you in forever."

"Awwww, wittle brother misses me?" she asked in a baby voice.

I grinned as I took a right at the next intersection. "Wittle brother is over a half foot taller than you."

"Yeah, yeah. Like you don't remind me of that every time I see you. And don't worry. I'll be home in May, and we can spend the entire summer together. I'll help you and Kassie get ready for the baby. Oooh, I want to throw y'all a baby shower, complete with stupid party games."

"Y'all?" I asked with a laugh.

I could hear her smile through the phone. Evie had the best smile, bright and impish. "Guess Texas is rubbing off on me. Definitely rubbing off on my ass. There's this little hole in the wall with the best tacos ever. I eat there at least twice a week, and I bet I've gained at least three pounds."

"Oh my god… three whole pounds?" I shrieked, making her laugh.

"Shut up, butthead. How is Kass feeling?"

"She's better. All the morning sickness is gone. I just left her house, in fact. Took her some ice cream."

"That's my boy. Treat her like the queen that she is. Have you decided on names?"

"We like Willow for a girl."

"Aww, that's sweet. What about Eve for a middle name?"

"Willow Eve? It sounds like a feminine product," I quipped.

Her squeaky laugh rang in my ear. "Yeah, that's true. What about for a boy?"

"Kassie likes Nicholas, but we're not going to need that because we're having a girl," I said confidently.

"Wait!" she yelled, making me flinch. "When did you find that out?"

"We haven't for sure, but I really want a baby girl. I'd be a kick-ass girl dad."

"You totally would, bro." Her voice turned wistful. "I sure do miss you, Mont."

"Miss you too, Evie. Hey, I'm pulling into the parking garage, so I'll talk to you tomorrow," I said, sliding the sleek silver car into my designated parking space.

"Love you, goofus."

With a mirthful roll of my eyes, I replied, "Love you too, Eve-ster Egg."

"Dad, can I come in?" I asked from the doorway of his home office.

His smile was warm and welcoming as he waved me inside. The walls were a pale mustard color, making the dark wood of his desk and bookshelves pop. Photos of me, Auburn, and Evie were everywhere.

"Of course, son. How was school today?"

"It was good," I said, rubbing the back of my neck as I sat in the burgundy leather chair across from him. "Dad, I have to tell you something important."

Paul Bouvier leaned forward, his arms resting on the leather-trimmed desk calendar as he gave me all of his attention. He always did that, focused on me when I said I needed to talk, whether the topic was which college I wanted to attend or how the Philly Cougars baseball team was doing. My words were always important to him.

"Go ahead, Monty."

I inhaled a breath and blew it out with my rapidly spoken words. "Kassie is pregnant, and we're going to get married."

Dad's lips tightened and his brow creased, but he never averted his eyes. Anxiety sat like a rock deep and low in my belly.

"Okay, son. That's... wow." He rubbed a hand over his graying hair. "You're both so young."

"I know. Are you mad?" My breathing halted as I awaited his answer. I hated disappointing my father.

"Well, it's not ideal, Monty. Are you still planning to go to college?"

"Yes, and I want to help Kassie too. She's so smart, I'm sure she will have all kinds of scholarships though."

He stared at the surface of his desk, his look pensive before raising his eyes back to mine. "I'm glad you came to me with this. As long as you plan to continue your education, I'll help you kids in any way possible."

The rock of anxiety broke into a fine dust and dispelled as relief filled the empty space. "Thanks, Dad. We didn't mean for it to happen, but I want to do the right thing." I rubbed my fingers against my jaw. "That didn't come out right. I want to marry Kassie no matter what. Not just because she's pregnant."

"Your timeline has just been accelerated, right?"

My head bobbed up and down in relief. "I love her, Dad. I know we're young, but I'm sure she's the one for me."

"Being young doesn't preclude falling in love. She's a lovely girl, Mont. Does she still want to be a lawyer?"

"Yes, sir. She does."

"If she decides to go into corporate law, there will be a place for her at *Bouvier*, if she wants."

"I appreciate that, but I think she wants to go into criminal law. Hopefully we won't have any need for that."

Dad chuckled. "Let's hope not. When are you planning to get married?"

"Married?"

The hairs on the back of my neck stood up as my mother's cold voice filled the room. *Shit.*

My head swiveled around to find Chloe Bouvier standing in the doorway, and my father stood and beckoned her forward. "Chloe, come in. Monty has some news for us."

"It better not be about marrying *that girl*. Because that will happen over my dead body."

Fuck.

Mother—not Mom or Mama because she insisted that *Mother* sounded more appropriate for "people of our standing"—entered the room but didn't sit. Rather, she leaned a hip against the desk with her arms crossed over her chest.

My mother was a beautiful woman, partly from good genes and partly from the miracles of Botox, but that did little to cover her ugly personality. None of her three children had any idea why our father stayed with her.

She was cold, bordering on mean at times, and I was actually happy that she didn't take too much interest in my life. Dad never missed a ballgame or awards ceremony, despite his extremely busy schedule, but Auburn, Evie, and I received very little maternal attention.

Evie actually took the brunt of Mother's wrath, most likely because she was jealous that the only daughter in our family was the apple of my dad's eye. Mine and Auburn's as well. We adored our sister, and though she was actually the middle child, we thought of her as our little sister.

Dad stood and rounded his desk, placing his hands on my shoulders and giving me a squeeze. Shoring up my bravery, I spoke.

"Mother, Kassie is expecting a baby."

She didn't move, didn't speak, just stared at me.

"We're, um, we're going to get married after graduation."

"No. You. Are. Not." Her words were chopped and deceptively quiet.

"Chloe..." my dad said.

"No!" she snapped, her narrowed eyes still on me. "You will not have anything else to do with that girl. I forbid it."

"But, Mother, she's pregnant."

She shook her head so hard, her normally perfect platinum blonde hair flew messily around her head. "If you want to live in this house, you'll do as I say. I won't have someone like... *her* in this family."

I went from shocked to angry in a split second, standing from my chair so quickly it would have tipped over if my dad hadn't been standing there. "Kassie *is* going to be family, so you'd better get used to it, Mother. You should be honored to have someone like her marry your son."

"Honored?" she shrieked. "She's trash, Monty."

"She is not," I yelled, shrugging off my father when he attempted to rein me in with a hand on my arm. I took a step toward the woman who had birthed me but had never been a mother. Had never shown me an ounce of affection. "Kassie is so fucking smart and has the best heart of anyone I know. She's going to be a lawyer."

"Her education paid for by you, no doubt," Mother sneered. "She's nothing but a goddamn gold digger, after your money and your status."

"You take that back," I growled, my anger bubbling over and seeping from every one of my pores.

Dad tried to break in. "Why don't we—"

"I will do no such thing. You're an ignorant, naive little boy who knows nothing about how those kinds of women operate."

"What kinds of women?" I asked, my voice low and dark. "Hispanic women?"

Mother doubled down, lifting her chin haughtily. "Yes, that's exactly what I mean. I know how they work."

"You know nothing about Kassie because you've never bothered to get to know her." Our eyes locked together in an epic battle of wills.

"Let me guess. She didn't want to use birth control because it's against her religion."

Ouch. She'd hit the nail on the head with that one, but I retorted, "Kassie would never try to trap me. She doesn't have a deceptive bone in her body. Unlike you."

Mother's eyes flashed with raw ire. "Get. Out," she seethed.

"Wh-what?"

"Get out. You're no longer my son."

My father stepped between us, facing his wife. "Chloe, stop it right now. You know you don't mean that."

"Oh, yes I do. Let's see how long little miss gold digger stays with him once he's no longer part of the Bouvier empire."

I was fucking stunned. She really wanted to kick me out of the house because she didn't like the woman I loved?

"Chloe," Dad bellowed, "in the other room. Now."

Dad marched from the room with my stuck-up bitch of a mother right on his heels. I sank into the chair with my head in my hands. I wasn't sure where in the house they went, but I didn't hear anything for about ten minutes, and then spurts of raised voices reached my ears, the words undetectable to me.

Surely Mother didn't really plan to kick me out. Then again, I wouldn't put much past her. She'd never given a damn about any of us kids.

I'd never had a hug from my own mother. Never. Not once in my life that I could remember. She basically acted like we didn't even exist unless we did something that would make her look good to her rich bitch friends.

Ohh, Auburn has a perfect grade point average this semester. Have you heard that my Monty is captain of the football team? We're so proud. Sweet Evelyn has been accepted to the most exclusive sorority at her college. Isn't that just grand?

My father, on the other hand, made up for her coldness with genuine warmth and kindness. We'd probably be a million kinds of fucked up if it weren't for the attention he'd freely given us growing up.

I worried about Auburn though, being the oldest. He'd grown up way before his time and had been like a second father to me. Ever since he'd left for college at Syracuse, he'd driven four hours every weekend to watch me play football. Never missed a single game.

But who took care of him? Who was there to support him besides Dad? What if he was so jaded he never found a woman to love who loved him back like he deserved?

I was pulled from my thoughts when I heard footsteps in the hallway, a single set. My father, by the heavy sound of loafers on the hardwood floors.

Looking up when he entered, I stood, feeling at least twenty years older than I had fifteen minutes ago as my eyes darted to the empty hallway behind him. "Where is she?"

"Your mother is lying down. She has a headache."

"Shocker," I muttered.

Dad tried a smile, but it didn't reach the blue eyes that were exact replicas of mine and Auburn's. He appeared to have aged decades in the past few minutes as well.

"Come here, son," he said, wrapping his arms around me.

I inhaled his scent, recognizing the cologne as one of the new *Bouvier* scents from our company. It was warm and comforting, like an expensive bourbon mixed with aged leather.

"Why was she acting like that? Is it really just Kassie she doesn't like or is it because she thinks I made a mistake and she can't tolerate imperfection?"

My father gripped my head with both hands and turned his fierce blue gaze on my own. "I don't ever want you to think you're less than perfect, Monty. Maybe you made an error in judgment, but you're standing up and being a man about it. I love you more than anything, and I'm so proud of you."

"Thanks, Dad."

He swallowed hard, his face looking pained. "Look, I want you to go and stay with Auburn for a while."

My stomach dropped to the dark wood floor. "You're kicking me out?"

"No, son. We just need to give your mother time to cool off. With both of your hot tempers in the same house, I'm afraid there will be bloodshed." He attempted another smile, but I wasn't amused at all.

"Then why don't you kick her out instead of me?" I'd never used that heated tone with my father, but I was hurt and so fucking angry.

"Trust me, if I could, I would," he replied cryptically. "I'll make sure you're taken care of."

"Other than being homeless, you mean," I bit out.

"You won't be homeless, son. You'll be living with your brother in a very nice house."

I pulled away from his hold and turned my back on him—exactly how he was doing to me—so he couldn't see the wetness gathering in the corners of my eyes.

"I can't believe you're choosing her over me."

I felt a tug on my arm, and suddenly I was whirled around to face him, looking into his haggard face. *Were those deep wrinkles around his eyes and mouth there when I entered his office earlier?*

"Never," he hissed ferociously. "I would never choose that woman over my children. Even when it seems like I am, I'm doing it for you and Evie and Auburn. Always." That last word quivered in the air.

"I don't understand, Dad. What the hell are you talking about?"

His eyes averted, staring at a spot on the floor a few feet away as his words came out quiet and low. "There are things you don't know, Monty, and I can't tell you right now."

Heaving in deep breaths and pushing them forcefully from my lungs, I clenched my fists at my sides, wanting to slam them into a wall.

"Ambiguous statements like that aren't helping."

"It's just temporary. Let her cool off, okay?"

His gaze was on mine again, the look so intense I wanted to shift my eyes away, but I didn't. Lifting my chin, I said, "No, if this is your decision, it's not temporary."

His eyes blinked rapidly behind his round, tortoiseshell eyeglasses. "Don't say that, son. Please just give me some time."

I retreated, taking three steps backward. "You can have all the time you want, *Paul*. I'm out."

I packed a suitcase with clothes and shoes before slipping my coat and gloves on. My eyes fell on the mammoth shiny wooden desk in the sitting area of my room, and I picked up one of my favorite photos, one of me, Auburn, and Evie from last Christmas.

It had been taken in front of the sixteen foot tree in the living room downstairs. Evie was in the center, and we all had our arms around each other, laughing at something she'd just said. Wrapping it in a sweatshirt, I placed it carefully in my suitcase before doing the same with the collage of photos of me and Kassie that Evie had helped me make. I opened my balcony door and took the outer steps down to the street.

I didn't want to run into either of my parents on the way out, not even my dad. I was so hurt, the betrayal stinging every inch of my face with even more potency than the sleet that was now coming down sideways.

Dragging my suitcase around to the parking garage, I spoke to the attendant before loading my suitcase in the back of the Beamer and climbing into the driver's seat. My phone pinged, and I checked the display, finding a text from my father. I didn't click on it, only reading the few words I could see: I love you, son. Please don't...

Nope. Don't care, old man.

I hit the button to call my brother, and he answered immediately. "Mont, you okay?"

"I guess Dad called you."

"Yes, what the fuck is he thinking?"

"I have no idea. I'm in my car right now in the garage. C-can I come stay with you?"

"Of course, bro. You don't even have to ask."

Relief flooded my chest, and I nodded to myself. "Okay, I'm on my way."

"Um, Monty, why don't you stop at the bank machine and get some cash. Dad mentioned something about... well, Mother is ranting about cutting you off completely. She has access to your bank account."

"Gotcha," I sighed, already feeling more weary than my seventeen years should allow.

Driving to the automated teller machine around the corner, I withdrew the maximum amount allowed, a thousand dollars, and headed out of the city. When a little light flashed on my dashboard, I cursed and found the nearest gas station.

I went inside the store and grabbed a bag of Flamin' Hot Cheetos and a Coke before going up to the counter and handing over my card. "I'm getting thirty in gas too," I told the clerk.

He ran the card and frowned before sliding it through the machine again. "Sorry, sir. It's saying insufficient funds," he informed me in a thick foreign accent.

The bitch had already cut my card off, and I silently thanked my brother for suggesting I pick up some cash on the way. I slapped forty dollars down on the sticky surface and waited for my change.

Well played, Chloe. Well fucking played.

CHAPTER 11

A MUTED VIBRATION BUZZED against my butt, and I wedged my hand beneath my mattress to pull out the cell phone I kept hidden there.

Monty had given it to me for Christmas last year. My parents didn't know, and while I hated deceiving them, I also wanted to talk to my boyfriend in between visits.

Sliding down on my bed, I pulled the covers over my head and kept my voice low when I flipped open the device and answered.

"Hey, Monty. You missed me, huh?"

"Always, baby." There was silence except for background noise for a few seconds.

"Am I on speakerphone?"

I could hear his sigh down the line. "Yeah, I'm on the way to Auburn's."

"Monty, he lives four hours away, and it's sleeting outside!" My nerves were suddenly frayed as I attempted to keep my voice down.

"I know, sweetheart, but..." I heard a long exhale.

"But what?"

"Things didn't go great with my parents, so I'm going to be staying with my brother for a while."

My hand went to the base of my throat as I tried to keep from throwing up. "D-did they kick you out?"

"Technically, my mother did. Dad took her to another room to talk, and when he came back, he said it would be best if I went to Auburn's and gave her time to cool off."

"Oh god, this is all my fault." I pressed my fist over my mouth to muffle my sob, but he heard it anyway.

"No, honey. It's not your fault at all. Don't ever think that. You're the best thing that's ever happened to me. And please don't cry, Kass. Please. You know it kills me when you're upset."

"I'm so sorry," I whispered, my voice a harsh rasp as I tried to stem my tears. "You can't lose your family over me."

"*You* are my family. You and our baby are my priority."

"But…"

His voice turned stern yet playful. "No buts, Kassie Ramirez-soon-to-be-Bouvier." That made me smile a little. "I love you with all my heart, and I promise I always will."

"I love you with all my heart too," I told him, feeling every single word.

"That's all we need to be happy, Kass. Don't worry about anything else. Let me handle it."

"I'll start working at the diner again so I can help with our expenses."

"You don't have to do that. I just want you to take care of yourself and the baby."

Now it was my turn to be stern. "I am young and healthy, Monty soon-to-be-my-husband Bouvier. Tons of women work right up until the time they give birth. I'm not some helpless little girl; I can contribute."

"I know you can, babe. We'll talk about it, okay? I need to go so I can concentrate on the road."

"Okay, please be safe and text me when you get there."

"I will. I love you, Kassie."

"Love you too." Holding my finger in front of me, I crooked it, pretending I was wrapping it around Monty's. "I'm doing the finger thing right now."

I could hear the smile in his voice. "I'm doing it too."

"Well, cut it out. Both hands on the wheel, mister."

His laughter in my ear made my heart do a flip in my chest. I loved Monty's laugh. It was deep, rich, and always full of joy.

"Yes, ma'am, boss lady. I'll text you."

"See that you do. Bye, Monty."

"Bye, Kasserole."

Chapter 12

ONCE I GOT OFF the phone with Kassie, the sleet began pelting my car with a vengeance, and it took me over five hours to make the drive to Syracuse.

The door to Auburn's home swung open before I could even knock, and he pulled me into a strong, brotherly hug.

"Shit, I was so worried about you, Mont. The weather turned bad really fast."

"Yeah, I drove slow," I said as he stepped back and let me inside the warmth of his apartment. The ceiling formed a high arch and was dotted with recessed lighting, while floor-to-ceiling windows overlooked a stunning lake that appeared to be frozen over.

"Wow, bro. This is nice."

"That's right. I forgot you haven't been to my new place. Come on, and I'll show you around." He picked up my suitcase and led me up a floating staircase to the room where I'd be staying. "It came already furnished, but I can change whatever you don't like."

"No, it's great, Auburn. I'm just..." I swallowed down my emotions. "Thanks for letting me stay here."

The room was painted navy-blue with bright white trim, and the queen-sized bed was covered with a navy-and-white comforter in a bold striped pattern. I stepped across the bleached wood floor and over the fluffy dark-blue rug to the white dresser.

"You okay?" My brother's eyes met mine in the ornate mirror as my fingers zigzagged over the textured surface of the furniture.

Overwhelming sadness strummed across my entire body and sank down bone deep. "I guess it just hit me that my clothes are going to be in *this* dresser," my lips twisted to the side in an effort to hold back my tears, "because I won't be living at home anymore."

Auburn flashed me a sympathetic smile. "Home is wherever we are together. You were going to be moving up here in the fall anyway."

"Having me here won't cramp your style?"

"Hell no. You can be my wingman."

"While I'd love to take you up on that charming offer, I'll be married and knee deep in diapers soon."

He shook his head and rubbed his fingers across his jaw. I was pretty sure with those blue eyes and his dark scruff, he wouldn't require a wingman to get girls.

"I can't believe baby Monty is going to be a dad."

"You and Evie just love to point out that I'm the youngest, don't you?"

"Yep," he said with an unashamed grin. "Come on, and I'll show you your bathroom."

The connecting room was decorated in the same color scheme as the bedroom, but there was a nautical motif, including a large iron anchor mounted over the pristine white bathtub.

"I guess I could stand living here," I teased, feeling a little lighter now that I was with my big brother.

"Let me finish showing you around, and then I'll make us a drink."

Auburn's bedroom suite was two doors down from mine, and a large study, complete with packed shelves of books, was at the end of the hall.

Besides the living room, the downstairs consisted of a dining room, a well-stocked kitchen, a laundry room, and a home gym large enough for my entire football team.

Indicating that I should sit on the ivory couch, Auburn poured us each two fingers of a brown liquid at the full bar in the corner.

I sniffed mine, and he said, "Bourbon. It's really smooth, so even a lightweight like you will enjoy it."

"I'm not a lightweight; I just don't drink much because of football."

"The season's over. Drink up." He lifted his glass in a salute. "To the guy who's going to be the best damned teen dad in the world."

I took a small sip and choked at the sting in my throat. Auburn sat down beside me and patted me on the back with a chuckle. "All right, bro?"

"Yeah," I croaked. "I just usually drink beer."

He swallowed half his glass without the hint of a flinch. "Trust me, hard liquor is the only way to deal with our mother. Now tell me how you're feeling."

"What're you, my shrink?"

My brother grinned at me over the top of his glass. "Something like that." He drained the rest of his bourbon and stood to pour another. "I know we're not super close because you're six years younger than me, but I'll always be here for you, Mont. Plus, I have the gift of wisdom on my side."

I tried another sip while he had his back turned, and that one went down more easily, seeming to seep instantly into my bones. My head pressed into the plush leather of the couch, and I let out a weary sigh as he sat back down.

"I guess I'm just confused. And..." I swallowed another fortifying gulp of the alcohol. "And it hurts my feelings that Dad didn't stand up for me."

My brother leaned forward and rested his elbows on his knees, head lowered as he stared down into his glass. "I'm really pissed about that. I only see Mother on holidays, but I'm still close with Dad. Now I'm thinking of completely cutting ties with him too. You're his fucking kid, and he didn't even—"

"No!" I almost yelled, bringing Auburn's head sharply around to me as I spoke fervently. "You can't do that. You have to take over *Bouvier* when Dad retires or, you know, if something happens to him. If you cut him out of your life, that bitch might get control of it."

His eyes hung on my matching ones for a long moment before he nodded slowly. "I guess you're right. Grandpop wanted us to run the company, you, me, and Evie."

"It was the very last thing he ever said to me before he died." My lips curled into a reminiscent smile. "Don't ruin all his plans because of me. I mean, if running *Bouvier* is still what you want."

He gave an affirming nod. "That's all I really want in life."

"You want a family too though, right?"

My brother's lips bent into a sardonic smile. "I'm not like you, Monty, all gung ho about having a wife and kids. As long as I have you, Evie, and our company, that's all I need."

"Well, we didn't exactly grow up with the best role models for a loving relationship," I said, and my brother snorted at the understatement. "I guess I just want to do it better. I want to prove that real love exists and that having money doesn't mean you have to have a cold marriage."

Auburn gave me a tiny smile. "I'm really happy for you, and I was serious about what I said earlier. You're going to be an amazing father to your kid."

I downed the rest of my drink. "Thanks, but now I'm worried about even having any money. *She* already cut off my bank account, so what if she revokes my trust fund? How am I going to support my family?"

"Don't worry about that. Dad's parents left us our trusts, and he has control over them. He'd never cut you off."

I blew out a gust of air from my pursed lips. "I'm not sure how he'll feel about me after the way I stormed out of there. He's probably so pissed he'll never talk to me again."

"I don't know about that, but are you forgetting your brother is already a millionaire? I'll pay for your education if that's what you need. You and Kassie."

A runaway tear bolted down my cheek, and before I could wipe it on my sleeve, my brother had his arms around me, his big hands pressing between my shoulder blades.

"Shit, I forget you're still a kid, Mont. It's okay to let it out."

And I did. I finally let all the emotions—fear, frustration, sadness, and some I couldn't even define—wrench from my chest. My tears dampened Auburn's cream cable-knit sweater as he tapped firm, even pats against my back. There was something soothing about the rhythm of it, almost like an external heartbeat.

As I cried in my big brother's arms, the large pit in my stomach shrank to a small one, still present but much more manageable than the throbbing mass that had threatened to fold me in half a few minutes ago.

Finally retreating, I swiped the heels of my hands down my cheeks to dry them. "Sorry I turned into a total pussy," I mumbled, my face heating with embarrassment.

Auburn swatted me lightly on the back of the head. "You're not a fucking pussy, Mont. You're handling this a hell of a lot better than I would be, and I'm twenty-three. If I'd gotten a girl pregnant, I'd be crying into my pillow every night."

"Thanks, man, and you don't have to pay for my shit. It's my responsibility."

My brother rolled his eyes. "Don't be stupid. Being responsible and mature doesn't mean you never ask for help. Hell, look at Dad. He's the head of *Bouvier*, but there's no way he could run the company by himself. He's good at men's clothing, but he can't design women's clothes for shit. That's why he brought in Devereaux."

I cracked a grin. "And he'd never make it to a meeting on time without Tony staying on his ass."

"Right? So don't let pride get in the way of accepting help. If it makes you feel better, when you come to work at *Bouvier*, you can pay me back."

"With interest?"

Auburn let out a long sigh. "No, you idiot. You're my brother; I'm not charging you interest."

"I don't mind."

"I do. Now shut up and get to bed. I have class in the morning, but we can go look at a couple high schools in the afternoon."

"Shit, I hadn't even thought of school."

"That's what you have a wise older brother for. I talked to a chick I know whose younger brother is finishing his senior year. She gave me the lowdown on the local campuses."

Great. Let's add starting a new school to the shitshow my life has become.

CHAPTER 13

"Do you know what Mrs. Haley wants with me?" I asked Lily as we walked down the hallway at our high school. Alva Haley was my favorite teacher. She taught English Three and was also the sponsor for our school's debate team.

"Not sure."

My teeth worried my bottom lip with tiny bites as we approached Mrs. Haley's door and paused out of viewing range of the small window.

"I'll wait out here," Lily whispered.

"Okay, thanks," I said, stepping forward and shaking out my nervous hands before lifting my fist to knock.

Before my knuckles could rap on the wood, my teacher noticed me through the dingy window and gestured me inside with a wave of her hand.

Blowing out a stream of tension, I pushed open the door and stepped inside.

"Good afternoon, Kassie. You can take a seat."

Wedging myself into a desk in the front row, I set my backpack on the floor beside me and blurted, "Hi, Mrs. Haley. Am I in trouble?"

She smiled and shook her head, the beads on the ends of the three cornrows over her left ear clacking with the movement. "Of course not. I have some news for you, but first, how are you feeling?"

News? What news? I want to know. Now! But apparently, we were doing small talk first. "Much better. Thank you for the teabags you gave me. The peppermint really helped me through my nausea."

"Good, I'm glad." My teacher picked up a manila envelope and held it in both hands as she leaned her forearms onto the surface of her desk. "Now, what I wanted to discuss with you…" She lifted her eyebrows. "I kinda did a thing."

"Okay, what thing?"

Mrs. Haley normally had a stern face—I guess that was an occupational necessity when you were dealing with large numbers of teenagers—but when she smiled, her entire demeanor transformed.

A tiny bit of my nervousness dissipated as her lips curled up and her hazel eyes sparkled back at me. It was the same look she would give me just after I'd won a debate competition.

"I hope you don't mind, but I took the liberty of submitting an application for you for the Boland Debates. I didn't tell you about it because I didn't want to get your hopes up. It's very difficult to be accepted into this particular competition, as you know."

"Right. Only the best of the best in the state." She'd probably called me in here to let me know I'd been rejected.

Mrs. Haley tapped the envelope on the desk twice as she gave me a crooked smirk. "Then I guess you're one of the best, Kassie, because you've been accepted."

My jaw dropped open so wide it ached, and I would have toppled over onto the floor if my hands didn't grip onto the edges of the desk.

"No way. You're joking with me."

Her grin widened. "I can assure you I am not."

"B-but…"

"No stuttering," she scolded, her eyes sharpening on mine.

I nodded and collected my words. "But the competition is always in February, and it's February now."

Mrs. Haley let out an exasperated sigh. "It's actually this Saturday. There was apparently some kind of mix-up, or your letter got lost in the mail. I'm not sure, but I received a phone call from the director today asking why they hadn't received your confirmation and payment."

My excitement plummeted to the floor at her last word. "Payment? How much is—"

"The school pays your entry fee, Kassie."

"Are you sure?" I asked, attempting to rein in the thrill that was trying to work its way down my spine. This could *not* be happening.

"I'm positive. Principal Griffin is ecstatic and said he would send the payment over as soon as you confirm that you want to compete."

Pointing at her phone, I commanded, "Yes. Call him. Now."

Mrs. Haley let out a loud laugh and stood, handing the envelope to me before picking up her cell phone. I held the paperwork against my chest like a lifeline as she made the call and then dropped her phone into her purse.

She leaned against the corner of her metal desk, her pretty eyes trained on mine.

"Kassie, I've been at this school for over twenty years, and no other student from here has ever been accepted to Boland during my tenure. In fact, I've only ever nominated two others in all that time."

That's when I burst into tears.

Grabbing a box of tissues from her desk, she set it on mine and placed a soothing hand on my shoulder. "I know. It's a bit overwhelming, right?"

"Yes," I croaked, swiping at my eyes with a wad of tissue. "Thank you so much for having confidence in me. I just can't believe this."

She bent at the waist until her face was inches from mine. "Believe it. You are the most talented debater I've ever had the pleasure of teaching, and I think you have an excellent chance at winning."

I'd been so flabbergasted at being accepted, the idea of winning hadn't even crossed my mind. But oh, it was crossing it now.

"The prize is a scholarship, right?"

"Full ride to the college or university of your choice," she confirmed, and my heart soared.

Though he didn't say as much, I knew Monty was worried about the money situation since he'd been booted from his home. If I could win this, our new life together would be so much easier.

I smiled as I hitched my bag onto my shoulders. "I promise I'll come out swinging," I told her, echoing the words of wisdom she told the team before every debate.

"See that you do, Kassie. I'll be there cheering you on."

CHAPTER 14

THE REST OF THE school day passed in a whirlwind of activity. I'd used my secret cell phone to call and tell Monty the good news and then used the school phone to call my parents. They were all ecstatic about the debates.

Then Principal Griffin let me push the button to send the payment to the Boland Institute. It was a simple moment, but it was so... *profound* I almost cried. Again.

Then there were photos, an interview with the school paper, and an intense coaching session with Mrs. Haley.

"She's really nice," Lily gushed as we walked down the main corridor of the school. "I mean, she's a total comma tyrant in the classroom, but you can tell she really cares about her students."

"Commas are important. They can mean the difference between *Let's eat, Grandpa* and *Let's eat Grandpa.*"

My friend barked out a laugh and pushed open the front door. "Thank goodness I have you to proofread my shit."

We'd only made it down two steps before she stalled, her eyes fixed on something near the street in front of our school.

As my gaze followed the trail of her own, my heart stopped beating for a few seconds. Monty Bouvier was leaning back against his silver sports car, legs crossed at the ankles and hands stuffed in the pockets of his khaki trousers.

He was wearing a burgundy sweater with a tan overcoat that probably cost more than our entire house. Classic Ray-Ban Wayfarers covered his eyes.

"Dayum, that man of yours looks like a model," Lily said from the corner of her mouth. "Are you sure his brother doesn't like younger women? Because we could totally be sisters."

"I know, right?"

Monty lifted his sunglasses, revealing bright sapphire eyes that were locked onto me, and his sexy mouth curved up into a smile that made my panties feel too tight. I swear, that man's mouth had me thinking some very unsavory thoughts. Ones I should probably mention in confession but wouldn't.

"Hey, Kasserole," he said, smoothly pushing away from his car and striding toward me. When he reached me, we did our finger-holding thing before he leaned in for a soft kiss.

"Hi," I breathed, unable to think of other words because *he's here.*

"Surprise, baby." He released my finger and looped his arms around my waist as mine curled around his neck.

"I'm definitely surprised. What are you doing here?"

"Thought I might take you out for a pizza after we shop for rings," he suggested, pressing our foreheads together.

I nodded, my cheeks aching with my happy smile. "This is officially the best day ever."

"I agree. I'm so proud of you, and I wanted to celebrate with you in person."

Monty took my backpack, hitching it over his shoulder as he looped an arm around my growing waistline.

"Pretty soon your arm isn't going to be long enough to go around me."

"Then I'll have to use both arms," he said with a wink before turning to Lily whose face was beaming like a thousand suns. She adored Monty. "Hey, Lil. You want to grab a pizza with us later?"

"No, I have to work at my parents' diner. You crazy kids have fun."

Once we were seated in the car, I quickly called my mom on Monty's phone to let her know where we were headed, then simply studied my boyfriend's face while he drove. I never tired of looking at Monty. He had dark hair and the most gorgeous blue eyes I'd ever seen.

His lips were full and the perfect shade of pink, with a defined cupid's bow that made me want to kiss him all the damn time. With a straight nose and a jaw that appeared to be made of steel, the man's face looked like it had been carved by a Renaissance artist.

"Should we go to Tiffany's?" he asked, reaching for my hand and entwining our fingers. His warm palm pressed against mine as his thumb toyed with my knuckle.

I scrunched up my face and shook my head. "No, there's a place a few blocks from my house. We can try there. It's not too expensive."

"That doesn't matter, baby. I'll get you whatever you want."

Letting out a long exhale, I brought our joined hands to my mouth and pressed my lips against the back of his. "I only want a simple wedding band, Monty. I don't need an engagement ring too."

"Kass..."

"No, seriously. We need to be careful about financial things until we get settled, especially with the baby coming. If you want to buy me one later, that's fine, but for now, I just want a wedding ring. Something that symbolizes our marriage."

His lips tightened as he nodded. "You're right. That's the only thing that matters right now, but I'm buying you a huge diamond as soon as I can."

Ten minutes later, we were standing outside the jeweler. The storefront was painted a pretty rose color, and the subtle lighting showed off the rows of jewels in the two windows on either side of the glass and metal door.

"It's not very fancy, but it's run by an elderly couple who has been in the neighborhood for years."

Monty took my hand and squeezed. "I like that, Kass. Supporting a family business."

It didn't take us long to find *the ones*. My eyes were drawn to the matching rings as soon as Mrs. James set the velvet-lined tray in front of us.

"Do you like these?" I asked, pointing to the bottom right corner.

Monty lifted the women's band first, and the third finger on my left hand literally itched for him to slide the ring onto it.

"That's a beautiful set," the elderly lady said, the wrinkles on her face revealing a lifetime of smiles. "It's eighteen karat gold and has fine milgrain detailing along the edges. It effortlessly combines both modern and classic elements."

I picked up the men's ring, my finger sliding from the cool, smooth center to the rougher grain at the edges. My mind could picture this ring on my future husband as he cradled our child in his big hands.

A tear escaped from my eye and made a long, slow trail down my cheek. Monty's thumb was there almost instantly, halting the wet path with a gentle swipe.

"Hey, what's wrong, Kass? We can keep looking if you don't like it."

"I love it," I sniffled. "I was seeing you wearing it in my head."

The kiss he pressed against my forehead triggered another tear to fall. It was such a tender moment, and I nestled my face against his neck and inhaled his masculine scent. In a few short months, this man would be my husband, and I'd never been more content in my life.

I heard his deep voice say, "We'll take these, please," and then the ring was removed from my fingers as Monty's arms pulled me close. My own wrapped around his waist, and the love between us grew until I thought I would burst.

As Mrs. James bustled off to find the correct sizes, my almost-fiancé's gentle fingers lifted my chin. "I know it's not time to do the vows yet, but looking at these rings together... I just... I'm feeling so many things. I know things may not be easy going forward, and our life may not be perfect, but I'm going to love you so hard until the day I die."

"If I'm with you, it's perfect," I breathed.

"Why did you go into the back room at the jewelry store?" I asked before taking a bite of my pizza. The saltiness of the ham combined with the sweetness of the pineapple and sang a glorious tune against my tongue.

"I wanted to talk to Mr. James about the engraving."

"What engraving?" I asked, taking a drink of my water while eyeing his bubbly Coca Cola with envy.

He slid his frosted glass across the table with an indulgent smile. "Here, have a sip."

My lips wrapped around the straw, and I took a greedy gulp. "I wish the man had to carry the baby so they would have to give up caffeine," I groused before handing his drink back to him.

His brow furrowed. "You're right, babe. I shouldn't be drinking this in front of you." He lifted his hand to signal for the server as I shook my head.

"No, it's okay, Mont."

He reached across the table and took my hand. "Nope, we're in this together, and if you can't have Coke, I won't drink any either."

"Fine, but I'm not putting up with any attitude from your caffeine withdrawals."

"Noted," he said with a laugh.

He was so damn sweet to me, and sometimes I found it hard to believe he was mine.

"Thanks for getting this done so quickly, Mrs. James," Monty said when we returned to the jewelry shop.

"Of course. I'm so happy to see young people in love." Her face beamed. "You make a beautiful couple, and we're happy you chose us to be a part of your special story."

He took the proffered black velvet boxes. "I plan to buy Kassie a diamond once we get settled a little more. I'll make sure to come and buy it from you guys."

The elderly lady's face scrunched up into a smile. "Nothing would please me more. Now, check the engravings to make sure they're to your liking."

Monty checked both rings before handing them over to me. "It's something you said earlier, and I really loved it, Kass."

I turned each ring around in my fingers, reading the matching words, and tears filled my eyes.

If I'm with you, it's perfect.

CHAPTER 15

"Okay, I think she's ready," Mrs. Haley whispered as she took her seat beside me in the huge university auditorium.

"I'm no expert, but it seems like she's been killing it all day," I said.

Kassie's teacher grinned like a proud parent. "She's been outstanding. That's how she made it to the finals."

My girlfriend had blown my socks off today. She'd made it through round after round of smaller debates, defeating one person after the other with what seemed like little effort. Even when her opponent would grow heated, Kassie remained calm before shooting holes through their arguments like a well-trained sniper.

"Are we almost done?" eight-year-old Luciana whined from her perch on my lap. "I'm hungry."

Kassie's mother was on the other side of me, and she pulled two packets of fruit snacks from her purse, handing one to Luci and one to Regi, who was on her father's lap.

"Here, mi hija. Only one hour left, and then we can go get dinner."

All heads turned to the stage as the final two participants were introduced. Kassie's heels tapped across the wooden planks as she strolled confidently to her designated podium.

She looked so tiny up there, but she also looked powerful as hell. A fierceness I'd rarely seen from her—aside from when we discussed pizza—gleamed in the dark brown of her eyes, making them seem to glow with determination.

We all stood and cheered like maniacs when Kassie's name and school were announced, and she gave a respectful dip of her chin before her eyes met mine. Her smile illuminated the dim auditorium, and a sense of pride filled me to the brim.

My eyes were drawn away from her when the opponent's name was announced. To my surprise, he was dressed in what I recognized as a *Bouvier* suit in a rich, black fabric with a pale blue tie.

"And from the Bainbrook Academy in Syracuse... Otto Baldwin," the announcer intoned.

My eyebrows lifted. Bainbrook was the school I would be attending, starting Monday.

"That school has a fantastic debate program," Mrs. Haley hissed in my ear. "They've won this competition five of the past eight years." I glanced over to see her chewing nervously on her thumbnail.

"What's the topic?" I whispered back.

The teacher's eyes widened. "Whether birth control should be provided in high schools."

"Oh shit," I muttered, and little Luci's mouth dropped into a tiny O. I pressed my index finger over her lips. "Shh, don't rat me out, kiddo. I'll buy you more Nerds next week."

"I want a Twix too," she demanded, and I happily acquiesced.

"Which side is Kassie arguing?" I asked Mrs. Haley.

"For, but that's a good thing. She loves arguing against her own opinions and beliefs. She thrives on the challenge of it."

Over the next hour, I watched as my girlfriend completely eviscerated her opponent. She was like a tornado, blowing away each argument and counterargument as if they were nothing more than leaves in a storm.

Don't get me wrong; Otto was good, but Kassie was fucking phenom-enal.

"She just wiped the floor with his ass, didn't she?" I asked Mrs. Haley, who grinned like she'd just won the lottery as she nodded.

"Yep."

Luci's eyebrows lifted. "You just said another bad word, Monty."

"Gummy worms?" I asked with an eye roll.

"Yup. The sour ones, please."

I kissed the top of her head. "You're a pretty good negotiator, Luci-Loo. You're going to be just like Kassie one day."

She turned her face toward the stage and found her sister. "I hope so. She's awesome."

I couldn't agree more, kid.

For the first time all day, I noticed Kassie showing signs of nervousness as her hands twisted at her waist. The debate was over, and she and Otto were standing at the front of the stage, awaiting the results.

Her gaze fell on me, and I lifted my index finger and curled it. She tilted her pretty lips upward and then subtly matched my gesture, her shoulders relaxing slightly.

A middle-aged gentleman in a suit walked out onto the stage to an uproar of applause from the audience.

"Thank you, thank you, everyone. We're so happy to see a full house this year for the forty-fifth annual Boland Debates."

Yeah, yeah, dude. Just get on with it.

"I've been hosting this event for the past..."

We don't give a damn, man! Just give us the results.

"And I've never seen such spirited..."

Oh for fuck's sake. Come on!

"As usual, besides the honor and prestige of winning, this year's award includes a full-ride scholarship to the college of their choice granted to the winner."

Wait. What?

Excitement began to build at the base of my spine, creeping slowly up and up until...

"And the winner of this year's Boland Debates is..."

The longest goddamn pause in the history of anticipation took over the room as everyone held their breath. My entire head was about to explode.

Fuck me, man. Hurry up!

"Kassie Ramirez!"

The auditorium erupted. Kassie looked stunned for a split second, her hands rising to cover her mouth. Then I lost sight of her because everyone was standing and cheering.

Except for me. I was still sitting numbly in my chair like a lump on a log. Remedying that, I pushed to my feet, letting out a loud whoop as I propped Luciana on my hip.

Otto was shaking Kassie's hand, his head dipped to whisper something in her ear, and she nodded politely.

I'm not sure how she maintained her composure, chin held high and not a tear in sight. Maybe she was in a bit of shock, though she shouldn't have been. She had to have known what a fantastic performance she gave.

After approximately eight thousand photos and handshakes, Kassie finally made her way down the stairs at the side of the stage where we were all waiting.

Mr. Ramirez got to her first, pulling her into a hug and whispering things that had Kass burying her face in her father's shoulder. They stayed like that for a long while until Mrs. Ramirez couldn't take it anymore and tugged Kassie away.

Then came hugs from Regina, Luciana, and Mrs. Haley while I waited with false patience until it was my turn. Finally, she walked into my arms, and I nestled my nose against her ear.

"I'm so freaking proud of you, Kasserole," I said in a low voice that was raspy with emotion.

"I'm kinda freaking proud of myself," she replied, her arms tight around my middle.

Lifting my head, I brushed away a strand of hair that had escaped from her prim bun. "Did you know about the scholarship beforehand?"

Her head bobbed up and down. "Sorry I didn't tell you. I didn't want to jinx myself."

I wanted to kiss her so badly, but her family and teacher were standing only a few feet away, so I reluctantly pulled back, taking her small hands in mine. "Your parents invited me to dinner. Is that okay with you?"

She nodded, her closed lips tipped up into a smile and her eyes bright.

"Okay, let's get out of here before Luci blackmails me for any more candy."

"What does that mean?"

"Tell ya later," I murmured, looping an arm around her shoulders as we followed her family from the auditorium.

Dinner with the Ramirez family was a noisy event full of laughter, chattering, and love. It was nothing like the customary meals with my family.

My egg donor—that was Chloe's new moniker in my head because she'd never been a mother—insisted that we have bi-monthly dinners at the latest hot spots in New York.

Only the trendiest restaurants for the Bouvier family.

She liked to be seen out and about with her famous husband and *perfect* kids. *Or I guess not so perfect in my case,* I thought bitterly.

Sitting here with the Ramirezes and Mrs. Haley at a small burger joint though, it was... fun. And there wasn't a tuxedoed maître d' or pristine white tablecloth in sight.

It certainly wasn't all bad growing up. I'd had fun meals with my father and siblings around our huge dining room table when the egg donor was away at one of her many "retreats." But when Chloe was present, the meals were subdued and laden with complaints.

Sit up straight, Auburn.

That's not the correct fork for this course, Monty.

Evelyn, you will not wear that hairstyle to this dinner table again.

My eyes trailed around the table at this cheap burger restaurant, and I was pretty sure I'd never had a finer meal. Regi and Luci were arguing over whether tater tots or french fries were superior while Mrs. Haley and Mrs. Ramirez recounted their favorite parts of today's debate.

Kass was taking ravenous bites of her bacon-jalapeño burger as her father quietly surveyed his family with pride. To be honest, I was feeling pretty damn proud to be here with these folks myself.

Leaning over, I whispered, "I want all of our family dinners to be exactly like this."

"Me too," Kassie said, dabbing a smear of mustard from the corner of her mouth.

Mister Ramirez, obviously having overheard, gave me a tentative smile and pushed the family-sized platter of fries in my direction. "More french fries, Monty?"

"Yes, sir," I said immediately, grabbing a handful, even though I was completely stuffed. It was a small gesture from him, but in my mind, it was big on acceptance.

Curling my arm around Kassie's shoulders, I pictured our future, and I wanted it to look exactly like this.

Mustard faces. Arguing kids who were slumping comfortably in their chairs. Normal conversations not built around things my mother could brag about later.

In a word: happiness.

CHAPTER 16

MONTY HELD MY HAND as he drove us toward the Hilton on a Saturday in early March. We hadn't been alone together in weeks, and I was *needy*. Damn hormones were making me crazy.

There was always someone at my house, and we could no longer go to his parents' apartment. The round-trip drive to my house from Syracuse was eight hours, so we'd decided to get a hotel room in New York for the day.

"You like your new school?"

"It's fine. The uniforms are hideous though. The jackets are dark green and gold, and I feel like I've just won the Masters tournament," he said with a grin. "Oh, I forgot to tell you. My tour guide on my first day was Otto Baldwin."

"The guy from the Boland Debates?" I asked in surprise.

"Yep, he was a pretty cool guy. Invited me to sit with him and his friends at lunch."

"He was really nice backstage and after the debate."

"Even after you kicked his ass?"

I nodded and laughed. "He was a very gracious loser."

"I really like my art teacher, Mrs. Benson. Our final grade for the semester is based on a project of our choosing. The only requirement is that it should be something that inspires us. I sat down and worked on it for three hours last night." His eyes flashed to me and then back to the road. "It was great. I actually felt like drawing for the first time in the past few weeks."

God I felt so bad for him. He'd lost his home and his relationship with his dad all because of me. And it was affecting his passion for drawing.

"I'm sorry, Monty." My chin dipped to my chest as he whipped his car beneath the brick portico. When a valet approached, Monty held up a finger for him to wait.

Reaching over and tilting my face up to meet his striking blue eyes, he asked, "What are you sorry for?"

"You're going through all this stuff, and I don't know how to help you."

He nuzzled his nose against mine. "Just be with me. That's all I need, Kassie."

Wrapping my arms around his neck, I gave him a fierce hug, pouring all my emotions into the embrace. "What did you draw?"

He pulled back and smiled shyly. "Wedding dresses." At my confused frown, he said, "For later. I know we're having a small ceremony at your church in a few months, but I want us to have a big wedding one day. And I want to design your wedding dress."

"Monty..." A tear slipped down my face, and he smudged it away with a gentle thumb. "I would love that so much."

"Good," he said, climbing out of the car and coming around to help me out. "I did three different ones, but the trumpet silhouette is my favorite so far. I still can't get the back of it quite right, but I have plenty of time to work on it. When I'm done, I'll show them to you, and you can decide which one you like the most."

Monty had checked into the hotel before he picked me up, and as we walked to the elevator, my core clenched in anticipation.

His footsteps stalled as we approached the gold doors. "Oh, I forgot to ask. Are you hungry? We can grab a bite to eat in the restaurant first—"

"No. I'm ready to go to the room. Now."

His sexy mouth curved into a slow smile as we entered the elevator.

As soon as the doors closed, he pressed me back against the wall and devoured my lips, his hands sliding down to cup my bottom. "I can't wait to be alone with you either," he murmured into my mouth. The ride to the top floor seemed to take only seconds, and after one final kiss, Monty wrapped an arm around me and led me out into the hallway.

Elegant light fixtures were mounted to the wall every few feet, bathing the corridor in a warm, yellow glow. Monty's left hand slipped into the back pocket of my jeans as he guided me to the right, and I loved the move. It told the world: *this girl—this one right here—she's mine.*

"This is us," he said, pulling a keycard from his pocket and tapping it against the reader.

When the door opened, I had to bite back a gasp. I'd only stayed in a hotel room once in my life, and it was nothing like this. There were no stains on the carpet or tacky, multicolored bedspreads.

No, this room was understated yet elegant. The covers on the king-sized bed were crisp and white, and there was actually a dining table, couch, and chair near the huge plate-glass window.

"Monty, it's beautiful! It's like a whole apartment in here!" I walked over to the window, dragging my hand across the pale red couch cushions as I went. There wasn't much to see outside the window, just more buildings, but the early March sky was bright blue and clear beyond.

Reaching for the white rods, I closed the curtains, dimming the illumination in the room to the two lamps on either side of the bed. When I turned back around, my boyfriend was staring at me, one finger rubbing back and forth along his bottom lip.

"Monty, this seems awfully expensive. I don't mean to be a Frugal Franny, but are you sure—"

"It was free, baby." He stalked slowly toward me and grasped my hands. "Auburn had hotel points, so it didn't cost anything. Don't worry about it, okay?"

"Okay," I said, relief easing through me before I was struck by what he said. "Wait. Auburn knows we're here?"

He nodded. "Yeah, my brother booked the room since I'm underage."

"What?" I practically screeched. "Does he know what we came here for?"

Monty lifted one eyebrow. "Well, I told him we needed a place to do arts and crafts, but I'm not sure he believed me."

"Ugh! I can't believe I'm marrying such a smartass."

"We all have our crosses to bear," he retorted, tugging me gently until my arms were around his waist. "Don't worry about my brother. He only wants us to be together and happy."

As always, I felt at home in Monty's arms and laid my head on his chest. "Okay, if you're sure. I don't want him to think badly of me."

"Kass, we're expecting a baby. I'm pretty sure he knows we have sex." I giggled as Monty ran his fingers through my hair. "Plus, it's not like us going to a hotel is going to shock or offend him. He's probably done worse before breakfast."

The mere mention of sex had my panties growing wet, and I tangled my hands in Monty's hair. "I think you should kiss me now."

He complied immediately, his lips brushing softly against mine. When my hands tightened and my body pressed against his, he took it deeper, plunging his tongue between my lips as his chest rumbled against me.

I loved when he made that noise, like he had a motor inside him that revved when things started heating up between us.

A sharp pinch shot through my abdomen like someone had looped a thread around my waist and tightened it. I winced, but it disappeared almost as quickly as it appeared.

"What's wrong, baby?" Monty asked, releasing my lips and frowning down at me.

"It was nothing. Just a weird feeling for a second. That book you gave me said that as the baby grows, things will start to feel different." I placed my hand on my belly and smoothed it up and down.

"Are you sure? Maybe you need to eat or drink something. Have you had enough water today?" His doting made me smile. Even before I got pregnant, Monty was always concerned about me, but he'd completely leveled up since we'd found out we were expecting.

"I've had about half a gallon already today." I rolled my eyes to the ceiling. "Actually, I probably just need to use the restroom after drinking all that. The book said that would happen too."

"Okay, sweetheart," he said, sweeping the back of his index finger down my cheek before tapping my nose.

I stepped into the bathroom and closed the door behind me, glancing around at the creamy tile and fluffy white towels. On the back of the door, there was a wooden hanger with a fuzzy bathrobe that I wanted to cozy up in.

In fact, maybe I would put it on now and then walk out of the bathroom wearing only my lingerie underneath. Then my hot-as-hell boyfriend could unwrap me. I shivered in anticipation.

After stepping out of my boots, I removed my socks and wiggled my toes against the coolness of the tile. Then I stripped off my black-and-red sweater and folded it neatly on the countertop before peeling off my black leggings and doing the same.

My breasts had seemed to grow overnight, so I'd had to buy a new bra this week. I'd found a pretty baby-pink one on the clearance rack and a pair of panties that were a shade darker but still looked good enough.

My forehead furrowed when I noticed a stain on the crotch of my brand new underwear, and I bent to get a better look. That's when I saw the trickle of blood sliding down my left thigh.

No!

I snatched up a washcloth and swiped the blood away—as if that would fix everything—but another stubborn trail appeared right behind the first. Pressing the thick cloth between my legs, I opened my mouth.

"Monty!" I could barely hear my own voice. Maybe because my brain was clouded with fear. Maybe because my voice was barely a whisper. Or perhaps both.

"Monty!" I cried again, this time louder, the word rounded and full like a balloon that had been overfilled.

He burst through the door, his eyes dashing around the room, looking for the danger. "Kassie! Wha—"

I held up the now bloody washcloth, and the panic was evident on every feature of his face.

"Kass, no. No."

"Monty, I'm..."

He turned in a circle one way and then the other, looking for god knows what. Under other circumstances it would have been comical. But it wasn't. Not even a little bit.

Monty seemed to gather his wits because he pulled the white bathrobe from the door, the wooden hanger clattering noisily to the floor. He managed to drape it around me at the same time he pulled out his phone.

"I'm calling an ambulance, Kass. Does anything hurt? Can you tell me what happened?"

My hands protectively covered our tiny baby in my belly, and a pain ripped through me, deep and hard. "Owwww!" I moaned, doubling over.

Monty caught me, lifting me in his arms and settling on the lip of the large bathtub with me in his lap.

He made the phone call, his voice sounding calmer than his face looked. I could tell he was freaking out but trying not to show it. He was trying to be strong for me.

I wanted to comfort him; I really did. But I couldn't do or say anything. The pain in my abdomen had dulled to one continuous cramp that had me clenching my teeth to keep from crying out.

Monty hung up the phone and wrapped me tightly in his arms, rocking me from side to side. "I've got you, baby."

"Don't. Leave. Me," I managed to eke out as tears clogged my throat and streamed down my face. My hands fisted tightly in his shirt as I buried my face in his neck. I felt like I'd just jumped out of an airplane, and Monty was my parachute, the only thing keeping me from crashing to the ground.

"I won't leave you, Kass. I'll make everything okay."

Turns out, he was wrong.

On both counts.

CHAPTER 17

WE'D LOST HER.

Our baby girl was gone. Our Willow.

I'd never known the true meaning of the word *devastation* before. I thought I was devastated when my mother kicked me out of the house. Then I wasn't sure things could get worse when she cut off my bank account.

I was wrong.

So. Very. Wrong.

This... this pain was indescribable. Unbearable.

But I *had to* bear it. I had to be strong for my Kassie. Because if I was devastated, she was completely broken.

I couldn't even imagine carrying a child inside your body, nurturing and loving her, and then having her ripped away.

Yes, our baby was a little girl; the doctor told us. I'd wanted to be a girl dad so badly. To lay her on my bare chest and feel her little baby breaths. To have tea parties with silly tiaras on our heads. To teach her to catch a ball and ride a bike and throw a punch at any boys who looked at her.

To *love her*.

I held Kassie's hand between both of mine. She was turned on her side, facing me in the hospital bed, finally sleeping, thanks to the pain medication the doctor had given her. But I still wanted her to feel me. Maybe it was as much for me as for her because I needed to feel her too.

Even in sleep, Kassie's face reflected her misery. Turned down mouth. Cheeks ashy with dried tear tracks. Eyebrows furrowed.

Unable to hold back any longer, I let the tears slide in hot, wet streaks down my face. My grief soaked the tweedy white blanket as I buried my head in the covers to muffle my sobs.

When I heard the hospital room door ease open, I swiftly wiped my eyes on the blanket before lifting my head. Kassie's parents appeared, Mrs. Ramirez's face already blotchy and her chin quivering as she approached me slowly.

"Ay, pobrecita," she whispered, looking down at her daughter even as she brushed a hand through my hair. The move was so maternal, it made my tears threaten to return.

"She's sleeping," I said quietly. "Would you like to sit here?"

The woman nodded. I kissed my girlfriend's limp hand and reluctantly handed it over to her mother as we switched places.

Mister Ramirez stood just inside the door, pressing his fingers against his mouth, and I walked over to stand beside him.

"How is she?" he asked quietly, his gaze not wavering from the hospital bed.

"Physically, the doctor said she'll be okay, but emotionally, she's... not great."

The big man shook his head from side to side. "What caused it? This thing that happened to my baby girl?" His voice was husky with his own grief.

"I don't know. The doctor said it happens in a certain percentage of pregnancies."

Mister Ramirez's hand rubbed against his chest, and he muttered, "Pobrecita." It was the same Spanish word his wife had used, and I was pretty sure it meant poor girl or something like that.

"The doctor did say she needs a procedure called... crap, what was it called?" I massaged my forehead and tried to remember what the doctor told me. Everything was so chaotic when we arrived. "A D&C, I think. It's supposed to help it to finish faster so she's not in so much pain."

"It?"

"The... the miscarriage." I could barely get that word out. It was agonizing to even say.

"And Kassie needs this... procedure?" The man's gaze finally met mine, and I saw the concern there.

"Yes, sir. The nurse can explain it better than me. Do you want to talk to her? They need a parent's permission before they can do it anyway."

He nodded and turned to the door. "Whatever is best for my daughter, that's what we'll do."

Two hours later, the papers were signed, and the D&C was done. Kassie was in the recovery room with her mother by her side.

I understood why, but I didn't like it. I wanted to be the one holding her hand. I wanted mine to be the first face she saw when she woke up.

"Mister Ramirez?" a young female nurse asked as she approached. We were in the hallway, waiting for Kass to be brought back to the room.

"Yes," he said, jerking upright from where he'd been leaning wearily against the wall.

"There's been a slight complication with your daughter."

My heart stopped in my chest, and I wasn't sure I wanted it to start up again. Not until I heard her next words.

"Kassie is going to be okay, but she had a reaction to the sedation."

"What kind of reaction?" I practically yelled at the poor woman, and she placed a soothing hand on my arm.

"I promise, she's going to be okay. It took a little longer than normal for her to wake up, and now she's having some vomiting. The doctor said he would like for her to stay overnight for observation."

"I'll stay with her," I said immediately, and Mister Ramirez's eyes jerked to mine and leveled me with a glare.

The nurse seemed oblivious to our standoff as she held out a white plastic bag. "Here are Kassie's clothes. Her underwear and robe are soiled, so they'll need to be washed."

"Robe? What robe?" he asked.

Oh shit.

"It's what she was wearing when she came in to the emergency department. Kassie and your wife should be back down here in a few minutes so you can see for yourself that she's okay."

She strode off, unaware of the bomb she'd just dropped. Directly on top of my head.

Mister Ramirez's jaw clenched, and he took a menacing step toward me. "Where exactly were you and Kassie today?" His voice was scarily low, but I raised my chin with bravery I didn't feel.

"We..." I cleared my throat. "We were at the Hilton."

"You took my daughter to a hotel?" he bellowed, drawing stares from a couple who skirted nervously around us.

"Nothing happened, sir. We were just spending time together." I consciously left out the fact that we'd gone to that hotel room to do precisely what he was probably picturing in his head.

His meaty fist clenched the front of my shirt, yanking my face to within an inch of his. "Listen to me, you pinche puto." I didn't know what that phrase meant, but the spittle dotting my face told me it wasn't complimentary. "I don't want you to—"

"What the fuck is going on here?" My brother's voice rang loud and clear, and I wasn't sure whether to be relieved or more nervous. "Take your fucking hands off my brother."

Auburn stomped toward us wearing an impeccable three-piece suit and looking like power personified, his eyes the color of ice. He'd had a meeting at our dad's office, and I had called him after we'd arrived at the hospital.

"This little asshole took my baby girl to a hotel room to do god knows what, and now..." The big man shoved me away, and I stumbled back two steps as his face fell. "And now my Kassie is in the hospital. Because of *him*."

The pain inside my gut intensified at that. *Is all this my fault?*

"That's bullshit, and you know it, Ramirez. Monty loves that girl and would never put her in harm's way."

"That girl is my daughter!" His voice rose as he jabbed a finger in my direction. "And I don't want *him* around her."

"Excuse me," a nurse hissed, marching up to our group with eyes of steel. She was probably in her early fifties and looked like she didn't take shit from anyone. "You are in a hospital. Don't make me call security."

Mister Ramirez's hands clenched at his sides. "Good, call them, and have this pinche perro kicked out of here."

My brother started to speak, but I held up a hand. I needed to stand up for myself. I pushed down my anger and chose my words carefully as I glanced down at her nametag.

"Nurse Shields, I understand why Mister Ramirez is upset, but all I want is to see my girlfriend. She needs me."

The woman's sharp gray eyes softened. "You're the father of Kassie's baby?"

Pinching my lips together, I nodded, only able to tamp down my impending tears when Auburn placed a warm hand on my shoulder and squeezed.

Kassie's father spoke up again, his voice slightly calmer. "Monty said he wants to stay overnight with her, but that's her mother's place."

Our new mediator nodded thoughtfully. "I understand. This is a horrible situation, but Kassie needs everyone to come together." She popped her hands on her ample hips. "How do you think she would feel if she overheard all this arguing?"

I dropped chastised eyes to the floor. "I don't want to argue. I respect Mister Ramirez, but I need him to respect me too."

"Hmmm. How about this?" the nurse said. "If it's okay with Kassie, her mother can stay the night with her. She may need a woman's touch for certain things she'll be going through." She turned to the large man across from me and waggled a finger at him. "But she's also going to want to see Monty. They've suffered a terrible loss, and they need time to mourn together."

After a long beat, Kassie's dad nodded with grudging acceptance. "Okay, fine."

A tiny smile of victory appeared on her lips. "Wonderful. Do you like Italian food?"

He seemed taken aback by the shift in conversation and answered with a tentative, "Yes."

Nurse Shields dug into the pocket of her pink scrubs and pulled out two wrinkled slips of paper. "My brother is the owner and chef at Antonio's. He gives me a few of these vouchers every week to give away to families of my patients."

Mister Ramirez fiddled with the collar of his denim work shirt. "I don't know..." he hedged.

"It's a family restaurant, so the dress code is casual. You look fine." She held out the vouchers, and he took them from her. "Take your wife and have a nice meal together. That will give your daughter the time she needs. It's only a block away from here."

"Okay, that's... that's very kind of you. Thank you." With one last look at me, he turned on his heel and strode off down the corridor.

"Wow," Auburn said to Nurse Shields, "you're good. If you ever decide you want a career change, you can come work at *Bouvier* to negotiate contracts."

She smiled at him. "Mister Bouvier, I adore my job." She stared down the hallway at Mr. Ramirez's retreating back. "But on days like today, that's a very tempting offer."

CHAPTER 18

Monty held the straw to my lips, and I sucked up a small sip of the bubbly Sprite before he set it aside.

"Can I get you anything else, baby?"

I nodded as another tear—one of a million I'd shed in the past few hours—slipped down my face.

"What is it, Kass? I'll do anything." His voice sounded pained and desperate, and I hated that he was hurting because of me.

Silently, I pulled back the blankets covering me, and he immediately pulled off his shoes before carefully crawling onto the bed beside me.

"Hold me."

Without a word, he wedged one arm beneath my head and wrapped the other around my body. The empty spot inside me, where our baby had been, was pressed against his warm torso, and I cried.

I cried my heart out.

Everything was raw, inside and out, including a place inside me I hadn't even known I possessed. It was a deep, dark vessel of pain that felt as though someone had scrubbed it with steel wool until it was bleeding.

"I know, baby," Monty whispered, pressing his cheek on top of mine. I felt his tears mingle with my own, and there was something comforting about that—sharing my pain with the only other person who understood. It didn't make this better; it simply felt... cleansing.

Then I puked on him.

He flinched at first but didn't recoil, even as I continued retching against his shirt. "I'm... sorry," I managed to heave out, but he simply rubbed my back, not letting me pull away.

"It's okay. Get it all out."

"God I'm so gross," I whined.

"No, you're sick, Kass," he said kindly. "I'll get the nurse to bring you some more anti-nausea meds."

I'd just vomited on my boyfriend, and his only concern was me. I loved him more than anything.

Ten minutes later, my bed linens were being changed as Monty wrapped an arm around me and led me into the small bathroom. His hands were gentle as he used a cloth to clean me up and help me into a fresh gown. Then he held my hair back so I could brush my teeth.

"Feel better?" he asked when I was done.

"Yeah." I reached for a clean washcloth and held it beneath the warm water before lathering it with soap.

Monty had stripped off his soiled shirt, but he still smelled like vomit, so I rubbed the soapy cloth against his bare chest.

"I can do that, Kassie," he protested, trying to take it away from me.

"Please let me." My eyes implored him. I needed this, to do something, to take care of someone. *Like I would have done for her.*

"Okay, sweetheart. Whatever you want."

My movements were slow, my strokes meticulous, as I cleaned and rinsed my boyfriend. His hands were steady on my waist, supporting me. Then I dried him, softly dabbing his skin before hanging the towel back on the rack.

"Thank you for taking care of me," he whispered, pulling me close and kissing the top of my head.

He got it. He got *me*.

"It's the least I could do since I hurled on you." My lips tried to form a smile, but it felt foreign, and I pushed it away.

We stood holding each other, taking and giving the comfort we both needed until...

Knock, knock, knock.

Holding me with one arm, Monty used the other to twist open the doorknob. One of the nurses held out a scrub top.

"There you go."

"Stop thinking about apologizing," he said once he'd taken the shirt and closed the door. Lowering his forehead to mine, he brushed feather-light kisses across my lips. "I love you, Kass, and I'd rather have a lifetime of messiness with you than one spotless minute without you."

"You're the most beautiful person I know, Monty." My eyes drifted closed, and my body sagged against him as the anti-nausea meds kicked in. "I love you," I slurred.

"I've got you," he said, carefully lifting me into his arms and grabbing the IV bag from the hanger on the wall.

As Monty laid me on the bed, I heard him murmur something to a nurse, and a couple minutes later, I pried open my eyes to find him unwrapping a small hairbrush from its clear wrapper. Then he proceeded to brush my hair in long, smooth strokes.

"I love having... my... hair brushed," I said through the yawn forcing my jaw open.

"I know, sweetheart."

"Stay with me till I fall asleep?"

"Do you want me to stay until your parents get back?"

The haze of medication was taking over me, drifting me toward the peaceful sleep that my body needed as much as I needed air in my lungs.

"No, I want to sleep. Can you come see me when I get home tomorrow?"

"Wild horses couldn't keep me away."

"M'kay."

The bristles of the brush scraped lightly against my scalp, and I carried his assurance with me into dreamland.

A sweet, cloying aroma flowed around me, and I tried to force my eyelids open. They were heavy though, and it took a few minutes for consciousness to fully take over.

A groan escaped me, my mouth unable to form actual words as I rolled only my back. When my eyes finally opened, someone was sitting in the chair beside my bed.

"Mrs. Bou—" My voice sounded like I'd swallowed a cactus, and I looked toward the small nightstand for anything that would help me clear it.

"Here you go, dear," Chloe Bouvier said, handing me a can of ginger ale with a straw.

Is this a dream? Is Monty's mother really sitting in my hospital room and handing me a drink?

I pushed up onto one elbow and took slow, careful sips, hoping the contents of my stomach would stay put this time. Puking on my boyfriend was bad enough, but in front of his mother? *Jesus, no.* The woman was so elegant and put together, I wasn't sure she'd ever vomited in her entire life.

The fizz of the ginger ale seemed to clear away the cobwebs in my mind, and I was able to push the button to raise the head of my bed.

"Hello, Mrs. Bouvier." I forced a placid smile on my face. I had no idea what she was doing here. The woman had barely spoken two words to me in the entire eighteen months Monty and I had dated.

"How are you feeling, Kassie?" Saccharine dripped off her tongue, deceptively sweet but with a bitter undertone that lingered.

"I'm okay. I get to go home tomorrow."

"That's excellent. Then you can get your life back on track." She brushed a nonexistent piece of lint from the sleeve of her perfectly tailored olive-green suit. "And my son can do the same."

The words left my mouth before I could stop them, perhaps because of the effects of the medication. Or perhaps because I was annoyed that she was here. "I thought he wasn't your son anymore."

Chloe's lips tightened at the corners. "Of course he is. He'll always be a Bouvier, even when he's being naive and letting himself be manipulated by a very clever girl." She leaned forward, the light over my bed catching the blonde highlights in her hair. "And you *are* a very clever girl, aren't you, Kassie?"

"I've never once manipulated Monty, Mrs. Bouvier."

She waved a manicured hand, dismissing my words. "That's a matter of debate. Speaking of debate, I heard you won a scholarship."

My head spun at the change in direction. "Yes."

"So you no longer need my family to pay for your education."

A metallic crinkle met my ears, and I realized I was squeezing the soda can so tightly it was bent in on the sides.

"I never wanted your family's money," I spat. "That's not why I'm with Monty. We're in love."

The woman actually laughed in my face. "Oh come on. My son doesn't love you. You're just the first girl who spread her legs for him. Men are so easily distracted by sex. I've got to hand it to you though; you played your hand well, Kassie. Ending up *accidentally* pregnant with his child."

Her implication was clear, and my hands shook with anger. "It *was* an accident."

"Hmmm, sure it was. But things have a way of working themselves out, don't they?" She glanced down at my belly, and I suddenly felt nauseous again.

"I think I'd like for you to leave." *Before I throw this can at you.*

The woman pursed her lips. "Not until I've said this. My husband is going to talk to our son. Now that all... *this*... is finished, he can come back home tomorrow. You had to have known it wouldn't last. You and Monty are worlds apart as far as status goes."

"Monty doesn't care about status," I argued, trying to keep my anger and fear under control. "We only want to be together."

"Don't be stupid, Kassie. He's a Bouvier, for god's sake. He never intended to marry you. Now that the pregnancy situation is resolved, he has no reason to stay with you. You were always just a dirty little fling for him."

I knew in my heart that wasn't true, but the woman was doing an excellent job of playing right into my insecurities. *What the hell does Monty even see in me?*

As if she could read the thoughts on my face, she continued. "You seem to be a smart enough young lady. Ask yourself what you bring to the table in a relationship like that. Besides embarrassing my son with your lack of breeding and culture. Can you even imagine going to a black tie dinner, dear?"

That last word sounded like she was trying to be kind, but I felt it pierce my heart like the sharp jab that it was. My debate skills failed me because I had absolutely no argument for that.

Chloe blinked several times before driving her point home. "Would you even know which is the fish knife in a twelve-piece setting?" *There's a specific knife to use for fish?* Reading the answer in my eyes, she continued.

"Save yourself—and my son—the embarrassment and get out while you can. This whole incident is an excellent excuse for a break."

"Incident? Are you talking about Monty and I losing our baby?" The words hurt to even say.

"Yes, such a tragedy," she replied with a simpering smile. "Like I said, this would be a good opportunity for you both to move on. There's a very nice girl that Monty has been talking to at his school. She's much more..." The woman tapped her French-manicured nail against her chin. "She's more *suitable* for Monty, but he's been holding back on letting things go further out of loyalty to you."

"Th-that's not true." *Could it be? No. Definitely not.* But she'd planted the seed of doubt and then watered it with her next words.

"Then maybe you're not as smart as I thought you were." She made an arrogant little tsking sound. "Of course there are hordes of young ladies that would be more than willing to marry my son. The sooner you get your head out of the clouds and realize that you're only holding him back, the better."

Averting my eyes, unable to look at her smug face for another second, I rasped, "Please leave."

"Okay," she said amenably, rising and tucking her designer handbag beneath her arm. "Just think about everything I've said. If you truly love Monty, then you'll want to do what's best for him."

Chloe Bouvier's high heels clacked across the tile floor. I'd have known the second she exited my room even if I hadn't heard the door close behind her. The atmosphere was somehow lighter without her here, as if her presence was a heavy, evil weight on each molecule of air.

Though the air in the room softened, there was a hard, oppressive force in my gut, and I reached for the basin beside my bed, heaving out the meager contents of my stomach.

Chapter 19

"Mi corazoncita," my mother's voice said, stroking a cool hand over my forehead. "Are you okay?"

Spitting one last time, I nodded, and she whisked the basin away.

"Was that Monty's mother we saw in the hallway?" my father asked, his arms crossed over his broad chest.

"Yes," I croaked, reaching for the ginger ale can and taking a fizzy sip. "She came by to talk to me."

"What the hell did that woman say to you?" Papá demanded, his voice taking on a growly timbre that only made me sob harder.

"N-nothing. It's not worth repeating."

My parents exchanged a look, and my mother shook her head before settling onto the bed beside me. "It's not important, Lucas," she chastised as she took me into her arms. "Just hush for now."

Mama's shirt was soaked by the time I was finished crying.

"We need to go home and pack a bag for your mother," Papá said softly. "Is there anything you need from the house?"

My head shook side to side. "No, and actually, I'd like to be alone tonight."

Mama gasped. "No, Kassie! I should stay here with you. You need me."

"Mama, I really want to be alone. I need time to process my thoughts." With great effort, I forced a smile onto my face. "I'll be fine."

Papá regarded me with his dark eyes, and I silently begged him to understand. Giving a subtle nod, he told my mom, "Lorna, let her have some time to herself. You know how our Kassie is. She needs the quiet to think."

"Okay, mi hija," she finally said. "If that's what you want, but I'm worried about what that woman said to you. You were so upset when we came in."

"It's been an emotional day, Mama."

She kissed each of my cheeks and squeezed my hand. "I'm going to make sure the nurses have our home number and your father's cell number. I can be here in minutes, so you tell them to call me if you need me. At any hour, understand?"

"Yes, ma'am," I replied. After one more round of kisses, she left me alone with my father.

"Do you want to talk about it?" he asked.

I shook my head but then changed it to a shrug. "Do you think I'm good enough for Monty?"

Papá's face reddened, and he squinched his eyes shut for a long moment. "Is that what that woman filled your head with?"

"Something like that," I muttered.

He opened his eyes, and I read the ferocious love of a father there. "You, princesa, are the most wonderful person I know. I know we don't have much money, but money doesn't make you a good person. You are kind, so smart, and... what's the word?" His eyes rolled to the ceiling for a second. "Driven. You have the heart of a warrior, my Kassie, and no amount of money can buy that. You're going to be whatever the hell you want to be in life, and the Bouviers can fuck off if they don't like it."

I dipped my chin at his praise. My father wasn't a man of many words, but the ones he did speak were full of love and passion.

"Thank you."

He pulled me close, and I nestled my face into the crook of his neck fighting off the urge to cry again. He smelled familiar and strong, and I loved him so damn much.

"Don't worry, mi corazoncita. Papá will take care of everything," he murmured into my hair. "I'll make it all okay."

I didn't know what that meant, but I clung to my father for a long while before pulling back. "I love you, Papá."

"I love you too, my sweet girl."

He stood and stared down at me. "We will see you in the morning unless you need us during the night."

Once he was gone, I rolled onto my side. That seemed to be the most comfortable position for me, but I needed something else.

My finger found the call button on the remote, and Nurse Shields entered a minute later. "Kassie, what can I help you with? Are you finally hungry?"

My face scrunched up. Food was the last thing I wanted. "No, thank you, but could I have another pillow?"

"Of course." She left and returned shortly, handing over my request. "Anything else, honey?"

"Yes, do you... do you have a cell phone I could borrow?"

I needed to talk to Monty. I'd tell him everything his mother had said to me, and he would tell me it was all bullshit and that he loved me. Then maybe I could find a little bit of peace on this dreadful night.

The nurse's gray eyes shifted to the door as she reached into her hip pocket. "I'm not supposed to have this while I'm on duty, so I'm trusting you to keep this our little secret."

I nodded and took the device, staring at all the icons on the screen. It was one of those new iPhones like Monty had, so I knew how to make a call with it. I pressed the phone button and froze.

What are the last four digits of his number?

Nine-five-something-something. Or was it five-nine?

I closed my eyes and tried to make my brain remember, but it wasn't coming to me. The number was programmed into my cell phone, so I didn't have it memorized.

Nine-five, and is there a four?

Gnawing on my bottom lip, I opened my eyes to see Nurse Shields staring at me with concern. "Do you need help dialing?"

A long sigh pushed from my lips as I reluctantly handed the phone back over. "No, I can't remember the number."

"Try to rest, sweetheart. Maybe it will come to you once your brain has relaxed a bit. If so, just hit that call button again, and I'll come running with the contraband. I'm on until midnight." She flashed me a sweet smile before leaving.

Bringing the spare pillow to my stomach, I held it there, pretending I was still pregnant with our baby girl. I finally seemed to be out of tears, thank god. My face was raw from crying so much.

My thoughts turned to Monty and his mother. I was pretty sure everything she said was complete crap, aside from the part about me not fitting in. That part was a hundred percent true.

There's a very nice girl that Monty has been talking to at his school.

I was convinced that was a lie. It *had* to be. His love for me was too deep and too real for him to be interested in another person.

You're just the first girl who spread her legs for him. Men are so easily distracted by sex.

That was also a load of bull. Monty had waited for over a year before we had sex. He was so sweet and patient with me, telling me he would wait forever, if that's what I needed. If all he'd wanted was sex, he certainly could have found a million girls willing to do it, but he waited for me.

I held the pillow tighter to my middle. He said he would come over tomorrow. We could talk then.

But... he never came.

Chapter 20

I STARED AT THE phone in my hand, confusion clouding my vision. Blinking a few times, I read the text again. It was still the same as the last ten times I'd read it.

> **Kassie: Can you please not come over today? I'd like to be alone for a while.**

A knock on my bedroom door distracted me from reading it an eleventh time. "Come in."

"Hey," Auburn said, opening my door and leaning against the doorframe. "Do you want to grab a bite to eat before you head to Kassie's?"

"I don't think I'm going."

My brother sighed. "If you need gas money, all you have to do is ask. In fact, I'm starting you a new bank account tomorrow."

"It's not the money. She texted and said she didn't want to see me."

He crossed to my bed and poked my shoulder. "Scooch over." I did, and Auburn sat against the headboard beside me, leaning over to look at my phone. "Hmmm, ask her if she's okay. Maybe she got sick and is afraid she'll blow chunks on you again."

I knew his gentle teasing was done to make me smile, but it didn't work. I tapped out a message and received a reply a couple seconds later.

After a few minutes, it became awkwardly obvious that she wasn't going to say it back, and Auburn pushed off the bed.

"Bet she's asleep. Let's go grab a pizza." When I started to protest, he thumped me on the head. "You didn't eat anything for breakfast, goober. Come on."

I forced down a single slice of pizza at the restaurant, glancing down at my phone every minute or so. When we got back home, I went upstairs to my room and pulled out my sketch pad.

I'd just picked up a drawing pencil when my phone rang. I snatched it up and was disappointed to see my dad's name displayed instead of Kassie's.

"Hello."

His voice was shaky when he spoke. "Monty, I talked to Auburn, and I wanted to let you know how sorry I am about the baby."

"Thanks, Dad."

"And please give Kassie my condolences as well. My heart is just broken for both of you."

"I will. I appreciate that."

We talked for a few minutes. He asked about my new school since this was the first time I'd talked to my dad since the night I left. It felt good. I'd missed him so much.

Until he said, "I really wish you would come home, son."

All the frustration I'd been feeling since this morning bubbled over like a pot left on the stove too long.

"Oh, so now that my baby is dead, I'm welcome to come back home?" I spat.

"No, n-no, Monty," he spluttered. "That's not how I meant—"

I hung up on him, so angry I broke my pencil in half. Tossing it in the trash, I selected another from my leather case and took a few calming breaths. My mind went instantly to the baby we'd lost yesterday, and a picture formed in my head.

Then my pencil began to move in smooth, round strokes, forming the face of what I imagined my newborn daughter would have looked like in a few months.

She had dark hair like me and Kass, and I sketched out dark eyes like her mother. Long, thick eyelashes and a cupid's bow mouth. Tiny ears. A button nose.

A tear dropped from my eye onto one of her cheeks, and I didn't bother wiping it away. It seemed to belong there, like my sadness was a part of her.

Two days later, I was sitting on my bed, scrolling through the text messages between me and Kassie, starting with yesterday's.

> **Monty: I'm not going to school today. I can come see you, if you want.**

> **Kassie: Not today, okay?**

> **Monty: Okay. If that's what you want.**

Then another later that day.

> **Monty:** *I hope you're having a good evening. I'd really like to see you.*

> **Kassie: I'm sorry. I'm just really tired.**

> **Monty:** *We don't even have to talk. I just want to be near you. I can bring my sketchbook and work while you sleep.*

And then this morning's text.

> **Monty:** *Good morning, baby. I sent you some flowers. Did you get them?*

It was almost noon, and I'd received no response.

"Fuck it," I muttered, rolling off the bed and putting my shoes on before heading downstairs.

Four hours later, I arrived at the Ramirez home and jogged up the steps. Two stuffed puppies were tucked beneath my arm for Regi and Luci. I'd wanted to get the girls a little something since I was sure they would be upset about the loss of the baby. They'd been so excited about becoming aunts.

As I knocked, I noticed the flower arrangement sitting on the small porch. The florist had done a beautiful job. I'd asked for something cheerful, and the multicolored blooms were bright against the dull brick.

Getting no answer, I knocked again.

"Monty, is that you?" The voice came from behind me, and I whirled around to find the Ramirezes' widowed neighbor on the sidewalk. She was wearing a thick, black, wool coat as she took her chihuahua for a walk.

I trotted down to meet her. "Hi, Mrs. Dupree. Do you know—"

"Oh, you dear boy," she interrupted, wrapping her chubby arms around my middle. "I'm so sorry for your loss."

"Thank you. It's been a terrible few days," I replied, patting her back.

"I can only imagine. I kept the little girls while Lorna and Lucas went to the hospital."

"That was really kind of you, Mrs. Dupree. Hey, do you know where Kassie is? I'm a little worried she's not home."

The old lady stuck a finger beneath her pumpkin-orange knit cap and scratched her head. "Well, they left this morning. Did you get the days mixed up?"

A nervous energy skittered down my spine. "Left to go where? Did Kassie have a doctor's appointment or something."

Mrs. Dupree shook her head, as if confused. *Yeah, join the party, lady.*

"Today was moving day, Monty. I was shocked when they told me they were leaving the neighborhood. They've been such wonderful neighbors."

My hand went to my throat, trying to push back the bile that was rising there. "Where did they go?"

The woman's eyes narrowed. "Didn't Kassie tell you? Did you two have a tiff?"

"No, ma'am. Not that I know of."

"Ah, she was so distraught, she must have forgotten since it all happened so fast. Such a sweet dear. Still, I would have thought she'd mention it to you."

Me too.

Trying to remain calm and not yell at this poor little old lady, I asked again, "Where did they go?"

She brought a gloved hand to her face and massaged her chin. "You know, I don't think they actually told me where they were going. It must be pretty far though because Lorna came over this morning and gave me the food from their refrigerator. Said it would spoil before they got there." She shrugged. "Wherever *there* is."

Attempting to keep the bitterness from my tone, I said, "There's been so much going on, I guess no one had time to mention it to me. Do you know when all this occurred?"

"The first I heard of it was yesterday when the moving van showed up. Then the whole family got in their vehicle early this morning with a couple big suitcases and left. I thought it was very odd that it all happened so quickly."

"I know how you feel," I muttered. "Thanks for the information, Mrs. Dupree."

Her smile was tentative. "I'm sure Kassie will call you soon and let you know where she is."

"I'm sure she will," I replied before walking toward my car.

But I wasn't sure at all.

Nothing.

That's what I'd heard from Kassie for the past week. I'd thrown myself into drawing... sketching and re-sketching the wedding dresses like a mad man.

My mind said maybe if I worked faster, made the dresses more perfect... then she would miraculously call me.

It didn't work.

I was equal parts panicked and heartbroken. I'd lost weight—I didn't even know how much, but my clothes hung limply off my frame—because I could barely eat.

Little did I know that things were about to get worse.

On a cool evening in late March, Auburn entered my room, his face as serious as I'd ever seen it.

"Monty, you need to sit down."

"Bro, I am sitting."

He glanced at me in my desk chair and nodded, a numb robotic movement. "Oh yeah. I guess *I* need to sit down."

My brother had a hundred percent of my attention as he sank onto my bed with his head in his hands.

"Auburn, what's wrong?"

"I-I have to tell you something."

"Okay. You're freaking me out a little bit."

He dragged his hands down his face until his fingertips covered his mouth, muffling his voice. "It's bad, Monty. So fucking bad." Tears pooled in his eyes, and my heart traveled north until it was stuck in my throat.

"Just tell me," I whispered, even though I was pretty sure I didn't want to hear what he was going to say.

Was there another terrorist attack? Did our dad have cancer? What the hell was it?

Then my brother reached into my chest and ripped out what was left of my heart.

"Monty, Evie is missing."

PART TWO

THE PRESENT

CHAPTER 21

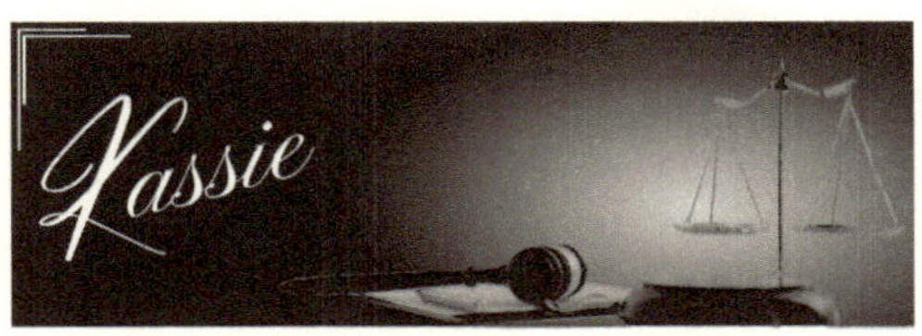

MY EYES SCANNED DOWN the document, and I made a couple corrections to the third paragraph. Then I reread the entire thing again until a hand tapped on my elbow.

"Mommy, I'm bored."

Pulling my fingers from the keyboard and hiding the document, I brushed a lock of sandy-brown hair from my five-year-old son's forehead.

"Only a couple more days of Christmas vacation, and you'll be back at school, Sully. You won't be bored then, huh?"

He smiled the cutest smile to ever cross a pair of lips, and I kissed his nose.

"I can't wait to see my friends again," Sullivan Ramirez said, his small feet tapping in a happy dance.

"You get to see Sid almost every day."

As if on cue, Sid's mother entered my office. "Aunt Lily!" Sullivan exclaimed, running to my best friend with his arms held wide.

She picked him up and cuddled him against her. "Hey, Sul. How are you getting so big?"

"My mama feeds me every day," he replied with all the seriousness in the world.

Lily put on her best shocked face. "For real? Every single day?" He nodded sagely as she sat in the chair across from my desk with my son on her lap. Her little boy, Siddhanth, was the same age as Sully, their birthdays only about a month apart, and they were best friends.

"Did you bring Sid to work with you?" my kid asked, his brown eyes bright with little boy hope.

"No, he's with his dad today. He's working from home." Sully's lips turned down into a frown, but Lily quickly added, "Why don't you come over and play with him tonight?"

"Okay," he happily agreed. "I'll bring my trucks."

"How's your mom?" I asked. Mrs. Ganjam was undergoing treatments for ovarian cancer, and she had chemo today.

"Dad called a little bit ago and said she's good. Not nearly as sick as last week."

"I made Nana G a picture," Sully announced, hopping off my friend's lap and sprinting to the small table where he'd been furiously working. He adored Lily's mom. Since Mrs. Ganjam was retired, she kept Sully and Sid when they were out of school and was like a second grandma to my son.

He returned to Lil with his picture of a brightly colored rainbow and a purple umbrella.

"You drew this all by yourself?" He nodded proudly, and Lily kissed the top of his head. "She's going to love it. Purple is her favorite color."

"I know," Sully said with his adorable little smile.

"You are the sweetest," she replied. "Just like your mommy."

Well he certainly didn't get it from his father.

Glancing back at my friend, I lowered my voice. "I was working on my remarks for the parole hearing."

With tightened lips and narrowed eyes, she said, "Print it out for me," as she rose. "Sully, let's see if Andi will help you type a letter for Nana G. I'll give it to her with the picture."

"Yes! I can use the curly letters to make it pretty," he squealed, bouncing on her hip.

Lily carried him to the door of my office and spoke a few words to Andrea, my paralegal, before handing my son over to her. Lily and I were both attorneys at the prestigious Owens, Kavanaugh, & Underwood law firm in New York City. Her specialty was family law, and I was a criminal defense attorney.

I had the document ready for her by the time she returned and slumped into the leather office chair to read. "Yep," she said with a nod as her eyes moved down the page. "That's good, and I like this third paragraph about the asshole violating the restraining order."

"Multiple times," I added wryly.

Lily's concerned brown eyes lifted to mine. "Do you have copies of the letters Wesley has been sending to you?"

Opening my top drawer, I pulled out a folder containing a thick sheaf of hand-written pages from my ex-husband. "Got his *love notes* right here."

"I really wish you wouldn't read them, Kass. It doesn't serve a purpose for you to get all upset. Just have Andrea put them into a file for when his parole hearings come up. Then you can hand them over to the board and let them read them."

"A good attorney never hands over something she hasn't read thoroughly," I said in a monotone.

She tilted her head toward the papers in my hand. "Anything new?"

"Just how much he loves me and wants to kill me," I replied, keeping my tone neutral even as my heart rate accelerated.

"It'll be fine," she soothed. "No way will they let him out after reading that bullshit he's spewing. When is the hearing again?"

"Not till March. I just wanted to get a head start on my thoughts. I'll add more and refine it when the time gets closer."

Lily's eyes sparkled with mischief. "Is there any way you can work in some kind of comment about his tiny penis?"

"Hmm, let me make a note of that," I said, clacking my short fingernails against the keyboard and pretending to type. "Vienna sausage dick... completely ineffective... and done!" I pulled my hands away from my laptop with a flourish and grinned across the desk at my best friend.

"I love when you let your inner smartass glow."

"Why, thank you, madam. I live to please."

At Andrea's knock on the door, I called for her to come in. She popped her head inside. "Sully is finished with his letter," she said with a barely restrained smirk.

"Okay, he can come back in now."

He shot into the room as soon as the words were out of my mouth, sheet of paper waving in his chubby little hand. "I finished! Andrea helped me spell everything right, but I typed it all by myself."

He handed it to Lily, and I watched as her eyes widened and her lips smashed together. "That's... nice, honey," she managed to say. "Why don't you show your mom?"

As Sully brought it around to me, Lily's upper body shook with silent laughter, and I wondered what in the hell he had written. I took the sheet from him and read the few sentences.

Dear Nana G,

I hope you like my picture. I hope you feel better. You are pretty even when you don't have any hair.

Love, Sullivan Ramirez

He beamed proudly up at me, and I ruffled his hair as I fought my own smile. "This is so sweet, baby."

"Do you think Nana G will like it?"

"Oh for sure. I think you covered all the major points here."

"I wish I could give it to her myself," he said, turning the puppy dog eyes up to the hundredth level.

I squeezed his little hand. "You know the rule. Nana gets two days of peace and quiet after she goes to the doctor. You can see her on Wednesday."

"Because me and Sid are wild boys?"

"You got it," I laughed. "Do you want Aunt Lily to take her your gifts, or would you rather wait and give them to Nana yourself?"

"She can take them. I want to make Nana smile while she's not feeling good."

"Mission accomplished," I quipped, handing the sweet, funny letter back to him.

Andrea cleared her throat from the door, and I gave her my attention. "Mister Bouvier is on the line for you."

I'd like to say I didn't get a jolt when the Bouvier name was mentioned, but I'd be lying. Even though I knew it was Auburn on the phone and not... *the other one.*

Lily rose and winked at me before taking my son's hand. "Sul, let's go to my office and sue some people."

"Okay," he agreed readily before looking over his shoulder at me. "Mommy, I'm going to sue some people."

"Have fun, baby," I called back before reaching for the phone. "Auburn, hello."

"Hey, Kasserole."

I laughed. "Are you in need of a criminal defense attorney this morning?"

"Not at the moment, but I'm about to head into a negotiations meeting with a complete jackass, so there's still hope. What is the penalty for assault these days?"

"Are you planning to use a deadly weapon?"

"No, I think a nice bitch slap would be more satisfying."

"Ah, that's a simple assault then. It carries one year in prison, but with me as your attorney, you won't do any hard time. Just probation."

"Great, I'll take it. Stay by the phone." We shared a chuckle before he got down to business. "I got a letter earlier saying the guy who does contracts at your firm is retiring."

"Collins, yes. He'll be done by June."

"They sent me a list of other attorneys that can handle my business, but I wanted to get your opinion on who to use. They suggested Cox, Richardson, or Watson."

"Shawn Watson is who you should use," I said without hesitation. "He's younger than the other two, but he's a real bulldog."

"Excellent. That's who I'll use then. I appreciate you always taking my calls. I know corporate law isn't your specialty, but I trust your opinions."

My chest swelled with pride. "That means a lot to me, Auburn. If you could just drop that little tidbit of information to the partners here at the firm, that would be great," I teased.

"I'm golfing with Edward Owens next weekend. I'll be sure to bring up your name." Switching the subject, he asked, "How is your son doing?"

"He's well. Thank you for asking. He's actually at work with me today. Mrs. Ganjam usually keeps him when he's not at school, but she had a chemo treatment today."

"Lily's mother? I didn't realize she was ill."

"Oh that's right. You know Lily; she handled the adoption for you."

"At your suggestion," Auburn said. "Gianna and I were so pleased with her. Please tell her we're thinking of her and her family."

"I sure will. How is your wife, by the way?"

"As gorgeous as ever," he said dreamily, a tone you didn't hear much from the billionaire CEO. But the former playboy was completely enamored of his new bride.

"I'm glad you've got her to keep you in line. How are Jaxon and Jane?"

"Really good. They've settled in since the adoption, and Janie is doing well with her physical therapy."

"When is her surgery again?" I asked, selecting a pencil from the cup on my desk.

"In March. We'll fly to Dallas a couple days before and stay with my cousin Blaire and her family. She'll be doing the surgery to fix Jane's leg."

I jotted down the date on my calendar so I'd remember to send something to the brave little girl. A question was on the tip of my tongue, but I swallowed it down like I always did.

Have you heard from Monty?

The first time I'd met with Auburn about a legal matter over a year ago, he mentioned that his brother was a detective down in Florida. We hadn't discussed him since, and I hadn't let my curiosity get the best of me, but it was like a burning flame in my gut now.

Opening the browser on my computer, my fingers hovered over the keys.

Don't do it, Kassie. Leave the past in the past.

I realized Auburn was still talking. "...so then they're hopeful she will be able to walk."

Finding my tongue, I said, "That's great, Auburn. I hope everything goes well. Those kids are so lucky to have you and Gianna."

"We're the lucky ones," he replied, his voice soft. "Listen, my meeting is about to start. Thank you for the advice."

"Any time," I replied as the middle finger of my right hand typed an M. "Talk soon." My fourth finger hit the O key.

"Bye, Kassie."

The flame in my gut was licking up the inside of my torso until it reached my chest, and I finished typing the name in the search bar as soon as we hung up.

MONTY BOUVIER.

Taking a deep breath, I allowed my pinky to hit *Enter*. Images filled my screen, and I let out a short gasp. "Holy shit, this is *not* fair," I muttered. "Men shouldn't be allowed to look like this."

It's like someone had taken every muscle on teenage Monty's body and blown them up to twice their normal size. He'd always been muscular, but *daaaaamn!*

And had he gotten taller? It seemed like it because he towered over every person he was photographed with. Scrolling down, I noticed that there weren't any pictures of him with women aside from other police officers.

For some reason, that pleased me. It shouldn't have, but it did.

Stop that train of thought right now, Kassie Ramirez. You have sworn off men. Forever.

Something else struck me about the photos. Detective Monty Bouvier never smiled. Not at all. He looked stoic and... hard. That was the best word I could think of to describe his expressions.

"Hey, boss. I saw you're off the phone," Andrea said, entering my office. I slammed my laptop closed and shifted in my chair like I'd been caught doing something wrong.

Because it is wrong, chica.

"Why's your face all red?" my paralegal asked, running her fingers through her short, sky-blue hair as she made herself at home in the chair and dropped her eyes to my closed laptop. "You watching porn or something, boss?"

What I was looking at was better than porn, I thought as I tried to ignore the stirrings between my legs, something I hadn't felt about any other person in a very long time.

"Of course not," I said indignantly. "You know I'm not interested in men."

"What about women? We've got room for you on our team. Jenna and I could introduce you to some of our friends." Her green eyes sparkled playfully, and I laughed at her teasing.

"I'm not interested in *anyone*," I said firmly, "though I appreciate the offer."

"Are you sure? That's the second time Mister Sexy has called here in the past few weeks."

"Mister Sexy?" I asked with lifted eyebrows.

"Hey, I'm bisexual and not completely blind," she commented. "Auburn Bouvier is hot as hell. Maybe he's interested in you."

"Only professionally," I assured her. "He's completely devoted to his wife. He only asks for me because..." I hesitated because no one at the firm besides Lily knew I had a history with the Bouviers. But I trusted Andrea as much as I trusted anyone besides my family and Lily's. "Because I knew him many years ago. I used to date his brother."

Her eyes rolled up to the corner of the room. "That's right. I'd totally forgotten there was another Bouvier brother." She snapped her fingers a few times. "Marty or something?"

"Monty," I corrected, the name feeling foreign on my tongue.

"Didn't they have a sister too? The one who disappeared?"

"Yes, Evie went missing around sixteen years ago."

Andrea's entire face seemed to droop with sadness. She was the most empathetic person I knew and wore her heart on her sleeve. "I remember it was all over the news. I was a preteen when that happened, but it really upset me. And scared me. That's when I asked my mom to enroll me in kickboxing classes."

"And now you're a total badass."

"Hell yeah, I am. By the way, are you coming to class tonight?" Andrea was the kickboxing and self-defense instructor at the gym she'd introduced me to.

"I'll be there. Lily invited Sully over to play with Sid. I hate missing classes. They're a great stress-reliever. They make me feel..."

"Empowered?" she suggested, and I nodded.

"Exactly. It's like you've turned my weaknesses into strengths."

Andrea leaned over, her palms flat on my redwood desk as her green eyes caught fire with passion. "You are strong, Kassie. One of the strongest women I know. On the inside, where it really counts. And now you have the body of a warrior to go with your inner strength."

"Thank you," I said, my voice almost a whisper.

"No problem," she replied, straightening as she adjusted her black blazer. "I want all women to know how powerful they can be."

As she turned to leave, my eyes fell on the folder of letters on my desk, and I stared at them until I heard the door close. Then I stuffed them back in the drawer where they belonged.

Fuck you, Wesley Campbell. I have the power now.

CHAPTER 22

Fuck me.

Pushing from the blue cloth-covered chair in the waiting area of the doctor's office, I approached the petite receptionist who was waiting by the door.

"I go by Monty," I informed her shortly.

"I don't blame you," she replied with a giggle. "The nurse is on the phone with a pharmacy. She asked me to take you back to the exam room."

"That's fine."

"So you're a policeman, huh?" she asked, looking over her shoulder at me as we walked down the pale green corridor.

What's with that color anyway? Who the hell decided that medical offices and hospitals should be painted in the most hideous green imaginable?

A small smile crossed my lips as I remembered a similar conversation with Evie many years ago. She'd dubbed the color *institutional green*, and her verdict was that they painted it like this to drive people away, keep them from lingering longer than necessary.

"You're awfully cute when you smile, Monty," the receptionist said, stopping beside a door and batting her eyelashes at me.

I eyed her up and down. She was cute. Blonde. Petite. Not my usual type, but she was definitely interested, if the way her tongue slid across her bottom lip was any indication.

"I can assure you, looking cute was not my intention."

"Then it must come naturally to you," she said, tapping me on the arm as we entered the room. "It looks like your last visit was two years ago. That's just before I started working here."

Rubbing a hand through my hair, I nodded. "Yeah, I'm a little behind. My captain insisted that I come in for my physical though."

"It's important, Officer Bouvier."

"Actually, it's Detective."

Her perfectly white teeth sank into a full, pink bottom lip. "Ooh, you're a detective. Nice." *Yep. Definitely flirting.* That was confirmed when she handed me a pale blue gown and said, "You can change into this. Let me know if you need help."

I chuckled. "I think I can manage. I'm a big boy."

"Yes, you are," she purred, her gaze scraping up and down my body before leaving the room with a wink over her shoulder.

I stripped down and put on the hideous gown with some kind of swirly pattern covering it. *The medical community is in severe need of a fashion and interior design upgrade.*

Once I was changed and seated on the exam table, a knock sounded at the door, and I called for the person to come in. I expected the nurse, but it was the flirty receptionist again.

"Just wanted to give you an update. The nurse should be here in about five minutes, Detective."

"Thanks," I told her, shifting the too-snug garment to try and make sure all my vital parts were covered.

She gave me another long look. "I'm not usually this forward, but since Dr. Cornehl is retiring, this is my last day here. I was wondering if maybe you'd like to help me... celebrate after work." Her hand drifting slowly down the front of her throat told me exactly what kind of *celebration* she had in mind.

I considered the offer. It had been a while since I'd gotten any action. I'd been covered up with work since being named head of the new task force a month ago, so I responded with, "We could have a drink after you get off and talk about it."

Her face lit up as she pulled a sticky note with her phone number on it from her pocket. "That sounds great. I'm Shana, by the way."

Sitting in a bar around the corner from the medical plaza, I nursed my whiskey neat. Like most of the drinking establishments in the mid-sized town of Marytown, Florida, my spirit of choice, Macallan, wasn't available, so I'd ordered something new.

The Henry McKenna single barrel bourbon I was drinking had caramel and vanilla notes with a hint of cinnamon, and I was surprised at how much I enjoyed it. When my bartender, Jeremy, walked by, I thanked him for the recommendation, and he gave me a nod of acknowledgment.

My thumb tapped on the Instagram app on my phone, and my lips twitched with an almost-smile when my favorite account popped up at the top of the feed.

The Adventures of Garfield and Snoopy.

I'd returned the follow from the account a few years ago, mostly because their content amused me as an animal lover. This particular one stuck out because it documented the best friend relationship between the account owner's pets, a cat and a dog.

But what caught my initial attention was the fact that the dog was named Garfield and the cat was Snoopy.

While I watched their latest video, I let out a quiet laugh. The big, goofy blond lab was on his back, grinning like an adorable dope as the black-and-white cat rubbed his belly with both paws.

I tapped out a comment: *We could all use a friend like Snoopy.*

A reply popped up almost immediately: *Snoopy is a recent graduate from the Feline Academy of Massage Therapy.*

The account owner's cheeky commentary never failed to entertain me. I checked the time and was immediately annoyed because Shana was almost an hour late for our meet up. I had her number, so I could call her, but I wasn't sure I wanted to put in that much effort.

One more drink, and then I'm out of here.

Raising my finger, I signaled the bartender for another McKenna before shifting my eyes toward the door when I saw a flash of red. Shana entered, and my annoyance rose. She'd said she was coming directly after work, but she had obviously gone home, changed clothes, and fixed her hair and makeup.

The sleek, blonde ponytail and nude lipgloss had been replaced with a head of loose curls and a full face of makeup. She was wearing a tight red bandage dress that accentuated her small curves but was a little too flashy for this low-key joint.

Her eyes searched the room until they found me sitting at the long, dark wood bar, and she reached up to fluff her hair with one hand. Making her way across the room, she put an extra swing in her step that I appreciated.

"Hey," she said, her tone breathy.

"I was just about to leave," I commented, turning to Jeremy when he dropped off my drink. "Whatever the lady wants."

"I'll have a white wine spritzer." For some reason her drink order aggravated me, but I inhaled and exhaled three times to get control of it.

In control. Always. That was me.

"Can I see your ID, please?" the middle-aged bartender, Jeremy, asked, and Shana pulled it from the small red handbag she'd placed on the wood surface. My eyes zoomed in on her birthdate when she handed over the card, and I did the calculations in my head. Twenty-six years old, a tad younger than I usually went for. At thirty-three, I preferred women with a bit more maturity, especially in the bedroom.

But whatever. I needed a fuck buddy for the night, and she was here. Finally.

Shana pursed her hot-pink painted lips into a pout. "Sorry I was late. I wanted to look nice for our date."

"I wasn't aware we were on a date. I thought we were meeting up for drinks to discuss our plans for the night."

My matter-of-fact tone didn't seem to bother her in the least. "I wasn't sure what you had planned, so I wanted to be ready for anything."

Lifting one brow, I regarded her. "Anything? Are you sure about that?" My voice was low and quiet but held an air of authority.

I noticed how her breath hitched as a blush of desire colored her exposed chest. "Yes, anything."

Her breasts swelled above the top of her dress, and I allowed my gaze to roam there, my meaning crystal clear. Even so, I didn't want any misconceptions about what this was, so I spoke the words aloud.

"I'm not looking for a date or a girlfriend. I'm looking for someone to fuck really hard for an hour or so. That's it. There won't be any second hookups or phone calls tomorrow. Only one night. I just want to make that perfectly clear."

She nodded eagerly, her eyes alight with lust. "That's all I'm after too. I'm at the fun stage of my life, not the relationship stage."

"Good. As long as we understand each other."

"Completely."

Jeremy set her fizzy drink on a cocktail napkin in front of her before departing, and I tilted my forehead toward it. "Finish your drink and then we'll get going. Do you live around here?"

She took a tiny sip and then her face scrunched into a look of apology. "I'm actually staying with friends right now until my new apartment is ready."

Fuck. I hardly ever took women back to my place. I didn't want them knowing where I lived. *It's fine. She understands the rules, and she's not looking for anything more than a hookup either.*

"All right. We can go to my house when you're done with your spritzer."

Forty-seven minutes. Forty-seven *fucking* minutes was how long it took Shana to drain her glass. In the meantime, I learned a lot of shit I didn't give two fucks about.

She has a sister two years younger than her. Her last day at Dr. Cornehl's office was today, but she had a new job lined up and was starting on Monday. Her favorite food is chicken strips dipped in ranch dressing.

Christ on a cracker.

Motioning Jeremy over, I paid the bill as Shana informed me that her new apartment was going to be "just the awesomest," and I found myself seriously second-guessing this entire night.

I hadn't fucked anything besides my fist for two months, and as I gazed down at it in my lap, I imagined him saying, "For fuck's sake, man. Get laid by a real woman and give a hand a break already."

As soon as Shana's full lips slurped up the last of her drink, I stood. "Why don't we get going?"

She rose and gathered her tiny purse, and I placed my hand on her back and led her outside, grateful to finally be headed to the main event.

CHAPTER 23

ROLLING OFF THE BED, I gave Shana a smack on the ass. "I'm going to hop in the shower. You can get dressed as soon as your legs stop shaking."

"Might be a while," she muttered, her back heaving up and down with her labored breaths. Her hand reached out to my left pec. "I love tats on a man. What does this one mean?"

I flinched away from her touch, turned my back on her, and muttered a complete lie. "Nothing."

After turning on my shower, I disposed of the condom and then stepped into the glassed-in enclosure. This was one of my favorite parts of my apartment, and I unwrapped a shower steamer disc and tossed it onto the ivory tiles at my feet. The aroma of spearmint and eucalyptus surrounded me, and I closed my eyes, allowing the hot water to beat down on my back and shoulders as I pressed my palms against the opposite glass.

Once I'd inhaled my fill of the fresh scent, I reached for a plush gray washcloth and lathered it with my favorite body wash, adding a hint of bergamot to the aroma surrounding me.

Despite over an hour of hard sex, my cock was still half erect. The encounter with Shana had been... unsatisfying, to say the least.

I cleaned myself, deciding I would jack off once I'd gotten Shana out the door. My poor hand would just have to deal with it.

After drying off, I pulled on a pair of gray sweatpants and strolled back into my bedroom. Shana was nowhere to be seen, and her clothes that I'd left in a pile at the side of my bed were gone.

Thank Christ. That would alleviate any post-sex awkwardness that some women felt afterward. I personally never experienced that because I was pretty much a dickhead who didn't give a fuck.

Shoving my phone into my pants pocket, I decided to make myself a snack. Opening the door to my bedroom, my heart dropped to my knees when I found Shana standing outside my spare room with her hand on the knob.

"What the fuck do you think you're doing?" I growled, stalking across the whitewashed wood flooring.

Her head jerked up and she patted her chest with one hand, but the other hand was *still on the goddamn doorknob*, twisting it back and forth.

"You scared me. I'm trying to see what's in here." She pulled a couple times on the locked door.

"Get away from there. It's none of your business," I snapped, pulling her away by the elbow. I gave myself some credit because I didn't have her slammed against the wall with my hand around her throat.

"Why is the door locked?" she asked as I herded her to the living room.

"It's private."

"But what's in there?"

I narrowed my eyes at her and gritted out, "That's where I keep the dead bodies. Would you like me to add yours?"

Her eyes rounded and then she laughed nervously. She should be nervous. No one was allowed inside that room except me.

"Jeez, you don't have to be such a grouch about it. I was just curious. I don't understand why you won't tell me."

"What part of 'It's private' don't you comprehend?" She didn't reply, and taking a page from Auburn's old playbook, I opened a ride-share app on my phone and found a car a couple blocks away. "An Uber will be here to pick you up in three minutes. Do you have your purse?"

Her lips parted in surprise, but she recovered quickly, tilting her head to the side and giving me a coy smile. "Why don't you cancel it, and we can grab something to eat together and hang out for a while."

"That wasn't what we talked about at the bar, Shana. I thought I made myself perfectly clear, and you agreed."

She flapped a hand in the air between us. "I know, but plans can change. That's allowed, right?"

"No, it's not. I have work to do."

"But it's a Friday night. You shouldn't have to work on a weekend," she whined, and my frustration rose to a fever pitch.

Thank god I heard a car pull up in front of my house, so I picked up her purse and handed it to her. "Your car is here."

My phone rang in my hand, and I answered, "Hello, bro. Give me just a second." Opening the door, I said, "Bye, Shana," my tone pointed.

"I'll see you soon," she mouthed before sashaying out the door.

Not if I have anything to do with it, I thought as I closed and locked it behind her.

"Who is Shana?" Auburn asked as soon as I was back on the line.

"Just a chick."

"Anyone special?" he pried.

"Not in the least."

"Why not?"

"Because she's not, Auburn. Number one, she makes horrible noises during sex; she sounds like a pig in a blender."

Auburn roared out a laugh. "Yeah, I can see where that would be a distraction. Shoulda stuffed her panties in her mouth."

"She wasn't wearing any," I replied dryly, "so I used a ball gag."

"God damn," he said, faking a little sniffle. "I feel like a proud dad right now."

It was my turn to laugh as I sat down and propped my feet on the beach beech wood coffee table. "Speaking of that, does Gianna ever… you know… call you Daddy?"

"I don't see where that's any of your business, little bro," he hedged, but I could hear the smirk in his voice.

"Oh, come on! You can tell me. I can totally see you putting off major Daddy vibes. Telling her what a good fucking girl she is. Maybe smacking that ass."

"Shit, now I'm hard. Gianna!" he called, and then a few seconds later, "All of it. Off. Now." His tone was low and growly.

"Dayum, bro. Is that your CEO voice or your Daddy voice?"

"Both," he replied before a quiet groan reached my ears.

"What? What's she doing? Let's switch to video so I can watch."

"Not a goddamn chance in hell, Mont." I listened as he spoke to his wife. "Your brother-in-law is a pervert, baby girl."

"Hi, Monty!" I heard in Gianna's soft southern drawl.

The sound of a palm connecting with soft flesh met my ears and I bit back a groan of my own. "Can you leave the line open so I can listen?"

"Negative. I'm hanging up now. Bye, Monty."

"Bye, Daddy Auburn."

His deep laugh was cut off when he hung up, no doubt to fuck his incredibly gorgeous younger wife over his desk. Besides being a brunette bombshell, my sister-in-law was also an absolute sweetheart who had turned my brother's life around.

I pondered on the complete reversal in the lives of the Bouvier brothers. It's like we'd switched personalities some time in the past sixteen or so years. Where Auburn was now a dedicated family man with a wife and two kids, I was currently playboying around South Florida.

On nights like these, I wondered who really had the best life. The younger brother with no commitments except to his job? Or the older brother who had someone to warm his bed and his heart every night?

I was so damned thrilled that Auburn had found a good woman, but that was no longer the kind of life I wanted.

I'd given up on that dream many years ago after the worst month of my life. Those events had broken me.

Sure, I'd put myself back together and built a life here in Florida, but I was like a piece of pottery someone had dropped and tried to put back together. The fragments fit, but there would always be chips and cracks that left my soul imperfect.

Though something about tonight made me think about my situation in a new light. My brother was with the woman he loved, and I was here alone and unfulfilled.

On the bright side, at least I'd never have to see Shana again.

As it turned out, that wasn't exactly the case.

Parking in the employee lot around back on Monday morning, I got out of my Range Rover, scanned my card at the door, and entered the station through the breakroom.

"There he is," Julian Silva called from his position near the coffee machine.

"Wassup, Jules?" I said, stealing the cup of hot java he'd just pulled from beneath the dispenser. "Thanks for this."

I took a long sip and eyed him over the rim of the plastic cup as he scowled. "How do you always know the exact moment I pour my coffee so you can nab it?" he demanded to know, pulling another cup from the cabinet.

"I have a caffeine radar," I informed him. Greeting Alice, Dylan, and Jimmy, three of our patrol officers who were about to go on duty, I headed through the metal door toward the offices.

As I strolled down the carpet-lined corridor toward my office, Captain Carl Snyder called to me from the Records Room.

"Morning, Cap," I said, pushing through the half-open door.

"Detective, I wanted you to meet our new records clerk."

My eyes shifted to the person sitting behind the desk, and...

Fuck me running.

A blonde ponytail dipped to the side as my Friday night hookup tilted her head and waved cheerily with a shit-eating grin on her face.

I only caught a couple of the captain's words as the few sips of coffee I'd drank threatened a reappearance.

"Shana O'Neil... Esmerelda retiring... administrative experience... so happy to have her..."

My mind attempted to process everything. Leo Olson had been the lead detective in our office, and his wife, Esmerelda, was our records clerk. I knew they were both retiring. Leo had actually been the one to recommend me to head the new task force that had been assembled. He'd been gone about a month, but his sweet wife had stayed on until we could find a clerk to replace her.

My brain tuned back in to what the captain was saying. "So when I called to make the appointments for the physicals, Shana here told me she was looking for a new job, and I asked her to come in for an interview last week. Thought you might want to welcome her aboard."

Turning my gaze back to the woman sitting there like a trip wire I needed to avoid at all costs, I said flatly, "Welcome aboard."

"I already know Detective Bouvier," she chirped, and I could feel my eyes burning into hers with a warning. *Don't fucking do it.* "I met him at the office on Friday." She stopped there, thank god, but she smirked like she knew a secret.

And she did. A big goddamn secret.

She knew what my cock tasted like. And what I looked like naked. And how my fingers bruised her ass while...

Christ, this is a nightmare.

CHAPTER 24

"HI, MAMA," I SAID, kissing her cheek as I entered her apartment.

"Hello, honey." She bent to scoop up Sully and pepper his face with kisses. "How is my precious grandson?"

"I'm good, Yaya. Did you make some mollies?"

She laughed merrily. "I did make tamales. You can go play while I finish up the rice." After setting him on his feet, her eyes turned sad and followed him as he scurried to his playroom. "I wish your father could have met Sullivan."

"I know, Mama. Me too."

"I can't believe he's been gone for seven years." Her bottom lip trembled as she stared off into space.

Placing my arm around her shoulders, I guided her to the kitchen. "Come on. I'll finish the rice while you keep me company."

"Oh, I can do it. I was just feeling sorry for myself. Besides, the rice is resting now. Only needs to be fluffed."

"Lucky for you, I'm a master fluffer." Taking the lid off the pan, I closed my eyes and inhaled the Mexican rice dish my mother had perfected long ago. The aromas of onions, spices, and tomato bouillon mixed together and smelled like home.

Grabbing a fork from the drawer, I ruffled it through the pan, fluffing the rice like Mama taught me when I was a little girl.

"How was your doctor's appointment today?" I asked, casting a glance her way.

"Bien. He said my blood pressure was much better, and I don't have to take medication for it any longer."

"Cutting back on your sodium really helped, huh?"

"Yes. I'm still getting used to that salt substitute you bought me, but at least it's better than having to take a pill every day." Mama scrunched her nose in revulsion at the very thought of it.

"If anything changes, I expect you to take whatever pills he prescribes. Papá's heart attack took us all by surprise, and I don't want to go through that again," I told her sternly.

"Yes, my bossy daughter."

Reaching for the plates, I winced when I lifted my arms over my head, and my mother noticed instantly.

"What's wrong, Kassie? Have you hurt yourself?"

"Just a little sore from kickboxing. I've been to three classes this week, and Andrea has been kicking my booty."

Her lowered brows indicated her disapproval. "I don't like you doing something so violent. Can't you just take an aerobics class?"

"Mama, you know I take those classes for self-defense as much as fitness. It's important to me."

"You're right," she sighed, stroking a hand down the braid that hung just below my shoulder line. "It's very important for you to be able to defend yourself. I know that, but I can't help but worry."

"A little soreness is worth my peace of mind," I replied, setting the plates on the counter as Sully zipped into the kitchen, skidding to a stop in front of his grandmother.

"Yaya, can we have mollies now?"

"Yes, mi nieto. You can have all the mollies you can eat," she told him, her face softening with a grandmother's love.

"That's enough storytime for tonight," I told my son, setting the well-worn copy of *Charlotte's Web* on his blue nightstand. It had been my favorite book growing up, and I was so happy Sully loved it too.

He turned onto his side and curled into a ball, his favorite sleeping position. "Mommy, do I have a dad?"

I was taken aback by the question. He'd never asked about his father before, but I should have known it would come eventually.

"You do, but he's not a part of our lives."

Sully's long, dark lashes brushed his cheeks as his eyes closed. "M'kay, but why?"

Smoothing his sandy hair away from his face, I formulated the best answer I could come up with. "Because he wasn't a very nice person, so I told him to take a hike."

His eyelids lifted slightly, and he smiled. "That's good. We only like nice people."

"That's right," I said soothingly.

"Like Sid and Aunt Lily and Uncle Praveen?"

"Exactly."

"Yaya and Nana G," his list was interrupted by an adorable yawn, "and Poppy G." My mother and Lily's parents.

"Yes, baby."

His words faded as sleep began to overtake him "And Andrea and Jenna."

I stayed seated on the edge of his bed until his lips parted and his breathing deepened, marveling at what a beautiful little boy I had. The question about his father had thrown me for a loop. I couldn't exactly lie and say he didn't have a father, but I thought my answer was pretty decent.

Sully had a lot of women in his life, but only two men of any note, Lily's father and her husband, and I worried about the lack of male role models in his life.

Mr. Ganjam wasn't feeble by any means, but he limited his daily activities to a brief walk around their Queens neighborhood.

Lily's husband, Praveen, on the other hand, was very involved in my son's life, often inviting Sully to outings with him and Sid. Praveen loved museums, which could get boring for two rambunctious five-year-olds, but they had fun anyway because they were together.

I just wished my dad was around to take his grandson to a baseball game or teach him to catch a ball.

You know what? Fuck that. I didn't need a man to take my son to a ball game or teach him how to throw and catch. I was a strong, capable woman who could do that my own damn self.

"What's in the bag, Mom?" Sully asked as we walked hand-in-hand toward the park. I loved holding his little hand and did it as often as possible because I knew one day he would be too big or too cool for such things. Kids grew up so damn fast.

"You'll see," I said as he vibrated with excitement beside me. Finding a spot near a large tree, I set the bag down and squatted beside Sully, my fingers adjusting the zipper on his blue and black jacket. It was unseasonably warm for January in NYC, and there were lots of people taking advantage of the nice weather.

"I thought we'd play some baseball," I told him, and his eyes brightened.

"For reals?"

"For reals," I assured him with a laugh.

A few minutes later, I realized that watching baseball and playing baseball were two totally separate things.

"You're not very good at this, Mom," Sully informed me, his eyebrows censuring me in their ascent up his forehead.

I jogged over and picked up the ball that had gone awry when I attempted to throw it. "It's fine. I just need to warm up."

"That lady throws way better than you, and she just got here," he said with brutal, childlike honesty, pointing toward a blonde woman who had just zinged a ball in her partner's direction. The guy caught it effortlessly, and I flattened my lips and looked away.

"Okay, well, be ready, Sul. This one is going straight in your glove!" I said with a confidence I didn't feel. I reared back and threw the baseball, which fell way short and rolled toward the other couple playing nearby.

"I'll get it," my son called, running in that direction. A split second before Sully reached my errant ball, the extremely tall man threw his toward the blonde woman. Hard. And it was on course to hit my kid directly in the head.

I had approximately forty-seven heart attacks before the lady reached over Sully and caught the ball expertly in her glove.

With my chest pounding, I broke into an all-out sprint, but the man reached them well before I did.

"You all right there, kiddo?" he asked, kneeling down and holding my son's small shoulders to look him over.

"Yeah, I'm good. That was an awesome catch!"

I was on the brink of certain death, but my son was completely unconcerned that he'd almost been beaned. Images of hospitals and bandages around his head were still flashing through my mind, and I placed a hand over my wild heartbeat.

The man looked up at the blonde lady with admiration and... something else in his eyes. "Yeah, she's totally awesome."

She winked at him before squatting down to address my kid. "No problem. I couldn't let the handsomest guy in the park get hurt," she told Sully, pinching his cheek.

My son dipped his head and gave her the cutest, flirtiest little smile. *Sweet Jesus, my kid's a little playboy.*

That's when I took a good look at the couple and recognized them.

Holy shit! That's Layton Lancaster! And Arizona Abbott!

Layton was a catcher for the Philly Cougars, and Arizona played softball for the Philadelphia Anacondas. Jogging up to the group, I bent to check on my son.

"Are you okay, Sul? You scared me to death."

"Why?" he asked, peering up at me with his big brown eyes.

"Because you walked right in front of that ball. You have to be more careful, okay?"

"She's right," Layton said, ruffling my son's hair. "It's no fun getting pegged in the head with a ball. Trust me, it's happened to me."

"That's so cool!" Sully said, looking awestruck at the very idea.

"Not as exciting as it sounds," the tall, dark, and handsome man said with a chuckle.

"I'm so sorry about him, Mr. Lancaster. And Miss Abbott, thank you so much for the save. That was a fantastic catch," I gushed.

"No prob," the woman said. "And call us Layton and Arizona." She turned back to Sully. "Do you play baseball?"

"I'm just learning. This is my first day. Mommy is trying to teach me, but she's not great at it. She's really smart though," he added to soothe the sting of his insult.

"Did you play any sports in high school?" Layton asked, flopping down on his butt and indicating for me to do the same.

"No, I was on the debate team," I told him, feeling kinda lame.

"Wow, seriously?" Arizona asked, her eyes widening. She was really pretty without a hint of makeup on her flawless face. "I'm not sure I could do that. I'd probably just end up rambling."

"You have no problem arguing with me," Layton commented.

"You make it easy," she retorted with a roll of her eyes, and I grinned at their interaction as Sully settled in my lap. I wasn't sure what the deal was between these two, but they were giving off some serious vibes.

"My mom is a lawyer. She argues all the time in court," Sully informed them. "I have a dad, but I don't know him because Mommy said he's not a very nice person. She kicked his stupid butt out."

I resisted the urge to shrink myself and crawl into a hole in the big tree so I could live with the squirrels till the end of time. "I'm so—"

"Hey, it's cool," Lancaster said to my son. "I never knew my dad growing up either. It's awesome that you have such a great mom, huh?"

Sully nodded happily and snuggled back against me. "She's the best. She makes really good hot dogs."

"It's a well-honed skill and the highlight of my parenting career," I commented dryly as the other two adults laughed.

"Tell ya what, Sully. Why don't you hang out with me and Arizona for a while. We'll show you some stuff."

"Oh, I couldn't ask you to do that," I protested, and Arizona swished her hand through the air in a gesture of dismissal.

"You didn't ask. It'll be fun."

For the next hour and a half, these two wonderful people taught my son how to throw and catch a ball, some fielding techniques, and how to properly break in his glove. I even picked up a few things myself.

"I can't thank you two enough," I said when Layton tossed us all a bottle of water from his cooler while Sully put our gloves and ball back in the bag.

"It was great. I love watching kids learn to love the sport before they get too competitive and jaded. It's refreshing," he said, eyeing my son with a softness in his eyes. "You should bring him to Philly this summer. The

Cougars and the Anacondas will be doing a doubleheader exhibition game. I think tickets are already sold out, but I can arrange for you to get some."

"That... wow... okay, I accept," I said, a bit flabbergasted at how kind these two superstars were. "Just tell me what to do."

"We're in New York to meet with some of the new owners of the Cougars. You've probably heard of them. Gianna and Auburn Bouvier?"

"I've heard of them," I replied, my lips quirking up at the corners. Seriously, who didn't know of those two? They were one of the biggest power couples in the city.

"Just get in touch with Auburn and tell him we requested VIP tickets for you and your son." He dug his phone from his pocket. "I'll mention it to him during our meeting but let me give you his number so you can call to set up how to get the tickets."

"I have Auburn's number. I know him through work."

"Great. It's all settled then." The man flashed a smile that had no doubt dropped a million panties. "Thanks for letting us play with your kiddo. He's adorable."

"I agree," I told them as Sully trotted back to us with the bag in one hand. "Buddy, can you say thank you to Arizona and Layton?"

He nodded and gave them each a hug around the knees. "Thank you for helping me. It was superduper fun!"

"For us too," Layton said, pulling his baseball cap off and placing it backward on Sully's head. "Why don't you keep this since you're a Cougars fan now?"

"Um, no. The Sull-meister is an Anacondas fan," Arizona argued. "Isn't that right?" She tweaked his nose and he beamed up at her.

"I think for baseball, I'm a Cougars fan, and for softball, I'm an Anacondas fan."

"Very diplomatic, kiddo," she said before unzipping her bag. "But I think you need some of my gear too." Pulling out a blue-and-white jersey and a marker, she poked Layton and said, "Turn around, superstar. Let me use your back."

He did as he was told, and Arizona used his back as a makeshift clipboard to sign the jersey with a flair.

"There you go, cutie," she said, handing over the shirt to my kid.

At my nudge, Sully thanked them both again, and we headed back home.

Later that night, once I'd climbed into bed, Monty's face popped into my thoughts. Younger Monty. The boy I used to love. I guessed the mention of his brother and his favorite baseball team today at the park had triggered it.

I'd been so hurt and angry at him back then, but when his sister went missing, all I wanted to do was reach out to him, comfort him. I would have pushed away all of my own pain to be there for him... if only I had a way to get in touch with him.

It doesn't matter now, Kassie, because Monty never showed up.

Over the years, I'd let that betrayal settle into the pit of my mind, and I kept it there. But some days it reared its ugly head and punched me right in the gut.

For a long time, I wished I could see Monty again and get some closure.

I was over it now though. I was a grown woman with a high-powered job and a son to raise.

But as I drifted off to that vulnerable space between wakefulness and sleep, my mind asked the question.

Why, Monty? Why did you abandon me when I needed you most?

CHAPTER 25

I'D MANAGED TO AVOID going into the Records Room all week, instead relying on the documents that had been scanned into the computer. But today I needed the physical records. I thought better with the papers and photos actually in my hands.

The first two days Shana was at the office, she waved and called out each time I passed her office, and I gave her a halfhearted lift of my hand to be polite. After that, I had resorted to taking the long way around the square layout of our station to bypass her domain.

Heading down the hallway, I was grateful that she wouldn't be working on this Sunday morning. And then I pushed the Records Room door open.

"Hi, Monty," the last woman I wanted to see purred, and my shoulders slumped in weary defeat.

Keep it professional, and you'll be fine.

"Morning. I need to get the file for 59223, please."

"Sure thing, boss," she said with a wink as she pulled out her keyring and opened the door behind her desk. A minute later, I heard her say, "Wow, there's a lot."

"Hold on. I'll come in and find the boxes I need." Rounding the counter, I entered the back room and located the row where Shana was standing, looking at the boxes lining the metal storage shelves.

My eyes scanned the labels. "I only need a few today. This one and... let's see... this one." I pulled the boxes and stacked them beside me. When I bent to get the third box, I felt something brush against my ass. Standing, I pushed out a sigh as I faced her. "Miss O'Neil, please don't."

"What?" she asked, blinking innocently at me. "You had some dust."

My teeth grinded together. "From now on, let me handle any dust that may or may not be on my butt. Or anywhere else on my body, for that matter."

"Whatever you say, Monty." She held both hands up in surrender. "I was just trying to help."

"And you can't call me Monty. It's Detective while we're in this building." I stacked the last box on top of the other two and then lifted them.

"Oooh, look how strong you are. So what about when we're not in this building? Can I call you Monty then?" she questioned.

"We won't be seeing each other outside of work," I said firmly, carrying the heavy load down the row.

"Whatever you say, Detective," she said, her tone still way too flirty for my taste.

"Thanks for the files," I said when I reached the exit.

And for the love of god, keep your mouth shut about what happened last weekend.

Two hours later, I had the three boxes sorted and the contents stacked across my desk like I wanted them. My newly formed task force was aimed at catching a serial rapist and murderer.

The rapes had started two years ago, and each case had been handled by a different detective, one of them being me. Then I'd been assigned to a second case and realized how familiar the circumstances sounded.

Going back to that unsolved rape from eleven months earlier, I found the facts to be eerily similar. Once I began asking around among the other detectives, we'd pieced together that every one of the nine rapes had happened early in the morning.

But that wasn't the only similarity. All of the women were housewives or worked from home, and a masked stranger had broken into their houses by picking the locks on the back doors after their husbands left for work. They were bound to their headboards by zip ties while they were being assaulted.

The positioning, the things he said, and the little bit of forensic evidence we found were all exactly the same.

I'd asked for a task force to be formed at that time, but the higher-ups had denied my request. Then the first murder occurred.

Emily Boyd's husband left for his job at a local warehouse at the same time she took their two daughters to school. Then she returned home to start on some housework. When Mr. Boyd came home for lunch, he found his wife on the bed, wearing only a tiara on her head. She'd been strangled to death.

The perpetrator used a condom every time, so there was no semen present, but in two of the cases, a blond pubic hair was found on the bed.

And that was all we had.

A couple hairs that didn't hit on any forensic websites. A *probably* blond man that could be anywhere from five-ten to six-two. The words "You're my good little princess" said over and over while he was raping them in a voice free of any distinguishable accent. And the weird-ass tiara thing.

The sexual assault and murder of Emily was a little over a year ago, and then the exact same thing happened to Fiona Warren three months later.

Killing Emily and Fiona seemed to satisfy the perp's tendencies a bit because he'd slowed down—going longer between attacks—but he'd escalated in the sense that he was now strangling the women to death while assaulting them.

By the end of last year, four more women were dead. In the past two years, we'd attributed a total of fifteen sexual assaults to the prick as well as six homicides.

The names and faces of the dead women rolled through my head: Emily, Fiona, Maeve, Haley, Anya, and Hua.

And then the women who had been assaulted but lived through it: Khaleesi, Anna, Amelia, Jia, Sara, Sarah, Kinsley, Shantae, and Vicki.

I had each of them memorized, and sometimes they haunted me in my dreams. Like they knew I was the one who would find the horrible predator who had done this to them.

God, I hoped so.

Filling in the final square on the spreadsheet, I leaned back in my chair and stretched, my mouth widening into a yawn.

Fuck, I needed some caffeine, but I didn't want to go to the breakroom for coffee in case Shana was there. Or maybe I was just being paranoid. Nevertheless, I stood and grabbed a Coke from the mini fridge in my office before focusing on the sheet I'd just made.

I had organized each victim according to their demographics. There had to be something here that linked all of these women. There *had* to be.

My eyes scanned each column, and I made notes on my yellow legal pad. Their ages ranged from twenty-five to forty-four, with the majority being in their thirties. Race didn't seem to be a factor. There were three Black women, two Asian, three Hispanic, four White, and the rest were of mixed race.

Sexuality? All were straight except for Khaleesi, who reported that she was bisexual. All were married, so that didn't help either.

Another commonality was that they were all mothers. Kinsley and Vicki had adopted their children, and Sara's kids were actually her stepchildren, but the rest had borne their offspring.

The kids... the kids... could it have something to do with them? Something niggled at the back of my brain. Maybe they were all involved in organized sports. The perp could be a coach or another parent.

Maybe...

"Hey, Monty. I mean, *Detective Bouvier.*" My brain shut down whatever train of thought it had been on when Shana appeared at the door of my office.

Clenching my fists beneath the desk, I attempted to keep the frustration from my tone. "Miss O'Neil, can I help you with something?"

"It's lunchtime. I thought maybe you'd want to grab a bite to eat?"

"No, I'm good. I've got a lot to work through here." I directed my gaze back toward my laptop, hoping she'd get the hint. She didn't.

"Anything I can do to help?" She strolled in like she owned the place and leaned her palms against my desk.

"Nope," I said, avoiding eye contact.

"Do you want me to go grab you some food?"

"No, but thank you." My jaw was clenched so tightly, it ached.

"I think I'll order a sandwich. I'll be back in a few minutes to keep you company."

Jesus fucking hell.

"Actually," I said, rising from my seat, "I think I'm going to head home for the day." I began gathering the stacks from my desk and organizing them neatly in the white cardboard boxes.

"You need to put those back in the Records Room?" she asked, tilting her head to the side.

"My closet has a lock on it, so I'll just keep them there for the time being."

"Okay, I'll see you tomorrow."

"Great," I muttered.

I knew I needed to do something about this situation. It had gone from uncomfortable to untenable. The woman was now affecting my ability to do my job. I'd planned to work here until at least five, but because of her, I was going home at one just to avoid her.

How the hell was I supposed to handle this though? *Hey, Captain. You know that new records clerk? Yeah, I fucked her before I knew she worked here, and now she's pestering me. Could you fire her or something? K. Thanks.*

I was pretty sure that would go over like a pimp in church. It was frowned upon for ranking officers to sleep with employees.

Fuck it. I was tired and couldn't think about this anymore. Maybe I'd find a solution tomorrow.

Shana popped into my office "just to say hi" no less than five times the next two days, and I was at my wit's end.

On Wednesday, I wrapped up a task force meeting and asked Julian Silva to stay for a few minutes to brainstorm with me while the other five members of my team worked on the tasks I'd assigned them.

The kid was only twenty-three, but he was sharp as a tack, his brain traveling on a slightly different track than anyone else's. He was going to be a fantastic detective one day.

"Okay, Silva. I want you to look over this spreadsheet I made. See if anything pops out at you. I thought I was onto something Sunday, but I couldn't get a grasp on it. Something to do with the kids."

He took the sheets and settled back into the chair across from my desk just as the door to my office opened.

"Hi, Detective," Shana chirped before she noticed Julian sitting there. "Oh, and Officer Silva. I just wanted to see if you guys needed anything from the Records Room."

"We're fine," I replied tightly. "And you need to knock before you enter someone's office, please."

"Of course," she replied with an awkward giggle before backing out of the room.

Julian's eyes met mine and held there. "She's trouble, boss."

"I'm aware," I sighed before an idea struck me. "Silva, why don't you move into my office until this case is over? We work well together when we bounce ideas off each other."

And you would serve as a nice buffer so I'm not ever caught alone with that woman.

The guy's eyes lit up, and he nodded eagerly. "Sounds good, sir. Where do you want me to set up?"

I had one of the larger offices here, so I told him I'd have a desk brought in for him to use. An hour later, it was done, and Silva was behind the small metal desk adjacent to mine.

We worked in companionable silence for another hour before Silva called my name. When I looked up from my computer, I found him scrawling on a legal pad with a furrowed brow.

"Whatcha got?"

His finger ran down whatever list he'd just written before he lifted his eyes to mine. "I don't know if it means anything..." he hedged.

"I won't know unless you tell me."

"It's just that every one of these women have daughters. Some have sons too, but there's not a single victim that doesn't also have a girl. It seems weird."

I nodded thoughtfully, my brain wrapping around the idea, and something restless slipped down my spine. "Yeah, statistically, you'd expect at least one family out of fifteen to be all boys."

"Could be like a dance class." Then he hastily added, "I mean, guys can dance too, but traditionally speaking, it's known as more of a girls' activity."

"No need to censor yourself with me, Silva. We're just spit balling here."

"Yes, sir. What about softball? Or an all-girls basketball team?"

I was making notes. "Any sport really. Maybe even Girl Scouts."

"Yeah. That's good." His tone lifted with excitement. "My niece is in a STEM group where they promote girls in engineering and science and stuff."

Tossing my pencil down, I ran a hand through my dark brown hair. Being in the South Florida sun had lightened it a bit over the years.

"It could be a million different things. I need to talk to these women and see if anything pops out."

"Yes, sir. I'll keep brainstorming while you're gone."

Rounding my desk, I smacked him on the back. "Actually, I'd like you to go with me. If you're still planning to become a detective one day, it's time you started learning the ropes."

"S-seriously?" he stammered, standing so quickly he knocked his chair over and then scrambled to right it.

Chuckling, I gave a mirthful shake of my head. "Seriously, kid. Let me give a couple of them a call and let them know we're coming. My first rule when speaking with a victim of sexual assault, especially when it occurred in their home, is to give them the opportunity to have someone with them. A husband or friend or whoever."

"That makes sense. It's gotta be hard to have strange men coming into their homes after... *that* happened to them." Silva's lips turned down in a frown. "I have sisters, and I couldn't even imagine that happening to one of them."

"It's not station policy, but it's *my* policy."

"You're a good guy, Detective. A little grumpy, but you have a good heart."

Well, he wasn't wrong about the grumpy part.

CHAPTER 26

KHALEESI SHAW SAT ON her blue-and-white striped couch, clutching her husband's hand.

"I don't see why you have to bother my wife again," James Shaw said, scowling across the glass coffee table at Silva and me. "It's been two years, and we're trying to heal from this."

"I understand, and I hate to dredge up old memories, but I want to catch this guy, Mr. Shaw. He's not going to stop until we do." My words weren't forceful, but they swelled with every bit of passion I felt inside.

Khaleesi's hand squeezed her husband's. "He's right, honey. I don't want anyone else to have to go through what I did. And now he's murdering women." Her dark brown eyes filled with tears as her chin lifted. "What do you need to know?"

"We've noticed that all the women who were attacked have daughters, so we thought that might be significant. Do your girls participate in any organized activities?"

"Um, Karlie, our seven-year-old, just started playing softball, but that was after... after what happened to me."

Probably not helpful then, but I asked anyway. "What's the name of her team?"

"The Bombers. Our nine-year-old, Kandace, is more of a bookworm, so not really into sports or anything."

"Does she go to the library, or is she a part of any kind of reading group?" Silva asked, and I gave him a mental high-five for the excellent question.

James Shaw shook his head. "No, we order her books from Amazon. She has a nook in her room beside the window where she likes to read."

"Anything else you can think of that might be significant from two years ago? I know you've probably been asked that a million times, but I'm trying to make sure all the bases are covered."

The couple shared a look, and Mr. Shaw shook his head and shrugged. "Not that I can think of. Karlie's birthday was a few weeks before, but that's about it."

"Thank you for your time. Here's my card in case you think of anything else."

Anna Suarez sat beside her sister at the kitchen table as we all sipped the tea she'd insisted on serving.

"Not really, Detective." She took a drink from a porcelain cup before setting it down. "Oh, wait. Maria is on the math team at her school. She attends Marytown Elementary. Is that helpful?"

"It might be. Thank you for letting me know. Anything else you can think of that might be significant from two years ago?"

Both women shook their heads.

We met with Jia Li at a local coffee shop because they were in the process of moving. In fact, over half of the families involved had moved after their homes had been invaded, which made me want to catch this guy all the more. Not only had he hurt their bodies, but now the women were too scared to even live in their own homes.

"My children are involved in several activities. My son is on a soccer team, and my daughter plays the flute in a youth orchestra program."

"Which team does your son play for?"

"The Marytown Tigers."

"And they are fourteen and twelve now, correct?"

"Yes, Detective."

"Is there anything else you can think of that might help us? Particularly anything from around the time of the incident?"

"No, Detective."

I couldn't get in touch with Sara Barnes, so we visited Sarah Jacobs next.

"My twin daughters have both played soccer for three years. They're nine now. And my eleven-year-old is on her school's robotics team."

My fingers flipped back through my spiral notebook when she mentioned soccer. Mrs. Li's son played as well, though he was older than the twins.

"Can you tell us the name of the soccer team and their school?"

"They play for the Marlins, and all three go to Westside Prep."

Damn. None of that matched.

Handing over my card, I told her to let me know if she could think of anything else.

That night I dreamed again, but it wasn't about the women. My sister appeared, walking through a white room toward me. When I ran to embrace her, I found there was a glass wall separating us.

She looked exactly the same as the last time I'd seen her when she was almost nineteen, and I wondered if that was significant.

"Evie!" I cried, my voice sounding hollow in the huge, blank space.

"You've got this, bro." Though the clear wall seemed thick, I could somehow hear her as if she was speaking directly into my ear.

"I've got what?" I asked, placing my hand on the glass. She did the same, directly over mine, and I could feel her warmth.

"You've got this. I promise."

Then she turned and walked away.

"Evie, wait!" She kept walking. "Evie, please! Where are you?" My voice was a frantic scream, but my sister continued walking away, the white dress she was wearing beginning to blend in with the background.

Before she disappeared, I slammed my shoulder against the barrier. It shattered, and...

I woke up.

"Goddammit," I panted, sitting up straight, my head swinging from side to side. I was in my room. Alone. Swiping the sweat from my face with both palms, I tried to control my heartbeat. "What the fuck was that?"

Feeling slightly dizzy, I flopped back down onto my pillow and checked the time on my phone. It was slightly after six, so I decided to go ahead and get up.

During my three mile run, my pace was off because my mind was too full of the weird dream. What did it mean that I saw Evie? And what was that message about?

By the time I got back home, I had to rush through my shower and morning routine to make it to the station on time. As soon as I sat down at my desk, Silva busted through the door like he was on fire.

"Boss," he panted, pressing his hands on his knees. "There's been another one."

Motherfucker.

CHAPTER 27

"Hey, girl!" Luciana said, opening the door to let me inside her apartment. As always, I gawked at the mile-high ceilings and elegant furnishings in my younger sister's residence.

But there was something new today.

"What did you do?" I asked, eyeing the golden streamers and large, shiny *Congratulations* balloon in the living room.

"Celebrating our big sister's win," she replied, hugging me as I entered.

"Miss Kassie, so lovely to see you," her butler said in his charming British accent, taking my coat as I shrugged it off.

I removed my camel-colored leather gloves, and he took those too. "Thank you, Thomas. How are the grandkids?"

"Growing up before my very eyes. Thank you for asking."

"Come on," Luci said, pulling me across the dark Spanish marble floor. "Regi's already here."

"Hello, counselor," my other sister said, entering from the kitchen with a silver bucket containing what appeared to be a bottle of champagne. "Congratulations."

She sat it down and embraced me warmly. "Ooh, you feel good. Why does February have to be so damned cold in New York?"

"Bennett and I are going to Gozo next week," Luciana informed us. "To get away from this frozen state."

"I don't even know where the hell that is, but can I go?" Regina asked.

"It's an island in the Mediterranean, in Malta."

"Okay, I'm going too," I announced, sinking onto the royal-blue couch that was more comfortable than it looked.

"That would be awesome," my younger sister squealed. "I'll talk to Bennett about it."

"We were kidding," I said as Thomas poured us each a glass of champagne. I still couldn't get over the fact that my twenty-four-year-old sister had a fucking butler.

"There's no way I can get away right now. We're low on substitute teachers at the school. Flu season and all that," Regi sighed.

"Yeah, and I've got another big case to work on." I lifted the crystal flute to my lips, allowing the bubbles to dance merrily across my tongue. "Holy hell, that's the best champagne I've ever tasted."

"It is good," Regi said. "Better than the thirteen dollar bottle I usually have at the end of the school year. I'm assuming this one costs a tad more than that?"

Luciana tilted her head to the side, her perfectly highlighted hair swinging over one shoulder. "I think it's eight hundred a bottle."

Regina choked and some of the liquid gold sputtered from her mouth.

"Careful, Regi. That's about eighty-seven dollars running down your chin," I told her with a laugh.

"Dammit, woman. Why did you tell me how much it costs? Now I feel like I need to bronze my mouth."

"Bennett told me last week that he'd like to bronze my mouth," Luci giggled.

"I don't even want to know what that means," I replied dryly.

"No, you probably don't," she retorted.

Speak of the devil, my brother-in-law strolled into the room, looking like he'd just stepped off the pages of a men's fashion magazine in his well-cut suit. Hell, his tie probably cost as much as the excellent champagne we were drinking.

"Kassie," he said, bending to kiss my cheek, "congratulations on winning your case yesterday. That was a big one."

I hunched my shoulders, feeling the giddiness that always came after a victory. "Thank you, Bennett. I knew there was no way my client killed her baby. The poor woman was practically catatonic the first time I met her."

Regina leaned forward to accept Bennett's kiss on her cheek. "How did you know the poor baby had an underlying heart condition?" she asked.

"I didn't. I just kept digging, talking to every pediatrician I could find. One of them referred me to a cardiologist who agreed to look at the autopsy results. So she's the real star here."

"Nope, you're the superstar," Luci said, her smile beaming with pride. "To Kassie!" She lifted her glass, and Regi and I followed suit before taking a sip.

Bennett took his wife's glass and clinked it with mine. "I hope I never need a criminal defense attorney, but if I do, I'm glad I have one in the family," he said smoothly before drinking some of the bubbly.

Luciana poked his arm. "Did I say you could drink from my glass, sir? I don't know where your mouth has been."

He looked at her like he was about to devour her on the spot. "Oh, sweetheart, I think you know *exactly* where my mouth has been."

He pulled her to her feet and kissed her. Like, *really* kissed her, and Regi and I shared a *here they go again* look. At thirty-five, Bennett was eleven years older than his wife, but I'd never seen a more compatible couple.

Except for maybe...

Nope. Not going there.

"Well, I'm going to need a cold shower now," Regina drawled as they broke apart, and I laughed at the look on her face—half jealousy and half disgust at seeing her sister with her husband's tongue down her throat.

Bennett smiled, a look of adoration and contentment on his handsome face as he looked down at his wife. He finally lifted his gaze and nodded at his sisters-in-law. "Ladies, I'm headed to work. I hope you enjoy your girls' night."

"Thank you," I replied as Luci walked him to the door. She returned a few minutes later with her face flushed and sat beside me.

"He said you two are welcome to come to Gozo with us. But in a separate house so we can have our privacy." She bobbed her eyebrows at us.

"Of course he did," I said. "That man would give you the world if you asked."

"He already does," she said with a blissful sigh.

"And trust me, we wouldn't want to share a house with you two pervs," Regi teased.

"No, you wouldn't," Luciana said with a light giggle. "So, how's work for you, Reg?"

"Oh, you know. Just living the glamorous life of a kindergarten teacher. I adore my kids though. They are freaking hilarious. If parents only knew the things their kids came to school and said."

"Like what?" I asked. My sister never had a shortage of amusing stories.

She shifted her legs beneath her in the cushy blue chair as a grin spread across her face. "I had one little boy last week who told me his mother really likes flowers. I told him that was nice, and he proceeded to inform me that she had an entire bouquet of roses in her bedside table—red, light pink, dark pink, and purple."

It was my turn to choke. "You think he was talking about the sex toy roses?"

"What other kind of flowers is she going to keep in a drawer beside her bed?" Regi said, lifting a wry eyebrow.

"And who needs four of the same toy?" I wondered.

"I have six roses," Luci informed us. "It's good to have a variety because each one has its own intensity and vibration. You never know which one your body is going to respond to on a particular day."

I fell over onto the couch, curling into a ball and holding my ears. "Make it stop! It's too much!" I cried dramatically, making my sisters laugh.

"Seriously, you're totally an oversharer, Luci."

She shrugged. "Sexual pleasure is nothing to be ashamed of."

"What is this *sexual pleasure* thing you speak of?" I muttered, pushing back to a sitting position.

"You poor thing," she cooed, standing from the couch. "Hold on. I think I have a couple extra roses I want you two to try."

"I hope they're not used," Regina called as our sister headed toward the master bedroom. "I love you, but I don't want to share coochie toys with you."

Luci returned a few seconds later with two rose-shaped devices—still in the package, thank god.

"Of course I'm not sharing my personal goodies with you two bitches. Not when you can have your own." She handed me the pale pink one and gave the plum one to Regi. "Use them in good health, ladies. This is the most powerful rose on the market."

I inspected mine. It would fit in the palm of my hand and didn't look all that powerful.

"I'll try it tonight. Sully is staying over at Mom's house."

"Coolness. Let me know how it goes."

The evening passed with lots of laughter and way too many drinks, which led to more laughter. Poor Thomas indulged us with patient smiles and tons of carbs, and at almost midnight, he called Luci's driver to take Regi and me home.

Once I was safely inside my apartment, I cleaned my new toy and settled on my bed, eyeing the thing in my hand. "Are you my new friend?" I asked it when I flipped the on switch, but it only buzzed in response.

"Say hello to my leetle frand," I said in my best Tony-Montana-from-*Scarface* voice, which turned me into a giggling maniac. It had been a while since I'd been drunk.

It had also been a while since I'd masturbated. I usually fell directly asleep when my head hit the pillow, weary from working and mommy-ing.

"Let's see what you've got," I told the small vibrator, spreading my legs and placing it against the lips of my pussy. "Ohhh, that's... that's good."

The device was supposed to simulate oral sex, and I'll be damned if it wasn't pretty freaking close to the real thing. It was like a pulsing, sucking, breathing entity that had my eyes rolling back in my head.

A soft moan ripped from my lips, and then a louder one when I hit the button for the next level.

"Fuuuck, that's... holy mother of god!" The intensity of the vibrations increased tenfold, and I came in less than sixty seconds.

"Shit," I panted, pulling the sucky little device away from my sensitive clit. "What the fuck is this thing?"

The package had informed me that the rose had ten levels, and I'd gone off like a rocket on level two. I couldn't even imagine what would happen on level ten, but I was certain it would kill me.

And wouldn't that be fun? I knew a ton of first responders, and I couldn't even imagine them finding me in my apartment, alone and dead and smiling like a motherfucker.

Or my mother. Lord have mercy, they'd have to bury us together because she would keel over on the spot.

Nope, I decided. *No level ten for this chica.*

Once I could stand—albeit on shaky legs—I went to the bathroom for a quick cleanup before stashing my new best friend in the small safe I kept in my closet.

I certainly didn't want Sully going to school and telling his teacher about the "flower" Mommy kept in her nightstand.

Crawling beneath the sheets, I grabbed my phone and texted Luciana before I went to sleep. It was a short message, only two words, but it would get my point across.

Thank you.

CHAPTER 28

I SAT AT MY desk and stared down at the newspaper from a neighboring town, reading the headline over and over.

Marytown... or Murdertown?

"Yeah, really fucking clever," I mumbled. Silva was out today for a dentist appointment, so I was talking to myself.

Fear was running rampant throughout the entire city of Marytown and the surrounding areas, and that pissed me off. I hated that our female citizens were living with that. Articles like this didn't help.

My cell phone rang, and I checked the display to see that Lita George was calling. She was the latest victim, but she miraculously survived the attack. As soon as the perp climbed on top of her, she headbutted him in the face. The fucker had rolled off her and ran out the back door, the same way he'd come in.

She must have busted his nose or his lip because we'd found blood on the floor along his escape route. We figured his signature black ski mask probably absorbed most of it, but he'd left behind a few droplets, the most promising forensic evidence we had to date.

Unfortunately, it led exactly nowhere when we ran the DNA profile through all our databases. It would be a key piece of evidence during a trial, but first we had to find the asshole.

"Mrs. George," I said, answering the phone. I'd given all the victims my personal cell phone number so they could reach me at any time. "How are you?"

"Detective Bouvier, hi. I'm okay, just taking it day by day, you know?"

"That's all you can do. Is there anything I can help you with?"

"Thank you, but I don't think so. Um, I know I gave you my day planner when you asked for it after... everything."

Her voice quivered on the last word, and my chest tightened at the sound of her distress. I fucking hated that this woman—*any* woman—had to be afraid. It meant I wasn't doing my job well enough, and I took that personally.

"Yes, I took photos, and then your husband dropped by and picked it up a couple weeks ago. Didn't you get it?"

"Oh, yes. I got it. That wasn't what I was calling about. About a month before the, um, the incident, I started using a calendar app on my phone. I used it for a couple weeks and decided I didn't like it. I prefer using my day planner because it has cute little stickers and stuff. Anyway, I just remembered that and checked the app and found a few things that weren't written in my day planner."

Tucking my phone between my cheek and my shoulder, I pulled up my spreadsheet. It was woefully incomplete because we'd paused our interviews with the previous victims while we focused on the most recent attack and the new evidence.

"Okay, go ahead," I told her.

"Let's see, the last week in December, I took the girls to the zoo. Then the next weekend, we had Jenny's birthday party, and the weekend after that, we went to visit my sister in Miami. I know none of that is probably helpful, but you said you wanted everything we'd done recently, no matter how big or small."

"Got it," I said, entering the information. "Was the zoo trip with a group of any kind?"

"No, I just took them because they were on Christmas break and bored. Do you have kids, Detective?"

Pressing my hand over my heart, I closed my eyes. "No, I don't." *But I almost did.*

"Ah, well, trust me. They get all excited about being off from school, but a few days later, they're whining about being bored."

Forcing a smile into my voice, I said, "I think I remember being the same way as a kid. Were there any other events or activities in the weeks prior to the attack?"

"No, like I said, I only used the app for a little bit before switching back to my day planner."

"Thank you for calling and letting me know. If you think of anything else, feel free to call me any time, day or night."

"I will, and thank you for everything you're doing. I know this is hard on you too, having to see and deal with the things you do." Her voice softened. "I couldn't even imagine, and I just wanted to let you know I appreciate you."

"That's really kind of you to say. I had a sister once—" *Why am I saying this?* "Anyway, I promise I'm doing everything in my power to catch this guy, Mrs. George."

There was a beat of silence. "I'm sorry about your sister, Detective," she said quietly.

"Thank you. If you need anything, you have my number."

We hung up, and I propped my elbows on the desk and ran both hands through my hair. March was approaching, and it was always a hard month for me. That must be why I mentioned Evie to a woman I hardly knew.

Blowing out a breath, I focused back on my computer. A trip to the zoo. A birthday party. A weekend trip to Miami. Not much to go on there.

But something was sparking at the back of my brain, so I read the words again, my eyes stalling on the second event.

Wait. Didn't one of the other victims mention their child's birthday?

Probably wasn't significant. Between the sixteen women, they had almost forty children, so surely some would have had birthdays around the times of the women's attacks.

Leave no stone unturned, Bouvier.

Right. I could at least check it out. But who was it that mentioned a birthday?

I could almost feel the gears grinding in my brain as I thought back to that week I interviewed the other women.

Was it Anna? No, I think it was someone with more than one kid.

My train of thought was derailed when the door to my office opened. "Hi, Monty."

Jesus fucking Christ.

"Miss O'Neil, is there a reason you came into my office without knocking?" My tone was icy, but I didn't give a fuck. She knew damn well she was supposed to knock before entering any office in this building.

"I thought we could talk since Julian's not in today." She shut the door, and my anxiety went through the roof.

"Leave the door open, please."

Ignoring me, she sauntered farther into my office, a sly smirk on her face. "I just want to talk to you, Monty."

"Detective Bouvier," I gritted out, standing and marching to the door to open it. "Now if you'll excuse me, I'm right in the middle of something."

I returned to my desk and sat, trying to refocus on what I'd been thinking about before the interruption.

Was it Sarah Jacobs? She has twin daughters. That didn't seem right though, and I reached for my notebook to see if I'd written it down somewhere.

But there was an ass on my notebook. Shana's ass, to be specific. She was perched right on the corner of my desk, her legs hanging off the side.

"Could you please move? I need my notebook."

"No. I *said* I wanted to talk to you."

"And *I* said I'm working, like you should be doing."

"I'm on a bathroom break."

"Well this isn't the fucking bathroom," I snapped, losing what little patience I had in reserve.

"Fine, if you won't talk to me here, we can meet up after work. You want to go to that same bar we went to last time?"

My frustration bubbled over. "No, as I've told you every time you have tried to corner me somewhere alone, I *do not* want to go anywhere with you."

"But we had so much fun together that night," she cooed.

"Listen to me, Miss O'Neil. That was a one-time thing. I told you that before anything ever happened, and you said you understood."

"Come on, Monty. Just one more night together, and I'll stop bugging you." She dragged a pink fingernail down my bicep, and I pulled away. "I promise."

"Not going to happen. It would be highly inappropriate since we work together. To be honest, it pisses me off that you knew you'd be working here, and *you* didn't divulge that to *me* before we slept together."

Her eyes narrowed. "Why are you acting like this?"

I wanted to scream at her, but there was no way I wanted the entire station to hear this shit. So I stood, my face only a few inches from hers as I lowered my voice.

"Because you're not fucking listening to me. There is nothing between us. Nothing. And there never will be. Do you understand what the fuck I'm saying? Hooking up with you was a mistake, and I wish it had never happened because you're driving me fucking insane."

I barely flinched when she slapped me across the face, her light eyes burning with ire. Before I could respond, I heard a voice from the doorway.

"Uh, is everything okay in here?"

Alice Cunningham, one of our patrol officers, was standing there with her eyes wide, and I clenched my teeth so hard they hurt.

"Sure, I was just leaving," Shana said, pulling her eyes from mine with a smug smile that made me want to strangle her.

As soon as she was gone, I fell back into my chair and scratched the back of my neck. "Officer Cunningham, I'd appreciate it if you wouldn't mention that to anyone. Miss O'Neil and I had a disagreement about... some records that were misplaced."

That was about the lamest fucking excuse I'd ever uttered, and Alice didn't look like she believed a word of it, but she nodded. "Okay, Detective."

"And would you close the door on your way out, please?"

Once I was alone, I rose and grabbed a bottle of water, holding it against my stinging cheek. I couldn't believe that bitch slapped me. Not that it really hurt; it was just the audacity.

Shaking my head, I decided I would deal with that shit later. I really felt like I'd been onto something before damn Shana interrupted me.

My fingers flipped through the pages of my notebook, and I found the one I was looking for.

Khaleesi. That's who it was. She'd mentioned something about Karlie's birthday being a few weeks before the attack.

Probably nothing, I told myself as I dialed her number.

"Hello?" She sounded like she'd been asleep.

"Mrs. Shaw, I hope I'm not bothering you. This is Detective Bouvier."

She sniffled, and I wondered if she was crying. "No, it's fine. Did you need another meeting?" she asked, her tone weary as hell.

"No, just a quick question. You mentioned when we spoke a few weeks ago that Karlie had a birthday shortly before the break in at your house."

"Yes, that was two years ago, so her fifth."

"Did you have a party?"

"Yes, we have a party every year for our girls."

I struggled to think of my next question. "Was it at a restaurant or maybe one of those places with all the bouncy houses?"

"No, we did it at our home, just finger foods and cake." Disappointment crashed down on me; I was really hoping something would come of this. Then she said, "We didn't have anything extravagant, foodwise, because the princess service we hired cost so much."

Furrowing my brow, I asked, "What's a princess service?"

"Oh, you know. They provide people dressed up as Cinderella or Elsa. Whoever your child's favorite princess is. They come over and read a book to the kids or act out a little skit. It's really nice."

"All right. Thanks for the info. I'm just trying to follow up on everything. You have a good day, Mrs. Shaw."

We hung up, and I leaned back in my chair, my hand stroking the beard I'd allowed to grow on my chin the past month. Princess party. Who the fuck knew that even existed?

We knew the perp was a male, so maybe the princesses had someone carry their gear for them or something. Tapping a number on my cell phone, I called Lita George back.

"Detective, long time no hear."

"Hi, Mrs. George. Sorry to bother you again so soon. I had a quick question. You said Jenny had a birthday in January. What kind of celebration did you have?"

She seemed taken aback by the question. "Oh. We had a party at our house and hired some characters to come and entertain the kids. She's six, so she's really into the princess thing."

A shiver ran down my spine so hard my entire body shook. "Where did you find characters?" My voice sounded hollow in my ears, as if I was speaking in a large cavern.

"There's a business here in town called Marytown Princess Parties. We actually hired three characters. Cinderella, of course, because she's just classic."

Holy fuck. I think I've finally found a possible link.

"And Aurora," Lita continued. "She's the one in the pink dress."

All the victims have daughters.

"Of course, Cinderella wouldn't be complete without her Prince Charming."

Prince Charming! My hands balled into fists on my desk, my knuckles turning white as she kept talking in my ear.

"It was so cute. He got down on one knee and fitted Cinderella with a glass slipper."

My hand shook when I unfisted it and reached for a pen. "And what did you say the name of the business was?"

"Marytown Princess Parties. A very nice lady named Chanel owns it."

I wrote down the information, barely able to read my own handwriting.

"Detective, are you there? Does this have something to do with what happened?"

Finding my voice, I said, "I'm just trying to figure out if any of the families have gone to the same places or used the same services. Covering all my bases, you know?"

Disconnecting with Lita, I called Anna Suarez.

"Hello?"

"Mrs. Suarez, Detective Bouvier here. This may sound like a weird question, but when is Maria's birthday?" The attack on Anna had been in April, two years ago.

"It's in March."

Mother of god!

"Do you remember what you did for her birthday two years ago?"

"Let's see. She would have been nine then… oh yes. We had a princess-themed party."

Excitement filled every cell of my body—the thrill of the hunt when you finally caught sight of your prey. "I've heard of those. Which characters did you have?"

"Elsa from *Frozen.* And we also had Prince Charming, even though those two don't really go together. I thought she would choose Anna since that's Elsa's sister, but..."

The rest of her words fell away as soon as she said Prince motherfucking Charming.

I've got you now, asshole.

I went down the rest of my list and called each of the surviving women I'd come to know over the past two years. Every single one of them had used Marytown Princess Parties in the two months prior to their respective attacks.

And there was one glaring similarity in each of their casts of characters.

"We had Belle and Prince Charming."

"Tiana was a huge hit with our girls, and they just loved Prince Charming too."

"Cinderella. Oh, and her prince, of course."

"We actually hired four characters. Elsa, Moana, Cinderella, and Prince Charming. The prince was so sweet and handsome."

"Prince Charming and Ariel."

Prince Charming.

Prince Charming.

Prince Charming.

Looking up the website for Marytown Princess Parties, I found the photo gallery and clicked on it.

And there he was. A man in a blue-and-white prince costume. Blue eyes. Blond hair.

Blond fucking hair!

I dialed Julian Silva's number as I stood and pulled on my suit jacket. His voice was garbled.

"Hewwo?"

"Jules, are you done at the dentist?" I asked quickly.

"Yes, just finished. My mouf is all numb."

"Send me the address. I'm coming to pick you up. We got the mother-fucker."

CHAPTER 29

I STOOD IN MY office at the law firm, my arms crossed over my chest as I stared at the news scrolling across my television.

He was on the screen. Monty Bouvier. I'd seen still photos of him online, but this was the first time in years I'd seen him in motion. The last time had been at the press conference after Evie's disappearance all those years ago.

My heart had broken into a million pieces that night for so many reasons. Because I'd lost the love of my life. Because Evie was missing. Because I was in a strange city with no friends. But mostly because the boy I loved looked so lost and scared. I ached for him.

"Hey," Lily said, entering my office.

"Hi," I replied, unable to pull my eyes from the screen.

"What are you... oh my damn. Is that..." She stared as the words *Detective Monty Bouvier* appeared beneath him. "That's fucking Monty. *Your* Monty." Her finger jabbed me in the arm.

"He's not *mine*," I protested, flinching away from her as we watched Monty walk to the podium on a makeshift stage.

"You know what I mean. Holy shit, he grew up well."

Absolutely no lies detected there.

Clicking the remote, I turned up the volume, and his voice filled the room. It was different from when I'd known him. Deeper. Richer. Harder.

Monty—excuse me, *Detective Bouvier*—spoke about the recent apprehension of a criminal named Jonah Lee Carver.

"This is big time," Lily said in a low voice. "He made the national news."

Monty was head of the task force assigned to catch a serial rapist and murderer, and my chest filled with pride as he expertly fielded questions from reporters.

He was wearing a baby-blue polo shirt that stretched over his wide shoulders and chest. His hair was lighter now, but his eyes were just as blue, though they lacked the good-natured twinkle they'd always held.

"He looks good with a beard," I murmured, almost forgetting I wasn't alone.

"Hey, you okay?"

Looking down, I found Lily's eyes filled with concern.

"Yeah, I'm fine."

Her dark eyebrows made a slow ascent up her forehead. "Are you being honest with me?"

I sighed and gnawed on my bottom lip. "I don't know."

She looped an arm around my waist. "It's gotta be hard seeing him. They say you never fully get over your first love."

"I'm over him." At her skeptical look, I insisted, "I really am, but seeing him, I can't help but wonder *what if?*"

"I get that. You never really got any closure."

My head bobbed up and down in agreement. "Exactly that."

"He's not bad to look at though," Lil said, and I fought a smile at her gross understatement. We turned our attention back to the television and watched as he answered question after question from reporters representing all the major news organizations.

"I feel really... proud of him right now. Is that weird?"

"Not at all. I'm proud of him too." My friend shook her head. "God, those poor women. Now they can finally sleep a little easier at night."

Monty pointed to a male reporter from CNN, and the man asked, "How do you feel now that Jonah Lee Carver is finally in police custody?"

For the first time, a smile crossed his face. The slightly crooked one that had always made my knees weak. And if I was being completely honest with myself, that effect hadn't lessened a bit. That tiny crook of his lips threatened my ability to stand upright, so I averted my eyes and stared at a uniformed officer in the background.

"Most of all, I feel relieved," Monty answered. "The surviving women are some of the bravest I've ever met, and this arrest never would have happened without their help."

A female reporter piped up. "How are the women taking the news about the arrest?"

"I've spoken with each of them, as well as the families of the murdered women. As a whole, they're glad it's all over." His eyes defocused as he seemed to stare out into space. Even after sixteen years, I could still read him like a book. He was thinking of sweet, funny Evie.

The entire room went silent as everyone seemed to sense the change in him, from the press of his lips to the tight grip he had on the edges of the podium.

Finally, he cleared his throat. "I'd like to ask you all to please give these women, as well as their families, the privacy they need to heal. I'm aware you have a job to do, but please consider this. If it was someone you loved, how would you want them to be treated?"

With that parting remark, he lifted a hand and announced that there would be no more questions. Then he turned and walked off the side of the stage.

He looked as good from the back as he did from the front, his broad back tapering to a slim waist.

Lily took the remote from me and clicked the off button. "I have a very serious question, and I don't want you to bullshit me."

"Okay, shoot."

Her mouth twisted into a sly grin. "If Monty Bouvier walked in here right now, would you jump on that beard and take a ride?"

"Lily!" I shrieked with a laugh, smacking her arm. "Stop it! You know I'm on a strict man ban."

"That wasn't a no," she sang.

"It's an unequivocal no. A hard no. A big, fat *hell no*."

"Methinks—"

"Oh shut the fuck up."

"You've got this," Luci said, squeezing both my hands before releasing them and fussing with the collar of my navy suit jacket.

"I know. This is my thing, convincing jurors to do what I want." I pushed a thin line of air from the corner of my mouth, blowing away an errant strand of hair from my cheek. "Only I'm trying to convince the parole board to keep Wesley locked up."

"You can do it, Kass. I have complete faith in you."

I pulled air into my lungs until they were at maximum capacity before letting it back out. "Thank you. I'm ready."

"Go get 'em, tiger," she said, making a little growly noise at the back of her throat that made me smile.

I went into that room with my head held high and my confidence brimming. I spoke for fifteen minutes without stopping, my speech flowing from my lips with eloquence and passion, never needing to look down at my notes even once.

When I was done, I was exhausted but happy.

"How did it go?" Luci asked, clinging to me like an excited puppy as soon as I exited.

"Really good. I showed them the letters, so there's no way they're letting him out."

Three days later, I was proven wrong when the board announced their decision.

My ex-husband, Wesley Campbell, had been granted parole.

Fuck.

CHAPTER 30

"Hey, Captain," I said, strolling into his office and taking a seat. "What did you need to see me about?"

He fixed me with a long stare as if analyzing me. "How are things going, Detective?"

I lifted one shoulder in a shrug. "Really good, actually. I feel like I can breathe easier now that Carver is behind bars."

"Excellent work on that, Bouvier." He was still staring at me, his drooping brown eyes looking more sorrowful than usual.

"Thanks, Cap. Is there something wrong?" My jaw flexed as a thought hit me. "It's not about the evidence, is it? Because I can assure you, everything was handled with the utmost of care, and we had a search warrant for everything we found in his house after the arrest. There's no way the judge will throw any of it out."

I mentally flicked through the catalog of overwhelming evidence. The blood droplets. The pubic hairs. The three pairs of leather gloves in Campbell's closet. One of Sara's hairs embedded in the ski mask we'd found. Everything was unimpeachable.

His big head shook side to side. "No, that's not it. There's something else." The captain's gaze dropped to a paper on his desk before lifting back to me. "There's been a formal complaint against you."

I sat straight up in my chair. "Oh, hell no! The arrest was executed perfectly," I protested, jabbing a finger toward him to punctuate my words.

"Every bit of it is on camera. I didn't even so much as put the cuffs on too tightly." *Though I'd secretly hoped the fucking sicko would resist arrest so I could tackle him.*

"It has nothing to do with the Carver case, Detective. It's a..." A tiny shake of his head told me he didn't want to finish that sentence. But he did anyway. "A sexual harassment claim."

The air around me grew thick. Oppressive. I could barely breathe because I felt as though I was inhaling pea soup. I was pretty sure I knew the answer already when I asked, "Who is the complainant?"

"Shana O'Neil."

Son of a motherfucking bitch.

Keeping my tone as measured as possible, despite the raging storm building inside me, I said, "That's complete bullshit, Captain. She's the one who's been harassing me. I should've filed a complaint against *her.*"

"But you didn't."

I flattened my palms against my black pants so I didn't ball them into fists. "No, I was handling it. I made it known in no uncertain terms that I wasn't interested, but she kept pursuing me, coming into my office for no reason, stuff like that. But I always made sure to leave the door open when she did, and I never laid a finger on her."

"So you've never had a sexual relationship with Miss O'Neil?" My eyes dropped to his thick fingers drumming against the papers on his desk, and I knew that he already knew the answer to that.

"Yes, but it was only once, and it was before I knew she was employed here."

Captain Snyder massaged his temples, the wrinkles on his forehead becoming more pronounced. "Fuck, Bouvier! Why didn't you come to me with this?"

"Like I said, I was handling it, and the, uh, incident occurred before she worked here."

"She tells a different story. Miss O'Neil reports that you've been relentlessly trying to get her to sleep with you again. And I understand there was a physical altercation in your office two weeks ago? We even have a witness to that."

A witness? My mind stretched back to the day that seemed a lifetime ago.

"Are you talking about Alice Cunningham?" Captain Snyder nodded. "I had asked Sh—Miss O'Neil several times to leave my office because I was on the verge of figuring things out with the Carver case. She refused, and I finally had to get firm with her. I told her to get the fuck out of my office, and then she slapped me. I guess Cunningham was walking by in the hallway right about then."

Snyder's eyes narrowed. "I've interviewed the officer, and she said it looked intense."

"I suppose it was. Like I said, Miss O'Neil refused to leave my office, and I got snippy with her. I was frustrated because she was interrupting me while I was trying to do my job." I lifted both palms in the air. "You know, what you're *paying* me to do?"

He let out a long, weary breath, leaning back in his high-backed leather chair as his eyes rolled to the ceiling. "For what it's worth, I believe you, Bouvier. I checked back through your personnel file, and there's never been even a hint of impropriety in the eleven years you've been with this department."

"I've never had a single reprimand," I confirmed. "If you believe me, why do I feel like there's a *but* coming?"

The captain let out a frustrated noise and leaned forward with his forearms on the wooden desk, apologetic brown gaze steady on mine. "I think you know the answer to that. We have to take these kinds of complaints seriously, Monty."

"And what about my complaint?" I asked as the anger inside me threatened to simmer over.

"You never filed one," he reminded. "And you did have a sexual relationship with an entry-level employee."

"*Before* she worked here," I gritted out. "In fact, Miss O'Neil knew exactly where I worked because I met her while I was getting my physical for the job. She never said a thing about her being an employee here. She's the one who should be fired for... deception or something."

The captain's eyes closed for a long moment. "Christ, this is a fucking nightmare, Bouvier. I don't want to see your record marred with something like this, and I also don't need this department to be dragged through the mud. We're on a high right now."

"Because my team and I found a goddamn serial rapist and murderer," I snapped.

"Right, and how would it look if the current golden boy of Marytown was dragged into the muck on a sexual harassment case?" he shot back.

I knew he was speaking the truth, but it still stung. "Where do we go from here?"

Snyder rubbed his large hand down his face. "Here's what I've come up with. I should be placing you on administrative leave right now." When I opened my mouth to protest that absolute bullshit, he silenced me with a raised palm. "*But,* I was thinking maybe you might enjoy a little leave of absence after wrapping up a very emotional case."

"You want me to leave," I stated. My next thought was coated in bitterness. *Why does this sound familiar?* But I held my tongue.

"I want you to take a step back. Voluntarily."

"Because it would look better for the department."

"And for you. Like I said, I believe what you said, Bouvier." He picked up the papers and flapped them around. "But I can't just sweep something like this under the rug. She'd run straight to the press."

My eyes shifted to the wall behind him, focusing on a gold-and-black plaque as my world seemed to crash down around me. "I've worked my ass off to get where I am, Cap."

"I know, Monty. Take a few weeks off and go down to the Keys. Lay on the beach and unwind. Drink mai tais or whatever the fuck you want to do."

"If I don't, I'll be kicked off the job anyway, right?"

"You'll be placed on administrative leave, pending the outcome of the investigation."

"And I could lose my job completely."

The lines around his eyes deepened. "Possibly. I don't want that to happen, but it could."

"Fine," I said sullenly.

"I'll need a written statement from you as well."

Standing, I pulled my badge holder from my pocket and slapped it down on the desk. "I'll have it for you by the end of the day."

Snyder stared at my badge before bringing his eyes back to mine. "I'm really sorry about this, Monty."

"Yeah, me too," I said, suddenly more tired than I'd been in years. This was my fucking career, and now it may be over. I couldn't even fathom what I was supposed to do now.

I knew one thing for sure. I never wanted to get involved with another woman for the rest of my life.

Returning to my office for maybe the last time, I stared down at my palm.

"It's just you and me now, buddy."

"Hey, bro. How's it going?"

"Good," I lied, leaning back against my headboard with one arm behind my head as I FaceTimed with Auburn. "I wanted to talk to Jane before her surgery tomorrow."

"Hold up; I'll take the phone to her." His image bounced on the screen as he walked through our cousin Blaire's house. "Janie girl, I have someone who wants to talk to you."

He handed the phone over, and my beautiful little blonde niece came into view. "Uncle Monty!" she squealed, her smile lighting up my world. This was exactly what I needed after the crap I'd endured today.

Jane and Jaxon were Auburn and Gianna's adopted children, and I fucking adored them. Janie was the sweetest little girl in the world, and her tenacity amazed me every day. The things that poor kid had been through...

At least she had parents who loved her and her twin brother now. They would never want for anything, especially love.

"How's my favorite girl?"

"I'm good. I'm having surgery on my leg tomorrow. Aunt Blaire is doing it."

"I know, sweetie, and don't you worry about a thing. Blaire is the best orthopedic surgeon I know."

Jaxon's blond head popped into the picture. "Hi, Uncle Monty. We're in Texas!" His precocious grin melted the ice that had been frozen around my heart since this morning. "We rode on an airplane and everything!"

I laughed for the first time in what seemed like forever, and the vibration of my vocal cords soothed me. "That's cool, buddy. What have you been doing?"

"We had barbecue today," Jane informed me, nudging her face in beside her brother's. "I ate ribs for the first time."

Over the next few minutes, they talked non-stop about the plane ride and their cousins, and in that short time, my anxiety seemed to fade away. These two were good for me, and I'd never even met them in person.

My heart was suddenly overwhelmed with the urge to do just that. To go see my niece and nephew and feel their small arms around my neck as I held them for the first time.

I hadn't been back to New York since I'd left sixteen years ago, but maybe it was time.

I slept in till ten the day after the meeting in Captain Snyder's office. Could be because I'd gotten stupid drunk after I got off the phone with Auburn and the kids.

Emptying two Tylenol into my hand, I swallowed them with the glass of water I'd just poured when I heard my phone ringing. I trudged back to my room, my chest tightening when I saw it was my brother calling. Jane's surgery should be done by now. It was the first thing I'd thought of upon waking, and I'd been waiting on this call.

"Auburn, how did Janie-Bug's surgery go?"

"It was fine. Blaire said everything went really well, and hopefully, she'll be able to walk in a few months."

"Thank god. I've been so worried," I said, sinking to the edge of my mussed bed. "How is Gianna holding up?"

"She's tired but doing okay. We're both glad this part is over. Look—"

"And Jaxon? Poor little fella. I know he's been worried sick." That kid was so protective over his twin.

"He's okay. He got to see her in the recovery room for a couple minutes, so that helped. Listen, I really need to talk to you about something."

"Okay, bro. Shoot."

I heard him inhale and blow out a long breath.

"Monty, something's happened. It's time to come home."

My brother sounded as serious as a heart attack, his voice tight, and I wondered if there was a complication with the surgery he'd neglected to mention.

"What's wrong?" I asked, my heart rate quickening.

"Our mother is dead."

CHAPTER 31

I WAS GLAD I was sitting down because that was the last thing I'd expected him to say.

"Whoa, okay. I—I'm not sure how to feel about that."

"That's okay. I'm the same, brother. I wasn't ever close to her, but I never wished her dead."

"Yeah, same." My mind was reeling. "What happened? Was she sick?"

Auburn let out a sound from the back of his throat. "No, it was a single car crash outside Atlantic City. I just talked to Dad. He said the state troopers contacted him this morning. They're still technically married, even though they've been separated for over a year now. Chloe has been dragging out the divorce for as long as possible."

"Yeah, I've been talking to Dad at least once a week the past year. Before that, he'd call me on holidays and we'd chat for a few minutes, but since he decided to divorce the egg donor... I don't know, I guess it soothed some of my raw nerves over what happened."

"I'm glad things are getting better between you two." After a slight pause, he said, "There's something else. She wasn't alone in the car. There was a man in there with her. A younger man. He also died."

"Wow. That's... wow. How does Dad feel about that?"

"He was worried about how it would play out in the press, but otherwise, it didn't seem to bother him all that much. I think I'll have the *Bouvier* PR people put out a statement. Say the family is saddened, blah blah blah.

And refer to Chloe as Paul Bouvier's estranged wife. Maybe that will make things seem less salacious."

"Good idea."

"Anyway, Mont, I think it would be a good idea if you came home."

"Okay."

He continued on as if he didn't hear me. "I know you couldn't stand her, and rightfully so, but I think it would be good for Dad if... wait. Did you say okay?"

"Yes. I'll come. I've been wanting to see the kids. And to hug your gorgeous wife. You think she's into brothers?" At his low growl, I laughed. "Stop sounding like an angry bear, Auburn. I was kidding."

"You better be, asshole."

"Do you know when the funeral will be?"

"Not sure. They still haven't released her body, so it will be a while. And Jane can't travel for two more days. We came on the private jet, and Blaire is coming back with us, along with a team of nurses, just to make sure the transport is comfortable for Janie."

"Okay, I'll book a flight for three days from now."

"I can send my plane for you, and then they can come back to Dallas to pick us up."

"Nah, that's too many flight hours for your pilot. I'll fly commercial. I can afford it."

More than afford it, actually. Our father had released my trust fund to me right after my eighteenth birthday, and I had barely touched it besides purchasing a house.

More funds came in every month because my brother insisted on profit sharing with me. I'd balked at first, but he said *Bouvier* was our family's business, and he wouldn't have it any other way. Hell, I hadn't looked at the account in years and had no idea how much money was even in there. I was fine living off my job.

Which I may not have any longer.

But somehow, that just didn't seem all that important right now.

I was going to see my family.

The *Welcome to New York* sign came into view, and I stopped in the middle of the concourse to stare up at it. Busy travelers bustled around me on their way to and from everywhere in the world.

The vibrancy of the city pulsated around me, even though I was still inside the airport. Miami was a vibrant place too, but the vibe was different.

"Mr. Bouvier?"

My head swiveled to the side and found a large man approaching. This must be the driver Auburn said he was sending.

"Yes, and please call me Monty," I said, sticking out my hand.

He shook it with a firm grip and smiled with perfectly white teeth. "I'm Cruz Estrada, your chariot driver for the day." He flipped open his ID and showed it to me, which I appreciated. I nodded, and he quickly stowed it back in his pocket and reached for my suitcase. "Let me get that for you."

"No, I've got it," I deferred. "Thanks for coming to get me. I told Auburn I could take an Uber."

He rolled his eyes good-naturedly. "Yeah, well, I've found it best not to try and argue with the man."

"He can be a bit stubborn. How is he to work for?"

"Really good," Cruz said, gesturing with one hand toward the exit, and we began walking. "He's demanding but fair, and he's gotten a lot nicer since Gianna came into his life."

"I've never actually met her in person, just on FaceTime. Is she really as nice as she seems?"

"Even nicer," he said as we left the building. "Don't get me wrong. She may be a sweetheart, but I've seen her put Auburn Bouvier in his place more than once. In fact, she's the only person allowed to boss him around. It's pretty hilarious to watch. Here we are."

We arrived at a black Bentley illegally parked at the curb, but the security guard nearby simply gave us a nod. Cruz reached for the back door.

"Do you mind if I sit up front with you?" I asked. "I haven't been driven around since I was a kid."

He stowed my suitcase and carry-on duffle in the trunk. "That'd be great actually. It will be nice to get to know the prodigal Bouvier son."

"I don't know about prodigal," I told him with a chuckle as we settled into the luxurious vehicle. "I'm just me."

"Your brother is really proud of you," Cruz said, casting me a glance before pulling out into the thick traffic. "He hasn't stopped talking about the serial killer case you solved."

I shrugged one shoulder. "I had a great team."

"Don't be modest. That was outstanding police work on your part."

Wanting to shift the subject away from me, I asked, "So what's your story?"

"Born and raised in Galveston, Texas. It's an island south of Houston. Joined the Marines right out of high school."

"I thought you looked like a military man."

He rubbed a hand over his crew cut. "The hair gave it away, right?"

"And the way you carry yourself. How did you end up working for Auburn?"

"He was looking for a personal guard and driver. I applied and got the job," he said with a shrug. "I'm also a reserve officer on the SWAT team."

"You see much action?"

"You know how it is. We're mostly used for high-risk search warrants, but sometimes we get into more engaging shit," he said, merging onto I-495. "Hey, do you know Florida Man?"

My brow furrowed as I looked out at the city I'd left behind all those years ago. It seemed bigger. "Who?"

"You know. The one you hear about in headlines, always doing crazy stuff. The fucker always seems to be from the Sunshine State. *Florida man steals car—naked.* Or *Florida man calls 9-1-1 because he has cocaine in his ass.*"

That made me laugh. "Oh yeah. Him. I've met him once or twice. One time we were called to a local McDonald's because some guy had a gun and was demanding they give him all the ketchup packets in the store."

Cruz shook his head. "Doesn't he know Micky D's is stingy with their condiments? He should've gone to Chick-Fil-A. They would have given him whatever he wanted and told him it was their pleasure."

"That's the truth. The kicker with this story though was that the guy was using a finger gun to hold up the restaurant."

"Did he have his hand in his pocket?"

"No, just like this." I held up my own finger gun and demonstrated. "And the workers actually called emergency services for that."

"People," Cruz said, rolling his blue eyes. "I guess Texas has their share of crazy stories too. There was one woman who posted on Facebook that she was selling a frozen armadillo."

My eyebrows hit the roof. "Seriously?"

"Yep. Some guy replied that he wanted it, so they decided to meet in the Walmart parking lot for the big varmint exchange. When he got there, the man said he didn't have the money to pay for it, so the woman proceeded to beat him with the frozen armadillo."

I barked out a laugh. "That's some funny shit. I think we should introduce Texas Woman and Florida Man. They could get married. I'm curious though. How much was she charging for it?"

"Fifty-one dollars and twenty-three cents."

"Well that's oddly specific."

By the time we reached my brother's apartment building, Cruz and I were talking and laughing like old friends, something I didn't have much of down in Florida. I had acquaintances and often went out for drinks with coworkers, but I mostly stayed to myself.

But this? It felt... nice.

"Monty!"

I recognized Gianna as soon as she opened the door. We'd chatted face to face many times over the phone in the past eighteen months.

The woman was even more stunning in person, though she was dressed down in black yoga pants and what appeared to be one of Auburn's old Syracuse sweatshirts, which hung off one slim shoulder.

Her dark hair was pulled back into a ponytail, and her green eyes sparkled as she yanked me into a neck-wringing hug.

"We're so happy you're here," she squealed before lowering her voice to a whisper. "Your brother especially, but don't tell him I said that."

I leaned back and looked down at her with a smile. "How long have you been in New York, Gia?"

"Two years, next month."

"You still have your accent."

She delivered a light poke to my ribs. "Shut up. You can take the girl outta Texas, but you can't take the Texas outta the girl."

Hearing a noise, I looked over her shoulder to see Auburn walking toward me down an arched hallway that I assumed led to the bedrooms. The grin on his face was nothing short of ecstatic, and it shoved my emotions directly to the forefront.

We stared for a long moment before we broke into a jog at the same time, as if it were choreographed. We crashed into each other, arms binding us together in the first hug we'd shared in years.

"Damn, it's good to see you," he croaked, pounding me on the back.

"You too." My voice was a near whisper as tears clogged my throat.

When he finally released me, both our eyes were damp, and a tremulous smile curled over his lips. "We're never going this long without seeing each other again, Mont. I don't give a fuck how busy you are or what excuses you come up with. I'm flying down to Florida to see you at least four times a year."

"Agreed," I managed to say because for some reason, the idea of being separated from my family no longer held the appeal it once did.

He patted my cheek and cleared his throat. "All right. That's settled. Let me show you to your room."

I walked toward the duffle bag I'd left beside the door and hauled it over my shoulder. "Actually, I'd like to see my niece and nephew first. I brought them some stuff."

"You shouldn't have done that," Gianna scolded, wiping wetness from beneath her eyes with her fingertips. "You sent them each a huge box of stuff for their birthday."

"Don't tell me what to do, ma'am. I'm a certified funcle."

"What the hell is a funcle?" Auburn asked.

"Fun uncle," Gianna and I said together, and my brother rolled his eyes.

"And where did you get your certification?"

"From the Funcle Conservatory in Paris. It's very exclusive."

My brother laughed and wrapped an arm around my shoulders as he led me down a hallway. I'd been back less than five minutes, and we were already back to our old selves.

"Jaxon was reading Jane a story, and she'd just fallen asleep when I left them," he said quietly as we approached an open door on the right.

I peeped in, and my nephew's eyes lit up. "Uncle Monty!" he mouthed, standing up on the bed and launching himself at me as I approached.

Dropping my bag, I caught him easily and buried my face in his hair. He smelled like cotton candy and little boy. *Why the hell did I wait so long to meet these two in person?*

"Hey, buddy. I'm so glad to see you."

"Me too." He nuzzled against my neck, and I swayed him back and forth for a long while, simply taking in the moment.

Jaxon was a solid weight in my arms, and I leaned back a little to look at him up close. "You've gotten so big. You're practically a man now."

He shook his head, his face serious. "Not really. I don't have hair in my armpits. Or on my balls."

I bit back a laugh and kissed his forehead. "Why don't you show me your room since Janie is asleep." Glancing down, I smiled at my niece's sleeping form. She looked like a little angel.

He pointed his index finger, directing me to his room across the hall, and I carried him with Auburn in our wake. "This whole room is mine," he told me, wiggling until I put him down. "The whooooole thing."

My heart broke a little, thinking of him and Jane living in that orphanage before my brother and Gianna adopted them. I was so happy they had everything they could ever need or want now. They were both amazing kiddos.

Jaxon's enthusiasm was contagious as he ran around the room, and I made a big fuss over everything, from a rock he found in the park to a signed baseball he'd gotten at a Cougars game.

He grabbed my hand and dragged me to his bed. "And see? That's the alligator pillow you sent me. I sleep with it every night. Janie loves hers too."

I patted the big blue gator-shaped body pillow. "Glad you like it, bud."

We heard a tiny voice say, "Daddy?" and all of us hauled ass back to Jane's room across the hall. As soon as she saw me, she sat up and pushed the covers down off her body like she was going to sprint across the room. "Uncle Monty! You're here!"

Jogging across the huge room, I sat on the side of her bed and gathered her to me. She was slighter than her brother and felt frail in my arms.

"I'm here, Janie-Bug." I held her as her thin arms wrapped around my neck. "You're even prettier in person," I told her, swiping the wetness from her sweet face. I may have dropped a couple tears myself.

"And you're handsomer in person. You look just like my daddy."

"I know I'm cuter than him. You don't have to say it out loud," I said in a faux whisper, making her giggle. "How are you feeling?"

"Good. My leg doesn't hardly hurt at all."

"She's been very brave," Auburn said, settling onto the bed beside his daughter. Jaxon crawled into his lap and held his sister's hand.

These two were so close, and my thoughts turned to my relationship with Evie. I remembered sitting beside her just like this after she had her tonsils out when she was seven.

"I brought you two some prizes," I sang, and both kids bounced with excitement as I retrieved my bag.

Most of it was touristy souvenir stuff, and I was amazed by how they were thrilled with even the smallest of things I'd brought them.

"These seashells are so pretty. You really picked them all yourself?" Jane asked, and I assured her I had. "I've never been to a beach before."

"Tell you what," I said, resting my hands on the last two items in the bag. "How about when you're all better, you can come visit me in Florida and we can go to the beach and..." I pulled the mouse ears from the duffle with a flourish. "Disney World!"

Their squeals almost burst my eardrums as they pulled the little hats onto their heads.

Auburn laughed as both kids started chattering over each other. "Can we for real, Daddy?" Jaxon asked, holding his dad's cheeks with both hands and peering intently into his face.

"Absolutely, if Uncle Monty is sure."

"I'm sure. I live a few hours south, but we can stay in one of the hotels in the park."

"Then we'll go as soon as Janie is able."

"I'm gonna work extra, superduper hard on my therapy," she announced, shimmying her shoulders.

Auburn kissed each kid's head, and my emotions swelled once again at seeing his softer side with his children. A tender, sweet Auburn Bouvier was something I never thought I'd see, but I loved it.

"I'm going to go help your mom with dinner. It's almost ready." He turned to me. "We've been eating in here because it's easier for Jane. The table and chairs are in her closet."

"I'll set it up," I assured him.

Thirty minutes later, the kids were on the bed with their spaghetti dinners on trays, and the adults were sitting at the folding table a few feet away.

"Sorry about the kid food, Monty, but it's Janie's favorite. She loves *baby meatballs*," Gianna said, taking a nibble of her garlic breadstick.

I held one of the tiny balls up and studied it. "Are they made from actual babies?"

Auburn snorted. "No, you weirdo. Gianna was teaching the kids how to make meatballs one night, and they kept rolling up these teeny ones. She fried them up anyway, and they turned out to be pretty good."

Eating mine, I chewed. "It is good. Kinda crispy."

"Anyway, you're probably used to nicer meals," Gia said.

"Actually, I eat a lot of takeout." *Alone on my sofa.* "So this is nice. Thank you."

My sister-in-law's smile showed a hint of sympathy, like maybe she knew. "We're so happy to have you for as long as you decide to stay."

Auburn swallowed his bite and nodded. "I hope you're not planning to leave right after the funeral. We'd like you to stick around as long as you're able."

"I'd like that too. Now that the big case is over, I'm taking some time for myself." It was the truth but not the whole truth. I'd tell him the rest later.

My brother looked pleased, and the more time I spent here with my family, the less appealing my return to Florida sounded.

CHAPTER 32

ANDREA POPPED HER HEAD into my office, her eyebrows sitting high on her forehead. "Mister Owens is on line one for you."

My face scrunched in confusion. "I thought he was out of the country." Edward Owens was my boss at Owens, Kavanaugh, & Underwood law firm, and he was supposed to be in Paris.

She shrugged. "He said it's urgent."

Taking a deep breath, I picked up the phone and pushed the button. "Edward, hello. I hope your trip is going well." He'd taken his daughter to France for her sixteenth birthday.

"Very well. Melinda is having a blast. I was calling with a request." Straight to business. That was Edward Owens.

"Of course. Anything."

"I've just been informed that Chloe Bouvier was killed in a motor vehicle accident a couple days ago. She's Auburn's mother."

Yes, I'm quite aware.

Attempting to infuse a sympathetic tone—that I didn't feel—into my voice, I said, "Oh, what a shame."

He made a little humming noise. "I'm going to keep my mouth shut on that." I pressed my lips together to contain my snort. Apparently Edward wasn't a fan of Chloe's either; I didn't know anyone who was. "Anyway, someone from the firm needs to be at the funeral, and seeing as though I'm in France, I need you to go."

"M-me?" I stuttered as my heart hammered in my chest.

Andrea, sensing something going on, made herself at home in the chair across from me and pressed the speaker button so her nosy ass could hear what was going on. I was too stunned to do more than shoot her a look.

"Of course. Auburn is very impressed with the way you handle things in my absence. I've told him you're our best and brightest criminal lawyer and not a corporate attorney, but he trusts your opinions. What Auburn Bouvier wants, he gets, so you're officially part of his team."

Andrea lifted both thumbs and grinned. That was quite a compliment coming from Edward Owens, but my mind was still stuck on the funeral.

"Right, yes. Thank you for saying that. And the entire family will be at the funeral?" My voice sounded higher than usual, and Andrea's mouth dropped open.

"Who died?" She mouthed, and I waved a hand at her.

"Well, yes. I'm assuming so, Kassie. I've talked with Auburn and explained I was with my daughter, and he assured me he wasn't upset that I can't attend." His voice turned stern, and I knew I didn't have much choice in the matter. "*Bouvier* is one of our most important accounts. It's vital that the family feels we are there for them at this time."

"I'd be happy to go," I said, hoping I didn't sound as miserable as I felt.

As soon as we hung up, Andrea pounced. "What was that? Who died?"

"Chloe Bouvier, Paul's wife."

"Wow, okay. Weren't they in the middle of a divorce?"

"That's the rumor," I said as knots of worry filled my stomach.

"Oh. Wait!" She snapped twice and then pointed at me. "You dated the brother, whatshisname."

"Monty," I supplied.

"That's why you were asking about the family being there." She gasped, her nude lips forming an O. "Monty Bouvier. That's the dude that caught the serial killer down in Florida. Why didn't I put that together before?"

"I don't know," I said, my entire body feeling like it weighed a ton.

Andrea's eyebrows inched closer together. "Are you all right?"

My jaw tightened to the point of pain. "Fine."

Her head tilted to the side in sympathy. "You're worried about seeing your ex again."

"It's… it's more complicated than I told you before," I said, my thumb absently rubbing my bare ring finger. "Monty and I were actually engaged."

Andrea's eyebrows were pressed so tightly together, they formed a single unibrow. "But you said you were just teenagers."

I met her eyes. "I got pregnant."

"Oh, honey." She rose, walked around my desk, and dropped to her knees in front of me before pulling me into a gentle hug.

"I miscarried near the end of my first trimester."

She sat back on her heels, her mouth twisting into a grimace. "I had one too, when I was twenty-two. It was hard enough then; I can't imagine how difficult it was when you were a teenager. Is that why your relationship fell apart? It's not uncommon after a loss like that."

My hands squeezed into tight balls in my lap. "I don't know what happened. Monty seemed as devastated as I was. He was so excited about the baby and even proposed to me the same night I found out I was pregnant. Then the day after we lost Willow, he was supposed to come to my house." I shook my head, still confused to this day. "He never showed up. I'd lost my phone at some point and couldn't even call to ask what happened."

"You just never saw him again?"

"No, and a few days later, we moved. My father got a promotion, and his job required him to move to Pennsylvania. Mama said it had been in the works for a while, but with everything that happened, they decided it would be better to go ahead and move as soon as possible. Fresh start and all that." The last part was delivered with a healthy dose of bitterness.

"Do you think maybe Monty got delayed or something? Did he know you were moving?"

My head twisted from side to side. "I didn't even know. It all happened so quickly. I tried to explain to my parents that I needed to be in my own house, not a new one. I needed the comfort of familiarity."

"Of course you did."

"My parents' decision may have had something to do with the visit Monty's mother paid me while I was in the hospital."

"His... the one who just died?"

"Yes, she said a bunch of shit about how I wasn't good enough for her son and that maybe this had all worked out for the best. I'm guessing he went home to Mommy and Daddy once he didn't have the burden of a fiancée and baby."

Andrea's cheeks bloomed with two patches of bright red. "Well fuck both of them! I hope he is there so you can kick him in the balls. Then I want you to go piss on Chloe Bouvier's grave."

I stifled my laugh behind my hand. "Andrea!"

"I'm serious. These sound like horrible people."

Picking at a loose cuticle, I stared down at my lap. "That's just the thing. Monty was nothing like his mother. He was an artist, very sweet and sensitive. He doted on me and told me he wanted to marry me even before the pregnancy. I just wish I knew what happened to change his mind."

"Maybe now you can finally ask him."

"Or maybe it's best to let sleeping dogs lie. It was a long time ago. I think I'll make an appearance at the funeral, sit in the back, and then leave."

Andrea stood and pulled me up with her, taking my shoulders and shaking them a little.

"Okay, but before you leave, promise me you'll kick Monty Bouvier in the balls."

Swiping the wetness from my face, I laughed and said, "I'll think about it."

CHAPTER 33

I SETTLED BACK ONTO the bed in Auburn and Gianna's guest room, the pale green comforter soft beneath me. Jaxon was at school, and Janie was napping after an intense physical therapy session with a bulldozer of a woman named Doctor Elaine.

The kid was absolutely amazing, gritting her teeth through the pain and smiling when she stood up for the first time with Doctor Elaine's assistance. The physical therapist was kind but pushed Jane, and my niece reveled in the challenge.

After dinner last night, my father came over, and it was... cathartic to say the least.

We'd hugged for a long time, and my brother and his wife retreated to their room to give us some privacy. Dad and I had a long talk, and both of us apologized for all the shit that had gone down between us. We'd gotten a lot off our chests.

He said he had a lot more to say now that Chloe was gone, but he'd like to do it with the entire family after the reading of the will. That would take place tomorrow.

At first, I wasn't sure how Dad would feel about the death of the woman he'd been married to for over forty years, but he seemed lighter somehow.

Tugging my phone from my pocket, I pulled up my Instagram account. The first post on my feed featured my favorite cat and dog duo. Snoopy the cat was riding on Garfield's back as he slid across a yellow slip and slide. The caption made me laugh.

How cats surf.

I replied with: *Kelly Slater ain't got nothin' on Snoopy.*

A knock at my door interrupted my scrolling, and Auburn entered a few seconds later, holding a garment bag.

"What's that?"

"A new suit for you. A *Bouvier* suit," he stressed.

"You didn't have to do that," I protested.

"Of course I did. I saw that off-the-rack shit you brought, and you're *not* wearing that to the funeral today."

"You're such a suit snob," I scoffed with a laugh, and he shrugged without an ounce of shame.

"I'm sure there will be press there, so I thought it would be nice if you, Dad, and I all looked cohesive. Also, there's this." He laid the bag on my bed and unzipped it, revealing a black suit, white shirt, and red tie. "Chloe's favorite color was blue, so we're wearing red."

I was unable to hold back my bark of laughter. "That's fucking classic, bro."

He shot me a sly grin and bobbed one eyebrow.

"Devereaux is excellent at estimating sizes by simply looking at a picture, but you might want to try it on and make sure he doesn't need to drop by and do any alterations." Auburn eyed my biceps in the tank top I was wearing. "You're pretty fucking jacked, dude."

"I run on the beach and hit the gym a lot. Not much else to do besides work." That sounded kinda sad when I said it out loud.

Taking the suit, I went into the bathroom to change before returning to the bedroom. My brother circled me, scrutinizing every inch as his fingers traced seams and tugged at hems.

"That's actually pretty damn good. Dev did a good job. What do you think?"

All at once, my former fashion artist self kicked into gear. "It's almost a perfect fit, though I'd like the sleeves to be let out a quarter of an inch. We can worry about that later though."

Auburn's gaze dropped to my sleeves, and he tapped his bottom lip with his index finger. "I think you're exactly right. I'll give him a call."

"It will be fine for today, Aub—"

He cut me off with a raised finger as he took out his phone. "No arguments."

"Bossy fucker," I muttered and heard him chuckle as he dialed.

An hour later, Devereaux finished the final stitch on the sleeve and handed me the jacket. "Try this on." I did, and he gazed appraisingly at the hems. "You were right, Monty; it's perfect now. You still have a good eye. So when are you coming back to *Bouvier* to work with me? I've been waiting forever."

I could feel Auburn's intent eyes on the side of my face as I answered. "I'm a cop now. I don't really draw anymore." *Not clothes anyway.*

"We'd love to have you, Mont," he said, and Dev nodded enthusiastically.

"It would be a pleasure. You were only a teenager, but the suggestions you made were always on point. I completely changed the way I made collars, thanks to you."

"Dev is a master of collars now," Auburn commented. "There's nothing I hate worse than an ill-fitting collar." He shuddered as if someone had handed him a suit made of dog poo.

"I'll think about it." I still hadn't heard back from the review board about the sexual harassment claim Shana had filed. I'd done an in-person interview the day before I left for New York and told them my side of the story. The truth, not the lies she was spewing.

But if the worst came to fruition, at least I'd have options.

My father, Auburn, and I entered the back of the church side by side. Gianna had stayed home with the kids.

Everyone was already seated in the gigantic room, filled with thousands of dollars' worth of floral arrangements. Every eye in the place turned as we began to walk down the carpeted center aisle.

Well, almost every eye. There was a woman in the back row with her head bowed, dark hair covering her face. My gaze was instantly drawn to her.

"Shit," I heard Auburn mutter. "I didn't know she was going to be here."

I was about to ask who when the woman lifted her head.

No!

Yes!

Oh my god!

My feet faltered as our eyes locked, and I probably would have fallen if Auburn hadn't secured an arm around my waist. Someone made a sympathetic sound in the background, obviously mistaking my stumble as a result of grief, but that wasn't it at all.

Kassie was sitting *right fucking there*. Her lips parted, and *sweet Jesus*, how is she still so beautiful?

Confusion and something else I couldn't put a name to had my body turning, but my brother physically twisted me around and hissed, "Later. Keep walking."

Kassie broke eye contact first, bending her head again so her hair obscured her face, and I was finally able to peel my eyes away and resume walking. Barely.

With my dad on one side of me and my brother on the other, I made my way down the wide aisle to the front pew.

As soon as we were seated, the pastor took the pulpit and began speaking. I didn't hear a word of it over the roar of *what the fuck* rushing through my head. And then he said, "Would you all please bow your heads to pray?"

Rather than bowing my head, I turned it.

Even through the crowd of lowered heads, she pulled me in like a rip current sweeping a swimmer out to sea. Kassie was staring directly at me, and she swallowed so hard, I was sure I could hear it from thirty rows away.

Her hand went to her throat as though she was having trouble breathing. I knew exactly how she felt. With great effort, I forced air in and out of my lungs as my blue eyes held her brown ones.

We were connected by some invisible force that I thought had been severed long ago. *Apparently not.*

Kassie's teeth sunk into her bottom lip for a second before mouthing, "Monty."

"Kassie," I replied without making a sound, and her chest hitched. My index finger instinctively curled around nothing but thin air, and I wanted to lift my hand so she could see what I was doing. But that would be a dumbass move, right? She probably didn't even remember that.

Dad squeezed my leg, and I twisted around to face him. "You okay, son?" he whispered, and I wasn't sure how to answer.

"I don't know," I answered honestly. Sometimes late at night, I'd imagined seeing Kassie again, and I assumed I would feel hurt and probably anger. I never expected to feel complete ecstasy, but that very emotion was bound tightly around my chest.

Auburn tilted his head toward mine. "I'm so sorry, Mont. I had no idea she would be here."

I processed his words. He didn't say *Holy shit, is that your ex? What is she doing here?* What I'd expect him to say if he hadn't seen her in sixteen years. No, it was more like he was surprised that she was *here* specifically.

My tie seemed to be attempting to choke me to death, and I slid my finger beneath the knot to loosen it as some woman sang some song I didn't give a shit about.

I could still feel the pull from behind me, and it took every ounce of strength I had to remain seated. My leg bounced a nervous rhythm until the pastor had spoken his last words. Then Chloe's casket was wheeled down the aisle, and a man in a suit directed us to follow.

Everyone stood, and *goddammit*, I couldn't see Kassie because of all the bodies in the way. As we approached the final pew, my gaze found only an empty seat.

She was gone.

Again.

"Someone better tell me what the fuck is going on. Right. Now." Those were the first words that left my mouth as soon as we were seated in the back of the limousine.

"Monty, I swear I didn't know Kassie would be here today."

"The way you said that… it sounds like…" I shook my head wildly from side to side.

"She's one of my lawyers."

My mouth gaped open in shock. "For how long?"

"I first saw her when all that shit was going down with Magdalena." Magdalena Lewis was Auburn's ex who had tried to blackmail him.

"But…" I did the calculations in my head. "That was eighteen months ago," I snapped.

"I'm aware. Edward had a kidney stone, so his office set me up with someone who was handling his accounts while he was out. I was stunned when I walked in and saw Kassie."

"And you never thought to tell me this?" My voice and my anger were rising at the thought of my brother being in contact with Kassie and not mentioning it to me.

He held up a finger. "Number one, every time I've brought up Kassie to you in the past, you told me you didn't want to talk about it. In fact, I think your exact words the last time I asked were 'I don't ever want to hear her fucking name again.'" One dark eyebrow lifted in a clear challenge.

"I was going through my angry phase," I muttered darkly. It had been a very long phase.

He raised another finger. "I'll say. And number two, Kassie asked me not to tell you."

That made my chest hurt, and I couldn't define exactly why.

"She doesn't want anything to do with me," I stated.

"I'm not sure that's it. She genuinely sounded concerned that it might dredge up bad memories for you."

Placing my knuckles against my lips, I stared out the window and wondered why Kassie had left so abruptly. The interior of the limo was silent until my father quietly asked, "Do you still have feelings for Kassie?"

"I don't know. I didn't think I did." Tilting my head over against the cool glass, I admitted, "I looked her up years ago and found out she was married. To some guy named Campbell. So I finally decided to put her behind me for good."

"She's divorced now."

My head jerked around at his words as my heart somersaulted inside me. "Divorced? What happened?"

"No clue. She said it was a long story." His eyes met mine. "Kassie told me she has a son. He was three then, so he'd probably be four or five now."

"I'll bet she's an amazing mother," I murmured half to myself.

The rest of the ride back to Auburn's apartment was made in silence. I was so damned grateful Dad had decided to forgo a graveside service because I wasn't sure I'd be able to stand still for that long.

I needed to take a long run and then hit the gym hard to work out my thoughts.

The only thing I knew for sure was that I had some serious unresolved feelings for Kassie Ramirez.

CHAPTER 34

I KNEW HE'D BE there, and I'd mentally prepared myself to see him. Or at least I thought I had.

Until I *actually saw* him.

God knew exactly what he was doing when he made the Bouvier men. They were striking, and that was putting it mildly. All of them had dark hair—Paul's with a heavy sprinkling of gray—and their bright blue eyes popped against jealousy-inducing eyelashes.

All three were devastatingly handsome in their perfectly cut black suits, but the one in the middle captured all my attention the second he entered the church.

As hard as it was to look away, I lowered my chin and stared at my lap, allowing my long hair to act as a shield. Until I couldn't take it anymore. My head lifted on its own, and our eyes locked with an intensity that had me holding my breath.

He looked shocked, and I guessed Auburn had granted my request not to mention me to his brother. Time froze as I stared at my past.

Monty Bouvier was still the most gorgeous man I'd ever seen, and I realized that no amount of mental preparation could have primed me for seeing him in person. He was no longer a boy. He was a huge, powerful man.

When he was seated up at the front, I canted my head to the side a little to keep sight of the back of him. He was hard to miss, slightly taller than his brother now, and his shoulders appeared to take up all the space in the room.

The pastor called for a prayer, but my head did not lower. Monty's didn't either. It turned toward me, and our eyes met once again. His face softened, and that almost broke me in two.

His name left my mouth in a silent appeal—for what, I don't know—and I saw his lips form my own. My pointer finger curled involuntarily in my lap. It was one of the most intimate moments of my life, even though we were surrounded by hundreds of people.

So I'd fled. During the song, I stood and quietly exited the church with my hand pressed against my belly.

Why the hell am I reacting this way? I'm over him. I've been over him for a long time.

"It's just the shock," I told myself as I climbed into my blue Lexus GX SUV. "What we shared together was real and strong, and this is the first time you've seen him in person. That's all."

I cranked my vehicle but didn't move. Not until they wheeled out the casket with the Bouvier men following. Monty's eyes darted from side to side, like he was looking for something.

Or someone.

As the parking lot emptied, I pulled out onto the street and headed for my office and reminded myself of one important fact.

You have neither the time nor the desire to have a man in your life, Ramirez. Especially one who left you broken.

Closing my laptop, I answered my ringing phone.

"Kassie, how did the funeral go?" Edward asked.

I have no fucking idea, Ed. I was too busy staring at my ex.

"Fine," I said, scrambling for something to say about the event I hadn't paid attention to. "The flowers were beautiful."

"Excellent. The reading of the will is tomorrow at two at Paul's house. I'll send you the address."

I blinked hard and shook my head. "Edward, I'm not an estate lawyer." I didn't mention that Trusts and Estates was my least favorite class in law school.

"Oh, I know that, but you should still attend the reading. Like I mentioned before, Auburn thinks highly of you, which is a definite check mark in your column when it comes time for partnership talks."

My heart did a little flip flop move in my chest. Edward had made vague references to partnership in the law firm before, but now he was dangling it like a pickle in front of a pregnant woman.

"I'll be there."

And so will Monty Bouvier.

Fuck.

Shield around the heart: Activated.

CHAPTER 35

"Do we really have to be here for this?" I asked as Gianna, Auburn, and I walked up the sidewalk to Dad's gigantic house.

He no longer lived in the apartment where we'd grown up, which was a mixed blessing. My memories of that place were tainted, but it was also the last space I'd shared with Evie.

"Yeah, it's not like she's going to leave anything to us. Not that I'd want it anyway," Auburn grumped.

"But Paul wanted to talk to us all after it's done," Gianna said in her soothing drawl. "What do you think that's all about?"

"He said he had answers to a lot of our questions," my brother replied. "Whatever the fuck that means."

"How are you holding up after today, Monty?" his wife asked, looping her slim hand around my forearm. I looked down into her green eyes that held nothing but concern and kindness and knew Auburn had told her about my seeing Kass at the funeral.

"I'm okay," I told her.

Both our heads whipped around when Auburn growled, "What the fuck are you doing here?"

His ex, Magdalena Lewis, was striding up the walk behind us, her blonde hair perfectly coiffed and her smile smug.

"I was contacted by the estate lawyer, who requested my presence." Her red-tipped nails fiddled with the collar of her crimson dress. "So nice to see you again, Gianna." Her tone was snarky as fuck, but Gianna Bouvier could hold her own.

"Likewise, Magdalena. You're looking well after your incarceration."

I didn't even attempt to hold back my snort, and Auburn looked down at his wife with pride. Magdalena had gone to jail briefly after her blackmail attempt on my brother. Her lips tightened, and I could practically hear her teeth grinding as she turned her attention to me, eyes raking up and down my six-foot-three frame.

"Well, I see the long-lost brother has returned."

"Yep," I said, turning my back on her when the large, wooden front door opened.

My father greeted us all with hugs, except for Magdalena, who he graced with only a curt nod. "We can do this in my study. Ezekiel, the estate attorney, just arrived."

We headed down the hallway when a knock sounded at the door. "I'll get it," I offered, pivoting around and walking back toward the entrance.

When I swung open the door, my intestines felt as though they wrapped around my stomach and squeezed. "Kassie."

She inhaled a long breath and then blew it out. "Hi, Monty."

If I'd thought she was gorgeous yesterday at the church, that was nothing compared to seeing her this close. I had to stuff my hands in my pockets to keep from touching her face.

"You look beautiful," my mouth said without my permission.

Her lips quirked up on one side. "And you look... big." Her face flushed adorably. "Sorry, that was weird."

I laughed, a whole fuck-ton of tension releasing from my body in an instant. "It's okay. I've grown up."

Kassie's eyes dropped to my pale blue button-down before returning to my face. "You have. I saw you on TV. The serial killer thing."

I nodded. "It was a difficult case. Those women and their families have been through so much."

"I'm sure they're really grateful to you." Her hand reached out and touched my arm. It was only for a split second, but the gentle brush of her fingers made my knees weak. "I'm proud of you, Monty."

"I'm proud of you too, Kass. Auburn says you're a kick-ass lawyer."

Her eyes rolled upward. "Your brother exaggerates."

I knew for a fact she was being modest because I'd spent some time looking her up online last night. Four hours worth of time, to be precise.

And what I'd found out was that Kassie Ramirez was one of the best litigators in the state.

"Uh, Monty? Would it be okay if I came inside?"

"Shit! I'm so sorry," I said, realizing she was standing out in the cold. I stepped back and let her walk into the foyer. "Please forgive me for being a jerk."

"You're forgiven," she said, a little smile shaping her lips into a pretty curve.

She shrugged off her navy peacoat to reveal a slim-fitting forest-green dress with a black belt that accentuated her curves. And, *damn*, she had some curves I'd like to sink my teeth into.

Cool it, man.

Finally remembering my manners, I took her coat and hung it on the rack near the door. When I turned back around, Kass was rubbing her hands together, and I reached immediately for them and frowned. "Your hands are like ice."

"Well, you did leave me standing outside for ten minutes, Bouvier," she retorted.

Fuck, I want to kiss that smart mouth of hers.

Her lips parted on a soft inhale, and I wondered if I'd said that out loud. My hands massaged some warmth back into hers as our eyes met again, and I did what felt natural. Taking a step closer, I pulled her arms around my waist and slid my hands up her arms and to her back.

This... this right here...

Kassie tilted her neck forward until her forehead rested against my chest, and I nestled my nose into the top of her hair. Hints of orange blossom infiltrated my nose, and I closed my eyes.

"Is this okay?" I whispered. It was damn sure okay with me. More than okay. It was fucking incredible to have her in my arms again.

She nodded her head. "Yes."

We took an infinitesimal step toward each other at the same time, and when our bodies were flush together, we both seemed to relax into each other.

I've missed you.

I'm not sure how long we stood embracing in the foyer, but we broke apart when we heard footsteps coming from down the hall.

Kassie cleared her throat and reached up to pat the sleek bun resting on the crown of her head. A couple small tendrils curled lazily in front of her ears and framed the face I'd tried to forget over the years.

She looked almost exactly the same, other than a few tiny lines around her mouth and eyes. But they didn't detract from her immutable beauty.

"Kassie, there you are. I thought maybe you'd gotten lost." A man of about forty in a brown suit and wire-rimmed glasses approached, his eyes roving up and down her body.

"Monty Bouvier," I said, stepping into his line of vision because I didn't like where that line was directed. At all. "I needed a word with Ms. Ramirez before we began. We're ready now."

"Nice to meet you, Monty. I'm Ezekiel Woods." He held out a hand, and I shook it. Firmly. Very firmly. I tried not to look smug when he winced and flexed his hand by his side.

Once we were in my father's office, Woods sat behind the desk and directed Kassie to sit beside him, which irked the hell out of me. I took the only open chair, the one on the left of a short row, beside Gianna.

"Well, this isn't going to take long," the estate attorney said, and my forehead crinkled. What the hell was he talking about? Chloe Bouvier was a very wealthy woman before she even married my father, and the distribution of her estate shouldn't be a simple matter.

"Paul, I understand, you're the owner of the apartment Mrs. Bouvier was living in at the time of her death?" My father nodded. "And her vehicles were in your name?"

"That's correct."

Woods stared down at the paper in his hand. "The only other assets are her personal belongings. Clothing, jewelry, and handbags. A few pieces of art."

Auburn and I looked at each other in disbelief, but Dad didn't seem to be surprised in the least.

"Mrs. Bouvier's will directs that all of those belongings should be left to one Magdalena Lewis. The approximate value is right at two hundred thousand dollars." He looked at us over the top of his glasses. "That's all."

Auburn spoke up. "I know Chloe had at least three bank accounts in her name. What happened to those?"

"They've all been closed due to insufficient funds," the attorney said, his dark-green eyes settling on each member of our family.

I was so confused. What happened to all that money? And her personal belongings that she'd accumulated over forty years should be worth way more than two hundred thousand. Chloe Bouvier only wore the finest clothes and jewelry.

"I think I can explain everything, but I'd like to speak to my family alone," Dad spoke up. "Ezekiel, if you could arrange for Miss Lewis to pick up her inheritance from Chloe's apartment, I would appreciate it."

Sensing his dismissal, the man stood. "Of course." Kassie and Magdalena stood as well, the latter throwing a smirk at us, like we actually gave a fuck that she'd been the beneficiary to the egg donor's estate.

It had obviously been orchestrated by Chloe as a slap in our faces, but I couldn't care less. I received nothing from her when she was alive, and I wanted absolutely nothing from her now.

As the trio began making their way to the door of the office, Dad stood and stopped Kassie with a hand on her forearm. "I'd like you to stay, please."

The surprise on her face reflected the expression I was sure was on my own, but she nodded, hovering awkwardly until Gianna stood.

"Here, Kassie. You can sit here."

Kassie's eyes fell on me as she walked slowly and sat in the chair next to mine. Gianna took Dad's chair on the other side of Auburn, and our father strode around his desk, staring out the window until the room was cleared.

"Does anyone need something to drink? Because this is going to take a while."

CHAPTER 36

"WHY AM I HERE?" Kassie whispered, fidgeting with the arm of the burgundy leather chair.

"I have no clue," I answered in a low voice as I reached for her hand and linked our index fingers. It felt perfectly natural to me and seemed to calm her discomfort.

"You're probably wondering why I asked you to stay, Kassie," Dad said, seating himself behind his huge oak desk.

"Honestly, yes," she replied, curling her finger more tightly around mine. I liked that subtle move.

"Parts of this story concern things that happened a long time ago, and I thought you deserved to hear it." He folded his hands on the desk and stared down at them for a while. No one spoke a word; he had our undivided attention.

"I guess I'll start at the very beginning." Dad rubbed two fingers across his distinguished gray-and-black goatee. "When I married Chloe, I was in love with her. It was a semi-arranged marriage. Our parents encouraged the union, but it wasn't set in stone. We started dating, and over the next couple years, we fell in love. It wasn't perfect by any means. I knew Chloe's shortcomings before we married. I was aware that she could be selfish, but what I didn't realize was that she would be more selfish of my time than my money."

He sat back in his chair and steepled his fingers beneath his chin. "I guess things started changing after Auburn was born." Dad cast a warm smile at my brother as the creases in his forehead smoothed out. "I was so in love with you, son, from the first time I laid eyes on you. My family became my entire world. Yes, I had a fashion empire to run, and I worked hard, but I loved spending every waking moment just holding you or watching you sleep."

My father's eyes lost a bit of their softness. "Chloe was extremely jealous of the time I spent with you because she was no longer the center of my universe. That's the first inkling I got that she may have been a bit narcissistic."

"No shit," I muttered darkly, and there were chuckles from around the room.

Dad continued, "Not that I neglected my wife at all. I still doted on her, took her on dates, that kind of thing, but she was resentful of any time I spent with our new baby. I tried to explain to her that I loved her dearly, but when you brought a new life into the world, you were responsible for them."

"We understand," Gianna said, sharing a fond smile with her husband. "Our life revolves around Jane and Jaxon now, and their needs come first—always—but it doesn't mean we love each other any less. If anything, adopting them has made us stronger."

Auburn lifted their joined hands and kissed the back of Gianna's. The love radiating from them was pure and so fucking profound it made my chest ache.

"I agree," he said. "Watching you be a mother to our children makes me love you even more." He gripped the back of her head and laid a kiss on her that threatened to set the room on fire.

Dad interrupted with a clearing of his throat. "Okay, lovebirds. The old man is trying to tell a story here."

The two broke apart with matching chagrined smiles. I'd never seen a couple more in love.

"Anyway," he continued, "Unlike you two, Chloe seemed to garner no joy from watching me with our boy. It made her jealous, and she became… I wouldn't say neglectful, but she wasn't as enamored of our new addition as I'd hoped she would be. I spoke with her often about it and even made sure to include her when I spent time with Auburn. I did everything I could think of to get her engaged in our new life. I finally suggested that maybe she was suffering from postpartum depression and offered to take her to see her doctor about it. She refused to even entertain the idea, and I think the seed of resentment inside me took root then because I realized that it was simply her selfishness coming to a head."

"Sometimes it's hard to see when it's someone you're close to," Gianna suggested, and my father gave her a wan smile.

"It is. When Auburn was six months old, I suggested that we take a two-week vacation, and Chloe perked up immediately. But when I told her we would be bringing the baby with us, she refused to go." He shook his head sadly. "There was no way I was leaving my infant son for two whole weeks, so I scrapped the idea."

Dad inhaled a long breath before releasing it. "The next day, I arrived home from work to a screaming baby. Chloe was sitting on the couch reading a magazine like nothing was even wrong. She'd left Auburn in his crib with a bottle. When I got to him, he had a dirty diaper, and the bottle was empty. She said she was teaching him to *self-soothe.*"

Kassie, who had been quiet up to this point, gasped, her hand covering her heart. "That's horrible."

My father's lips tightened. "I was so fucking angry at her, and we had a huge fight. I immediately moved out of our bedroom and took up residence in the guest room next to Auburn's nursery. The next day I hired a nanny, a lovely young woman named Estrella, because there was no way I was going to let my son be neglected like that."

Auburn lifted one finger. "Wait…" His eyes narrowed in deep thought. "Straya?"

Dad smiled. "Yes, that's what you called Estrella when you couldn't pronounce her name. I'm surprised you remember her."

My brother pursed his lips. "Vaguely. When you said her name, it triggered something. Did we make cookies together?"

"Yes, when you were a toddler. Chocolate chip ones. You were almost permanently attached to Estrella's apron strings. You two adored each other."

Auburn nodded. "Sorry I interrupted. Go ahead, Dad."

Our father crossed one ankle over the other knee and fiddled with his shoestring. "So, when Auburn got out of the heathen stage of toddlerhood, things began to get better. Chloe certainly wasn't a doting mother, but she at least paid some attention to him. She asked me to move back into the master bedroom, and I agreed. Looking back, I don't think I was in love with her anymore, but I was desperate to make our family work."

"That had to have been hard," I remarked, and Dad's eyes met mine.

"It was. I began drinking quite a bit. Every night, in fact."

Auburn and I shared a concerned glance. We'd never seen our father take a drink of alcohol. Ever.

"When your mother became pregnant with Evie, I was understandably concerned, but I hoped maybe Chloe had changed. She'd never been around babies much, so I thought maybe she was just overwhelmed by motherhood the first time around."

Dad's fingernail flicked against the tip of his shoelace with audible clicks. "I couldn't have been more wrong. As soon as we found out we were having a girl, I was over the moon, but Chloe was… less than happy. This time, she moved out of our bedroom and hired a team to construct a second master suite downstairs. I knew then that our marriage was effectively over."

"Wow," Auburn said. "For as long as I can remember, you two had separate bedrooms. I thought maybe it was because one of you snored or something."

Our father shook his head. "I was at my wit's end with her." He lifted his hands and let them fall to his lap in exasperation. "I began to despise the woman, but I stayed in that farce of a marriage anyway because I stupidly thought divorce was the worst thing in the world for a kid. Turns out that's not true." His tiny smile was the saddest thing I'd ever seen.

"Because your parents stayed together until they died," I said softly, and Dad nodded.

"Yes, and they died within a month of each other. I guess I thought that fairytale marriage was still attainable, but I slowly started to become aware that wasn't going to happen in my case. A narcissist will never change their true nature, and it's difficult to love someone like that."

My father lowered both feet to the ground and rolled his chair beneath his desk, meeting each eye in the room. "This next part is difficult, so I hope you'll be patient with me." Silent heads nodded all around. Dad propped his elbows on the table and wrapped his hands around the back of his neck as he stared at the leather blotter on his desk.

"As soon as Evie Bouvier was born, she lit up the entire world." His voice broke a little on my sister's name, and Kassie shifted her hand until all our fingers were intertwined as Dad continued. "While Auburn had been a pretty quiet baby, my daughter loved the sound of her own voice."

"That's our Evie, loud as hell," Auburn commented, adding a touch of levity to the moment.

Our father looked up and gave my brother a small smile. "She was the happiest little thing, babbling and cooing constantly. Everyone who met Evie fell in love with her." His voice quivered with the strain. "Except for Chloe. I can count on one hand the number of times I saw her even hold our daughter. She was just so fucking cold."

I sensed Kassie's breathing pick up, and I pulled my eyes from my father to look over at her. Her lips were pressed into a thin line as she swallowed hard. We were still holding hands, but I reached over with my other hand and stroked her forearm, bringing her gaze to me.

"You okay?" I mouthed, and she attempted a weak smile and nodded. Sandwiching her hand between both of mine, I reverted my attention back to my father who had begun speaking again.

"By the time Evie was a few months old, I was working my ass off every day at the office and then coming home to take care of two kids. Estrella stayed with them during the day, but at night, I was on my own. When I'd get them down for the night, I'd drown myself in bourbon. It's not something I'm proud of, but that's the truth of it. I used liquor as a crutch."

He pushed to his feet, turning away from us, and I sensed that the story was also about to take a turn. I was right.

With his hands stuffed in the pockets of his navy dress pants, my father stared out the window behind his desk. "This isn't easy to say, and I hope you all don't judge me too harshly."

"No judgment, Paul," Gianna said softly. "You were doing the best you could."

He nodded, eyes fixed on something in the distance. "I know you don't want to hear all the details of this, but one night, when I was drunk, I allowed Chloe back into my bed. It had been almost a year since... well, I think you get my drift."

He huffed out a sigh and pressed his forehead against the triple-paned glass. "I felt so fucking guilty about sleeping with her." I could see the anguish in his eyes through his reflection.

"Jesus, Dad," Auburn said. "There's nothing to be ashamed of. You two were married."

Our father turned slowly—as if in slow motion—to face us, though he didn't quite meet our eyes. His words came out in one long, rushed sentence. "The thing is, I'd started developing feelings for another woman, but I couldn't sleep with her because I was married, so I got sloshed and slept with the woman I despised. It was... a moment of weakness." I could see the guilt shining in his blue eyes.

"You were in love with someone else?" I asked.

He met my eyes and shook his head. "No, not yet, but I cared very deeply for this other woman." His hand scruffed through his perfectly styled hair, mussing it up. "It was Estrella, our nanny."

He glanced around the room, looking for judgment on our faces, I guessed, and finding none, he continued. "She was the kindest woman I'd ever met, and she absolutely adored Auburn and Evie. She treated them like her own children, not like they were a job she was hired to do. I think that's what drew me to her."

Dad leaned his hands on his desk and dropped his head. "The day after Chloe and I slept together, she left to go on an extended spa vacation. With a five-year-old and an infant, she just fucking left. Over the next few months, things began to escalate between Estrella and me."

"You had an affair?" Auburn asked, but our father shook his head.

"Not physically, though the attraction was certainly there. We never kissed or held hands or anything inappropriate. She would stick around after I got home from work and help me with the kids, even though she was scheduled to leave by six every night. We had dinner together. We talked for hours, and my feelings grew for her. I fell deeply in love with Estrella."

We all listened with rapt attention as he spilled out his emotional story. "One night she told me she was going to have to find another job be-cause..." Dad pushed out a long breath. "Because she was in love with me."

"Oh my god," I heard Gianna say in her soft drawl.

"I finally confessed my feelings to her, and it was like a weight was lifted off my shoulders. I could almost reach out and touch the freedom, and I told Estrella that I would get a divorce so we could be together."

My heart was in my throat as Dad turned and faced the window again, lost in his thoughts. "I sent the divorce papers to Chloe at the retreat where she was staying in Vermont. She came home that Friday night, and I told her in person what I'd wanted to say for a very long time. That I didn't love her anymore, and I wanted out."

The room was silent for a full minute as I did the calculations in my head. Evie was only a few months old. My parents slept together. My birthday was roughly nine months later.

"But she was pregnant with me," I blurted out, and Dad nodded.

"Yes."

The weight of the world landed directly on my shoulders at that moment, and I stood. "So you stayed in a loveless marriage because of me."

Chapter 37

MY FATHER WHIRLED AND marched fiercely around his desk, taking my face in his hands. "Do not put this on yourself, Monty. From the very second I learned about you, I loved you. The circumstances didn't matter. You were my flesh and blood, and you were my priority, just like Auburn and Evie."

I stared mutely at him as his blue eyes burned into mine. "I love you, Monty, with all my heart." His arms wrapped around my middle, and after a second, I returned his embrace. A tear slipped down my face and made a dark spot on the shoulder of my father's light-blue shirt.

"It's all my fault you had to stay with that woman," I whispered, my voice hoarse and gritty.

Dad leaned back and rested his palm on my cheek, his thumb catching the next tear that was threatening to fall. "No, son. It's not. There's more to the story, if you guys aren't tired of hearing me ramble."

I swallowed hard. "I'd like to hear the rest of it."

He gave me a soft pat. "Sit, and I'll finish. I need to backtrack just a little." Dad leaned back against his desk and rested his hands beside his hips as Kassie looped her finger around mine. The simple gesture grounded me just a little as I settled into the soft leather of the chair.

"The day after I served Chloe with divorce papers, I felt free to finally kiss Estrella for the first time. Then one thing led to another, and we ended up consummating our relationship. It only cemented how we felt about each other. We were very... compatible."

Auburn held up one hand, his nose scrunched in distaste. "Please spare us the details. I don't think any of us want to hear about old man sex."

A smile curled my dad's lips up as he lifted a brow at my brother. "Remember, this is when I was thirty-three, so I was younger than you are now."

Gianna giggled at the look of horror on her husband's face. "Please continue, Paul, while my *old man* does a little self-reflection."

"I'll give you an old man when we get home," he muttered, and we all laughed.

As the hilarity died down, my dad's face once again turned serious. "Like I said before, Chloe returned on that Friday. I'm not sure how, but she knew about me and Estrella." His lips tightened until they turned white. "She threatened to go to the press if I went through with the divorce."

"Jesus," I uttered, shaking my head at the balls on that woman.

"Estrella was young, about eight years younger than me, and she was my employee. The optics of that alone were not good. Then Chloe informed me she was pregnant. She drew a picture of how that would play out in the press. The billionaire CEO having an affair with a younger woman—his nanny, no less—and the poor, pitiful, jilted wife with two small children and pregnant with the third."

Dad walked around his desk and took a seat, looking weary as hell when he scrubbed his hands up and down his face.

"But, of course, with Chloe, there was more. She said if I still decided to divorce her, she would..." His voice hitched, and he closed his eyes as he attempted to rein in his emotions. "She said she would take my children away."

A sob broke free from his chest, and my insides went cold. My poor father. He'd only been trying to do what was best by staying with Chloe.

He truly had been putting his children first, and I felt like a fucking dog for the things I'd said to him the night my egg donor had disowned me.

Auburn rose and went to stand behind our dad's chair, resting his hands on his shoulders. "You don't have to go on, Dad. I think we all understand now."

He reached for a tissue on the corner of his desk and blew his nose. "Just let me finish up, and then I think I'd like to lie down for a while. I'm getting a headache." Tossing the wadded tissue in the trash beneath his desk, he rested his forearms on the surface. "Chloe's parents had moved to Europe a few years before, and she threatened to take my babies away and go live with them."

"Why couldn't you have fought her in court, Paul?" Gianna asked, her tone gentle.

"You have to remember; this was over thirty years ago. Mothers had the advantage in most custody cases. There was a very real chance I would lose my children, especially given my *tawdry affair*, as Chloe called it."

"So you were stuck," I said, and he breathed out a long sigh.

"Yes, I was stuck. But I told her I wanted to think about it for a few days. I needed to talk to Estrella, since this affected her too. Her name would be dragged through the mud if our relationship went public. Plus, I wanted to speak with my lawyer and see if I had any chance of keeping my kids."

"What did he say?" Kassie asked.

"The same things I already knew. That there was no guarantee I would get custody of my children, and also that my company would take a hit. The pressure I felt was so immense, I thought it would break my spine. I had to think about all the employees I was responsible for. I had to think about Estrella, the woman I loved. And most importantly, I had to think about my babies being taken across the ocean and living with a woman who didn't give two shits about them."

Auburn's hands tightened on Dad's shoulders. "I'm sorry you had to go through all that. You were put in an impossible situation."

"Me too. On Monday morning, I waited for Estrella to show up for work. I wanted to talk things through with her. She was young, but she was very bright, and I didn't want to make any decisions without talking to her."

We all waited to hear what happened next, and our father sagged, seeming to shrink a couple inches in his chair. "She never showed up. I got worried and called in sick to work so I could go to her house to see if she was okay. When I arrived, her cousin, who lived next door, informed me that Estrella had lost her job and moved away to be with her parents."

I was confused. "Lost her job?"

Dad's head bobbed sadly up and down. "Yes, apparently your mother took it upon herself to fire Estrella without my knowledge. She also told her she wouldn't be getting any references from us and that we'd decided to keep our marriage intact because of the baby."

"Before you even had a chance to tell Estrella yourself? Oh, that poor woman," Kassie breathed. "So you stayed with Chloe."

My father's lips twisted to the side. "Yes. Estrella was gone without a word to me. I was so angry at Chloe and almost went through with the divorce out of spite, but that wouldn't have done my kids any good."

I felt his pain to the depths of my soul. Parts of his story were so similar to mine and Kassie's.

"Dad, I appreciate all the sacrifices you made for us," Auburn said, walking around our father's chair and leaning against the edge of the desk. "It was a very selfless thing for you to do, but I have a question about something. Why did you let her kick Monty out when he was seventeen? She couldn't play the *I'm moving to Europe and taking your kids* card anymore because Evie and I were already adults, and Monty almost was."

Paul Bouvier grimaced and massaged the spot between his eyebrows with his fingers. "This is the part I was dreading telling you all the most." He glanced at me across the desk. "That night, letting you go, was one of the hardest things I've ever done, Monty."

Then why did you do it?

A few minutes later, I had the answer to my unspoken question. "After I made the decision to stay married to Chloe, we... coexisted. I guess that's the best word for it. I raised you kids with little interference from her. She hired another nanny—an older, very unattractive woman," he said with a small smile. "Chloe and I would make public appearances together when necessary, but otherwise, we lived separate lives."

"I remember she was away a lot," Auburn said.

"Yes, and I was grateful for that," Dad said. "Anyway, a few years later, she came to me with a proposition. She said we both had needs and suggested that we, uh, take care of those outside the marriage. Very discreetly."

"Like an open marriage?" I asked.

"Exactly," my father said. "Hell, I was still a young man, and..." He closed his eyes and shook his head. "Christ, this is embarrassing."

"Dad, it's okay. We understand," Auburn said, patting his shoulder. "We've all been horny before."

That broke the tension a little, and everyone laughed, including our dad.

"Thank you for putting it so eloquently, son. Anyway, it took me a month to gather up the courage to do it. Even though there was no love between us, it still felt strange to break my marriage vows. There was one bar I frequented sometimes, and there had been a woman there who had been flirting with me during the previous couple of weeks. One night I flirted back, and we went back to her hotel room together."

His weary eyes glanced around, and I gave him a subtle nod. No way was I going to judge him for what he did after everything he'd given up for his kids.

"When we were finished, she... she asked me for two hundred dollars."

"Holy fuck! She was a prostitute?" Auburn gasped, and Dad covered his eyes with one hand.

"Yes. I had no clue. Please believe me, I would have never been with her if I'd known."

"We believe you, Paul," Gianna replied. "What did you do?"

He lifted both hands in resignation and let them fall to the desk with a thump. "What the hell else could I do? I paid her. I'd never been involved with something like that before, and I had no clue what was going to happen. Was some pimp about to come into the room and break my legs? I tossed a couple hundreds on the nightstand and hightailed it the fuck out of there."

My mind was whirling about five steps ahead, and I blurted, "Chloe found out, didn't she? That's what she was holding over your head all these years."

Dad pointed a finger at me. "Nailed it. Chloe must have set it up because she had video of everything."

Auburn pushed away from the desk and paced back and forth a few times, the anger radiating off him in waves. "That fucking bitch. I wish I could dig her up so I could slap the ever-living shit out of her, and then bury her alive."

"You'd have to stand in line," I gritted out through clenched teeth. "I can't fucking believe she would stoop so low."

"She was diabolical," Dad said. "She'd have done anything to keep the money and power she was used to. For the record, I've never taken another drink of alcohol since then."

"Speaking of money," my brother snapped, "what the hell happened to all of Chloe's? You've told me she was very wealthy before you two married."

"Gambling," our father answered. "She started going to casinos—Monte Carlo, Atlantic City, Vegas—about fifteen years ago and playing blackjack. She liked playing in high stakes games but didn't know when to quit. When she ran out of money, she began selling off her jewelry and stuff to keep feeding her addiction."

"Wow, okay. That's about the last thing I thought you'd say," I mused as another question popped into my head. "So why did you finally leave her? Did you get hold of the evidence she had or something?"

The smile that crossed his lips was slightly wicked. "No, around that time, I ended up with some information she didn't want anyone to know, so we... came to an agreement."

"What was it?" Gianna asked, leaning forward. "You know I'm nosy, Paul. You have to tell us."

"I'm aware, my dear." He flashed his daughter-in-law a grin as he leaned forward conspiratorially. "I found out the reason she wanted Auburn to marry Magdalena so badly. I'm sure it stems back to her running out of money. Long story short, the two were in cahoots to get their hands on *Bouvier*."

Auburn craned his neck forward, his eyes popping wide open. "Are you fucking kidding me? She wanted our family business?"

"Yep," Dad said, popping the P. "You'd grown the business so much since I retired. Those two had dollar signs in their eyes and wanted the whole damn pie. I'm sure they would have come up with some scandal or something to force you out, and then, as your wife, Magdalena could take over everything."

Auburn scoffed. "That never would have fucking happened because I would have had an iron-clad prenup. I would have left my shares to Monty, of course, and never let Magdalena Lewis get her dirty little hands on them."

"I know, son. I don't know the extent of the plan, but I had enough evidence to make Chloe back off and accept that we were getting divorced."

"Thank god she's gone," I muttered. "What about the evidence she had against you?"

"We came to a mutual agreement and each put our evidence in two safe deposit boxes. The keys were to be handed over to the other party at the time of our deaths. I retrieved it today."

Kassie spoke up for the first time in a while. "I can't believe how diabolical Chloe was. I mean, I guess I should have known when she came to my hospital room that night after—"

She stopped short and covered her mouth with her fingers, her wide brown eyes finding mine.

My blood ran cold in my veins. "After what, Kassie?"

Her lips pinched together, and she shook her head.

"Answer me." She remained silent as the ice in my veins turned to boiling lava. "Did she come to the hospital after we lost our baby?"

Kass stared at a spot on the floor and nodded miserably. "Yes," she whispered.

Holy fucking shit!

My eyes were fixed on Kassie, but I felt Gianna's gentle hand on my back. "We're going to go get Paul something for his headache. Auburn, why don't you come help me."

"You know where Dad keeps his medicine."

Her voice turned stern. "Now, Bouvier!"

"Oh, right. We need to... okay. Gotcha." He squeezed my shoulder as he walked by, and I watched with dismay as a tear made a long track down Kassie's pretty face.

And then we were alone.

Chapter 38

I was numb. I couldn't believe I'd blurted that out in front of Monty and his entire family.

Once the room was cleared, he took my hand and led me to a soft, tufted maroon sofa at the side of the room.

"Would you like something to drink?" His gentle tone belied the anger I could feel running through his veins.

"Yes, please. Something strong."

"I think Dad keeps some bourbon here for guests," he said, and I heard bottles clinking as he rummaged around a side table.

Returning a minute later with two glasses and a bottle, he seated himself beside me. I could feel the warmth of his body, and I simultaneously wanted to move away and closer.

I took the smooth, double-walled whiskey glass and downed the contents in one go, wincing slightly before holding it out for a refill. This one I sipped more slowly.

"Can you tell me what happened that night?"

"It was really no big deal. I'd rather not talk about it."

A gentle finger stroked along my jawline to my chin and then tilted my face. His blue eyes were as mesmerizing as ever. "I'd really like to know, if it's not too painful for you to talk about."

"Okay," I sighed, turning my head and breaking eye contact. I pressed my knees together, leaned my forearms on my thighs, and stared down into the amber liquid in my hand. "It was after you left but before my parents got back from dinner."

"I thought you were asleep, or I wouldn't have left," he said, inching closer until my shoulder was flush with his bicep.

"I was, but I woke up, and your mother was in the room."

"What the hell did she want?"

I swiveled my head to face him. "First of all, she wanted to discuss how I manipulated you. Then she proceeded to tell me that you never loved me. You were only there for all the leg spreading I was doing."

Monty's eyes practically popped from their sockets. "She fucking said that to you?"

"She did," I said, looking away and taking another fortifying sip of the bourbon. "After that, she suggested that the... the miscarriage was life's way of working things out."

I closed my eyes when his warm hand pressed against my back. "Kassie, I am so sorry. That's the most vile thing I've ever heard. How could she say that to a girl who'd just been through what you'd been through?"

"Because she's sick and manipulative," I snipped out. "Didn't you hear anything your father told us tonight?"

"Every damn word." He tossed back his own drink in one gulp and swiped his mouth with the back of his hand. "What else did she say?"

I shook my head and lifted the glass to my nose, inhaling the oaky scent of the bourbon. "I think you get the point. There's no need to rehash shit from sixteen years ago." The next sip went down smooth, like warm butter.

"Kass, look at me." It was almost impossible not to when his voice came out as a pleading demand. "What. Else?"

I stared him dead in the eye and lifted my chin. "After she insulted my lack of culture, she told me about the other girl you were interested in."

"What girl?" he snapped.

"I have no idea," I said, lifting my chin. "Was there more than one?"

"There was only you, Kass. You know that. There was only you and Willow."

I sat in stunned silence for a moment at the mention of her name. In my head, Monty had dismissed all thoughts of me and our baby long ago. "You remember her?"

His brow furrowed. "Who?"

"Willow."

Monty stood and paced away before spinning back to me, his blue eyes ablaze. "What kind of fucking question is that, Kassie?" He threw his hands up and let them fall. "How could you even question whether or not I remember our daughter?"

"I-I just assumed you'd forgotten."

My eyes dropped to his fingers, which were unbuttoning his light-blue dress shirt. *What the hell does he think he's doing?*

"There," he growled, yanking the sides of his shirt open to expose his bare chest. "Does that look like I've forgotten her?"

I stood, and my legs moved without me telling them to. Even from several feet away, I could tell the tattoo on his chest was a willow tree, but as I grew closer, I could see the date arced over the top.

The date I knew all too well.

The date I lost my first little love.

"Monty," I breathed, "it's beautiful. A work of art." With tentative fingers, I traced the outline of the dripping tree, and a thought occurred to me. Raising my eyes to his, I asked, "Did you draw this?"

He nodded solemnly. "I interviewed five different tattoo artists before I found one I trusted to do it. Did you look closely at the bark?"

My head tilted to the side as I inspected it. "There's a K."

"And?"

I stepped even closer, and his masculine scent made me want to bury my nose against his skin and sniff my damn life away. But I didn't, instead tapping another spot on his tat.

"I see an A and an M. Kam?"

His smile was barely there when he brushed an errant strand of hair behind my ear. "Keep looking."

The more I stared, the more the subtly hidden letters began to pop out at me, and my lips parted as I found each one. "Both our names," I said aloud when I realized.

Monty's voice was husky with emotion. "Yeah, because we were both a part of her. And you're both a part of me."

Oh. My. God. He never forgot us. He literally imprinted us on his skin.

My hands dropped to his waist, the skin there warm and familiar as I kissed every inch of his beautiful tribute. A strong muscle flexed beneath my mouth, and his hands lifted to cup the back of my head.

"Kass," he groaned, the sound guttural and gritty. When my eyes lifted to his, something shifted—the entire Earth, I think—and he pressed his forehead against mine.

I'm not sure who closed the last inch, but in the next instant, our lips were fused, tongues meeting and tasting. Small testing licks at first, and then more. So much more.

Cool air hit my bare bottom, and I realized Monty had jerked my skirt up and we were moving. My knees hit the velvety surface of the couch as he settled there with me straddling his lap.

Monty Bouvier was still the most attractive man in the world to me, and I found out the feeling was entirely mutual as he began to harden between my legs. With hips moving on pure instinct, I grinded slowly against him, earning me another groan from him.

"I never forgot," he whispered into my mouth.

"I know. I'm sorry I said that." I pulled back an inch to stare into his fiery blue eyes. "I'm so sorry."

"Shh," he hushed me, cupping my thong-covered ass with both hands as he took my mouth again.

Monty lifted his hips, pressing his hardness against my center, and *sweet lord almighty!* He'd grown up *everywhere.* My hands smoothed over his chest, the dark hair there softly abrading my palms, before sliding up his neck and tangling in his hair.

Leaving the emotional baggage behind us for now, we lost ourselves in the physical, our bodies moving like we'd never been apart for a day. My clit received all the attention she needed as I rode against the steel rod in Monty's pants.

A little voice in the back of my head told me this wasn't a good idea, but I told her to sit down and shut the fuck up. It had been a very long time since I'd felt a man's hands on my body, and I was primed for it. *Especially this man.*

Monty and I were like the severed ends of a livewire that had been fused back together, allowing the current to flow smoothly between us once again. My orgasm was on the horizon, and I reached for it as our bodies moved in sync.

"That's it, baby. Ride my fucking cock like you own it." My pace stuttered, but he gripped me tighter and guided me back and forth over him. He'd never talked like that to me before, but I'd be lying if I said it didn't turn me on.

"M-monty, what are we doing?"

His right hand remained on my ass with bruising strength while his left lifted to my face, tracing the outline with a tenderness that almost undid me. It was a wicked dichotomy that I never knew I needed.

"We're feeling, baby. Does it feel good to you?" I groaned and nodded, and Monty's thumb smoothed over my bottom lip. "Use your words, Kassie. I want to hear you say it."

"It feels perfect. I just don't know—"

I stopped talking when his thumb settled firmly over my lips and then pushed into my mouth. "We don't need to know everything right now. We have time. I only need to know if I'm making you feel as good as you're making me feel."

My head nodded as I scraped my teeth over the rough flesh of his thumb and then swirled my tongue around it. His eyes darkened, as did his tone. "Words, Kass."

I released him from my mouth and retorted, "I was using my words, and then you shushed me with your thumb."

He chuckled, the deep sound vibrating through my body. "You're right, baby. I did, and I'm sorry. I just wanted you to stop overthinking and just feel me... feel *this*." He lifted his hips, pressing firmly against me and I groaned.

"I definitely feel that." *It's pretty fucking hard to miss the damn thing.* We began moving again, our bodies taking over and doing what felt natural to us. So perfectly natural and right.

"I swear to God, if I had a condom with me, your sweet pussy would already be spasming around my cock." His filthy words made me grind more deeply against his hardness, taking what I needed so desperately from him.

"Good girl," he growled, both hands back on my hips. My knees pressed hard into the soft surface of the couch as I rubbed my clit against the hard cock beneath his black dress pants.

"Look how beautiful you are," he crooned, his tone soft and demanding at the same time. "We are not leaving this room until your wet spot is staining the front of my pants."

His lips trailed up and down my throat before coming to rest at the soft spot beneath my right ear. I was in a frenzy, twisting his soft hair between my fingers as what I'd been reaching for was finally in my grasp.

"Monty, I'm coming." My words were broken into harsh syllables as his rough tongue circled against my soft flesh. When he bit me lightly, I reached that pinnacle, that peak that I needed more than air.

"What a good fucking girl you are. You take my breath away when you come for me, Kass."

I trembled as he guided my hips effortlessly, and wave after wave of pleasure consumed me. My vision seemed to be fading in and out, and I clutched onto the back of his head for balance.

As my climax began to fade away—wringing the last remnants of desire from my weakened body—Monty's hands dragged slowly, sensuously up my body until he was cupping my face.

"Where is your son?" he asked, and I opened my startled eyes.

"He's at my mother's."

"Is he staying the night?" I nodded yes, and he gifted me with that boy-ish, crooked smile. "Good, then come home with me. I need you beneath me as soon as possible."

I sat up straight, my brown eyes searching his blue ones. "Monty, I can't. This..." I waved a finger between us... "this can't happen."

Deep lines formed across his forehead like tiny waves. "I hate to break it to you, sweetheart, but it just *did* happen."

My face heated. "I know that, but I mean it can't happen again. We can't be together."

"Why the hell not?" he demanded, and I stared at him incredulously.

"Because I don't trust you, not after what you did."

He grunted out a frustrated sound. "Kassie, I told you there were no other girls. I swear my life on it. Surely you don't believe a word of that bullshit my mother was spewing."

I felt as frustrated as he sounded. "No, I didn't believe that. I'm talking about you leaving me when I needed you the most."

His eyebrows smashed together as he fixed me with a glare. "I didn't leave you, Kassie. You left me, remember? You didn't even tell me you were moving away. I had to find out from your damn neighbor."

I glared at him as well. "I would have if you would've shown up."

"I did show up, but you weren't there," he argued.

"You're confusing me, Monty."

"You're confusing me too," he said, stroking his hands over my shoulders and down my arms until we were holding hands. "I'm not sure we're on the same page. Why don't we start at the beginning. Tell me what happened after my mother left."

"I threw up again. My parents came in right about then. They had seen your mother in the hallway, and I guess they put two and two together. My dad was angry and wanted to confront her, but my mother calmed him down. I decided I wanted to be alone to think things over, so I told my parents to go home."

"Did anything else happen that night?"

"I tried to borrow one of the nurse's phones, but I couldn't remember your phone number to call you. I just wanted to talk to you and have you tell me everything was okay."

He lifted one of my hands and kissed the back of it softly. "I would have. What happened the next day?"

I thought back to one of the several horrible days that changed my life forever. "When I got home, my parents informed me that we were moving to Pennsylvania almost immediately. There was a big job starting there in a few months, and they wanted my dad to be in charge of it. Mama said he was trying to put off the move until I graduated high school."

"So what changed their mind?"

"I think it was everything that happened. My mother kept saying that I needed to be protected from all the toxicity. I'm assuming she was talking about your mother."

"Why didn't you tell me, Kassie? I could have taken the train down to Pennsylvania and seen you as often as possible."

My eyes narrowed. "I would have if you'd have shown up the next day like you said you would."

Monty's eyes matched my slitted ones. "I would have, but you told me not to."

Jesus, we were going around in circles. "I never told you not to. What are you talking about?"

"The texts you sent, Kassie. You said you needed time."

"I didn't send you any text messages. I couldn't even find my phone. I don't know if I lost it at the hotel or at the hospital, but it wasn't in my purse. To be honest, I don't even remember putting it in my purse. I usually didn't bring it when I went out with you because you were the only person I talked to on it."

Monty pressed his thumb into his temple and massaged little circles. "My mind is so jumbled right now. I sent you multiple messages and you answered me back. You told me you needed time and to please give you some space."

Pressing my lips together, I quiet-screamed in frustration. "Why aren't you listening to me? I just told you I did not have my phone. The first thing I did when I got home was to check under my mattress for it because I needed to talk to you. I wanted to hear your voice. But the phone wasn't—"

"The phone wasn't what?" he asked.

My thoughts swirled round and round in my head as I whispered, "The phone wasn't there." The realization struck me, and an angry flush rose up my neck and burned the tips of my ears. "I've got to go," I said, climbing off his lap and tugging my dress down with as much dignity as I could muster.

"Kass, where are you going?" he asked, his handsome face perplexed.

I reached up and straightened the lopsided bun on top of my head, my voice turning cold. "I need to talk to my mother."

CHAPTER 39

I BUSTED THROUGH MY mom's front door in a frenzy. "Mother," I bellowed, "I need to talk to you."

"Okay, mi hija," she replied, looking startled.

"When I was in the hospital, did you find a phone hidden beneath my mattress?"

"You were in the hops-pittal, Mommy?" I was suddenly aware of Sully at my hip, tugging on my dress. *Shit.*

I lifted him and kissed his sweaty forehead, lowering my voice. "It was a long time ago, baby. Mommy's okay now."

I caught movement at the corner of my eye, and noticed my sister Regina standing from the couch, her eyes as wide as dinner plates. She approached and poked Sully in the ribs, making him giggle.

"Okay, stinky McGee, you smell like armpits and feet. Why don't we go give you a bath?"

"With extra bubbles?" my kid bargained.

"Of course with extra bubbles," she scoffed. "What do you think this is? Amateur hour?"

"Call me later," she mouthed as she took my son from me and headed down the hall.

When I cast my gaze back toward my mother, her face was pale, but she attempted a smile. "Kassie, sit down."

"I'd prefer to stand, thank you," I said, crossing my arms over my chest. "Now answer me. Did you find a phone?"

"You mean the phone you had been hiding from me and your father?" she pushed back. At my angry nod, she replied, "Yes, I found it when I was changing the sheets on your bed." I'd never worried about that before because I always changed my own sheets.

"Did you use it to send text messages to Monty?" I asked point-blank, and red spots appeared high on my mother's cheeks, signaling her guilt.

"You know I didn't have a cellular phone back then. I was no good at texting."

I lifted a skeptical eyebrow. "What about Papá? He had one for work and knew how to text."

"Kassie, you have to remember that was a very difficult time for all of us."

"Especially me," I snapped before lowering my voice so Sully didn't hear me. "I had just lost my child."

"I know, honey. Your father and I didn't think you needed any more stress in your life."

"So you moved me away from everything I ever knew? My home? My friends? Monty?"

"Monty's family," she snapped back, "were the wrong kind of people. Your father and I didn't like seeing you hurting."

"So you decided to inflict even more pain into my life? Yeah, that makes a ton of sense," I fumed.

"That was not our intent, Kassie."

I propped my hands on my hips and scowled. "Did Papá message Monty and tell him I didn't want to see him?"

"I-I don't know what your father did. All he told me was that he handled it."

I tossed my hands in the air and marched around the room with no particular destination in mind. I just needed to move. "I can't fucking believe this."

"Kassie Ramirez, you watch your language!"

"Sorry, Mama, but no. I will not watch my fucking language. I can't believe you'd do this. I can't believe you let *him* do this."

"Your father was always very protective of you, mi hija. God rest his soul." She did the sign of the cross. "He didn't think that boy was right for you."

"That was *not* his decision to make. I was almost an adult."

"But you were still our daughter."

"You moved me to Pennsylvania and made me finish out my senior year by homeschooling. You wouldn't even allow me to use the house phone to call Lily. I was all alone at the time I needed someone the most."

"You had me and your father. And your sisters."

"Ah, yes. I should have just discussed my miscarriage with a couple of elementary schoolers. Great idea." My teeth grinded together so hard they hurt. "I needed *him,* Mama. I needed Monty."

"I know, honey. I didn't agree with everything your father was doing, but he was my husband and I had to support him." Another sign of the cross.

"What about supporting *me*?" I questioned, smacking my palm against my chest as a stupid tear slid down my cheek. I hated angry tears; they appeared at the most inopportune times. "You isolated me."

Mama's chin trembled. "I realized that too late. You left for college and barely called home for two years."

"Because I was depressed! Thank god Lily transferred to Penn and kicked my ass into shape." My best friend had truly been my saving grace.

"How did you find out?" she asked. "About the messages?"

"Monty and I talked about it, and our stories didn't match up. He said he had wanted to come see me, but I told him I needed time. I knew I hadn't sent those messages."

Mama shook her head. "I did feel for that poor boy. He looked so broken that night at the hospital."

"But you decided it was okay to take control of our lives and separate us? You decided it was okay to drive the knife further into our backs?"

"That's not what I was trying to do. Your father said—"

"My father isn't here, so you have to answer for what happened."

She shook her head sadly. "I can't. Like I said, I didn't agree with everything your father was doing, but that boy's mother had poison running through her veins. I didn't want that poison to hurt my daughter."

"Monty had no contact with his mother."

"But we didn't know how long that would last. Rich people are different. They stick together because of money but have no idea what true loyalty is."

I rolled my eyes at the ridiculousness of that statement. "Well, I'm rich now, Mama. Are you saying I'm like that?"

"Of course not, but you were raised differently, mi hija."

"That's very prejudiced," I said, slashing my hand through the air. "You're no better than people who judge other people because of the color of their skin. You can't paint everyone with the same brush."

My mother hung her head, tears of shame falling from her eyes. "I know that, and I'm sorry for what your father did. But I don't like to hear you insulting his memory." She crossed herself once again, which was starting to annoy me.

"Just because Papá is dead, that doesn't mean I don't get to have feelings about this. It doesn't mean I don't get to be pissed as hell at him. I will always love Papá, but I am so angry at him right now. He ruined my life."

"Is your life really so bad? You have a good job and a son."

"I also went years floundering, Mama. I was so depressed. I did nothing but go to class and come home my first two years of college."

"I was so sad to see you unhappy, Kassie."

"Then you should have done something about it. You should have told me that Papá was manipulating things. I've gone years thinking Monty just didn't give a shit." I forced back the sob that was threatening to erupt from my chest. "You could have saved me a lot of heartbreak."

My mother's face dropped as she looked down the hallway from where we could hear Sully splashing and laughing with his Aunt Regina.

"I know you've had a hard time. There have been so many times when I wished you had never met Wesley Campbell, but then I remember if you hadn't, we wouldn't have our little Sullivan."

My eyes followed her line of sight. "Trust me, Mama, I have that exact same thought all the time. It's hard to fathom something so good could come from something so bad."

I sat alone in the graveyard, the moonlight streaming down and glinting off the dark headstone etched with my father's name in a bold font.

"I'm mad at you, Papá," I said aloud. "Mama did the sign of the cross at least thirty times tonight. She said I shouldn't speak ill of the dead, but I told her the dead shouldn't keep secrets."

I pushed out a sigh. "Then she did the sign of the cross again. Apparently I was being very blasphemous tonight."

I smiled and thought maybe that line would have made my dad smile too.

"Why did you do it?" I asked. I knew I wouldn't receive an answer, but I had to ask the question anyway. I had always seen people talking to their dead loved ones at the cemetery, and I never understood why until now. Asking unanswered questions out loud gave me a kind of power. I could speak my thoughts without interruption. I knew the questions were rhetorical because he couldn't respond, but it felt good to say.

"Why couldn't you have just given us a chance, Papá? Mama says you were trying to protect me, but from what? From the boy who loved me? I think we could have made it work. But we had all these outside influences working against us. You. Monty's mother. God. See? That's where the blasphemous part comes in."

I smeared away a couple tears from my cheeks. "My relationship with God was broken for a long time. I didn't understand how he could've taken everything away from me at the same time, but now I know that it wasn't only God. You had a hand in it too. I have forgiven God. I'm certainly not as devout as Mama would like me to be, but I do take Sully to Mass sometimes. And I'll forgive you too, Papá, I will. I'm just really mad right now."

An owl hooted in the distance, and I looked up as he took flight from a nearby tree, his wings spread as his shadowy form crossed the blackberry-colored sky.

"I'm done with letting men control my life, Papá. You. Wesley." I stared in the direction where the owl had disappeared, my eyes defocusing in the darkness.

"The only man who never tried to control me was Monty, and he was taken away from me. And now I can't even trust him because my vision is so blurred by everything that's happened to me."

Leaning back on my hands, I closed my eyes and allowed the cool March breeze to dry my tears. "I guess being alone is my only option."

I rose and laid my hand on my father's headstone. "Even when I'm mad as hell, I still love you, Papá."

Smiling, I did the sign of the cross. "That's from Mama."

I pummeled the punching bag with furious fists, one after the other, until my arms ached. And then I switched to kicking the shit out of it.

"Jesus, what did that bag ever do to you?"

I whirled around, crouching into a fighter's stance until I saw Andrea crossing the gym with a smirk on her face.

"Easy, killer. It's just me."

My shoulders relaxed, and I shook out my Jell-O-like arms and legs. "Just working through a few things."

"Anything you want to talk about?"

She tossed me a bottle of water and cracked open her own as I held mine against the heated skin of my neck. "If you don't mind listening."

"I never mind," she replied. "Is it Wesley?"

My ex-husband had been out of prison for a week now, and I hadn't heard a word from him.

"No, still no contact, thank god."

"Okay, then what's going on?"

I sank to the ground, and Andrea did the same, facing me as I straightened my legs and bent over them in a deep stretch. She watched in patient silence as I did the same with my arms before twisting open my water.

The liquid was ice cold and soothed my throat and my ragged nerves.

Then I spilled the whole sordid tale as she listened, the lifting and falling of her eyebrows her only response.

"Well, that's fucked up," she said, and I laughed for the first time in what seemed like forever.

"That about sums it up."

"So Monty is back, and you know now that he didn't abandon you."

"Yeah," I said, shrugging my shoulders and taking another long swig. "So?"

"Soooo, what's stopping you from being together? Do you not have chemistry anymore?"

My lips curled up at the corners as I thought about our tryst on the couch a few hours ago. "That doesn't seem to be a problem."

Andrea rubbed her hands together. "Ooh, that sounds like a story. Do tell."

"We kissed," I admitted.

"And?"

"And it was hot as hell, you nosy bitch. Things got pretty steamy for a bit, and then we started talking."

"See? That's where you fucked up. Don't talk; just do."

"It would never work."

Her face turned serious, and she regarded me intently. "Tell me your thinking on that."

I took another long glug of the water before wiping my mouth with my thumb. "I'm a mom and a lawyer."

"Oh right." She nodded as if she understood. "I forgot that mom-lawyers aren't allowed to have relationships."

"You're such a smart ass."

She patted her blue hair. "I know. It's part of my charm."

"I can never allow myself to *not* be in total control. Ever again."

My friend/paralegal/trainer blew out a long breath.

"Kassie, I know I'm a little younger than you, but I went through a lot of shit before I met Jenna. I learned something I'd like to share with you, if that's okay."

"Of course," I said.

She pushed her lips together and released them with a little pop. "Sometimes the only way to exert control is by giving up that control and trusting someone else. By ceding your power to someone you can trust, you're *allowing* something to happen rather than *making* it happen. It can be very freeing, especially in sexual situations."

She downed the rest of her water and pushed to her feet, closing the few steps between us before tugging my sweaty ponytail. "Just think about that, okay?"

I looked up at her sweet face, filled with concern for me, and nodded.

"I will."

CHAPTER 40

I RECEIVED A PHONE call from Kassie around noon the next day, and I snatched up my phone and answered it faster than a gunfighter in the old west.

"Hello."

"Monty, hey. It's Kassie."

I knew that because I had her number programmed in my phone. It's possible I sneaked a peek at Auburn's contacts and stole the number, but I wasn't about to tell her that.

"Hi, it's good to hear from you. Are you okay? You left kind of abruptly last night."

"I'm sorry about that. Some things started clicking into place, and I needed to talk to my mom about them."

"Did you get everything straightened out?"

I heard her long sigh over the phone line. "I have to tell you something. You remember I told you I couldn't find my phone when I got home from the hospital?"

"I remember."

"It turns out my dad had the phone. He's the one who was sending you those messages."

I was quiet for a beat. "Holy shit. Why would he do that? Was he that pissed that we went to a hotel together?"

"That may have been part of it. I wish I could ask him myself, but he died a few years back. I didn't know if you knew that."

"Auburn told me. I'm so sorry for your loss."

"Thank you. From what my mother said, Papá was trying to get me away from the, and I quote, toxicity."

"In other words, my mother," I said flatly.

"Yes," she said quietly.

"That's just one more way she fucked up my life," I observed bitterly.

"Between her and my dad, I'm not sure who I'm more pissed at."

"It's a toss up for me too." My finger circled the hole in the knee of my jeans. "Would you like to get together some time? We could talk about it in person. Or we could talk about something else. Whatever you want."

Anything. Just say you'll see me again. My skin was literally itching to spend more time with Kass.

Her voice was so quiet, I had to strain to hear her. "I don't think I'm ready for that yet. I'm still processing the fact that my father betrayed me. I just thought you should know the truth."

I closed my eyes against the disappointment. "I understand. I'm here though. Anytime you need to talk."

"Thanks, Monty. I appreciate it."

After hanging up, I tossed on some running clothes and headed outside to try and clear my head.

Two hours later, my phone rang again, but this time I stared at it like it was a bomb. *One ring. Two rings. Three.*

Finally picking it up, I answered, "Hello, Captain Snyder."

"Monty, how are you? I was so sorry to hear about your mother."

A muscle twitched in my jaw at the mention of her. "Thank you, sir."

"Did you see the floral arrangement we sent from the department?"

In all honesty, I'd been so distracted by Kassie's appearance, I hadn't even looked at the flowers. The Pope could have sent an arrangement with his big hat on top, and I would have missed it.

So I lied. "Of course. They were lovely. I appreciate the thought."

"Good… good." He was stalling, which wasn't a good sign. "Are you still in New York?"

"I am."

"Good. That's nice. It's important to spend time with your family."

"Cap, just get on with it."

I could hear the raspberry he blew over the phone line. "Monty, I'm afraid I have some bad news. The review board found that both you and Miss O'Neil acted inappropriately."

Even knowing it was coming, hearing the actual words stunned me into silence.

"I'm really sorry about this, but you're both being let go."

Let go. I was being fired.

"She's been there for two months. I'm sure it's heartbreaking for her," I said sarcastically.

"And you've been with the department for over a decade, Bouvier. It doesn't quite seem fair, does it?"

"No, Cap, it doesn't." *Fuck, fuck, fuck my life.*

"Son, there's something else." In my mind's eye, I could see him pulling at the back of his neck in discomfort. "Miss O'Neil is being given a… severance package."

I read between the lines. "Hush money."

He huffed out a humorless laugh. "She's having to sign a nondisclosure agreement not to talk to the press or anyone else about it."

"Great," I replied flatly.

"It's to protect you as much as it is to protect the department."

I was done with this conversation. If it kept on, I was afraid he'd tell me Shana was being named governor of Florida for her "troubles."

"Thanks for letting me know."

His voice dripped with humility. "Again, I'm really sorry about this. I hate to lose a good man like you."

"Well, you did." I couldn't contain the bitterness that had taken over my tone. "Maybe use this as a teaching tool for new officers. Tell them they have to remain celibate for the rest of their lives. Otherwise, they risk the off chance that some random woman they're with may work in the department sometime in the future. And then they'll get fucking fired."

"It's a shitty situation, and I'm as frustrated as you are. It's not right."

"Thanks," I sighed, "and I'm sorry I took it out on you. I know you advocated for me."

"A hundred percent, and if you ever need a reference, make sure to give them my name specifically. I'll do you right."

"'Preciate it, Carl." It felt weird calling him by his first name, but for the first time in over ten years, he wasn't my captain.

After we hung up, I roosted on the side of my bed with my hands buried in my hair. *Fuck! What am I supposed to do now?*

Being a cop was all I'd known for my entire adult life, and now it was over. I wasn't even sure if I wanted to try to start again at another department. Where would I even go?

Miami? Hell, at this point, I wasn't even sure I wanted to go back to Florida. I'd loved being here in New York with my family the past couple weeks.

And Kassie is here.

That thought went from the back of my mind straight to the forefront in an instant, and suddenly the entire loss of my career was infinitesimally less daunting.

Yet still horribly painful.

I needed… something. Something to take my mind off this.

Heading next door, I peeked my head into Janie's room. "Hey, kiddo." Her smile instantly lifted me, as always. Jane was a light in the world.

"Uncle Monty! You want to have a tea party with me?"

"There's nothing I'd like more," I said with complete honesty.

She clapped her tiny hands. "Yay! You can get the stuff ready, and I'll brush my hair," she informed me, reaching for the hairbrush on her nightstand. "The tea set is in the kitchen, and the costumes are in my closet."

Costumes?

Ah, fuck it. Let's go, kid.

And that's how I found myself sipping apple juice from a dainty, pink floral teacup while wearing a fluffy purple feather boa and a tiara that looked to be made of genuine Swarovski crystals with a large magenta stone set high and center. Janie said her dad bought it for her.

I swear, Auburn Bouvier was a bougie motherfucker.

In addition to my "costume," I was also sporting a huge grin. In my mind, I was designing an entire wardrobe of tea party clothing for kids. Guess my brother wasn't the only bougie one in the family.

And every bit of tension in my body was fucking *gone.*

"This tea is fantabulous, dahhhhling," I said, and my precious niece giggled.

"I agree, dahhhhling." She'd insisted that we use posh accents during our most excellent tea party. I was also informed that I had to lift my pinky finger while drinking.

I had that finger lifted—per my instructions—and the tiny cup held to my lips when a flash went off.

"Oh, this is totally going in the family scrapbook," Gianna said, grinning down at her phone. "I may even put it on my Instagram account."

"Oooh, speaking of the 'Gram," Janie said, "are there any new videos of Garfield and Snoopy?" I'd showed her my favorite account, and we'd spent hours laughing at the antics of the goofy dog and crazy cat.

Pulling up the latest on my phone, I handed it over to Janie. "This one is hilarious. They found a field of flowers, and Garfield is hopping around, trying to catch butterflies."

While my niece watched and laughed, my sister-in-law adjusted the tiara positioned atop my head. "We're so glad you're here, Monty. The kids love having you."

"But I've overstayed my welcome?"

Her eyes widened in horror. "No! Not even a little bit. Auburn and I were just talking about it last night. We wish you could stay forever."

Yeah, babe. Me too.

"I'm glad you called," I said, climbing into the back of the cab. "I needed a night out."

"Me too," Cruz Estrada said, holding his hand out for a slap. "Had a big night last night."

"Really? What... oh shit! Were you in on that raid I saw on the news? The mafia thing?"

He nodded, a hint of smugness in his smile as he lowered his voice. "Yep, we took down the entire Cappitani crime family. The dad, Luca, was killed, the fucking piece of shit."

"Some pretty bad stuff?"

His face turned grim, and his blue eyes lost some of their sparkle. "We found two girls locked in a room. Luca was on top of one when we busted in. He pulled a gun from beneath the pillow, and I took him out."

"Fuck."

"Yeah, it was intense."

"Did you say girls? As in underage?"

Cruz's jaw tightened. "One was seventeen, and the other just turned nineteen. They'd both been held there for over a year. Daily rapes by Cappitani and his men."

"God, that's fucking disgusting. He's in his sixties, right?"

My friend's nose scrunched up in distaste. "Yeah, and he's a big, bloated piece of shit." His head shook sadly. "Those poor ladies are back with their families now, but it's going to take a very long time before they're even close to okay."

Nausea rose up in my stomach, and I clamped my lips together to keep from spewing bile all over the back seat.

"You all right?" Cruz asked, his forehead creasing in concern.

"I... My sister went missing sixteen years ago. Every time I hear a story like this, I can't help but wonder if she went through..." I couldn't even finish that sentence.

"Fuck, man. I'm sorry. I remember hearing Auburn talk about her occasionally." His hand clasped my shoulder and gave me a light shake.

"Is it horrible of me to hope that maybe she was killed instantly instead of suffering like that?"

"No, buddy, it's not horrible." He cracked his knuckles one by one, staring down as each one popped. "I have a younger sister, and I'd never want her to go through something like that. This is the worst part of the job. The victims." He glanced up at me with a wan smile. "But you know all about that, don't you?"

"Not anymore. I was fired from my job two days ago," I blurted out.

Cruz's eyes widened, but before he could reply, the cab driver said, "We're here."

I paid the man, and Cruz and I entered the pub, looking around at the dark wood walls and furnishings. It smelled exactly like you'd expect an Irish pub to smell... like stale beer and greasy food.

We took a seat at a dimly lit table near the back and ordered two pints of Guinness from the waitress.

"What happened?" he asked as soon as she was gone, and I dropped the entire story in his lap as he listened with rapt attention.

"So now I'm feeling kind of lost," I concluded.

"That's some damn bullshit," he spat. "It happened before she even started working there. Can you appeal?"

I was silent as the female server dropped off our beers and took our orders for Irish nachos. "I'm not sure I even want to. I'm thinking I might move back to New York?"

That last bit came out as more of a question than a statement, and it earned me a grin and a slap on the shoulder from my new friend. "Fuck, dude. That would be awesome. I mean, I hate that this happened to you, but I'd love having you here, and I know your family would too."

My body sagged back against my chair. "I told Auburn and Gianna last night, and they said the same thing. They offered to let me live with them, but I'm thinking I need to get my own place."

"You should live in our building. Your brother set me up there so I'd be close, and the amenities are awesome." His excitement was palpable, and mine grew at the thought of living so close to my family.

"That would actually be really great," I said. "I'll look into it. See if there's a unit available."

"You know your brother owns the building, right? I'm sure he'd boot someone out and give you their apartment."

I laughed. "I wasn't aware he owned it. I wouldn't put anyone out of their home, but if there's an apartment vacant, I think I'll take it." A thrill shivered down my spine, and I knew I was making the right decision.

"Here ya go, fellas," the red-headed waitress said, eyeing me up and down as she set the huge platters in front of us. Then she leaned over with both hands on the table, allowing her ample breasts to spill out over the top of her bustier top. "Can I get you *anything* else?"

"Two more beers," I said flatly, averting my eyes and pulling my plate closer to me.

She sauntered off, and Cruz jabbed an elbow into my side. "She was totally giving off some *fuck me* vibes, dude."

"Not interested," I said, forking up a mound of crispy, golden potatoes smothered with cheese, corned beef, and a bunch of other delicious shit.

"You interested in someone else?" he asked, digging into his own food.

"There's someone, but I'm not sure if it's gonna work out."

"Is that someone here in New York?"

I nodded and diverted. "How about you? You got a lady?"

Cruz chewed slowly and shook his head before tilting it back and forth. "No, but yes. I really like someone, but I don't know if she likes me, so I guess we're both kinda in the same boat."

"Have you asked her out?"

"No, she gives me signals, but I don't know if she'd be into the same things as me. You know..." he lowered his voice and blushed beneath his darkly tanned skin, "sexually."

"You into BDSM or something?"

Cruz shoveled in another bite and shook his head. After swallowing, he rimmed the top of his glass with his finger. "Not that. Something different. I have trouble finding women who have the same tastes as me."

"If you need to talk about anything, The Bouvier Institute for Higher Learning in the Art of Female Pleasure is dedicated to helping young lads such as yourself."

A snort puffed from his nostrils. "The Bouvier Institute for Higher Learning in the Art of Female Pleasure?" I grinned and nodded as I stuck another bite of potato in my mouth. "How the hell do you fit all that on your letterhead?"

"We use small font," I popped back. "I'm sure there are women out there for you, Cruz. You just have to know where to look."

"Like a sex club?" he asked, leaning forward and dropping his voice even lower.

"Maybe. Or on online sites."

He drummed his fingers on the table, staring at a neon sign over the bar before bringing his gaze back to mine. "I have a buddy who goes to one of those clubs. He assures me it's not sleazy or anything. It's really upscale. Just a place to find other people who like what you like."

I bobbed my head up and down in understanding. "I used to go to one when I was younger. To get, you know, acclimated to the lifestyle."

"You're a dominant, right?"

My chuckle was low and dark. "That obvious, huh?"

Cruz tilted his head and lifted an eyebrow in a *duh* gesture. "It kinda oozes from you."

"Great. I ooze. Maybe I can put that on my resumé."

He tilted back his chair and belly laughed. "Fuck, man. You're crazy." Lowering back to the ground, he leaned his forearms on the table. "Hey, would you like to go to the club with me? My friend has been trying to get me to go, but he goes with his wife, and I don't want to be a third wheel. But I also don't want to go by myself."

Cupping my jaw in one hand, I massaged the beard I'd been growing out since I returned. "I'm not really interested in picking up anyone. I've kinda sworn off women since everything happened in Florida."

Except for one woman, the little devil on my shoulder whispered. *She could crook her little finger, and you'd drop to your knees for her.*

"I don't know if I want to either, but I'm curious as hell. Maybe I could find someone that likes the same weird shit I do."

"Hey, don't do that," I scolded. "Don't kink-shame yourself. Everyone has something that turns them on, and that's okay. As long as it's not anything illegal."

Cruz's eyes widened, and he shook his head vigorously. "No, nothing like that. I'm just... different."

"Like you wanna fuck Pokémon or something?"

He slapped the table and barked out a laugh. "Naw, man. I don't want to fuck Pokémon. Is that a thing? Because you're actually making me feel like maybe I'm not such a freak."

"Ain't a damn thing wrong with being a freak. As long as you've got a freaky partner."

His smile was a little sad. "That's the problem. I'm sure the girl I'm attracted to wouldn't be into the same shit."

I was so goddamn curious, but I didn't want to pry. Cruz would tell me when he was ready, but until then, I wanted to help him find his fellow freaky chick.

"You know what? I think I will go to the club with you. It'll be fun. If nothing else, I can check out the voyeur room and maybe get some new spank bank material."

Not that I was having trouble in that department. Since that night on the couch, I'd practically rubbed my dick raw to thoughts of Kassie Ramirez.

Cruz's smile took up his entire face. "Okay, good. I'll let my friend Bryson know. He said there will have to be a background check and everything."

"That's standard at the nicer places. The sketchier ones allow anyone in and trust me, you don't want to go there."

He wrinkled his nose. "Nope, definitely not. I'll message you with whatever info he needs, and we can get it set up for a couple weeks out."

"Sounds like a plan."

Two weeks later on a Saturday night, Cruz and I were inside Club E. The place was seriously swanky as fuck, and the accommodations were primo. We'd just finished the tour, given to us by a petite blonde named Everly.

"Okay, gentlemen. That's the end of the formal tour. You're welcome to return to any of the areas that caught your eye. Tonight's visit is free, courtesy of your guest passes, unless you decide to use one of our private rooms. Then it will be charged to the card you have on file."

"Thanks, Everly," Cruz said, and I gave a nod of acknowledgment.

"Membership information will be emailed to you in case you decide to join us on a more permanent basis. And we certainly hope you do." She winked one of her big, green eyes before waving a hand at a brightly lit storefront behind me. "This is our toy shop, where you'll find any and everything you could ever dream of. Just ask Elle, and she'll help you if you need it." With a cute wiggle of her fingers, she sashayed off.

"See anything you like tonight?" I asked, stuffing my hands into the pockets of my black pants and rocking back on my heels.

Cruz tilted his head and took in the vast downstairs room, which was basically a bar and dance club. "I don't know. The women here are gorgeous, but I feel like I'd be cheating on Lehra. Is that bizarre, considering we haven't even dated?"

"Lehra, huh?" My friend's eyes widened as he realized what he'd said. I tapped my smirking lips with one finger. "Seems like Auburn mentioned someone named Lehra that works at *Bouvier.*"

Cruz blew a sharp breath from between his lips. "Busted. She's the receptionist there, and she's just so gorgeous and sweet. Her smile..." His blue eyes turned dreamy, and I patted him on the shoulder.

"Your secret's safe with me, man. Why don't you ask her out and see what she says?"

His teeth sank into his bottom lip. "I'll think about it. I'm gonna wander around, maybe get a drink. You want one?"

I shook my head, jerking a thumb at the area behind me. "I'm going to check out the store."

"Good, bro. Get you a new whip or something."

In reality, I needed a new bottle of lube, hopefully something more viscous than the almost-empty bottle I'd bought at the drugstore a few weeks ago.

I was still laughing at the whip comment when I turned to enter the store.

My laughter quickly turned to fury as I opened the door. I didn't know what the boiling point of anger was, but I was rapidly approaching it.

My eyes were glued to the woman standing near the back, wearing next to nothing.

Oh, no the fuck she didn't!

CHAPTER 41

"I can't believe I let you talk me into wearing this scrap of material, Elle," I said, tugging at the minuscule dress that barely covered my ass.

"Oh, please. You can't rock up in here in one of your business suits and not stick out like a sore thumb. You blend," she commented, doing her best Marisa Tomei impression.

"It really is beautiful though. Thank you for loaning it to me." The flesh-colored dress hugged me like a glove and was overlayed with a luxurious black lace, so it looked like you were bare beneath it. "This is the sexiest thing I've ever worn."

"It's a *Bouvier*," she whispered, bobbing her eyebrows at me. "I thought you might like a little Bouvier all over your body."

"You're so ridiculous," I said, rolling my eyes.

"What brings you into my fine establishment tonight?"

"I need some new toys." I wasn't about to tell her I used my rose so much over the past couple weeks, it no longer worked.

She tapped her delicate face with one finger. "You like water play?"

"Um, what does that mean?"

"Do you like to play downstairs deejay while in the tub?" She moved her fingers back and forth. "You know, like doing the wicky-wicky on the old turntable?"

"Oh, yeah, I like water play. My bath is sometimes the only alone time I get."

"Mmhmm, you need an aqua stimulator," she said, working her way around the displays of... *things.* Picking up an item that looked like a penis-shaped slide, she wiggled it in front of me. "You hook this to your spout, and it directs the water directly where you need it the most." She dragged an elegant finger down the curve. "No more scooching down in the tub and practically drowning yourself to try and get the running water to hit your lady bits."

I took the translucent pink plastic in my hands and inspected it. "So it's like an extension of your waterspout."

"And it's shaped like a dick, so you get visual stimulation too. How is your dildo supply?"

"This does not seem like a normal conversation, Elle."

"Because you're in a sex store, Kassie," she retorted, looking up when the door opened and a handsome man wearing only a pair of tight black silk shorts poked his head in.

"Can I get you ladies anything?" he asked.

"Thanks, Nick. We'll have more of those new cocktails."

"Yes, ma'am," he said practically bowing. Elle was like royalty around here.

"I already had two," I protested when Nick left.

"Then this will make three. See how that works? It's the magic of math."

"Smartass," I muttered. "I'll definitely take the water slide of pleasure."

She took it from me and placed it on the counter before leading me to what I liked to call The Great Wall of Penis. They seemed to be arranged from left to right in order of ascending size.

"What do you prefer?" Her hand performed a twirly little wave. "Regular, jumbo, or rip-your-vagina-in-two?"

Um, ouch.

"Probably regular since my cooter is now like that old, haunted house on the street corner in every neighborhood. You know, the one that all the neighbors avoid because of the cobwebs and broken doors and strange squeaky noises coming from inside."

"Just gotta oil the hinges, and you'll be all right," Elle said. "I'll grab you a bottle of our best lube. You get quite a bargain if you buy it by the half-gallon."

"Sold." I grinned at her before returning my gaze to the wall. "Dear god, what is that one?" I asked, pointing toward a giant purple monstrosity on the far right. "That looks like it could make a male elephant jealous."

"Ah, the Flounder Pounder 3000. An excellent choice. Its only drawback is that it's loud as hell, so you can't use it discreetly on the bus or anything."

"On the bus?!" I shrieked.

Elle waved her hand dismissively and picked up an unpackaged Flounder Pounder from the display setup. "You'd be surprised how many people are walking around this city with something buried inside them on a daily basis. Men and women." She lifted one perfectly arched eyebrow as she handed over the toy.

I literally had to use both hands. "Good grief!"

"Yeah, it's a lot to take. This one isn't recommended for anal use." *No fucking shit.* "Luckily, there's a clit tickler that helps distract from the pain."

"I don't mind having my clit tickled," I commented, "but—"

"What the fuck are you doing here?"

The growl came from behind me, and I instantly recognized the voice. Elle's huge brown eyes were fixed over my shoulder, her mouth gaping wide. "Holy shit."

I whirled around to face the sneaky newcomer, and *holy shit, indeed.*

Monty Bouvier was the quintessential man in black, sporting the hue from head to toe. His pants were fitted, hitting right at the ankles to reveal that he wasn't wearing socks with his dress shoes. The matching jacket looked perfect on him, as did the black shirt that was unbuttoned just enough to show off a hint of his chiseled chest.

His hair was styled back away from his face, and his eyes were burning blue lava as they scraped up and down my body like they had all the time in the world to peruse me.

"I could ask you the same question, Bouvier," I snapped, poking him in the chest.

He looked down. "Why are you stabbing me with a giant purple cock? It better not be used." His eyes lifted to meet mine, and I caught a hint of sparkle behind the anger. "Unless it's been inside *your* hot little pussy. Then you need to raise it a few inches so I can lick it clean."

I may have peed my panties just a little at that point.

"Holy fucking shit," Elle whispered behind me. I swung the heavy toy backward to shut her up and heard her grunt. "Ow, dammit. You hit me in the pussy with that thing."

Normally I would have snorted in laughter at that comment, but Monty's eyes had me under their spell as Elle took the big dick from my hand.

"I asked you a question, Kassie. What are you doing here?"

Lifting my chin defiantly, I said, "Same thing as you, I would assume." It was a complete lie, but *how fucking dare he* judge me for being here when he obviously came here to get laid.

His eyes narrowed to near slits, and I could feel the waves of frustration and disbelief roll off him. "Oh really? Which floor do you frequent?"

My mind scrambled for an answer, and I propped my hands on my hips. "Floor two."

An unholy sound emanated up from his chest, and before I knew what was happening, Monty dipped his body and had me thrown over his shoulder like a sack of potatoes.

I shrieked in utter shock. "What are you doing? Elle, help me!"

She giggled. "Sorry, babe. You two need to work out your shit. And the best place to do that is on the second floor."

"That's where the fuck we're headed," Monty replied, pivoting and striding toward the door like he didn't have a grown woman tossed over his shoulder.

Elle teetered after us in her ridiculously high heels, snatching the aqua stimulator from the counter and shoving it into my hands. "You forgot your toy."

"I haven't paid for it yet," I said stupidly, as if that was the issue here.

"Charge it to my card on file," Monty said, never breaking stride. "Name's Monty Bouvier."

The last thing I saw was the smug grin on her pretty face. "Oh, honey. I know *exactly* who you are."

The trip up to the second floor was made amid a million questions from me—that went unanswered, by the way—and me calling Monty Bouvier every dirty name I could think of.

His hand stayed firmly on my ass to provide me a modicum of modesty, which I probably would have appreciated if I wasn't being manhandled.

Monty's hand slipped into his pocket, and he pulled out a key card that I knew held all his information. Twisting my head, I looked around to find that we were standing in front of a door with a green light overhead, signaling that the room was unoccupied. As he slid the black card against the reader, the light turned red, and there was the snick of an unlocking door.

Then we were inside. Alone. Placing a hand on my back, Monty slid me gently to the floor and stood in front of me. "This? This is what you like, Kassie?" One long, elegant arm waved in a slow arc as my eyes took in the room.

Holy hell! What is all this?

Of course, instead of admitting that I'd never been in one of these rooms, my stubborn ass doubled down. "Yes, I love it here."

His thick arms crossed over his chest, threatening the threads that held his jacket together as his tongue circled against the inside of his cheek. "Oh really? Then what's that called?"

Monty's dark head nodded toward a large wooden wheel with a giant X on it against the far wall. There were black leather straps near the edges.

I swallowed hard and turned back to him, nose high in the air. "That's the wheel of fortune."

He puffed out a short burst of air as he chuckled. "The wheel of fortune?"

God, Kass. Cut your losses and admit you don't know what it is. What any of this is.

But no.

I shrugged as if I discussed large, strappy sex contraptions every day. "That's what I call it because I feel very... fortunate when I get to use one. It's not like I have one of these in my house." I flicked my fingers in that direction, holding his gaze.

His thumb and forefinger stroked through the short beard and regarded me with shrewd eyes.

"Are you a Domme?" When I didn't answer, he quirked one dark eyebrow at me. "Do you like to bend naughty boys over a spanking bench and whip their asses?"

My eyes almost bugged right the fuck out of their sockets, and I shook my head vigorously. "No," I managed to say.

"Hmmm, then you're a submissive." His perfect white teeth scraped against the dark pink flesh of his bottom lip. "That works out perfectly."

His already huge body seemed to grow before my very eyes as he took my hand and led me to the corner of the room where there was a small red pillow with two curved dents. "I think you know what to do, Kass."

I'd seen those movies about Christian Grey. It had been years, but I remembered enough to know what Monty wanted me to do.

Kneel for him.

Are you really going to do this, you crazy bitch?

When my feet slipped from my black stilettos, I silently answered my own question. As I began to lower myself, he stopped me, taking my hands in both of his as his brow furrowed.

"I'm not sure what your other Doms have allowed, but you'll be naked when you kneel for me." Wetness pooled in my panties, and I wondered if I'd lost my damn mind. That calm, bossy tone should not have turned me on.

Monty pressed his cheek against mine, the soft roughness of his beard pleasantly abrading my overly sensitive skin. "Unless you're wearing some lingerie that pleases me," he whispered into my ear, "and then you may leave it on until I decide to remove it myself."

I should have balked at being told what I *may* or *may not* wear, but again, the thought made me drip.

He pulled back and brushed my hair away from my face with the backs of his fingers. "Is that clear, Kassie?"

"Yes." At the slight furrowing of his brows, I amended that and said, "Yes, Sir."

Monty's eyes closed, and he let out a deep groan of satisfaction that made my nipples tighten into rigid diamonds. When he raised his lids, the blue of his irises had darkened to a bottomless navy.

"You're going to be such a good fucking girl for me, baby." His mouth took mine, but where I expected ferocity, he gave me softness. Gentle sucks pulled against my lips over and over, making my knees weak and my muscles flaccid.

Why was this dominance he had over me so... *serene?*

"I'd like you to undress for me now," he murmured, taking a step back and shrugging off his jacket. He tossed it aside, the heavy fabric making a thunking sound against the gray marble floor. He seated himself in a large black leather armchair and rolled up his sleeves.

With legs spread wide, one hand resting over the wide arm of the chair and the other resting on his belt buckle, he watched me with rapt attention.

I was about to ask for help unzipping my dress when I realized the zipper was already down near my waist.

When the hell did he do that? Smooth bastard.

My movements were slow and deliberate as I pushed first one sleeve down and then the other, exposing my shoulders and chest. The rise and fall of Monty's chest quickened, which infused me with a confidence I didn't know I could feel in this most vulnerable situation.

"You're beautiful. Keep going," he encouraged, and I rolled the dress down my body as his gaze ate me up. The room was so quiet, I could hear the harshness of the air entering and leaving his flared nostrils.

When I was finally bare down to my fancy black lingerie—a gift from Elle—I stood tall for him, not feeling awkward in the least.

"Do you want these on or off?" My fingers traced over the tiny white pearls edging the panties and bra.

"On." It was only a single word, but it was intense. His eyes flickered to the kneeling pillow in a silent command, and I stepped over to it, hesitating for only a second.

Guess we're doing the damn thing, Ramirez.

I lowered to my knees and immediately felt a kind of energy surround me, wrapping around my body like a cozy blanket.

What am I supposed to do with my hands? My mind flashed back to Dakota Johnson's character in the movie, and I placed my hands on my thighs and dropped my eyes to the floor.

Holding that position, I concentrated on my breathing. In and out. In and out. A few minutes later, a pair of shiny black shoes appeared in my frame of vision, and a hand stroked over the top of my head.

"You are perfect."

With those words, the shoes disappeared, and my lips lifted in a smile. I heard the quiet slide of a drawer, and my body tensed.

"Relax, sweetheart," Monty said from behind me, and I resisted the urge to turn my head to look at him. Gentle fingers and a soft brush ran through my hair, fashioning it into what felt like a messy bun on top of my head.

Then the shoes were back, and his fingers were beneath my chin. "Look at me, pretty girl."

My eyes rose, taking in every inch of him and stalling at the bulge behind his zipper. There seemed to be a *whole lot* of inches in there. Bigger than I remembered.

"Kassie, I need to see your eyes," he urged, and I continued the upward glide of my gaze. He'd removed his shirt, and his hard, cut abs made me pause there to admire them before resting on that exquisite tattoo.

He finally leaned down until we were eye-to-eye, and his next words infused every cell of my body.

"While we're here, I'm in control, Kassie. But don't forget for one second that *you* are the most powerful person in this room."

CHAPTER 42

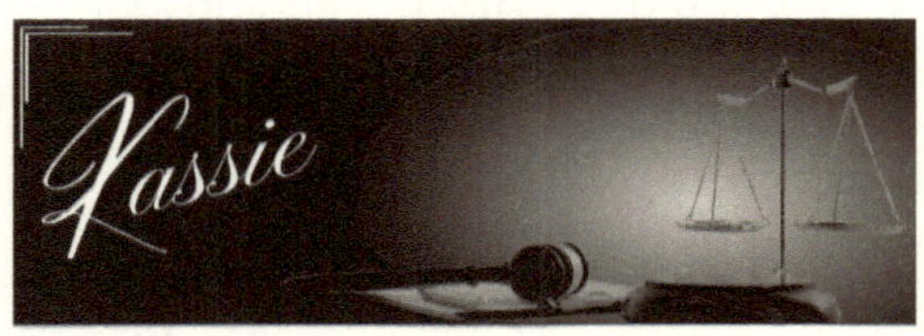

WHEN MONTY PRESSED A soft kiss to my forehead, I felt the power swelling inside me. This must have been what Andrea was talking about that day.

With a barely there touch, his fingers stroked the skin just above the upper line of my strapless bra. "You are exquisite in lace," he murmured, tracing a finger up my chest and around to the back of my head. "And I like your hair up so I can see your neck. So I'll be able to see the flush of pleasure I plan to put there."

A full-body shiver shook me, and Monty laid a comforting hand against my cheek. Once again, I was staring at the floor between his feet until he said, "You don't have to avert your eyes from me, Kassie. I want to see them."

My gaze lifted, and his face mirrored the serenity I was feeling. Like this was what we both needed.

"I apologize for my caveman behavior before. I saw you standing in this club and..." His eyes squished shut, as if in pain, before he opened them again. "I knew I didn't want any man but me to touch you. To feel your soft skin. To make you scream in pleasure. Is that what you want, Kassie?"

Scream in pleasure? Sounds good to me.

Instead of saying that, I asked, "Is it what you want? Sir?"

"More than I want air," he replied, the muscles in his jaw tightening. "However, what I want is irrelevant. I brought you to this room to fuck you into oblivion, but I'll only do that if you're a hundred percent sure that's what you want too. You can say no, and I'll dress you and take you back downstairs."

A million electric currents sizzled across every inch of my skin, and I said the words. "I want it too, Sir."

He swept me off the floor like I weighed nothing, cradling me in his arms as his nose nuzzled mine. "What are your limits?"

Limits... limits... what are my limits? When Monty held me like this, so close to his hot skin, as if I were a treasure, I wanted to shout out that I didn't have any limits when it came to him, but I forced my brain to function rationally.

"No choking," I breathed, and he nodded as he began to move across the floor. Toward the wheel of fortune thingy.

"Noted. No breath play. Are straps okay?" When my eyes widened, he clarified. "Around your wrists and ankles."

The thought of being strapped down and at his mercy had me answering immediately. "Yes, that's fine."

"Anything else I should know? I'll take it easy on you this first time."

"F-first time?" I stuttered, and he flashed me a boyish smile, which softened the hardness of his face.

"Sorry, I'm being a bit presumptuous, aren't I?" He set me on my feet and cradled my face with his large hands. "One time with you will not be enough for me, Kass. I can already tell. Unless you decide otherwise. I may be bossy, but you're the boss. If you say no at any time, I will stop. Are you familiar with the green-yellow-red system?"

I may have never done this before, but I knew what that meant at least. "Yes, Sir."

"Good girl."

Gahhh! Why did those two words make my thighs clench together? Monty brushed his firm lips across my forehead... my nose... my lips. "Is there anything else you need me to know?"

"I-I don't want you to leave marks on me. Like with a whip or anything." The thought of that didn't turn me on in the least.

He shook his head. "I don't want to hurt you like that, Kass. I'm a dominant, not a sadist." His eyes dropped to my breasts, which were swelling from the tops of my bra cups. "I would like to mark you with my mouth though."

"Yes," I whispered, desperate to feel his gorgeous mouth on me. "Just not where they will show. You know... for work." The last thing I needed was hickies all over my neck while I was standing before a judge in the courtroom.

"Of course," he said, backing me against the cool wood behind me. "The real name of this is a St. Andrews Cross. Most are free standing, but this one is attached to a bondage wheel." His lips twitched. "Or as you like to call it, the wheel of fortune."

My face heated in embarrassment, but he didn't notice because he was focused on my right arm. His hands stroked from my shoulder to my hand—taking his sweet time—before fastening a soft cuff around my wrist. Then he did the same thing with the left, his full concentration on his task.

Kneeling down, he parted my legs with gentle hands and attached a strap around my right ankle and then my left. His long fingers were nimble and sure, and I was pretty sure he'd done this before. Numerous times.

Pushing that thought away, I watched him. Watched his eyes take in every inch of my body. Heat infused my skin, and he let out a low groan.

"You look like a dream, Kassie. Do you have any idea how many times I thought of having you like this? At my mercy?"

"M-me?" I stammered, and he met my gaze, looking up from his knees in front of me.

"You," he replied simply. Then he began to touch me.

He started at my feet, his fingers trailing over each arch and up to my ankles. Strong hands cupped my calves which were muscular due to my kickboxing training.

His gaze intently followed his hands, and I'd never felt more exposed in my life. For some reason that I couldn't fathom, I liked it. I liked the way he looked at me and touched me with reverence.

Enormous goosebumps appeared on my thighs when he caressed me there, and he leaned forward to brush his tongue over the pebbled flesh, groaning as his face moved higher.

"I can smell your arousal, baby. I can smell how much you want my face buried in your pussy."

Oh dear god, yes! I almost came on the spot from his words alone.

"Is that what you want, Kassie? Do you want to drown me in your sweetness until my face is covered with you?"

"Yes, Sir," I gasped as his teeth closed around the tendon at the very top of my thigh. His beard brushed the crotch of my panties, and I squirmed against the restraints holding my arms in place. I wanted to rip them from the wall and sink my hands into his thick, dark hair. Hold him to me and force him to eat me until I came.

He bit me again and then sucked until I was sure he'd left a mark. It wasn't brutal. It was... worshipful.

"Monty, please," I begged, thrusting my hips forward as far as I could.

"Let me clean up this mess you made first, sweetheart. You're dripping down your legs." With slow, patient strokes of his tongue, he licked the inside of my thighs, groaning in ecstasy every few seconds.

Every time he got to my panty line, he stopped and lowered his head again to lick up every droplet of my desire. He was very thorough, and it was driving me fucking crazy.

"Please," I whimpered again, and he growled against my hip before twisting one hand in the front of my panties and ripping them from my body.

Tiny pearls scattered and hit the hard floor with little ticking sounds. "Goddammit, Kassie. I can't resist you and your demanding little cunt." His tongue swept through me once. "Is this what you want?"

"Yes," I breathed. "Yes, Sir."

"Fuck me. You taste better than I remember," he muttered, sliding his tongue deep between my pussy lips as his blue eyes met mine and held me captive. "Sweet." *Lick.* "Delicate." *Lick.* "Fucking delicious."

Then he went absolutely feral, devouring me in a way I'd never experienced. Teeth. Tongue. Lips. They all worked together like my very own pleasure-inducing machine.

Pressing his tongue inside me, he fucked me with it as his hands slid up and down my sides. Then he gripped my ass with force, fingers digging into my flesh, throat filled with carnal groans. His attention went a hundred percent to my clit, his teeth scraping me before sucking hard.

Damn, the rose toy ain't got nothing on Monty Bouvier.

"Coming," I squeaked.

His growl was deep and vibrated against me, more intense than any sex toy I'd ever experienced. My body was writhing out of control as the orgasm spread up my torso and down my legs. I jerked my hips forward in tiny pumps to ride out the pleasure.

"Oh my god," I panted. "That was so fucking good."

Monty's big hands spread my thighs impossibly farther apart, and he stuck out his tongue about an inch below my center. "Drip onto my tongue, Kass. Let me feel it."

I didn't know how to do that, but when his hands inched up my body and pulled my bra down, I could feel even more wetness pooling inside me. Then he pinched my nipples, pulling them hard as my desire trickled from my body.

"Mmm," he groaned, twisting my nipples before tugging on them again. Looking down, I could see droplets of... *me* coating his tongue. He pulled it into his mouth and grinned proudly up at me, like I had actually done something special. "Status?" he asked, and it took my foggy brain a second to catch up.

"Green," I announced, and his smile widened.

"Good. You'll come again for me."

"Again? Monty, I don't know…" My protest ended with a squeal when he slowly spun the big wheel until I was upside down.

"Do as I say, Kassie," he snarled, sliding two fingers inside me. "Squeeze this perfect little pussy around me while I finger fuck you and suck your clit. Come for me like the good girl you are."

Sweet Jesus, this man and his filthy mouth…

His hand began moving, his fingers finding my G-spot with ease and curling against it as his tongue fluttered as quick as a hummingbird's wings. The muscles in his thick, tanned arm flexed as he worked me over with hard, rough thrusts, and I probably could have come from that visual alone. Add to that his hot mouth surrounding my clit as he sucked and battered it with the slick velvet of his tongue, and I was a goner. In minutes.

My back ached from arching it so hard as I screamed his name to the room. That climax was somehow stronger than the first, and my legs—which were facing up toward the ceiling—felt like they were made of marshmallows.

My head was slightly below eye level with his crotch, and he palmed the bulge with his free hand as he continued to eat me, more gently now. I wished he would unzip his pants and let me give him even half the pleasure he'd just given me.

When the last tremor had left my body, he pulled his fingers from me and licked them clean, one hand still on his rock-hard dick. Giving me time to adjust, he turned the wheel a few degrees at a time until I was upright again.

"I've never had an upside-down orgasm before," I panted, and he grinned wickedly as he pushed to his feet.

"There's a first time for everything," he retorted, stepping closer until our upper bodies were touching. His skin was on fire, and his smattering of chest hair rubbed against my sensitive nipples. "Lick my lips, Kass."

I hesitated for only a second before leaning forward and lapping at his mouth, tasting myself. It was erotic as hell. He must have thought so too because he gripped the back of my hair and sucked my tongue into his mouth with a harsh groan.

"You're so fucking sexy," he mumbled. "And your pussy tastes even better when I suck it from your tongue."

He kissed me then, and it was hard and bruising, our lips crushing together like we couldn't get enough of each other.

"I need to fuck you, baby. What's your status?"

"Green, Sir."

I'd barely gotten the words out before he bent to unhook my legs from the straps holding them. A few seconds later, his belt was off, and his pants were unfastened, the waistband down around his hips.

My mouth dropped open at the sight of his bare cock in his hand. He squeezed the thick base of it before giving himself three long strokes. *Very* long strokes because the damn thing was enormous.

"I'll go slow," he promised, reading the trepidation in my eyes. "Just like our first time together."

My breath caught in my throat before I remembered how to breathe again. "I think about that night sometimes," I admitted, and then immediately wished I could take the words back.

His eyes filled with emotion as he stepped forward and rested his forehead against mine. "Me too, angel. It was the best night of my life, feeling you surrounding me for the first time."

The sweet, gentle boy I'd known all those years ago was back with me, not the hardened, demanding man he was now. Our eyes locked, and something passed between us. Something old and yet somehow new at the same time.

"I'm ready," I whispered, and he nodded before reaching beneath my butt and lifting me with one arm.

"Wrap your legs around me." I did and felt the smooth tip of him find my entrance. His hips pressed forward and up, taking his time as his thick head entered me.

He stretched long-unused muscles inside me, and it hurt, but I smashed my lips together to hold back my whimper.

"Dear god, you're fucking tight," he grunted, withdrawing and pushing in again. "Kass, look at me."

I hadn't even realized I'd closed my eyes, but I opened them to find his concerned blue gaze intent on my face.

"Am I hurting you?" I swallowed hard and started to shake my head in a lie, but his eyes narrowed and his voice turned hard. "I expect the truth, Kassie."

"A little."

Pulling back about an inch, he circled his hips. "I never want to hurt you, so you have to tell me. Always be honest with me."

"I will," I promised as he worked himself inside me with aching slowness as his free hand thumbed my clit.

A gush of wetness met him, and he smiled, his eyes closing. "There it is. You feel so perfect, sweetheart." Then his lids popped open as he inhaled a sharp breath. "A little too perfect. I'm not wearing protection. Shit, Kass. I'm sorry."

As he started to pull back, I made a snap decision. "I'm on birth control." Monty's eyebrows shot to the ceiling in surprise, and I tightened my legs around his waist. Maybe it was completely fucked up, but I wanted him like this. Raw. "I take the shot every three months, and I'm clean."

"I'm clean too. Are you sure this is what you want?"

I rolled my hips, taking him deeper. "I'm sure."

His hands clasped my ass with bruising strength as a muscle tightened in his square jaw. "How are you so fucking perfect for me?" He withdrew to the tip and thrusted into the hilt. "How do you fit me so well? You're like the lock to my key."

I groaned and threw my head back in bliss as he filled me. Monty was right. He was my key, the only one who could unlock me and set me free. And that's exactly how I felt right now. *Free.*

Lowering his mouth to my neck, he nibbled and licked, drawing my desire to the surface. "Monty... harder."

He growled against my throat as his hips picked up the pace and hammered against mine. His cock was tunneling into me like a freight train, his hardness stretching me with every deep stroke.

Everything felt so, so right except... "Monty, my arms hurt."

Holding me up with one arm, he immediately unhooked my right wrist and then my left, and I wrapped them around his neck, my fingers finding his soft, thick hair. The blood flowing to my limbs made them tingle, or maybe that was my impending orgasm.

"Look at how beautiful you are," he said, his soft voice contradicting the pummeling he was giving me down below. "Your skin is so flushed. You're about to come on my cock aren't you, baby?"

"Y-yes," I stuttered as I clung to him. "Make me come."

"I will, Kass. I want mine to be the only name you can fucking remember when I'm done with you."

Monty pinned me to the wall with his huge body, and he fucked me harder than I ever thought possible. The sound of skin slapping skin was a perfect, erotic cadence as he turned into an animal, sinking his teeth into one nipple and stretching it out as his wet tongue worshiped it.

When he sucked it into his mouth and looked up at me with those mesmerizing blue eyes, I fucking lost it, croaking out his name as the walls of my pussy clamped down on him.

Every inch of me was aware only of him, and I felt his throbbing cock jerk inside me.

"I'm coming. Goddammit, you feel good, Kassie." His voice sounded strangled as he let out a loud moan against the side of my neck.

His warmth filled me, and I pressed my forehead against his broad shoulder as my vision went dark around the edges.

With his large, strong body trembling against mine, my last thought was that I never knew losing control could make me feel so powerful.

CHAPTER 43

MY SWEET KASSIE... THE little liar.

I knew she had never been a submissive from the minute I saw her mouth drop open in shock when we entered the room. But she fucking went for it, and I loved that so damn much about her.

Fuck, I could have easily come on the spot every time her pretty mouth called me Sir. I'd never been more turned on in my life.

I'd gotten rough with her at the end, and she had taken every single bit of what I gave her. After her last orgasm, her body melted against mine, and she leaned her head against my shoulder. Then it was lights out.

Hell, I almost dropped to my knees in exhaustion as well. The woman had wrung me dry.

Now I had her in my arms and was walking us over to the oversized bed that was the focal point of the room. My cock was still buried inside her heat, and I wasn't sure if I ever wanted to let her go.

After shucking my pants and underwear one-handed, I pulled back the buttery-soft dark gray covers and carefully climbed onto the bed. Lying on my back with her on top of me, I removed her bra, covered us with the sheet, and stroked her back as she nuzzled her cute little nose against the side of my neck.

"Mon-ty," she yawned, and I kissed the top of her head.

"I'm here, baby. Just rest."

"Yes, Sir."

Goddamn. My dick grew about two inches at those sleepily delivered words. *Calm down you idiot.*

I closed my eyes and concentrated on Kassie's breathing, the deep, even movements of her back beneath my hands, and I drifted off myself.

My internal clock told me I'd been asleep for about thirty minutes when I became aware of someone watching me. Peeling my lids open, I found a pair of brown eyes and a shy smile.

"Hi," Kassie said.

"Hey. You okay?" I traced a line down her forehead and over the swoop of her nose.

"I'm okay." She stacked her hands on my chest and rested her chin there, regarding me.

"What's on your mind, baby?"

"You've changed."

I pulled my bottom lip between my teeth and nodded, feeling a bit vulnerable at her observation. "I have. Are you disappointed in me?"

Her lips parted in surprise, and she pushed herself forward, letting my dick slip from her warm body. "No, Monty. I'm not disappointed at all. I'm just trying to understand what changed you."

She trailed her fingers in a wide, gentle arc from my forehead to my jaw before kissing me with the utmost tenderness. It had been a long time since anyone had touched me with such... care, and I leaned my face into the sweet touch, knowing she needed an explanation.

I closed my eyes and let the words spill from me. "All those years ago, I lost almost everything important to me within weeks. I moved to Florida at eighteen and was pretty much alone, but I liked it that way. Or at least I thought I did."

Kassie's hand brushed through the hair over my ear, silently encouraging me to continue, so I did. "I struggled with any kind of intimacy because all I wanted was what I couldn't have. At the same time, I had the normal hormones of a young man and no outlet for them. I was overly aggressive and got into a lot of fights. When I started working a couple years later, a fellow officer who was a bit older than me recognized my struggles and invited me to a club similar to this one."

I opened my eyes and found Kassie's filled understanding. "I found an outlet and a purpose at the same time. The club was big on education, so I went to every seminar they offered on the lifestyle. I learned that a huge part of being a Dom is being responsible for another person, giving them what they need, which in turn, gives you what you need."

Kass laid her cheek back on my shoulder. "Thank you for telling me. So you found this club in New York and came here for an... outlet tonight?" I could hear the hurt in her voice that she was trying to hide from me.

"No, I came here with a friend."

Her head jerked up, eyes becoming mere slits. "Oh really? Is your *friend* waiting outside the door for her turn?"

Ah! She's jealous. That made me pretty fucking happy. "I came with a *male friend*, Kass."

Her look turned to one of confusion. "I guess I didn't realize you were into that."

"Into wh—" I shook my head and laughed. "No, baby. I'm not into guys. I'm only here for moral support for a friend. I didn't come here to get laid." I pressed a hard, firm kiss on her lips, deciding to be completely honest with her. "I haven't thought of any woman besides the one currently on top of me since I've been in New York."

Her face relaxed, and her swollen lips curled up at the corners. "Sorry I jumped to conclusions."

"It's okay. Though you shouldn't judge me when you came here looking for a Dom." I effectively hid the smirk trying to creep over my lips.

Her mouth dropped into an O before she averted her eyes. "That's not why I came here. I've... I've actually never done anything like this before." She waved her hand vaguely, and I captured it, pressing a kiss to her wrist.

"I know, Little Miss Wheel of Fortune," I said, finally letting myself smile.

She giggled. "Okay, I'll admit I kinda liked the wheel."

"I could tell," I teased, and my curiosity got the best of me. "What were you doing here tonight?"

"You know Elle? The woman I was with in the store?"

"I was aware there was another woman nearby, but I didn't notice anyone else but you."

Kassie's face flushed with the compliment. "Well, Elle, the owner of the, um, toy shop, is my sister."

"Your sister?" I asked, not understanding. She only had two sisters that I knew of, and they were both—

"Elle is Luciana."

My brain almost exploded. "What the fuck? Little Luci-Loo owns a sex shop?"

Kass laughed. "Little Luci-Loo is twenty-four and married to the owner of this club, Bennett Laird. He's very protective of her and doesn't want anyone to know her real name. So she's Elle when she's here, kind of a derivative of her first initial."

I flopped back against the pillow with my arm over my eyes and groaned, "I can't deal with this. Next you'll be telling me Regina is a dominatrix."

Kassie's laughter shook her entire body. "No, Regi is a kindergarten teacher."

"Thank fuck," I muttered, pulling my arm from my face and rolling us to the side so we were facing each other. My fingers played across her cheek. "Do you have to get home to your son?"

She shook her head. "No, he's staying the night with Lily."

I smiled at that. "Your friend from high school?"

"Yes, we went to our last two years of college together and then went to the same law school. We both work at the same firm now, but she's a family lawyer. She actually handled the adoption for Gianna and Auburn."

"I love that you're still in touch with her. I always liked Lily."

Kass turned her face and kissed my palm. "She's been an awesome friend. Her son is the same age as Sully, and they're attached at the hip."

"Stay the night here with me."

Her hesitation was like a knife to the heart. "Monty, I'm not sure if that's a good idea."

I twisted a tiny piece of her hair around my index finger, my eyes locked on that movement. "Is it because you're still in love with your ex?" I asked quietly, and her face instantly closed off.

"No, I'm not in love with Wesley."

Finally meeting her eyes, I asked, "Then why won't you stay with me?" My voice sounded raw and vulnerable, and I didn't like that. Vulnerability was a foreign concept to me.

Kass nestled against my bicep beneath her head. "Because I don't want to get too attached to you." I could see the pure honesty in her eyes. "You're going to leave to go back to Florida, and—" She stalled, closing her eyes and pinching her lips together.

"What if I told you I'm moving here?"

Her eyes popped open. "You're moving to New York? What about your job?"

Fuck, here we go.

Though it pained me to do so, I told her the story behind my firing, fully expecting her to judge me harshly. But she didn't. Instead, she went into outraged lawyer mode.

"That is absolutely ridiculous," she fumed, leaning up on one elbow. "They can't fire you for something you did outside of work that wasn't even illegal."

"Well, they did," I grumbled.

"We'll appeal it," she declared, her mind whirling. "I'm not licensed in Florida, but there are ways around that. I can—"

"Kasserole," I said, taking her chin between my fingers, "it's okay. I don't want to go back. I want to stay here."

The scowl lines on her forehead smoothed out. "You do?"

I nodded. "I do. Cruz set up an interview for me with the police department in a few weeks. It's time I came home. I want to be closer to my family." I paused before adding, "And to you."

Her brown eyes searched my face. "You want to be closer to me?"

"More than anything. I know we'll have to go slow and get to know each other again, but I can't even imagine letting you go," I told her with brutal honesty.

She pushed out a shaky breath. "Whew, I'm not sure how to feel about that."

"Do you hate the idea of me being back here?"

Her head shook slightly. "No, I don't hate the idea."

"Then tell me what you're comfortable with." I glanced around the room. "If all this was too much for you, I can just... take you to a movie or something." I was floundering a bit. I didn't really date.

"I don't really date," she said, echoing my previous thought. Kass's cheeks flushed a rosy red. "It wasn't too much for me. Tonight, I mean. It was something I didn't know I needed." She smiled shyly up at me. "Can we maybe come here again?"

My heart soared and sank at the same time. She didn't want to date me, but she wanted to fuck me.

Turning my tone to a teasing one, I said, "So you just want to use my body for sexual purposes? I'll have to think about whether or not I want to be your own personal fuck boy. Okay, yes."

She laughed at my immediate response. "I'm glad you thought long and hard about it."

"Speaking of long and hard..." I pressed my erection firmly against her belly, and her eyes caught fire.

"Again?"

"If you can take more."

Her bottom lip dented around the bite of her teeth. "I can take it."

Fuck me. She's so goddamn hot.

"Before we start, when can I see you again?" An anxiousness burned deep inside me at the thought of being apart from her for any length of time, which confused me. I was a self-imposed loner, but if she said she wanted to see me again tomorrow, I would jump at the chance.

She tilted her head in thought. "I'm wrapping up a case this week. It should be done on Thursday. I'm always antsy after I finish one, so maybe coming here would, I don't know... calm me?"

"Thursday it is. I'll take care of you, Kass. And you'll stay here with me tonight? Because I want to fill you up. I want you to sleep with my cum inside you all night long." I wedged my knee between her legs and could feel her growing wet with arousal.

"Yes, I'll stay with you."

Those five words were music to my fucking ears.

Chapter 44

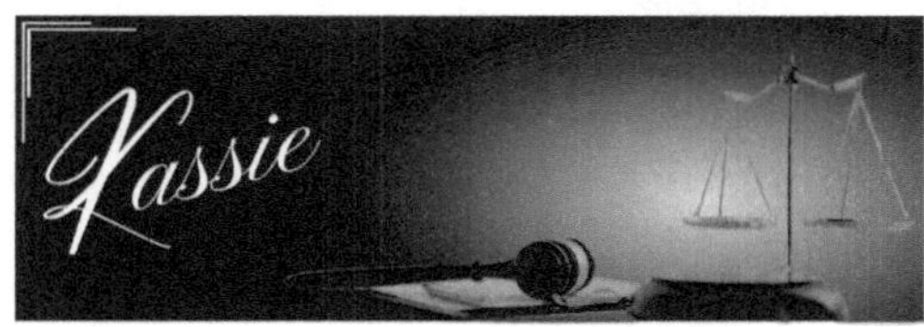

On Wednesday, four days after my marathon sex night with Monty, it hurt to pee.

"Where are you going?" Andrea asked as I walked by her desk.

"Bathroom."

"This is the third time you've been on your lunch hour," she said to my back, and I paused with my hand on the doorknob.

Turning back and walking to her desk, I lowered my voice. "It hurts when I pee. And only a little bit dribbles out, despite me feeling like I could flood the room with urine."

Her eyebrows pushed together and then shot upward. "You had sex!" she practically shouted.

"Shhh, shut the hell up," I hissed, waving my palm at her.

"You did! You got nailed, and now you have a UTI. Did you pee afterward?"

Rolling my eyes, I admitted, "I did after the third time, but not the first, second, or fourth."

"Christ, who did you fuck? The Energizer Bunny?"

"Something like that," I muttered, shifting at the discomfort low in my belly. "You really think I have a urinary tract infection?"

"I'd bet money on it. You need to get to a doctor ASAP."

"I can't today. I'm due back in court in twenty minutes."

"Kassie..."

"No arguments, Andrea. This case is almost done, and I don't want to ask for another continuance. The prosecutor has gotten two already, and my client doesn't deserve to be hanging out in the wind for god knows how much longer until we can get another court date."

I marched down to the restroom and managed to expel about a half a drop of pee—and an alarming amount of blood—before heading back to the courthouse.

After a fitful night's sleep, I got up the next morning and drank two glasses of cranberry juice before getting dressed for my final day of work for the week. I was in constant pain, and I was pretty sure I had a fever.

"Your face feels hot, Mommy," Sully said when he kissed my cheek outside his school.

Forcing a smile I didn't feel, I said, "Yep, the weather's getting warmer, huh?"

"I guess," he said, probably confused because I'd made him wear a jacket due to the coolness of the day. "Love you, Mom."

"Love you too, baby. Have a good day. I'll pick you up from Boys and Girls Club this afternoon," I told him as he climbed out of the car.

If I'm still alive.

I managed to make it through the end of the trial on Thursday and walked out of the courtroom with yet another win under my belt. Actually, it was more of a limp because I felt like absolute dog crap.

As soon as I entered my office in the early afternoon, Andrea stood and took my elbow, turning me back toward the door.

"What are you doing?"

"Taking you to the doctor. I already called them, and she's expecting you." She snatched her purse from the desk and waved her hand at a huge bouquet of red roses sitting there. "Oh, you got a delivery. Your name was on the envelope, but there was no card inside. I checked."

"Of course you did," I muttered. "Nosy ass."

"Good grief, woman," Doctor Lee said, entering the examination room. "Do you have any idea how much blood is in your urine sample?"

"A lot, I'm assuming," I told her wearily.

"A whole lot. Any idea what brought this on? Are you drinking enough water?"

"I drink tons of water, but... well, I had sex Saturday night. Multiple times."

"You go, girl. Did you urinate directly after each time?"

"No," I muttered, and her face turned stern.

"You know better than that, Kassie. Or maybe you've forgotten since your vagina has been on hiatus for years."

"Thanks for pointing that out," I said sarcastically. Janet Lee had been my doctor since before Sully was born, and we had an excellent rapport. She was honest to a fault and had a wicked sense of humor that made her seem more like a friend than my OB/GYN.

"You know I'm teasing. I'm happy you've brought the old girl out of retirement. Someone special?" She held the flat end of the stethoscope against my chest and closed her eyes as she listened.

"Maybe. I want him to be. I think."

"Well that clears that up," she said, moving the stethoscope around to my back.

"You know I'm leery of getting involved with anyone."

Her smile was sympathetic but not patronizing as she pulled the ear-pieces from her ears. "I understand. You've been through a lot. But you can't let the past color your present. Or your future."

"He's someone I knew a long time ago. He's recently moved back to town, and he seems to want to reconnect."

"Okay," she said easily. "Do I need to run an STD panel?"

Oh yikes! I didn't even think of that.

"I, uh, I don't know. We didn't use condoms, but he said he was clean."

"And do you trust what he said?"

I thought about it for a split second before answering. "I do trust him. He would never purposely hurt me."

Doctor Lee's thin lips formed a smile. "That's good, Kassie, but we'll do some blood work just to be on the safe side."

Her fingers flew over the keyboard of the small laptop on the counter as her eyes scanned the vitals the nurse had taken. "Dammit, your fever is one-oh-four. I'm tempted to put your little butt in the hospital."

"Please don't," I begged, and her eyebrows narrowed in consternation.

"Okay, fine, but I'm putting you on two different antibiotics, and I want you to increase your water intake *and* drink at least sixteen ounces of cranberry juice per day until you're all cleared up. You'll start to feel better by tomorrow, but make sure to take all the antibiotics, even if you're feeling fine."

"I promise."

"I'll call to check on you tomorrow, and if you're not feeling better, I'm admitting you to the hospital." She pursed her lips. "And don't even *think* about going to work until at least Monday."

I shook my head. "I'm off tomorrow anyway. I just finished up a case today."

"Good girl," she said, and I felt myself blush. Would I ever be able to hear those two words without thinking of Monty?

I could barely stand upright by the time Andrea helped me into my apartment and led me to my bedroom.

"You get undressed, and I'll bring you your medicine and some cranberry juice."

"I need to get—"

"Sully, I know. I'll pick him up and drop him off here." She tilted her head as I sat on my bed and unbuttoned my suit jacket. "Unless you want me to take him to your mom's. I would keep him, but I have two classes to teach tonight."

"He'll be fine here. He's good at self-entertaining."

"You sure?"

I nodded, but it made me dizzy, so I croaked out, "Yes."

After Andrea medicated and hydrated me, I fell into a deep sleep, waking when I heard my friend's whispered conversation with my son.

"But what's wrong with Mommy?"

"She's got a tummy ache. She'll be okay, but she has to rest, so you need to play very quietly, all right?"

"Can I sit in here and play with my trucks so I can keep an eye on her?"

A hot tear slipped down my cheek. My baby was the sweetest little boy in the world. With some effort, I pushed up on one elbow and dashed the wetness away.

"Hey, Sul."

"Mommy!" He ran and climbed up on the bed, throwing his arms around my neck. "I'm sorry you're sick."

"I'm okay, baby. Why don't you get your cars and come play in here. I probably need someone to keep an eye on me."

He nodded solemnly. "Okey doke, and I can help you to the bathroom if you need to throw up."

I brushed a hand over his sandy-brown hair. "Thank you, my lovey."

He kissed my forehead like the sweet little man he was and ran off to his room.

"You're raising the best kid in the world," Andrea said, leaning against one carved post of my four-poster bed. "Are you sure you don't want me to take him to your mom's?"

Collapsing onto my side, I said, "No, I want him to stay with me."

"All right. I'll come check on you after my last class to make sure you don't forget to take your bedtime dose."

"I am a grown woman, you know."

"And you're also sicker than I've ever seen you, so shut the fuck up and accept help when it's offered."

"I love you, bitch."

"Love you too, ya little cum bucket."

I couldn't help but chuckle at that.

When she was gone and Sully was sitting beside me making quiet little *reeeer reeeer* car noises, I sent a text to Monty, letting him know I couldn't meet him tonight.

Then I drifted off to sleep, only waking when I felt something on my arm. I opened my eyes to see Sully driving a dark-blue 1965 Mustang up and down my bicep.

"Hi, Mommy. I'm hungry."

A glance at the window told me it was dark outside and probably way past my kid's dinner time. "Sorry, honey. I didn't mean to sleep that long. What do you want?"

"Fancy mac n' cheese."

"I think I can handle that," I said, sitting up and trying to get my bearings.

"Why is your hair all wet?"

I ran a hand through it, and it was indeed damp at the roots, and my face was covered with a thin sheen of sweat. Probably a product of my fever.

"Just a little sweaty," I told him, making my way to the en suite bathroom. I almost screamed when I saw my reflection in the mirror. I looked like death warmed over, so I pulled my hair back in a haphazard ponytail to get it off my neck.

"Great. Now I look like death warmed over with a shitty ponytail," I told the ghoul staring back at me with red-rimmed eyes and rosy cheeks.

My body was racked with a sudden case of the shivers, and I grabbed my dark-red fuzzy bathrobe off the back of the door and tied it over the T-shirt I'd slipped on earlier.

"I'll draw you a picture while you're making dinner," my son said, dashing to his room. Oh, if I could only have an ounce of his energy on a daily basis.

Holding onto the wall, I made my way down the hallway toward the kitchen, but I halted when there was a knock at my front door.

Probably Andrea coming to check on me. She had a key in case of emergencies, so I had no idea why she would knock.

Rerouting, I paused by the couch when a wave of dizziness overtook me, and I blew out a stream of air.

You can do it, Kassie. Just a few more feet.

After that mini pep talk, I lugged myself to the door and opened it to... *not Andrea.*

What the actual fuck?

CHAPTER 45

I STARED AT THE phone in my hand as my annoyance rose. Kassie had texted me a couple hours ago, but then ignored every return message I'd sent.

> **Kassie: I'm sorry, but I'm not going to be able to meet you tonight.**

> Monty: Why, baby? What's going on?

> Monty: Kassie?

> Monty: Hellooooo?

> Monty: Would you please just answer me?

I was a little pissed that she'd canceled on me and wouldn't even tell me why. I was also worried as hell that she'd changed her mind about us.

Stuffing the phone back in my pocket, I knocked on the door to her apartment. If she was going to dump me, she was going to do it to my face.

As soon as the door swung open, every bit of frustration fled my body, only to be replaced by panic.

"Monty?" Her voice was weak and scratchy, but that was the least of my worries. She was drenched in sweat and seemed to be shivering at the same time.

"You're sick."

"Thanks for the update," she said, her eyelids drooping low over blood-shot eyes. She swayed precariously, and I grabbed her around the waist.

"Whoa, sweetheart. I got you." Sweeping her into my arms, I kicked the door shut behind me and carried her over to the large blue plaid couch. When I settled her onto my lap and kissed her damp forehead, her skin practically scorched my lips. My level of panic shot through the roof. "You're burning up, Kasserole. I need to get you to the emergency room."

She shook her head and leaned against my shoulder. "I just got back from the doctor."

"What did they say? Do you have the flu or something?"

Breathing out a weary sigh, she said, "I have a urinary tract infection. Can happen when women don't pee after sex." She tried a weak smile, but it fell way short.

It hit me. *This is all my fault.*

"What's the treatment? Antibiotics or something? Should you be in the hospital?"

"M'okay. I have medicine." She tried to wet her dry lips with her tongue, but it didn't seem to have much moisture either.

"Let me get you something to drink," I told her, moving her onto the couch when I stood. She curled onto her side with her hands wrapped around her middle, and I wished like hell I could take her pain away.

Kassie's kitchen was adorable, designed like a 1950s diner, complete with ceramic salt and pepper shakers shaped like vintage cars. I crossed the black-and-white tiled floors and pulled open the refrigerator. The door looked like an old-fashioned fridge, but the inside was modern with clear shelves and drawers.

My eyes fell on a bottle of cranberry juice on the bottom shelf, and I pulled it out. I knew that was supposed to be good for urinary infections. I was also aware that women were supposed to urinate after sex, but I'd completely forgotten that fact while I was with Kass.

That will never fucking happen again, I promised myself.

"Who are you?"

I almost dropped the bottle in my hand, but I recovered quickly and looked down to find a little boy standing near the bar with a scowl on his face. He was Kassie's mini-me, except his hair was a few shades lighter.

Setting down the bottle of juice, I squatted so I wouldn't look so intimidating. "I'm your mom's friend. I was getting her some juice."

"She's s'posed to drink the berry juice. I heard Andi say that."

"Who's Andy?" I asked, my jealousy rising like a phoenix from the ashes.

"She works at Mommy's office."

She. I pushed the jealousy back down, feeling a bit like an idiot. "That's cool. My name is Monty Bouvier. You must be Sullivan."

"I go by Sully. Unless Mommy gets mad, and then I'm Sullivan Lucas Ramirez." I held back my laughter as he said his full name with a sharp voice that I could imagine his mother using.

"Nice to meet you, Sully. What do you have there?" I nodded at the white sheet of paper in his hand.

"I was drawing Mommy a picture cuz she's sick, but I'm not a very good drawer." He frowned down at his work. "She looks like a mouse."

He turned it around, and I nodded at the droplet-shaped body and pointed head. "A little bit. You could add some round ears and a tail and call it Mommy Mouse. She'd probably think that was cute."

His eyes brightened. "Yeah, that would be awesome. I still wanted to draw a real picture of her though."

"Let me get your mom comfortable, and then I'll help you."

"You know how to draw?" he asked skeptically, and I nodded.

"I'm not bad."

"Okay. Do you like to draw with crayons or colored pencils?"

"Whatever you like, kid." I wasn't about to tell him the last sketching pencil I'd bought cost over seventy dollars.

Sully's little head tilted to the side. "What did you say your last name was?"

"Bouvier."

He jumped up and down a couple times. "Oh my gosh! Do you know Jaxon and Jane?"

"I'm their uncle," I said. "How do you know them?"

"I met them in the park one day. Their mom and dad talked to my mom while we played. Jane can go really fast in her wheelchair, but her mom always tells her to slow down."

"That sounds about right," I chuckled, pushing to my feet.

"Whoa, you're really tall," Sully said, tilting his neck back to look up at me.

"Because I eat a lot."

He glanced around the kitchen, looking for something. "Do you know if my mom cooked my dinner yet? She said she was going to." His look turned wistful. "I didn't want to wake her up, but I had grumblies in my tummy."

"We can't have that. I'll take care of it," I said, ruffling his hair. As I poured a glass of cranberry juice, I asked, "What was your mom making for dinner?"

"Fancy mac n' cheese."

Great. Some gourmet shit that I'd probably fuck up.

"No problem. Why don't you go get your drawing stuff, and I'll get your mom back in bed."

The kid's chin trembled a bit. "Is she gonna be okay? My mommy never gets sick."

Squatting back down to his level, I looked him in the eye and made a promise. "She'll be all right, bud. I'll take good care of her." I held up my hand, and he smacked it.

"Okay, thanks, Monty." He took off out of the kitchen like a shot. Pulling my phone from my pocket, I quickly Googled UTIs, and then I made two phone calls before heading back to the living room with the cranberry juice.

Kassie was curled up into a ball on the couch. Her hair was awry, and the color was high in her cheeks, but she still took my breath away with her raw beauty.

I sat down and pulled her into my lap before gently patting her cheek. "Can you wake up and drink some juice, Kass?"

She peeled her eyes open and blinked a few times. "How did you get here?" she slurred.

"I walked," I told her, picking up the clear glass and holding it to her lips. "Drink for me."

Taking a sip, she scrunched her nose. "I really don't like cranberry juice very much."

"I don't either," I admitted, "but it's good for you."

Once she'd managed to drink the entire glass, she looked around the room, and I could see the panic rising in her eyes. "Sully."

"He's fine. He's drawing you a picture."

"I need to feed him dinner," she said, attempting to get out of my lap.

"I'm handling it. Would you just relax?"

Her body sunk against mine even as she said, "I can do it."

I leaned my cheek against the top of her head. "I have no doubt you can, Superwoman, but I'd like you to rest now."

"I'm so tired," she whispered, and I tightened my arms around her.

"Then sleep, angel."

I held her in silence as she napped against my shoulder until Sully appeared beside the couch. He set down the paper and pencils on the coffee table, and his eyes shifted back and forth between Kassie and me a few times before he climbed up and kneeled beside us.

Taking his mom's hand, he laid a soft kiss on the back of it, and my heart almost burst at the sweetness of it.

"Go put your stuff on the table in the kitchen, and I'll put your mom in bed," I whispered, and he nodded.

I stood and held Kassie's overheated body against me as I carried her down the hallway. Peeking in one door, I found what was obviously Sully's room before continuing to the room at the end of the hall.

Looking around, I felt Kassie's presence in this room, from the feminine, pale pink sheets on the four-poster bed to the photos of her son on every flat surface. I managed to get her robe off without waking her and then placed her gently beneath the covers.

After brushing my lips across her temple, I reluctantly left the room and went back to the kitchen to find Sully spreading out his paper and colored pencils.

"I don't know how to draw faces very good," he informed me.

"Do you know your shapes?"

He nodded. "Uh-huh. I'm in kindygarten."

Selecting a black pencil, I drew two shapes on a blank sheet. "Does your mom's face look more like an oval or a circle?" I asked, pointing at each.

"Oval?" He glanced up at me for reassurance.

"Exactly right," I told him. "Let me see you draw one." He did, and it was surprisingly well-shaped and even. "Really good job, Sully. Now I'll show you an easy way to do eyes."

A few minutes later, he was happily coloring in his sketch while I rummaged through the refrigerator. I found a package of American cheese slices, a bag of shredded cheddar, and a pack of Swiss from the deli.

"Uh, Sully. Do you know what kind of cheese your mom uses in the fancy mac n' cheese?"

"She uses the sprinkly kind."

What the fuck is the sprinkly kind?

"Do you think you could show me?"

He stood and walked over to me, taking my index finger in his fist. "It's not in there, Monty. It's over here," he said like I was some kind of cheese doofus.

Leading me to the pantry, he opened the door and pointed at a familiar blue box. "The sprinkly cheese is in there. Then you just add the fancy sauce after you cook the noodles."

"Ah, gotcha," I said, pulling the box of Kraft from the shelf. "Do you know what's in the fancy sauce?"

He stood on his tiptoes and tried to reach a shelf above his head, so I picked him up and propped him on my hip. "This is it," he informed me, grabbing a small can of tomato sauce. "It's super good."

Boxed mac and cheese with tomato sauce. I could handle that.

"We probably need to eat a vegetable too. You can pick."

"Corn," he announced immediately, and I snagged a can from the perfectly arranged shelf.

Twenty minutes later, his picture was complete, and we were feasting on the simple—but surprisingly good—meal.

"That was really delish," Sully announced, wiping his mouth with a napkin. "You make better corn than my mom, but don't tell her I said that."

I mimed zipping my lips, and the kid laughed. He was really fucking cute.

"You did a great job on your picture. Do you want to hang it on the refrigerator so she can see it in the morning?"

"Okay," he agreed, taking his plate and fork and placing them in the sink. Kass was raising an amazing kid.

After he put the picture on the fridge with a magnet, I announced that he needed to get ready for bed. He groaned, but otherwise didn't complain.

Once he was fast asleep, I closed his bedroom door and headed back toward the front of the apartment, stalling when I heard a key in the front door.

A woman with cropped, light-blue hair stepped through and then halted when she saw me, her eyes growing round. "Who the fuck are you?" she asked, propping her hands on her hips.

"I'm Monty. Who the fuck are you?"

"I'm Andrea, Kassie's paralegal and friend. Why are you here?" Her tone was wary and demanding.

"I... Kassie's not feeling well."

"I know that. I was coming over to check on her and Sully."

"They're both sleeping."

She marched past me and peeked into each bedroom before walking back into the living room where I was waiting.

"They're asleep," she announced, and my lips twitched.

"That's what I said."

"I was just checking," she replied, her eyes narrowing. "You never told me why you're here."

"I came over to check on Kassie, and she could barely stand up, so I put her to bed."

Her face softened into concern. "I've been so worried about her, but I had classes to teach tonight. Was Sul okay?"

"Yeah, I fed him and got him ready for bed."

"*You* fed him and got him ready for bed?"

"Yes, Andrea. I am semi-domesticated."

She snorted out a laugh. "Good for you. Guess you're more than just an Energizer Bunny." *What the fuck does that mean?* "Did he have a bath? Brush his teeth?"

Tucking my hands in my pockets, I said, "Yes to both. He said he could bathe himself, so I waited outside the door to make sure he didn't drown or something. And I supervised the brushing of the teeth."

"He's such a little man," she said fondly. "I'm convinced he's going to move into his own apartment by the time he's ten."

"He's an awesome kid. What kind of classes do you teach?"

"Kickboxing and general self-defense for women."

I smiled at her. "That's excellent. I wish every woman could take self-defense."

Her return smile was tentative. "Agreed. Do you know if Kassie took her antibiotics before she went to sleep?"

"No, she's been out for a few hours. Where are they, and I'll make sure she takes them?"

She eyed me for a long moment. "I put them in her bathroom. The directions are on the bottles. How long are you planning on staying here?"

"Until she's not sick any more," I said firmly.

"You care about her." It wasn't a question.

Dipping my chin, I stared at the floor before looking back up at Andrea. "More than she knows."

"What's all this?" she asked, pointing at the sturdy oak coffee table.

"I had a couple things delivered. For Kassie."

She opened the deli bag and sniffed. "Chicken noodle soup?"

"I wanted her to have something to eat if she woke up."

"What's in the brown package?"

"A heating pad. I read that it can help with symptoms."

Andrea's grin widened across her face. "You might be all right in my book, Bouvier." Then she lifted one eyebrow at me and said, "Just don't hurt her, or I'll jack you up."

I huffed out a laugh. "Noted."

CHAPTER 46

I AWOKE TO A delicious warmth around my middle and reached down to find a fuzzy heating pad wrapped from my belly around to my back. It was heavy, and I realized it was one of those weighted ones.

Pushing it off, I followed the cord with my hand and turned off the remote. Where the hell did this come from? I didn't have one of these.

I smiled as I sat up slowly. Andrea must have brought it while I was asleep. With my back slightly stooped, I made my way to the bathroom. Urinating was slightly less painful than it had been the past couple days, and I sent a silent thanks to Dr. Lee for doubling my antibiotics.

As I stood, a hazy image flashed through my head, one of Monty holding me in his lap. On my couch. Did that really happen?

Making my way out into the hallway, I pushed open the door to Sully's room and saw his small form curled on his bed with the Spider-Man bed covers tucked beneath his armpit. Someone—again, I assumed Andrea—had even turned on his Batman nightlight, the Bat Signal cast on the ceiling with a warm glow.

I bent to kiss him, and he smelled squeaky clean, like the fruity soap and shampoo he used in his bath.

Hearing noises from the kitchen, I made my way there, and my mouth dropped open at the sight. Monty Bouvier was standing at my sink, washing dishes. I blinked a few times, but the image didn't change.

Sensing my presence, he turned and graced me with that adorable smile of his while wiping his hands on a dish towel.

"There she is. I was just about to come wake you to take your medicine."

My mouth was agape. I hadn't dreamed his presence after all. He was really here. Still unable to form any coherent words, I stared at him as he crossed to me and kissed my forehead.

"Hmmm, your fever seems a little better. How are you feeling?"

Before I could answer, he popped a thermometer in my mouth, pulling it out when it beeped so he could check the display. "A hundred and two. A little better. Are you hungry? I have some soup I could warm up for you."

My growling stomach informed me that was a good idea, and I nodded. "I could eat a little bit."

"Good." Monty lifted me by the waist and set me on one of the vinyl bar stools before placing a tray in front of me. It held a small saucer with four pills and a glass of water. "These two are your antibiotics, and the other ones are Tylenol for your pain and fever," he said, pointing them out before turning back toward the refrigerator. I watched him intently as he took out a container of soup and poured the contents into a saucepan on the stovetop. Then he wrapped a biscuit in a paper towel and popped it into the microwave.

He was wearing fitted jeans and a white, long-sleeved T-shirt and looked so damned at home in my kitchen. I wasn't sure how to feel about that.

"Monty, why are you here?"

Glancing over his shoulder as he stirred, he simply said, "Just helping out a bit." Then he turned back to his task. "Take your meds, babe."

With shaky fingers, I picked up two of the pills and swallowed them with a drink of water before taking the other two. The water was cool against my parched tongue, and I drained the rest of it before standing to get a refill.

"Ah, ah. Sit, please." Monty was on me in a second, herding me back to my seat as he took the glass from me.

"I can get my own water," I complained as he filled my glass from the jug of filtered water in the fridge.

"I know you can, but I want to do it for you. How are you feeling?"

"Semi-human. Did Andrea come over?"

"She did. She's nice."

I scoffed. "Maybe you met the wrong Andrea. The one I know called me a cum bucket."

Monty laughed and pulled a bowl from the cabinet before dishing up some of the delicious-smelling soup. "Nope, that's definitely the same one."

"How do you know where the bowls are?"

"I saw them earlier when I was looking for dinner plates."

I blinked up at him when he sat the soup in front of me, along with the biscuit on a saucer. "Why were you looking for dinner plates?"

He brushed a stray strand of hair behind my ear. "I assumed you didn't make your son eat from a bowl on the floor like a puppy, so I put his dinner on an actual plate. I'm cool like that."

"Such a smartass. Andrea must've rubbed off on you," I grumbled. "You fed my son dinner?"

He took the saucer that had held the pills and rinsed it off in the sink before putting it in the dishwasher. "Yep. Fancy mac n' cheese. Also made a can of corn because I figured he needed a veggie."

I flushed in embarrassment as I stirred the soup in my bowl. "I know it's not the most nutritious meal. I usually feed him better than that. It's one of those *Mommy's had a long day and is phoning it in tonight* kind of things."

"If you think I'm judging you, stop it. Sully loved it. Said it was his favorite food." Monty crossed the room and stood behind my chair, massaging my shoulders. "He's an awesome kid with an awesome mom." Pressing a kiss to the side of my neck, he whispered, "Eat, please, or I'll feed you myself."

My body and mind relaxed as his thumbs found a sore spot I hadn't even known was there, and I scooped up a huge bite of soup. The broth had just the right amount of salt, and the chicken was juicy and savory.

"Mmm, this is delicious."

"It's from the deli around the corner. I had it delivered, as well as the heating pad. Did that seem to help?"

I turned my head slowly to look up at him. *What the actual hell is happening right now?* "You ordered me a heating pad?"

"It's supposed to help."

My heart fluttered in my chest as my feelings for this incredible man grew by leaps and bounds. He'd come over without me asking and taken care of me and my son, who he didn't even know.

"You didn't have to do all this, but thank you," I said, lifting my hand and stroking his soft hair.

Monty pressed a series of soft kisses against my lips. "I'm not very good at talking about my feelings. I'm better at *showing* you how I feel about you."

"And how is that?" I asked, my heart beating a quick staccato in my chest.

He ran his tongue over his bottom lip. "I don't know, to be honest." His eyes searched mine. "All I know is that I think about you all the time, and when I found you sick..." He swallowed hard. "It physically hurt me."

"That's fair enough," I said, kissing his chin. "We don't have to define anything."

His grin turned wicked. "You're definitely more than my cum bucket though."

A giggle escaped my mouth, and I shook my head, turning back to my soup. "You're certainly a smooth talker, Monty Bouvier. Those are the words every woman wants to hear."

After I was done eating, Monty insisted—despite my protests—on putting away the leftovers and the dishes. Then he led me down the hall with an arm wrapped tightly around my waist.

"Back to bed, Miss Ramirez," he commanded, straightening my messy sheets.

"Yes, Sir," I said, giving him a little salute.

His chest rumbled as he leveled me with a glare. "Could you not use that word while you're out of commission?"

I stifled a grin. "Yes, boss."

"Not much better," he complained, stripping off his shirt.

As always, I was in awe of his perfectly toned body, and I gaped at him like a dummy for a second before finally saying, "What are you doing?"

"Getting ready for bed." He paused with his hands on his belt buckle. "Unless you want me to sleep on the couch. I don't want to make you uncomfortable."

"No, you can sleep here," I told him. There was no way I was making him sleep on the couch after all the kindness he'd shown me tonight. "We're both adults here."

His eyes dropped to my bare legs, and I became aware that I'd been walking around only in a T-shirt and panties. "We are. And you don't have to worry about me. I'll be a good boy."

"There's a first time for everything," I quipped, climbing onto the bed.

Monty undressed down to his boxer briefs and slid in behind me before turning off the lamp and cuddling against my back. "Do you want the heating pad back on?"

"No, you're warm enough," I murmured as his hand rested firmly against my belly.

I lay awake until his breathing evened out against the back of my neck, and then I allowed myself to fall asleep in his arms.

When I awoke, I realized two things. First, I was alone in my bed. And second, it was way past time to take Sully to school.

"Shit," I muttered when I checked the time on my phone and saw that it was after nine. Rolling off the bed, I was hit with a wave of dizziness that had me gripping the edge of the nightstand until it passed. Dammit, I hated feeling weak.

Making my way down the hallway as fast as I could manage, I called out, "Sully! Get up! You're late for school."

When I pushed open his door and found his room empty, I went into a full-fledged panic. His bed was neatly made, but I pulled back the covers and searched for him anyway. Stumbling from the room, I checked the bathroom, but I knew he wasn't there either. The apartment had that empty feeling that told a person they were completely alone.

Tears streamed down my face as I checked the living room and then the kitchen. *My phone. I need my phone to call the police.*

The front door opened, and Monty entered, his hands full. "Hey, Kass. I got—" He dropped everything on the floor and had my face in his hands in an instant. "What's wrong, sweetheart. Are you hurting?" His eyes reflected the same panic I knew mine held.

"Sully's gone. Someone kidnapped him and made his bed and took him," I babbled.

I tried to pull away, but Monty held my face tightly, and I slapped wildly at his hands. "Kassie, he's at school. Calm down, baby. I promise, he's okay."

My racing heart stuttered and then began beating again. "He's at school? How do you know?"

He pulled me into his arms and stroked my hair. "Because I got him ready, and then Lily came to pick him up."

I melted against him like a snow cone in the Sahara. "Li-Lily?"

"Yes, I'm so sorry, baby. I left you a note in the kitchen in case you woke up before I got back."

I buried my face in his chest. "God I was so scared I must have missed it. I'm sorry I freaked out. And you're a hundred percent positive he's with Lily?"

"Hold on," he said, pulling back and taking his phone from his back pocket. "I have proof."

I took the phone and saw a photo of Sully and Sid standing in the hallway of our apartment building in their matching school uniforms. Closing my eyes, I held it against my chest before looking at it again. The boys had their arms around each other and were grinning like little monkeys.

"Sid wanted me to take a picture and show it to you because he lost a tooth last night. See?" Monty tapped the screen.

Zooming in, I laughed as my heart rate left the range of full cardiac arrest. "He sure did. How cute."

"He also told me to tell you he didn't cry at all and that he got five dollars from the tooth fairy. He seemed to think the five bucks was quite a big deal and wanted you to be aware."

"I'll make a big deal of it next time I see him." I handed his phone back over. "Can you send me that pic?"

"Already done, babe." His lips tipped up on one side. "If you'd checked your phone..."

"I only looked at it long enough to see the time." Crossing my arms over my chest, I said, "I have questions."

"What's that?"

"How did Lily end up with my son this morning?"

"Andrea called her last night and asked if Sully could ride to school with them so you could sleep in." He held up his hands in surrender. "Totally her idea to have your son kidnapped. My part was to feed him breakfast and make sure he was dressed in time for the abduction."

I giggled at that. "Okay, maybe I did overreact a bit, but waking up to your kid missing…"

"Totally understandable, and I'm sorry. I should have taped a note to your face. What are your other questions?"

"Only one more. Where were you just now?"

"Oh, that's right. I totally forgot when I walked in and saw you crying. You scared the shit outta me." He walked back to the bags he'd abandoned on the floor. "I got us some breakfast. I felt like bacon and didn't see any in your fridge. And I got you these to cheer you up." His smile was a bit shy when he handed over a bouquet of fresh flowers.

I accepted them and took a long sniff. "They're beautiful. Thank you. But you already sent me flowers this week. I'm sorry I forgot to thank you, by the way. With everything going on."

Confusion flooded his handsome face. "I didn't send you flowers, Kass."

My brow furrowed. "You didn't send red roses to my office yesterday?"

Monty's lips pressed together so hard they turned white. "No but guess I should have since I apparently have competition."

And the jealousy monster raises its crazy head.

I stepped closer to him and wrapped my arms around his waist. "There's no competition, Monty. I've only dated once since my divorce, and that was three years ago." A bit of the tension left his taut muscles, and he kissed the top of my head.

"Who did you date so I know who to hate till the end of time?"

Laughing at his pouty voice, I stood on my tiptoes and kissed his jaw. "No one important. We went out once and I decided not to go out with him again."

"Why?"

"There was no chemistry. All he wanted to talk about was his fancy new car, and I was bored to death the whole time."

"And you feel chemistry with me?" he asked, sounding slightly more mollified.

I reached around and swatted him playfully on the butt. "If you don't know the answer to that, you're a terrible detective, Bouvier."

Taking the to-go bag from his left hand, I held up my index finger. His face broke into a smile as he looped his around mine, and we headed to the kitchen.

CHAPTER 47

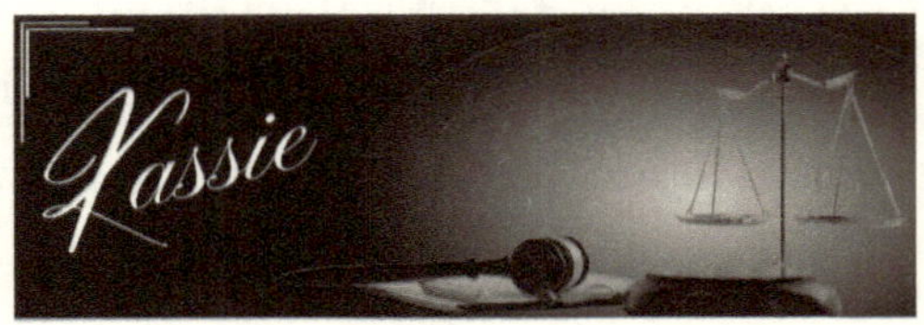

MONTY TREATED ME LIKE a queen all day on Friday. He drew me a bath, washed my sheets while I napped on the couch, and drove me to pick up Sully after school.

For dinner, he fired up the grill I've never even used on my patio and cooked pork chops. And Sully trailed after him like a puppy dog the entire time.

After dinner, he insisted I lie down while he and my son drew pictures. I rested on the couch, turning the volume down on the TV so I could listen to their laughter and banter. They got along so well, and I wished...

Nope, not gonna go there.

Monty had jetted over to Auburn and Gianna's for a few minutes to pack a bag, and he'd stayed the night again, holding me close to him as we slept. I woke feeling refreshed on Saturday morning.

"Did you sleep well, Kass?" his deep, grumbly, morning voice asked against my shoulder.

"Better than I've slept in a while," I replied, turning over to face him.

"What do you want to do today?"

"Something really exciting," I teased. "I need to repaint my toenails. They look terrible."

Monty lifted the covers and peeked down at my feet. "You're right. They're hideous." I smacked him on the shoulder as he let the sheet billow back down. "Let me do it."

"You want to paint my toenails?" I asked skeptically.

"Hell yes. I'm a fabulous toenail painter."

Thirty minutes later, I discovered that was a complete fabrication. "You're really terrible at this," I informed him, eyeballing the mess he'd made of my toes as I reclined back against my padded headboard.

"Just give me a minute. I'll fix it." His teeth bit into his bottom lip in concentration as he used a Q-Tip dipped in polish remover to try and clean up the hot-pink polish smeared on the skin around my toenails.

"Your career as a pedicurist is crashing and burning before my very eyes."

"Shut up, smartass," he shot back. "Close your eyes and let me work in peace."

"Okay, but while they're closed, I'm going to make a wish."

"What are you wishing for?"

"That my toenails don't look like they were painted by a blind man without opposable thumbs."

"That's it. I've had enough of your abuse, woman." He swung around and sat on my shins so I couldn't move. He'd put on light gray sweatpants before he started, but he was bare from the waist up, gracing me with a view of his tan, muscled back. Broad at the top and tapering down to a trim waist, the man didn't have an ounce of fat on him.

"What are you doing?" I shrieked when I felt something wet on the top of my foot.

"Hold still," he grunted, wiggling his fine ass against my legs when I tried to escape.

"Are you painting my foot?" I asked in outrage, though there was laughter behind my words.

"Yep." I attempted to buck him off, and he leaned down and lightly bit my big toe. "Be still or I'll tie you down."

"Promise?" I sang in my flirtiest voice.

He shot me a look over his shoulder. A look filled with fire and need. "When you're better, I'm going to introduce you to my handcuffs."

Whew! Did it just get hot in here?

Unable to move his large body even an inch, I resigned myself to lying still while he did... whatever to my foot. A minute later, he unseated himself from my legs and held my ankle up with pride so I could see his handiwork.

My mouth dropped open. "You wrote *Monty's foot* on me with nail polish?"

"Yep," he said with a cheeky grin, dragging one finger up my leg until it reached the inside of my thigh. "Would you like to know what I'm going to write here?"

"No doubt something dirty."

He lifted one dark eyebrow but didn't have a chance to reply because my son busted through the door. "I heard yelling." Climbing up on the bed, Sully gave me a sweet hug and kiss. "Morning, Mommy."

"Good morning, my lovey. Did you sleep well?"

"Uh-huh." Abandoning me, he turned and stood, wrapping his arms around Monty's neck. "Good morning, Monty."

Tears threatened the rims of my eyelids when Monty placed a large hand across my son's back and closed his eyes, his face the picture of serenity. "Good morning, little man," he said, kissing the side of Sully's messy head.

My kid extricated himself from the embrace and flopped down onto the bed with his legs crossed, pointing at my decorated foot in joyful amazement.

"Did you do that?"

Monty cleared his throat. "Sure did, and I was just about to do the other one."

"Good grief," I complained but didn't move when the big man winked at me as he shook the bottle of polish with a playful glint in his eye.

When he was done, my skin was adorned with bright pink letters proclaiming my left foot as *Sully's foot*.

My son fell back on the bed, holding his little tummy as he laughed hysterically. And was there a better sound in the world than hearing your child's unfettered joy?

Monty brushed a wild lock of hair back from Sully's face and said, "Why don't you go brush your teeth and hair, kiddo, and I'll meet you in the kitchen. We can make your mom breakfast in bed."

Once my boy had hopped off the bed and dashed to his room, my man crawled up the bed and straddled my body. With his mouth against my ear, he growled, "I can't wait till you're better so I can claim the rest of your body. And I can assure you, it won't be with toenail polish."

Yep, it's most definitely getting hot in here.

By Sunday I was feeling pretty much like myself again, and I accompanied Monty and Sully to the park. I sat beneath a tree and watched them play catch as I tried to fight my feelings for the man. He made it difficult not to fall for him.

He made it difficult not to dream of more.

Two and a half weeks passed, and I was frustrated. Sexually.

I'd mentioned going back to Club E like we'd planned, but Monty simply kissed my nose and told me he thought we needed to wait a little longer.

He was attempting to be chivalrous, and it was getting on my damn nerves.

"This chivalry shit is for the birds," I muttered to my computer.

"What the hell are you talking about?"

My head popped up. Andrea was standing in the doorway with a perplexed look on her face.

"I... nothing."

"The patriarchy getting you down?"

I chuckled and shook my head, eyeing my friend. Besides Luciana, Andrea was the most liberated person I knew when it came to sexual matters.

"Can you close the door? I want to talk to you about something."

"Yes!" she exclaimed, slamming the door shut and rushing to sit across from me. "Spill the tea."

Blowing out a raspberry, I tapped a pen on the surface of my desk. "I told you Monty and I were together a few weeks ago."

"Uh-huh. For the marathon night."

"What I didn't tell you was that we were at," I lowered my voice, "a sex club."

She leaned forward a little more. "The one your sister's husband owns?"

"That's the one."

"Oooh, this is juicy. Tell me more."

"That's the problem," I said flatly. "There isn't any more. Not since my UTI."

The metaphorical light bulb went off over her head. "Ah, I get the chivalry comment now. He's worried about you."

"Yes! He won't even touch me. He's come over almost every night for dinner the past couple weeks, but he hasn't made any move to, you know..."

"Lay some pipe on you?"

I rolled my eyes. "I wouldn't put it quite like that, but yes."

"Have you asked him?"

Rubbing the back of my neck with my fingers, I said, "I've told him I'm ready. I took my antibiotics religiously for ten days, and I even went back to the doctor for a follow up. My urinalysis was totally clean."

"You have to find his weak spot. And I think we all know most men's weak spot." She cupped a hand around her mouth like she was imparting a great secret. "Their penises."

"Very profound observation," I said dryly. "He does seem... interested when we kiss good night."

"He gets a boner, you mean."

"Good grief, Andrea! But yes."

She gnawed on her bottom lip and then grinned naughtily. "Woman, you've gotta strut into that club like your ass is for sale and the rent is due."

My eyes widened even as I snorted out a laugh. "The problem is actually getting him there."

"Hmmm," she hummed thoughtfully, staring over my shoulder before snapping her eyes back to mine. "I think I have a foolproof idea."

Well, this oughta be good.

CHAPTER 48

SITTING AT THE DESK in my room at Auburn and Gianna's house, I allowed my pencil to move across the page. The image was practically drawing itself; my fingers were simply the facilitators holding the tool.

I'd bought a new sketchbook last week, and the damn thing was already almost full. I hadn't drawn this much in years, but the ideas were flowing out of me like a dam had broken.

At the knock on my door, I called, "Come in," and my brother entered.

"Hey, Mont. Am I interrupting anything?"

"Nah, just piddling around," I said, twirling the pencil between my fingers.

He crossed the room with his long stride and set a brown, paper-wrapped parcel on the desk. "You got a delivery." When his eyes fell on my drawing, I attempted to put my hand over it, but he stopped me. "What is this?"

"I don't know. Ideas, I guess."

Auburn leaned down with one hand on the back of my chair and one on the surface of the desk. "Jesus, Mont. That's a fine ass tuxedo. I want to wear that, like... *now*."

"Ya'think?"

"Hell yes. Are you thinking white or ivory?"

"Ivory," I replied, tilting my head to survey my work. "I was trying to decide whether I liked the jacket with ivory buttons or black to match the pants."

"The monochromatic is fucking cool, but we could offer both."

"What do you mean *offer both*?"

"*Bouvier* is making this suit. It's fucking fantastic." He grinned down at me. "Don't worry. You'll be well-compensated. In fact, I think you'll make a damn fortune off this."

"I'm not worried about that. Like I said, I was just messing around."

Auburn's long finger tapped the corner of the page. "May I?"

I felt a little awkward letting someone else see my designs but said, "Sure, I guess."

He flipped through page after page, occasionally asking a question or two, before finally stopping on my favorite design so far, a long, flowing dress with intricate beading along the bodice and hem.

"Christ, that's beautiful." He stood, one arm around his middle and the fingers of his other hand drumming against his lips as he stared down at the drawing. "Color?"

"I was thinking somewhere between cherry and crimson."

Auburn nodded his approval. "I'd also like to have one made in a deep pine. Can you just imagine? For the holidays?" His head was bobbing up and down constantly as his mind worked. Then he turned his intense gaze on me. "Are you okay with me showing these to Devereaux so he can get started on some samples?"

"Oh, uh, if you want."

He chuckled and pulled out his phone, dialing a number.

"Tony, get me a billboard in Times Square for the day after Thanksgiving... Jesus, stop yelling in my fucking ear. I'm aware how much it will cost... Okay and get me a copy of our contract for designers but leave the dollar amounts blank. I'll negotiate those myself... The name for the contract?" My brother grinned and winked at me. "Montague Bouvier."

As soon as he hung up, I asked, "What the hell, Auburn? You can't put my designs in Times Square."

"I most certainly can. I'm the CEO, remember?" He slapped me on the shoulder. "I just wish I could get you to join us full time."

"About that…" I started, rubbing the space between my eyebrows. "I'm not sure I want to be a cop anymore."

My brother pulled up a chair and straddled it, leaning his forearms on the back. "Talk to me."

"We've discussed me moving here."

"Yes, and I told you there's an apartment on the thirtieth floor, ready for you to move into."

Gnawing on my bottom lip, I tried to gather my thoughts. "I don't think I want to work for NYPD. I liked working for a force that was on the smaller side. But I don't know. Maybe it's time for me to hang up my badge for good. I just need to decide what I want to do for work."

"Perhaps you could be a full-time designer for the fastest-growing fashion company in the world?" he crooned, his smirk barely contained.

I stared at his hopeful face for a long moment. "You'd really hire me?"

"Jesus, Mont. You don't even have to ask that. This is your company too. Even though you've been gone for a long time, I still consider us fifty-fifty. That's why I send you your profit payments every month. Do you even know how much money is in your account?"

"No," I admitted. "I've been living off my salary from the police force."

"Trust me, you don't need to work. You're set for life, as am I. But I love this company, and I love my job. I just want the same thing for you."

"I haven't been in love with my job for a long time. I think we're both aware of why I was drawn to police work in the first place."

Auburn hung his head and nodded, his voice so quiet I could barely hear it. "Yeah, bro. I know."

"Maybe it's time I stopped chasing ghosts."

My brother placed a hand on my knee and squeezed. "You've done good work, Monty. You've helped so many families find the closure we never got."

I hauled in a deep breath and let it out slowly as our matching blue eyes met. "I felt a little piece of her smiling at me every time I solved a case."

"I also think she would smile if she knew we were together as a family."

Pressing my lips together, I swallowed down the lump in my throat. "I think so too."

I stared down at the object, testing the weight of it in my hand. I knew who it was from even without reading the letter inside the package Auburn dropped off, but I read it anyway, my cock hardening with the very first line.

Dear Sir,

I'll be waiting in room 2-B at Club E at seven o'clock on Satur-day night.

I do hope you can join me.

I believe you'll recognize me. I'll be the one on my knees.

She didn't sign it, but she didn't have to. There was also a standard list of limits that she'd filled out, and I memorized it to the letter.

The flogger Kassie sent was a nice one with a sturdy handle and lambskin tails. She'd done her research, or else she'd gotten her sister to help her pick one out.

This one was perfect for what I wanted. Removing my pants, I tested it on my thigh over and over to perfect my strikes. I wanted to stimulate, not injure.

But, *ohhhh*, that ass was going to be the prettiest shade of red when I got done with it.

CHAPTER 49

I ENTERED ROOM 2-B in full Dom mode, my back straight and my eyes hard. My gift was held loosely in my right hand.

She was already there waiting for me like a good little sub, kneeling on the pillow with her hands on her thighs and her eyes downcast. Oh, and she was gloriously naked.

"Good evening, Sir. I see you got my invitation."

"Why aren't your eyes on me?" I asked, my voice holding firm consternation.

Kassie immediately lifted her soft brown eyes to mine, and I smacked the flogger against my palm. Her lips curled upward, the little vixen.

I held her gaze, daring her to look away. She didn't.

"You look lovely."

"Thank you, Sir."

Walking slowly toward her, I lifted her chin with the handle of the flogger. "Did you follow all the instructions I sent you?"

"Yes, Sir. I drank extra water, ate what you told me to, and stretched before you arrived."

"Good. Impact play can be intense, and I want to make sure you're safe. That's my number one priority." Leaning down until I was only inches from her face, I said, "I read over your limits. Do you have any questions for me?"

"No, Sir."

"What will you say if it's getting to be too much, and you need me to back off?"

"Yellow."

"And if you need me to stop immediately?"

"Red."

Brushing my lips softly against hers, I whispered, "Good girl." I shifted my right hand behind her and dusted the soft fells of the flogger down her back, earning me the most delicious shiver that traveled the length of her spine.

Then I trailed the tails across her firm, round ass. Back and forth. Back and forth. Until her hands were clenching her thighs in expectation.

Straightening, I abruptly turned away and placed the flogger on a small, round table, directly in her line of sight. As I shrugged out of my jacket, I heard her harsh exhale and smiled to myself.

Anticipation is key.

Schooling my expression into one of impassivity, I turned back around and began rolling up the sleeves of my pale gray dress shirt. Kassie's eyes followed the movements as I exposed my thick forearms.

Keeping my gaze glued to hers, I unbuckled my belt and reveled in the sight of her chest moving with her rapid breaths. Then I pulled my belt off through the loops, folded it in half, and snapped it hard.

She startled at the cracking sound, and I tossed the leather aside and approached her.

"Take my cock out," I commanded, and her small hands reached for me, fumbling a little as she unfastened the button and zipper. When she reached into my black boxer briefs, I twitched in her grasp.

"I love your touch, Kassie," I groaned. "I want you to stroke my dick while you suck on my balls."

With her eyes locked on mine, she spat into her hand before wrapping it around me, and *goddamn,* my knees almost buckled.

"Fuck," I bit out between clenched teeth as she lowered her head and sucked one of my testicles into her warm mouth. She twisted her hand, coating my length with her saliva as she began an achingly slow hand job. "Fuck, that's good, baby."

Kassie's soft tongue rolled around and around my ball before she switched to the other side, never pausing the slick slide of her hand up and down my shaft. She had me right on the edge in minutes.

"That's enough," I panted, tugging lightly at her bun until she released me with a pop of her pink lips. I offered my hands, palms up, and she took them, rising to her feet.

Retrieving the pillow, I led her to the lefthand wall where there were a series of hooks on slides. "Kneel for me," I instructed, placing the pillow down and holding her hands once again as she lowered herself. "I think I promised you some handcuffs."

Her smile was a little bit sweet and a whole lot wicked when she held her wrists out in front of her. Reaching behind me, I unhooked the leather cuffs from the back of my pants before strapping them onto her.

I lifted her hands above her head and secured the cuffs to one of the hooks. "Is that too tight?"

"A little bit," she admitted, and I slid the hook down a couple notches.

"Better?" I asked, and she nodded. "Words, Kassie."

"It's better."

"Good," I said, removing my clothes and placing them on a nearby dresser. Then I placed my palm against her cheek, my thumb firmly parting her lips. "I'm going to fuck your mouth, and you're going to take my cock down your throat like a good little slut, aren't you?"

The color rose in her cheeks, and her thighs pressed together. I could smell her arousal even from six feet up. "Yes, Sir."

With one hand against the dark-blue wall, I straddled her legs with my feet, pulling at my cock with long, tight strokes. "Let me see that beautiful tongue, baby."

She did as I asked, and I tapped my head against the velvety surface a couple times, leaving droplets of my pre-ejaculate there before sliding it inside. Her lips closed around me, and my breaths turned into scraping heaves.

"Kassie," I groaned as I began to saw my hips back and forth in an easy rhythm. "You have the hottest, sweetest little mouth. I'm going to fill it up with my cock and then come down your throat."

She made a hum of approval around me, and the sound vibrated up my shaft. With both hands against the wall, I pushed deeper into that heavenly cavern as her cheeks hollowed with her suction.

"That's it," I encouraged. "Take every fucking inch of me."

Kassie's back was arched in this position, and her soft tits jutted forward, making my mouth water for the taste of them.

My pace increased as I fucked her willing mouth, and her eyes lifted to mine. "Goddamn, you're sexy when your mouth is stretched wide and taking my fucking dick. I'm so hard for you. All for you, my filthy little angel."

The tip of my cock hit the back of her throat, and I pushed deeper. She didn't even gag, and that sent me into a frenzy. "Fuck, I'm almost there."

Lowering one hand to the back of her head, I fucked her mouth with long, rough thrusts as a trickle of ecstasy shot down my spine.

I was only able to grunt out, "Coming," before I spilled myself down her throat. My entire body threatened to collapse, and I leaned my forehead against the textured wall as I unhooked her cuffs.

Kassie's arms lowered, joined hands resting against my abs as I trembled above her. When I was finally able to stand without the assistance of the wall, I straightened and pulled out of her mouth. Her tongue darted out and licked up a droplet of me from her lower lip, and I cupped her chin.

"You are perfect." Her already flushed face reddened even further at my praise.

Scooping her up into my arms, I carried her to the bed and laid her face down after removing the cuffs from her wrists. Her skin looked beautiful against the navy-blue of the thick duvet, and I wrapped my hands over her slim shoulders as I sat astride her lower back.

Working my hands up and down her arms, I massaged her gently, knowing she had to be sore. "Does that feel better?"

"It does. Thank you."

I chuckled as I lifted enough to turn her over and then kissed her swollen mouth. "No, thank *you*, baby. You know, I've heard that orgasms do wonders for sore arms."

Her eyebrows lifted as a smile crossed her face. "I've heard the same thing. I think we should try out the theory."

Winking at her, I slid to the floor on my knees and hauled her to the edge of the bed. "Put your feet on my shoulders."

Kassie's pussy was a mess, the tissues swollen and wet with desire, and I'd never seen a more beautiful sight. Flattening my tongue, I lapped at her, wrapping my hands around her thighs to keep her legs open when she tried to squeeze my head.

I speared her with my tongue, tasting her from the inside as things below my waist began to come back to life. When my thumb gave her clit some much-needed attention, Kassie's toes curled into my shoulders, her hips lifting off the bed.

"Fuck yeah," I mumbled into her center as her fingers sank into my hair and pulled hard. "Take what you need, baby girl." She grinded against my mouth as I tongue fucked her faster, loving the feel of her coating my face and dripping down into my beard.

Kass had already been needy before I even buried my face between her legs, so it wasn't long before she was crying out my name, writhing through her orgasm as I lapped at her.

I kissed my way up her body, pausing to give some extra attention to her breasts. They were round and supple beneath my fingers, her skin like the finest, pale silk, and her rosy nipples pebbled against my tongue.

When I reached her face, her sated smile made my cock jerk. There was nothing I loved more than pleasuring her and putting that look on her face. She cupped my face and leaned up for a kiss, which I willingly gave, tasting myself on her tongue while her flavor still clung to mine.

"You're really good with your mouth, Mr. Bouvier."

I stroked my thumb along the bottom curve of her lips, still puffy from me fucking them. "You have quite a talented mouth yourself, Miss Ramirez. Do you need to rest for a bit?"

She shook her head back and forth. "No."

"No what?" I gently reminded her, and her cheeks pinkened even more.

"No, Sir."

Pushing off the bed, I squeezed her firm thigh. "I'm going to get you some water, and then we'll continue."

Once she had downed an entire bottle, I carried her to the blue and black apparatus in the corner. This room was set up differently than the last one we'd been in, and I'd been pleased to see a spanking bench when I walked in.

"I'm going to bend you over this and flog you, and then I'm going to fuck you until your throat hurts from screaming my name," I informed her in a calm tone, even though my excitement had me feeling anything but.

Her teeth sank deep into her bottom lip. "Okay, Sir."

"Kneel here and put your arms on these pads." Once I had her positioned like I wanted her, I kissed the back of her neck. "I don't have to use the straps if you promise to be a good girl and not squirm around too much."

She tilted her head, a coy smile on her lips. "Use the straps. I don't plan to be a good girl."

I lifted an amused eyebrow and chuckled as I began to fasten her arms and legs to the bench. "I think you like when I strap you down, Miss Ramirez."

"I think you're correct, Sir."

When I was done and Kassie assured me everything was comfortable, I stood back and surveyed my handiwork. I'd adjusted the bench so her ass was higher than the rest of her, putting her pink pussy on full display.

I arranged a lamp to the side of her and turned down the overhead lights. "Turn your head and look at the white wall, Kass."

"I see our shadows," she mused.

My anticipation was thrumming through my body as I took the flogger from the table. It felt right in my hand. Approaching the bench, I drifted the fells down her back, and she tensed.

"Relax, sweetheart," I crooned softly. "Just watch our shadows." I pulled back the flogger and struck her lightly on the left buttock. Kass flinched a little but settled easily, so I did the same on the right.

She let out a little whimper, and I soothed her with a gentle hand on her back. "Color?"

"Green," she said quietly, and I rewarded her with tiny kisses up and down her spine.

"That's my girl."

I delivered two more strikes. "You should start to feel more relaxed," I told her. "That's the endorphins being released from your brain."

"I feel it," she replied, and I knew she was telling the truth. Her body was soft and pliable beneath my hands.

Endorphins, I knew from my research, produced feelings of relaxation and wellness. They were also natural painkillers. Flogging was supposed to produce those effects in the receiving person, but I knew the person holding the flogger received the same benefits. At least in my case.

I wanted to watch our shadows but kept my eyes firmly on Kassie as I continued to flog her perfect, round ass with increasing impact, making sure not to let the tails hit her back. I didn't want to bruise or injure her.

When her skin was the ideal shade of dark pink, I tossed the flogger aside and turned my focus to *shadow me* on the wall. Every bit of tension had eased smoothly from my body. Except for my cock. He was standing at attention.

I stroked it, and Kassie groaned.

"Can you see that, baby? You see what you do to me?"

Moving my hand up and down my stiff dick, I put on a show for her, knowing she could see my shadow on the wall. With my free hand, I reached down and dragged my fingers through her center.

"Goddamn, Kass. I love making this sweet, pink cunt drip for me. You like me turning your ass red, don't you?"

"Yes."

I slapped her pussy. Hard. "Yes what?" I asked sharply, and I felt her clit throb against my fingers.

"Yes, *Sir*. I love when you flog my ass."

Mother of god, this woman... She turns me on like no one ever has.

Kassie had made a note at the bottom of the list she'd sent me to remind me she'd been on antibiotics, so I quickly donned a condom. I didn't want anything between us, but I knew some antibiotics could alter the effects of birth control.

Pressing my thumb down on my cock, I aimed it at her entrance, the head slipping in easily before her tightness halted my intrusion.

"This is my pussy," I growled. "Let me in, Kassie." Her walls relaxed around me on my command, and I pushed in to the hilt, pausing to let her adjust.

My hands closed around her slim waist, and I pulled my hips back before shoving inside her with a rough thrust.

"Yessss," she hissed, and I looked down to see her knuckles whiten as she clenched the pads where she was restrained.

"Color?"

"Green," she moaned. "So fucking green."

I grinned like a damn fool as I began fucking her hard and fast, turning my head to watch my shadow take hers. It was the most erotic thing I'd ever seen in my thirty-three years.

The slap of my skin against hers only heightened the sensations of euphoria coursing through my veins, and my grip on her waist tightened. I tilted my hips a couple inches, leaning forward until I found just... that... perfect...

"Oh god! I'm coming." Kassie screamed my name, and I fucked her harder, my thrusts bordering on brutal.

The image of her round ass on the wall—taking me so perfectly—had me gritting my teeth against the need to blow my load inside her. *Well, actually inside the condom*, I thought, feeling a little bitter that that thin piece of rubber was separating me from her. Though I completely understood why we had to use it.

I'd never once had the urge to fuck without wrapping my dick. The idea actually repulsed me. But not with her. Not with my Kassie. Being bare inside her was... special. *She* was special.

With that realization ringing in my head, I draped myself over her back, rolling my hips slowly. "I want you to come again for me, baby girl. Your pussy is gripping me like a vise, and I'm so close."

"Monty..." she breathed, and I covered her lips with my own, tasting the mixture of our arousal on her tongue.

"Please, baby. I need to feel you come with me." I reached beneath us and circled her clit with my fingers.

Her hips lifted an inch, allowing me to go impossibly deeper, both physically and metaphorically. I'd never felt more in tune with another person in my life.

Kassie's hot walls clenched around me, and I took her lips again, focusing only on her. The slow, sensual stroke of her tongue in my mouth. The firm softness of her ass beneath my rocking hips. The wetness flooding my cock and fingers.

And we came. Together. Our bodies were fused, but it was more than that.

I was a hundred percent positive I was in love with Kassie Ramirez. In fact, I wasn't sure I had ever stopped.

CHAPTER 50

"HOW ARE YOU FEELING?"

I reclined back against Monty's chest on the huge bed and closed my eyes, completely exhausted. "Get back to me in three to five business days, and I'll let you know."

He chuckled in my ear. "I'll check back."

My finger smoothed along the edge of the dark-blue cotton sheet.

"I like these sheets, but I'm a little surprised. I guess I thought a sex room would have satin ones."

His lips moved against my temple, in a smile and then a kiss. "I guess that would be a bit cliché. Would you like another strawberry?"

He lifted one of the chocolate-covered treats to my lips, and I bit down. Smooth sweetness met juicy sweetness on my tongue, and I hummed my approval.

"You don't have to feed me, you know."

Monty tossed the stem on the tray and tilted my head around with a tender grip on my chin. "I want to. Not just as a Dom providing aftercare, but because..." He hesitated, swallowing hard. "Because I really care for you, Kass. A lot."

Despite his roughness, he'd proven that tonight. Making sure I was fed and hydrated. Rushing me to the bathroom as soon as we were done and ordering me to pee.

His vulnerability made me feel like I had a rash deep beneath my skin, one I couldn't quite reach no matter how hard I scratched. So I deflected with a tease.

"You care about what's between my legs."

"No, I don't." His face broke into a cute smile. "I mean, I *do*. You have a really nice set of legs, and what's at the apex makes me fucking ravenous."

Oh mercy. The growl of those words made me feel the need to do the sign of the cross, something I rarely did anymore.

But the thought of his mouth between my legs was an unholy one. Monty Bouvier ate pussy like a man who wasn't sure where his next meal was coming from.

"You're a pussy glutton, Bouvier," I informed him, and he smiled.

"Guilty as charged, counselor." He snagged another strawberry from the tray, bit into it, and smeared it on my left nipple, twisting the berry until a thin line of chocolate ringed my peak.

"What the hell are you doing?" I asked.

"Don't take that indignant tone with me, Miss Ramirez. Not when you've made such a mess of yourself." His voice was stern as he maneuvered me until I was sitting astride him. "Luckily you have me here to look after you and clean you up."

When his mouth closed around my tip, I tilted my head back and groaned. "Very lucky." His cock was already hard between my legs, and I rolled my hips over him, feeling the slick glide of our bodies.

"Damn straight," he mumbled around his mouthful before pulling back with a hard suck. "Can you take me again?"

"Yes, Sir."

Monty snagged a condom from the bowl beside the bed and rolled it on before laying me carefully onto my back. Then he covered my body and cradled my head with his hands.

"Don't call me Sir right now. This isn't about that."

I blinked up at him and asked, "What's it about?"

He pushed inside me, burying his face against the side of my neck and whispering, "Fuck if I know. I'm still trying to figure that out."

And my feelings for the man skyrocketed to DEFCON Five. Or was it DEFCON One? I could never keep that straight. But whichever one meant that I was in deep doo doo... that's where I was.

I awoke in the darkness with Monty at my back. His arm was around my waist, and his index finger curled sweetly around mine.

"Go pee," he muttered against the back of my neck, and I giggled.

"Those are the words every woman wants to hear when she wakes up naked with a man."

He rolled halfway over and flipped on the lamp before leaning up on one elbow and glaring down at me. "Could you not be such a smartass first thing in the morning?"

"I'll think about it, Sir."

He swatted me lightly on the bottom. "Go, woman, before I make a meal out of you. Speaking of that, I'll order us some food while you're in the bathroom."

I rolled off the bed and pulled on the plush black robe hanging on a hook. "They serve meals here?"

"Yep," he said, reclining back and pulling his phone from the nightstand. The sheets pooled around his waist, showing off his delicious body and doing nothing to hide the bulge beneath. "It's like a bona fide bed and breakfast."

I set my hands on my waist and popped out a hip. "For your information, I've been to bed and breakfasts, and none of them had a wheel of fortune or a spanking bench," I told him dryly.

"I'm about to put your ass back on the bench if you don't go," he said, pointing a finger at the white door.

"Bossy ass."

He winked at me as he brought the phone to his ear. "This is Mr. Bouvier in 2-B. I'd like two full breakfasts delivered to our room... uh-huh... hold on." He covered the phone with his hand. "You want waffles or French toast?"

I sauntered toward the bathroom, calling over my shoulder, "I can't hear you over the needs of my bladder."

"Swear to god, Kassie," he grumbled before going back to his phone conversation. "Yes, we'll take the French toast. Extra syrup, please." As I closed the door, I caught the evil glint in his eye.

Thirty minutes later, we were sitting cross-legged on the bed as we devoured our meals.

"This applewood smoked bacon is delicious," I said, biting off the crispy end.

"Uh-huh," Monty said, cutting his food into itty bitty pieces. He seemed distracted.

"What do you like better? The green eggs or the ham?"

"Yeah, that's good."

Yep, definitely distracted. My stomach squeezed around the food I'd already eaten. "Monty, can you look at me?"

He jerked his head up and gave me an apologetic half-smile. "Sorry, I was thinking."

I took a sip of my fresh-squeezed orange juice to wash down the lump forming in my throat. "Anything you want to share with the class?"

"Actually, yes." He breathed in through his nose and out through his mouth as my anxiety ratcheted up about ten notches. "I got an apartment in Auburn's building and hired movers to pack up my house in Florida and ship my stuff here."

"Okay."

Monty's eyes darted all around, finally landing on his plate. "All except for one room."

My shoulders relaxed. "I think I understand. Is it a room like this?" I circled my finger in the air. "And you don't want anyone else seeing it?"

His gaze lifted to mine, his brow creased. "What? No, it's nothing like that." Shrugging one huge shoulder, he said quietly. "It's personal, and I want to pack it up myself. And I'd like for you to go with me."

"Me?" I squeaked, poking myself in the chest with my index finger.

Monty cracked a grin. "Why are you pointing at yourself?"

"I'm just verifying because it sounded like you asked me to go to Florida with you."

"I did. It's important to me."

His blue eyes bore into me, and before I knew it, the words spilled from my mouth. "I'll go."

"Excellent," he said, leaning forward to kiss my lips. "Let's go take a shower. Bring the syrup."

I waltzed into my office on Monday morning, feeling on top of the world. Until my eyes fell on the two dozen red roses on Andrea's desk.

"Another one?" I sighed, and she nodded.

"Yep. You really need to call the police and report this. Wesley is violating his restraining order."

"He violated it ninety-two times with the letters he sent me while in prison, and the parole board still let him out," I snapped. "What makes you think anyone will do shit about it now."

"You're a lawyer. You know you need a record of this."

I scrubbed at my eyebrow with my index finger. "You're right. I'll call."

Andrea stopped me with a hand on my forearm. "Wait. How did it go on Saturday night?"

"It was… fantastic." My voice sounded dreamy even to my own ears.

She clapped her hands in glee. "Yay! I knew he wouldn't be able to resist you for long."

"There's something else," I said, fidgeting with a button on my coat before meeting her eyes. "I'm going to Florida with him."

The googly-eyed look on my paralegal's face made me laugh. "Shut the front door! When are you going?"

"Next month. You know how I had taken a few days off work to be with Sully at the end of the school year?" She nodded. "Well, Lily and her family invited him to go to Philly with them. They're doing all the touristy things. Independence Hall, the Liberty Bell, the Rocky statue."

"So you have some free time to go gallivanting down to Florida with your hottie."

"Something like that," I confirmed with a smirk.

"Excellent. Do you need me to arrange a flight for you, or is loverboy doing that?"

"Loverboy and I will be traveling on the Bouvier's private jet," I told her, buffing my nails on my shoulder.

She licked her finger and pressed it against my arm, making a sizzling sound with her mouth. "Look at you." With a push between my shoulders, she said, "Go make the phone call to the po-po, Jetsetter, and let me know what they say."

Once in my office, I picked up the phone and called the nearest precinct. After I was finally able to talk to a live person, they transferred me to someone else, who put me on hold for twenty minutes. Then she rerouted my call to another officer, who turned around and did the same.

By the time I finally spoke with Officer Peterson, I was beyond frustrated, but the man was kind and respectful, which soothed my frayed nerves a bit.

All the questions were asked and answered. No, I can't prove it was Wesley. No, I've had no other contact from him since he was released from prison. Yes, I saved the envelopes that came with the flowers.

Surprisingly, the officer called me back within the hour. "Hi, Ms. Ramirez. I wanted to let you know that I spoke with the manager of the flower shop, and she said the flowers were ordered by someone who left money in her mailbox with instructions."

"Cash?" I asked, my shoulders deflating.

"Yes, I'm sorry. There's no way to trace that, and she didn't save the envelopes the notes and money came in. I also contacted the halfway house where Campbell is staying, and they said he checks in every night and hasn't broken any of the house rules."

"I appreciate you trying, Officer."

"Let me give you my direct line so you don't have to go through all the rigamarole of the phone system, in case you need to contact me again."

"That's very kind of you," I said, jotting down the number when he rattled it off.

"My sister went through something similar."

"I'm so sorry. Was it ever resolved?"

"Yes, he went back to prison, but not before putting her in the hospital for two months. It's a fucking shame these assholes keep getting let out. Pardon my French."

"God that's horrible. I hate to hear that happened to her. And don't worry about it. I speak French from time to time myself."

"Okay, ma'am. I've started a file, so call me if there's any more suspected contact from your ex."

After hanging up, I relayed the information to Andrea who was as frustrated as I was. "Have you told Monty about this?"

"No, I didn't want to worry him. He's got enough on his plate."

"I think he'd like to know, Kassie," she said, giving me the patented Andrea scowl.

I was saved from the argument by the sound of my cell phone chiming on my desk. Closing the door, I answered with a flirty, "Hello, Sir."

"Well, hello there, beautiful. How are you feeling today?"

"I feel like someone defiled me for hours this weekend."

"That's weird. I feel the same."

I giggled. "That will teach you to hang out with wicked women."

"Woman," he corrected. "One woman."

I liked the sound of that more than I should have.

"I was calling to see if you wanted to come over to my new apartment this weekend. Auburn and Gianna are coming and probably a few more people too."

"Hmmm, I'll see if I can arrange a babysitter."

"No need. Sully can come and play with Jaxon and Jane."

I couldn't help my smile. "Really?"

"Of course. If you couldn't tell, I like the kid. And his mom isn't too bad either."

"Gee, thanks."

He chortled in my ear. "So you'll come over?"

Hanging out with his family felt like we'd hit a new level, and that made my heart beat just a little bit faster.

"I'd love to."

CHAPTER 51

"Good grief, Sully. We left home five minutes ago. How did you already get dirt on your face?"

Licking my thumb, I rubbed at the smudge of dirt on his face, and he scrunched up his cute little nose. "Mommy spit is sooo gross," he complained.

Kid, if you knew how you got out of my body, some saliva would be the least of your worries.

The door swung open right as I was attempting to smooth down an unmanageable chunk of hair on the back of my son's head.

Monty stood there with a beaming smile on his face, looking like a male model in faded jeans and a lightweight brown sweater. *Brown! Who the hell looks like a supermodel in brown?*

He stepped forward and placed a very appropriate kiss on my cheek while his hand slipped around to my butt and gave me a very *inappropriate* sneaky squeeze.

"You look gorgeous. And look at this big guy!" He bent and picked up Sully. "I'm so glad you could come."

"Mom spitted on my face."

"I feel for you, man. She spitted on me one time too."

I choked, slapping my hand over my mouth, and gave Monty the wide eyes, to which he simply winked at me.

When I found my voice again, I waved my fingers at Sully's head. "I tried with this hair. I really did."

Monty inspected my son's hair before reaching up with his fingers and mussing it all over the place. "There, that's better." It wasn't. It looked ten times worse than when we'd arrived.

Sully giggled and retaliated by screwing up Monty's hair with both hands, and I couldn't help but roll my eyes. "You two look like you've been attacked by a pack of wild opossums."

Monty nodded seriously. "That's the look we were going for. Come on inside." Holding Sul on one hip, he led me inside and linked his fingers between mine.

I stared in awe at the high, vaulted ceilings and the picture windows taking up one wall of the living room. He'd only moved in this week, so I expected sparse furniture and stacks of moving boxes scattered around, but this place could be featured in a magazine.

The largest sectional couch I'd ever seen was in the center of the room. It was a deep eggplant color and was dotted with oversized ivory throw pillows. A hand-tufted rug in the same colors lay beneath a chest-style coffee table. The floors were dark walnut and polished to a high shine.

"Wow, Monty. This is gorgeous."

"You like?"

"I love. It's so stylish but comfortable at the same time."

His hand squeezed mine. "That's what I was aiming for."

"You're here!" a voice squealed, and I looked up to see Gianna practically skipping toward us. She engulfed me in a hug before turning to my kid. "Sully, do you remember me?"

He nodded vigorously. "You're Jaxon and Jane's mom."

She shot me a wry look. "That's my official name now."

"Same situation here," I replied.

Auburn's wife was stunning, fifteen years his junior, but it didn't seem like it. The two were perfectly matched. She had brilliant green eyes and legs up to her damn ears. I felt like a dwarf next to her.

After introducing Sully to their driver and security specialist, Cruz, who I'd already met, Gianna introduced both of us to her father, Tony, and his partner, Tora. The latter was a short man with huge, expressive eyes who greeted me like he'd known me forever before turning to Sully.

"You can call me Lolli, and this guy is Pops," he said, placing an arm around Tony's waist. "That's what the other kids call us."

"Nice to meet ya," Sully said, holding out his hand to shake theirs like I'd taught him.

"What a darling little gentleman!" Tora exclaimed. "You want to go to the kitchen with me so we can sneak some food?"

Sully's eyes lit up as he looked to me for permission. The kid loved to eat. "You can go," I told him, "but remember your manners."

"Okey doke," he said, squirming until Monty set him on his feet. He took Tora's proffered hand and headed toward what I assumed was the kitchen.

I smiled at Gianna's dad. "Tony, I've talked to you on the phone, but it's so nice to put a face with the name." He was Auburn's personal assistant, and from what Monty told me, there was some initial drama when Tony's boss started dating his much younger daughter.

"Likewise," he said, glancing between me and Monty with shrewd eyes. "I'm so happy to see you two together."

Monty's arm slipped around me, and he pulled me tightly to his side. I looked up at him, and my knees weakened at his sexy smile. "It makes me happy too," he said, his blue eyes full of affection.

And for the first time in a long while, I could say I was genuinely happy. I hadn't been exactly sad before. I had my career, my family, and some good friends, but Monty had brought so much more to my life this past month and a half.

Our moment was broken when someone knocked on the door. "That's probably Dad," Monty announced, taking me with him as he strode back to the entrance. With his mouth close to my ear, he whispered, "I don't think I've told you how edible you look tonight."

I suppressed a shiver because he opened the door just then. His dad was standing on the other side, and he pulled me into a hug immediately. "Kassie," he breathed, "I'm so happy you're here."

"Thank you, Paul. I'm happy I'm here too."

"Stop flirting with my woman, old man," Monty said, and I could hear the smile in his voice.

I shot him a look as I hooked my arm in his father's. "Now that my *real* date is here, we can start the party."

Monty's eyes narrowed in warning, but the corners of his lips twitched. I felt a swat on my ass as he followed us into the living room and knew I'd pay for that comment later. *In the most delicious of ways, I'm sure.*

"Where are my grandkids?" Paul asked, looking around the room with a sparkle in his blue eyes.

"They're in the playroom," Monty informed him, pointing down a hallway off the living room. *Playroom?* "First door on the right."

His dad patted my hand. "Sorry, dear. Grandbabies trump everyone."

I laughed. "I totally understand. My mom is the same with Sully. It's like I don't even exist."

Tora reappeared holding my son, who had two pigs in a blanket in his left hand and another—which he was cramming into his mouth—in the right.

"Dese are good," he said around a mouthful as Tora set him down.

"Sully, don't talk with your mouth full," I scolded, wiping a bit of mustard from his cheek. I swear, this kid couldn't stay clean for two seconds. "Swallow that bite and then say hello to Monty's dad. This is Mr. Paul."

He chewed and swallowed before wiping his hand on his jeans and extending it. "Hi, Mr. Paul. Nice to meet you."

The older man chuckled. "Nice to meet you too. I've heard a lot about you."

Confused by that statement, I glanced up at Monty to find his cheeks pinkening as he gave me a half shrug. "I may have mentioned my little buddy a few times. In passing."

"Yeah, in passing," Paul scoffed, and his son leveled him with a playful glare.

"Why did I even invite you here?"

"Because I'm an excellent babysitter," he shot back. "Come on, Sully. I'll show you where Jaxon and Jane are." As they walked off hand in hand, I heard him say, "You can call me Grandpa."

Something thick and heavy clogged my throat as I looked up at Monty. He was watching my son and his father retreat with a fond smile on his face.

"This is how it always should have been," he said so quietly, I wasn't sure he meant for me to hear it. But I did.

Blowing out a breath, he looked down at me and smiled. "Come on. I want to show you the rest of the apartment."

We peeked in on the kids, who were building a Lego tower so high it was threatening to topple over. I was relieved to see that Jaxon's shirt was misbuttoned, and Jane had a stain of what looked like ketchup on the collar of her shirt. At least my kid wasn't the only hot mess.

"I set up the playroom for when the kids come over. I also have three extra rooms," Monty told me as we continued down the wood-floored hall. "I'm not sure what I'm going to do with this one," he said as we passed an empty room.

"You could put a home gym in there," I suggested.

"Already have one of those. It's on the other side of the kitchen. This one is a guest bedroom." He opened the door to a sunny room with yellow walls and a white comforter.

"It's really pretty."

He opened the door across the hall. "I thought so. And this one is... well, I thought Sully could stay in here."

I gaped at the navy-and-white room with two double beds. "My Sully?"

"Well, yeah. Unless you know of another Sully with a hot mom that I'd like to have in my bed." He stepped closer, cradling my face in his hands. "I want you both to be comfortable here because I want to see you more often. A lot more often."

I wound my arms around his neck and kissed his jaw. *Could this really be happening?* "I want that too."

Moving slowly, he covered my mouth with his own. The kiss was sweet and steamy and filled with so many feelings. Feelings I could easily put a name to but didn't. Not yet. We were still too new.

But they were there, right beneath the surface and straining to break free.

We returned to the party, my hand grasped in Monty's and smiles firmly on our faces. "I need to go check on the food," he said, but then his head turned toward the door when someone knocked.

"I'll get the door. You get the food," I told him. Making my way across the floor, I opened the door to a familiar face. "Lehra!"

"Kassie, hey," she said, stepping over the threshold with a bottle of wine in her hands. I'd met the gorgeous blonde receptionist a couple times when I met Auburn in the lobby of the Bouvier building on business. She lowered her voice. "I'm not sure why I'm here. Auburn just told me his brother invited me."

"Well, it's a party," I said. "Come on in."

Her steps faltered, and her straight, white teeth sank into her bottom lip as she stared at something over my shoulder. I glanced in that direction to see Cruz stand with wide eyes and a dreamy look on his face.

Ahhh, something going on with these two? They were giving off some serious vibes. I guided her in that direction, and Cruz's smile broadened.

"Hi, Lehra." His voice was all breathy in a way I'd never heard from him before. *Yep, definitely some attraction there.*

"Hi, Cruz," the pretty blonde said, her cheeks blushing furiously. *These two are just too dang cute.*

I took the wine from her. "I'll put this in the kitchen."

Cruz's face fell when she hurried after me, announcing, "I'll go with you."

Monty passed us with two trays of food and a smirk on his face when he saw Lehra. I was pretty sure I knew now why he invited her.

"You could have stayed out there and talked to your friend," I commented as we entered the kitchen. It was homey and modern with dark-green countertops, fancy appliances, and frosted-glass-fronted cabinets.

"He's not my friend," she said quickly before amending that. "I mean, he *is* my friend, but *only* my friend. That's all."

Gianna strolled into the room, wine glass in hand. "What's up? Are we talking about why Cruz was literally panting after Lehra?"

"He was not!" she protested, and Gianna rolled her eyes in my direction. "Kassie?"

"Oh, he was definitely feeling you," I said, grinning as I located the wine fridge in the corner and put the bottle on the top rack.

"Come on, Lehra, don't you think Cruz is hot as fuck?" Gia cajoled.

Lehra folded her lips between her teeth before finally smiling. "Okay, he's nice to look at," she admitted. "He's Cuban but has those blue eyes that are just soooo..." Catching herself almost drooling, she cleared her throat and schooled her face. "They're blue."

Gianna winked at me. "His blue eyes are blue. Excellent observation, Lehra."

"Oh shut up," she said with a giggle, sitting on a barstool with her chin in her hand. "Let's talk about how Monty looked like he was about to gobble Kassie up in a single bite."

I couldn't remember the last time I'd laughed so hard. Gianna and Lehra were hilarious. We'd stayed in the kitchen gossiping for almost an hour before we got hungry and headed back to the party.

We checked on the kids in the playroom. Someone had brought them food, and they were eating happily. In the living room, Auburn was playing bartender while everyone laughed and talked. It was one big happy family, and my heart swelled that Monty wanted me here. Me and my son.

I had been reluctant to rejoin the dating pool after my divorce, especially after one man who was interested in me backed off when he found out I had a kid. Or "another man's baggage" as he so rudely put it.

But Monty Bouvier accepted us both.

A small hand tugged at the hem of my red shirt. "Mommy, Jaxon asked if I could spend the night with him. His parents said it was okay." Sully's big brown eyes pleaded with me.

Gianna was standing behind him and nodded in agreement. "We'd love to have him, and don't worry about clothes. He can wear some of Jaxon's."

An hour later, I said goodbye to my son as he left with the Bouvier family. They were the last ones to leave, so I found myself alone with Monty.

Wrapping his arms around me from behind, he kissed my neck. "I want to give you a bath. I think you're really going to love my tub."

CHAPTER 52

KASSIE'S HAIR WAS PILED on top of her head, and she was naked in my enormous jacuzzi tub. I'd placed a bath pillow behind her, and she was reclining back with her eyes closed. Fragrant steam rose from the water as she inhaled deeply.

"You're right. This tub is amazing. And this bath soak. Mmmm, what is it?"

"Fig and ylang ylang."

She opened one eye and grinned lazily up at me. "You should get your ylang ylang in here with me."

I laughed. She was so fucking adorable. Retrieving the aqua stimulator from the cabinet, I wiggled it at her. It was basically a penis water slide. She'd accidentally left it behind on our first night in Club E. "I thought we'd try this."

Her eyebrows lifted. "I forgot all about that."

"Spread your legs for me," I instructed as I kneeled and attached it to the faucet. She gasped when I adjusted the device so the water flowed directly onto her clit.

"Oh my god. That's... ohhhh." Her eyes closed, and I scooted toward her head, stroking my fingers up and down her torso.

"That feel nice, baby?"

She moaned, and my jeans were suddenly way too tight. "It's better than nice." With parted, smiling lips, she tilted her head back as the water flowed exactly where she needed it.

I leaned over and kissed her, my tongue toying with hers and my fingers plucking at her nipple. Kass gripped my head with both hands, soaking the back of my hair, and I tugged harder at her hard peak.

"Let go for me, angel," I murmured against her lips, and with fingernails digging into my scalp, her body began to tremble as she came slow and long, her sweet sounds vibrating through my mouth. I greedily swallowed each one.

"That was amazing," she panted into my mouth. "Officially my new favorite toy."

"I thought I was your favorite toy," I teased, pulling back to take in her flushed cheeks, drowsy eyes, and sated smile.

"Okay, my favorite non-human toy. Speaking of that, I want your ylang ylang now."

"Let me bathe you, and then you can have all the ylang ylang you want." With a purple bath pouf, I cleaned every inch of her body using a milled coconut soap I'd purchased especially for her. Then I helped her out of the tub and dried her with a large, fluffy white towel.

"Best bath ever," she said, tugging my shirt over my head and tossing it aside before reaching for my pants.

"Look how eager my girl is to get bent over and stuffed full of cock." She had my jeans pushed around my ankles, and I shoved them off before reaching for her full breasts. "Or maybe I'll fuck these and come all over your neck. Would you like a pretty pearl necklace, baby?"

I dragged one hand up and lightly cupped her throat.

And she kicked me right in the nuts.

"Ohhh, fuck," I grunted, doubling over at the waist and cupping my genitals. I was always down for some rough play, but this was too fucking much. "Kass, what the hell, baby? That's not funny."

But when I looked up at her, she wasn't laughing. My girl was backing away like she was... afraid? Of me?

"I said no choking," she yelled, holding one palm out toward me.

All the pain between my legs instantly shifted to my heart as I understood. She was scared of me. *Oh god, no!*

Dropping to my knees, I placed my hands behind my back and spoke quietly.

"You're safe, Kassie. I won't touch you."

A sob broke from her chest and almost killed me. "I didn't want you to choke me."

I dipped my head to my chest as my heart broke in two. *She's afraid of me.*

"I wasn't going to choke you. I swear to god, Kassie, I'd rather take my own life than betray your trust." I looked back up, meeting her tearful gaze. "I'm sorry. So sorry."

She pressed her hands over her mouth and approached me slowly, her eyes widening in horror. "Oh god, I hurt you, Monty. I-I didn't mean to. I just fr-freaked out." She kneeled in front of me, her soft hands touching my face.

"Baby, I'm fine. I'm worried about you. I shouldn't have put my hand near your neck at all. I didn't realize it would trigger you."

Kassie wound her arms around my neck and rested her cheek on my shoulder. "Would you hold me?"

I wanted nothing more. "Are you sure?" She nodded, and I could feel her tears dripping down my chest. Every one threatened to cut me wide open. "Okay, baby. I've got you."

My hands went slowly to her back, holding her gently, like she was made of glass. I kissed her temple and attempted to tamp down my anger.

"Give me a name, Kassie. Tell me who did this to you, and I'll make him pay."

She didn't say anything for about half a minute. "It was my ex, Wesley. He already went to jail." A shiver passed through her body, and I pulled back to look at her.

"I want to know what happened, but let's get you dressed first."

Cradling her in my arms, I stood and carried her to my bedroom before gently dressing her in one of my soft T-shirts. Then I pulled on a pair of boxers and led her to the bed.

"Is it okay if we sit here?"

She nodded, lips pressed tightly together. I leaned back against the headboard with Kass curled in my lap, staying silent until she was ready to talk.

"Wesley and I started dating in my final year of law school. He was a few years older than me, and we met at a law firm where I worked on the weekends for extra money."

Her fingers twirled through my chest hair. "While we were dating, we talked about having kids. He said he wanted a houseful. We used to joke that we'd have enough for a baseball team."

She paused for a long moment. "We got married right after I graduated, and he changed almost immediately. Became more possessive. He told me he changed his mind about kids because he wanted it to be just us."

What a fucking asshole.

"I didn't know what to do. I thought it was settled before we got married, but... I don't know. I guess I was a little afraid of being pregnant because of what happened with Willow, so I didn't mind waiting for a while."

She peered up at me, and I kissed the spot between her eyebrows. "That's understandable."

Her face curled back down to my chest, and I rubbed her back with soothing strokes. "I wasn't going to church at all then, and I'd totally abandoned the Catholic teachings, so I was on birth control pills. About three years into our marriage, Wesley and I were going away one weekend, so I went to the pharmacy for a new pack of pills on that Friday. There was some kind of shortage of that particular one, so they called my doctor, and he said it was okay to substitute another brand."

Kass puffed out a long breath. "No one told me that I needed to use another form of birth control for the next month until my body got adjusted to the new pills."

"And you ended up pregnant."

"I did. I was so nervous at first, but then I got excited. I waited a couple weeks to tell my husband. I was trying to wait until he was in a good mood, but it seemed like he was *never* in a good mood anymore. His career wasn't taking off like he'd hoped."

Kass looked up at me, her lips tipped up on one side in a sad smile. "Wesley wasn't a very good lawyer, to be honest. On the other hand, my career was going extremely well. I was a fairly new associate, and I'd already won a handful of big cases. He was jealous and resentful, so I didn't talk about work at home because I was tired of hearing him rant about how I only got the good cases because I was a woman."

"What a fucking prick," I bit out.

"Yeah, he was. I'd finally decided I was telling him after work one day because it was only a matter of time before he started noticing the changes in my body."

Her chest heaved with a huge intake of air, and I ran the backs of my fingers down her cheek. "I know this is hard on you, baby. You don't have to tell me."

She shook her head and pressed her face against my neck. "No, I need to get this out. Before I could get home that day, he found my prenatal vitamins in my makeup case. He was so fucking pissed."

Jesus, I already want to slit this guy's throat.

"As soon as I got home and walked up the stairs, he threw the vitamins at me and started screaming. Then... then he..." She blew out a thin stream of air. "He pushed me down the stairs. I landed at the bottom, a little dazed but still conscious when he—"

"He choked you?" I finished because I didn't want her to have to say the words.

She nodded. "Until I lost consciousness, and then he left the house. When I woke up, I called an ambulance immediately. The police came to the hospital, and I told them the whole story. Wesley had bruised my neck, and we had a security camera over the front door that caught him leaving shortly before the ambulance arrived, so the evidence against him was pretty solid."

"Christ, Kass."

"I was so scared I was going to lose Sully," she whispered, her voice trembling.

"But you didn't. You have a healthy, wonderful little boy."

Some of the tension left her body. "Yeah, I do. He brings light to every day."

"So what happened with fuckface? Did he take a plea deal?"

She shook her head. "No, the idiot refused and was sentenced to prison after the trial." Kassie hesitated for a long moment. "I have a restraining order against him, but that didn't stop him from sending me letters from jail."

"What kind of letters?" I asked, my voice tight with restraint.

"Not very nice ones."

I hated this guy more with every passing second. "Make sure to take those with you and present them when he comes up for parole. Shit, what am I saying. You're a lawyer; you know that already."

"I did take the letters, and they let him out anyway."

It was all I could do not to shout, but I was trying to remain calm for Kassie. "When?"

"A few weeks ago."

"And has he tried to contact you? Has he sent more letters?"

"No letters, no." The way she said it made me think she was holding something back.

"Kassie, tell me." My tone was gentle but left no room for argument.

"You know when I thought you had sent me flowers? Right about the time I got sick?" I nodded. "I think they were from Wesley."

Fuck me, this guy's got a death wish.

"What makes you think that?"

She gnawed on her bottom lip before admitting, "Because I've gotten two more bouquets since then. None of them had a card."

I gritted my teeth. How the hell had she not told me this? "Have you reported it?"

"Yes, and there's not much they can do. He left cash in the mailbox of the florist with instructions on where to send the flowers."

"And he's sending them to your house?" The fear was making me nauseous.

Her head shook back and forth. "No, to my office. He doesn't know where I live."

I lifted her chin gently. "Kass, how long do you think it will be before he finds that out too?"

Her eyes blinked rapidly and slid away from mine. "It's been six years, and he hasn't so far."

"Move in with me." Her gaze jerked back to mine, wide and disbelieving. I knew how she felt. The words that fell from my mouth surprised me as much as they did her. But I warmed quickly to the idea. In fact, I fucking loved it. "You and Sully move in here so I can protect you."

Kass huffed out a humorless laugh. "We can't move in here. Do you have any idea what it's like living with a five-year old? He would have this place destroyed in a day."

"I. Don't. Care. All that matters is that you two are safe."

"We are. I've been protecting us since before he was born."

"While Campbell was in prison, but he's out now, baby."

"Thank you for offering, but no." She shifted until she was straddling my hips, her fingers running through the hair over my ears. "Why are you so sweet to me?"

Because I'm in love with you.

"Because I have feelings for you, Kass." I swallowed hard. "Very real, very deep feelings."

"Me too," she whispered, resting her forehead against mine with her eyes closed. "I don't know how to process them. It's like," she opened her eyes, and I read everything in the brown depths, "the old feelings."

Neither of us were saying the actual word, but it hung between us, heavy, raw, and real.

I could taste that four-letter word on her tongue when she leaned forward and kissed me tenderly. I could feel it in every brush of her fingers through my hair.

"Monty, will you make love to me?"

And there it was. *The word*. In a different context, but there nonetheless.

"Yes, baby." She was wearing only my T-shirt, and I dragged it up and over her head. Her hips lifted long enough for me to remove my boxers, and then we were completely bare. Body and soul.

"Do we still need to use protection?"

She shook her head. "I called my doctor, and she said it's fine. Unless you want to."

"I don't," I told her, tracing her spine with my fingertips. I wanted nothing but Kassie touching me. She tilted her head back, and I peppered her neck with feather-like kisses. "I would never hurt you, Kass. Never."

It was both a promise and a plea.

"I know. I reacted out of instinct earlier, but I know you would never hurt me."

"You did good, baby. Most of me was very proud of you. One part was not so excited though."

She bit her bottom lip, a smile hinting at the corners as she reached down and wrapped her hand so fucking gently around my cock. "I'm so sorry about kicking you. Is it okay now?"

I was already hardening in her fist. "I think it's safe to say he's good to go. Just don't bounce too hard."

"I'll be gentle with you," she cooed in my ear, lifting her hips and dragging my tip through her wet center. Back and forth, teasing us both until our breaths were ragged and quick.

When she lowered herself onto me, our eyes locked. "You're so beautiful," I uttered, and she leaned forward, sucking softly against my lips.

"You are too."

My hand rose to the back of her head, holding her close as our bodies began to move. It was slow. Sensual. Worshipful.

The only sounds were the slight creak of the bedsprings and our quiet moans. But the feelings between us were loud and clear.

Kassie took her time, sliding up my shaft with aching slowness before lowering herself onto me as our lips fused. She was so damn tight and wet, her body sucking me in like it couldn't do without me.

I pulled her closer with one hand on her bottom, and her breath caught when her clit rubbed against my pubic bone. Lowering my head, I closed my lips around one nipple and tenderly sucked.

Kassie's body tightened around me, and she added a roll of her hips on every downstroke. "Yes, right there," she whispered against the top of my head. I gave some attention to the other breast, and her hips stuttered.

Dropping both hands to her ass, I guided her, rocking our bodies together until she yanked my head up and crashed her lips onto mine. The kiss was fierce, wanton, and I felt myself twitch inside her slick heat.

Our moans mixed as we both reached our peaks at the same time. We kissed deeply, our bodies slowing and finally stopping.

Kass rested her cheek against my shoulder, and we held each other in silence, hearts beating fast against one another's chest. Like they were having their own private conversation.

I didn't want to move. Like, *ever again*, but... "Wrap your legs around me," I told her, pushing off the bed.

She whined her displeasure at the interruption. "Why are we moving?"

"Bathroom," I said simply as I carried her.

Once she'd done her business, I placed her back in my bed and spooned against her back, my arms snug around her sated body. She was warm and soft, and I never wanted to let her go.

Once her breathing had evened out, I quietly called her name. Getting no response, I buried my face against the back of her neck and whispered the words I had struggled to say.

"I love you."

Turns out, it was easier than I expected. Much easier.

Chapter 53

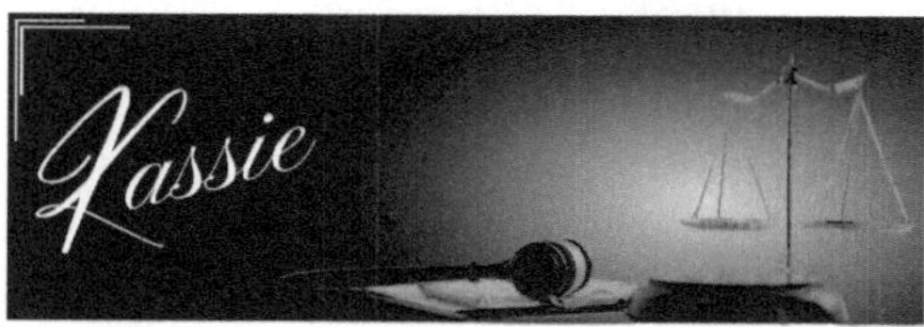

I STOOD AT MY kitchen counter and flipped through the mail. Bill, bill, baby shower invitation, bill, square envelope with no return address.

Tossing the others down—they could wait till I got back from Florida—I opened the cream envelope and pulled out a square card with the letter T in a large, bold font.

"What the hell is this?" I asked aloud, turning it over and finding it blank on the other side. Before I could think much about it, the doorbell rang, and I jogged to the front door and swung it open.

Monty grinned at me, wearing a baby-pink button-down and khaki shorts. How the hell a man could look so damn good in pink was beyond me.

He stepped inside and pulled me close, tilting my head to the side so he could greet me—with his tongue in my mouth.

"Good lord, there are children present," came a voice from behind him, and we reluctantly broke apart. Lily was standing in the corridor with one hand over Sid's eyes and one over her own.

"It's safe to look now," I informed her, and she peeped through her fingers before lowering her hands.

"Hey, Lil," Monty said, dropping a kiss on her cheek before squatting down. "What's up, Sid?"

"Hi, Monty," he said brightly. "Is Sully here?"

About that time my son came busting through the living room, dragging his Batman suitcase behind him with a whirring of wheels. "I'm ready," he yelled, releasing the suitcase and throwing his arms around his best friend.

Lily's smile was beaming as she looked down at our sons embracing. "Sid has been beside himself with excitement."

"We're gonna see some dinosaurs!" Sid announced, his little body shaking with excitement.

"I know!" Sully said, crouching his legs and making short dino arms in front of himself. "I'm a Sully-saurus Rex!"

His friend giggled and affected the same posture. "And I'm a Sid-asaurus Rex." Then they proceeded to stomp around the living room, circling and growling at each other.

I shot Lily a wide-eyed look. "Well. Good luck with all *that*."

She giggled. "Praveen printed out some dino facts and puzzles for them to go over in the car. Hopefully, that will keep them quiet."

Sully clomped over and looked up at Monty with an evil little grin. "Human! My favorite food," he growled and then bit him on the thigh.

"Sullivan Lucas Ramirez," I snapped in my best mom voice. "You apologize right now."

"It's okay," Monty said, lifting my son sideways and gobbling his tummy. "This human bites back." My kid screeched in delight until Monty settled him on his hip.

"Monty, are you my dad?" he asked, and I choked on my own spit.

But the man seemed unfazed. "No, buddy. I'm not."

"I didn't think so," Sully said, nodding with all the wisdom a five-year-old could muster. "Mommy said my daddy wasn't very nice, and I think you're really nice."

A little snort came from Lily's direction, and I shot her a glare.

"I think you're pretty nice too, Sully-saurus," he said, pulling him close and kissing the top of his head. "Are you going to be good for Aunt Lily?"

My son lifted his head and nodded. "I will."

Monty held out his index finger. "Promise?"

Sully looked down at it for a second before wrapping his small finger around the larger one. "I promise."

I had to swallow the damn golf ball that had somehow become wedged in my throat. Monty handed my dino kid over to me, and I stamped kisses all over his face.

"Mommmm, that's like, a thousand-million kisses," he complained, but I dropped one more on his adorable nose.

"There, now you have a thousand-million and one. I'm not going to see you for four days."

His demeanor sweetened, and he patted my face. "It'll be okay, Mommy. You can call me if you miss me too much."

I blinked back tears. "Every night," I promised, pressing my nose into his hair for one last mom-sniff. "I love you so much, baby."

"I love you too, Mommy." To my surprise, he held out his arms for Monty, who took him.

Wrapping his arms and legs around Monty, my son gave him a kiss on the cheek. "Love you, Monty."

My hand snapped up, covering my lips with my fingers, but my man didn't hesitate for even a second. In fact, his face melted a little as he pressed his lips to Sully's forehead.

"I love you too, little man."

My heart squeezed and released in an abnormal rhythm as my two favorite guys beamed at each other. Lily's hand brushed my back, and I glanced over to find a grin widening her lips. "So sweet," she mouthed, and I nodded before turning my attention back to Monty holding my son.

It looked... right. More right than I could have ever imagined.

Sully broke the moment when he asked sweetly, "Will you bring me a soubenir from Florida?"

Monty laughed at the mispronunciation. "Of course, we'll bring you a souvenir. Sid too."

The boys both yelled, and *good lord, why are boys so damn loud?*

Monty set my kid down, and I hugged him once more before embracing Lily and Sid.

Then the trio was headed down the hallway where Praveen was waiting by the elevator with the bags as I stood and watched.

"Sully!" I called, and he looked over his shoulder at me. "Don't bite any more humans."

He grinned. "'Kay, Mom! Bye."

"Things I never dreamed I'd have to say as a parent," I muttered, walking back inside the apartment once the group was in the elevator.

"You all right?" Monty asked.

"Yeah. A little sad, even though I know Sully is fine and he's going to have a blast. I always feel guilty when I do something without him too. Sounds weird, I know."

He twirled my ponytail around his hand and pecked my lips. "It's okay for you to go and do adult things, and it's also okay to miss your son at the same time."

"I like how you never invalidate my feelings, even when they don't make perfect sense."

"Feelings aren't always supposed to make sense. That's why they're called feelings and not facts. And yours will always be valid to me."

This damn man...

Fidgeting with the collar of his shirt, I said, "I hope Sully didn't make you uncomfortable when—"

"He didn't." His voice was quiet but firm, his blue eyes holding his truth.

I wrapped my arms around his middle and smiled up at him. "Tell me more about these adult things you speak of."

He gave me a swat on the butt. "Let's go get on the plane, and I'll show you all manner of adult things."

Adult things, indeed. There was a damn bedroom on the jet. And we used it. Twice. *Mile high club, anyone?*

"This is your house?" I asked, dipping my head to look out the window as we pulled up the driveway of a beachfront home with hip roofs and a terracotta walkway.

"No, this is a rental," he said, driving into one side of a two-bay garage. "My house is about a mile south. There's no furniture there, so I thought this would be more comfortable. I'm too old to be sleeping on the floor."

"So what's the plan, old man?"

"I thought I'd take you out for some seafood, and then maybe a walk on the beach?"

"Sounds good. I'm hungry."

"We can go to my place tomorrow."

"And you're not going to tell me what's in the room at your house?"

He reached across the console and squeezed my hand. "It's easier to show you."

The next morning we walked up the steps to Monty's house, a gorgeous white stucco building with a wrap-around deck and floor-to-ceiling windows.

My nerves were on high alert because I still had no idea what he was going to show me.

He unlocked the front door, and we entered a spacious living room with high ceilings and pendant lights. The space smelled of cleaning solution.

"Looks like the cleaners have already been here," he noted. "I kept the electricity turned on until I could pack up this last room."

"The mystery room?" I asked, and he smiled down at me as he took my hand and led me down a hallway floored with light-colored wood.

"Won't be a mystery for much longer," he said, unlocking a white door. He took a deep breath with his hand on the door handle. "No one has ever been in this room besides me. And now you."

He opened the door slowly and stepped back to allow me to enter first. My eyes flashed around the room and my heart stalled.

There were full-color drawings on three walls of the room. Monty's drawings, I could tell.

"You can start here," he said quietly, pointing to a sketch on the left wall with three faces. Me, Evie, and an infant.

Willow.

The caption written in a pretty script above the faces read: *Even when my heart is empty, it still beats for you.*

I could feel his pain in every word, every line, and every curve. Reaching a shaky hand out, I hovered my fingers over what I knew in my heart was our daughter's face.

"She's beautiful," I breathed. "So perfect."

"I drew that one after I lost all of you sixteen years ago."

My heart shattered for him. For us. Turning, I buried my face in his chest, my tears soaking his ivory linen shirt.

"I'm so sorry. We lost so much time."

Monty tilted my face up with his thumbs. "But we have each other now."

"I love you," I blurted out.

His eyes widened, and then his tear-streaked face broke into a huge smile. Wrapping his arms around me, he lifted me off the ground, and I encircled his waist with my legs.

"Do you have any idea how happy that makes me?" He leaned forward until our foreheads were touching. "I love you too, Kass. You're my reason for breathing. I never thought I would love anyone again. Not until you came back to me."

"Actually, I think you came back to me," I said, and he chuckled.

"You always have to argue with me."

"Would you have me any other way?"

He shook his head. "Not in a million years. I love you just the way you are."

My heart swelled as our lips met, love and desperation in every stroke of his tongue against mine. When we finally broke apart, I rubbed my fingers through the short beard on his jaw.

"Will you show me the rest of the drawings?"

Monty lowered me to the ground and turned me around, resting his chin on top of my head. "I drew this one on Willow's first birthday," he said, pointing at the second picture. "Or anniversary? I'm not sure what the correct term is."

"I like birthday," I said, staring at the drawing. She still looked like a baby but older than in the first picture. My eyes dropped to the bottom right of the canvas where there was a tiny drawing of a willow tree. "Is that a replica of your tattoo?"

"Yeah. I guess I wanted a special signature, instead of just signing my name. So I put it on all of them."

"I love that."

"When I drew that first one, I never planned all this, but then on her second birthday, I sat down at my desk and started on this one. After that, it was just something I did on March first of every year."

The next picture was of a toddler with puffy dark pigtails on each side of her head. She had a chubby face and a toothy grin.

"She's so precious," I said, my heart swelling with love for my baby girl and for the man holding me in his arms. The man who had shared this incredible treasure with me.

"For some reason, I drew her with blue eyes in this third one," he said, gesturing toward the next sketch. "Sometimes I pictured her with my eyes and sometimes with yours. I just drew what I was feeling at that particular time, so each one is a little different."

We walked around Willow's own personal art gallery filled with pictures of our daughter at each stage of life. Sixteen of them, one for each birthday she would have had.

"She looks like me here," I murmured when we got to the last one.

He stared at sixteen-year-old Willow. "That's how I pictured her this year. Looking like her beautiful mom at that age."

"I always picture her as a baby. Of course, I've kept up with the years that passed, but in my head, she was always a newborn." My eyes scanned the pictures from left to right, and I shook my head in wonder. "I never got to see her grow up, but now... now I get to see that. You gave that to me."

Monty kissed my temple, letting his lips linger there. "I would give you the world, Kassie."

Closing my eyes and folding my arms over his, I smiled because I believed him.

CHAPTER 54

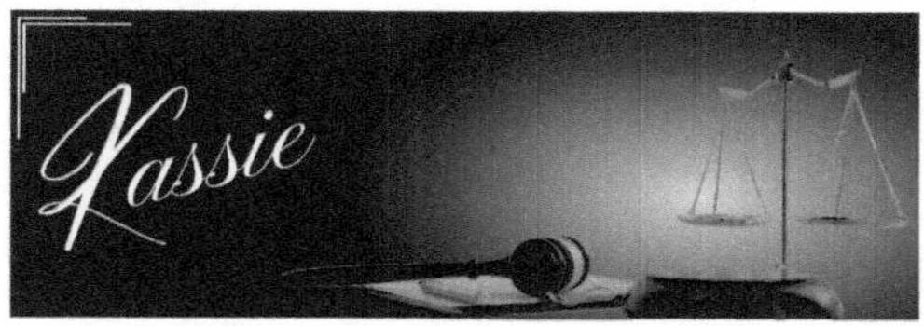

A CLOUD MOVED ACROSS the moon, almost completely shrouding us in darkness. Monty and I were shoulder deep in the ocean. Well, shoulder deep for him; the water would have covered my head if I wasn't wrapped around him.

We had just made love, and my head was nestled on his shoulder as he walked us toward the shore enough that I could stand.

"I'll run up and grab our clothes," he said, kissing the corner of my mouth and letting me slide down his body.

This had been an impromptu skinny-dipping tryst. We'd been strolling along the beach in the moonlight after dinner, one thing led to another, and voilà! We were naked and fucking in the ocean.

That meant we didn't have towels.

Monty's head swiveled from side to side, looking for any other beachcombers before jogging out of the water, butt-ass naked. I noticed him stop and walk a few yards to the left, then to the right, his dick bobbing in the moonlight.

"What are you doing?" I yelled.

"I'm looking for our clothes," he called back.

"They were on that rock right there."

"I'm aware of that, Kassie, but they're not here now."

What the fuck?

He waded back out to me until his lower half was once again shielded by the water. "Apparently, some asshole stole our clothes," he said grimly.

"What?" I shrieked.

He held up a palm. "It'll be okay. I'll just run up to the house and get us some towels."

"You're naked," I reminded him.

His eyes narrowed. "I'm quite aware of that, Kassie. It's either that or we live in the ocean for the rest of our lives. And then my dick would be all pruny."

I burst into giggles, earning me another glare. "Okay, you're right. It'll be fine," I told him, my cheeks hurting from trying to control my facial expressions. "I'll be your lookout."

Monty inhaled a deep breath and searched the beach once more before dashing from the water with his hands over his family jewels. Though he dropped one hand behind him to flip me off when I catcalled him.

I was so busy laughing and watching his fine ass, I didn't notice a man approaching from the left. A man with a hat.

A policeman's hat.

Oh shit!

I couldn't hear the words, but the man obviously called for Monty to halt because he did, his shoulders sagging as he turned around.

Fuck, fuck, fuck. He's going to jail, and I'm going to have to pray I turn into a mermaid because there's no way I'm getting my naked ass out of this water. Ever.

With Monty still cupping his crotch, he and the policeman had a prolonged conversation, during which he bobbed his head toward the rock and then in my direction.

Shit. What if I get arrested and my mom finds out? Or my son when he's old enough to use the internet? And could I be disbarred for this?

Dipping down into the water to make sure all my vital areas were covered, I lifted my hand in a wave.

"We're very nice people!" I called. "This is the first time we've ever done anything like this. Please don't arrest us!"

I was pretty sure I heard laughter, and then the cop shook his head, said something to Monty, and strolled off down the beach. My very naked boyfriend shot a look back at me, and I gave him a cheery thumbs up.

Even in the dimness, I could see his shoulders shaking before he turned and ran up the wooden steps toward our rental house, his white butt shining.

He returned a few minutes later wearing a pair of swim shorts and carrying my royal-blue bikini.

"We coulda used these earlier, huh?" I asked, and he rolled his eyes.

"You are the worst lookout in the history of skinny-dipping," he commented.

"I was admiring your butt," I admitted as I hooked the top around my breasts and slipped on the bottoms.

"Very helpful," he said dryly.

"How did you get away without getting arrested? Was it because I yelled out what nice people we are?"

"No, you goof. I knew the guy. From when I worked on the force."

"That was fortunate."

Monty turned and squatted down. "Hop on." I climbed onto his back as he started wading toward the shore. "Drew—that's the cop I was talking to—said this has been happening on the beaches lately. They think it's probably kids."

"Thank god we left our phones up at the house instead of putting them in our pockets." I nestled my nose into his neck, inhaling the scent of the ocean and Monty. "You know, I'm going to have to stop hanging out with you if you're going to be a streaker. I don't think I can be associated with someone like that."

"I have no idea why I put up with you," he grumbled, jogging up the stairs with me clinging to his back.

"Because you love me."

He turned his head and pecked me on the lips. "Yeah, I do. Though remind me to never go on a stakeout with you."

The rest of our weekend passed without any more public indecency or near arrests. In fact, it was pretty damn perfect.

After carefully wrapping and covering the drawings, we spent the rest of our time eating, swimming, and walking on the beach.

And having sex. A lot. Now that all the barriers between us were demolished, we couldn't keep our hands off each other.

"I need to return these to the station before we leave," Monty said one morning, holding up two dark-blue uniforms wrapped in clear plastic. "I wore them when I helped out with patrol duties."

My finger drifted down the buttons on the front of one before I raised my gaze to his. "I wish you didn't have to take them back. They're kinda hot."

His eyes twinkled, and one side of his lips tilted up in a sexy grin. "You planning on committing some crimes later, Miss Ramirez?"

"I'm considering it. Maybe evading arrest. You have handcuffs?"

"Always," he said, stripping off the plastic covering the garments.

"I thought you had to take them back."

"I'll send the department a check," he grunted, pulling on one of the uniform shirts. He paused while buttoning and lifted one eyebrow at me in warning. "You better start running, woman."

And with a happy squeal, I did.

As we disembarked from the plane at the private airstrip in New York, we found Cruz waiting for us beside a black Town Car. "Hey, you two. Did you have fun?" he asked brightly.

"We did," Monty said, eyeing him suspiciously. "You're awfully chipper."

Cruz shrugged with a huge grin on his face. "It's just such a nice day."

"Whatever you say." He winked at me and mouthed, "He totally got laid."

"So did you," I whispered, patting him on the butt.

"Maybe that's why I can't wipe this smile off my face."

Monty had a specialty shipping service meet us at the airport with a van to transport the drawings, and after he supervised the loading, we climbed into the car.

"What time is Sully getting home?" he asked as I tilted my head over onto his shoulder.

"Not for another few hours," I said around a yawn. My eyes drifted shut, and it seemed like only minutes had passed before Monty was shaking me awake.

With my middle fingers, I cleaned the crust from my eyes and rested my head back against the plush leather while the guys got our suitcases from the back.

"You ready, sleepyhead?" Monty asked, holding out his hand to help me from the vehicle.

When we entered the lobby, I said, "Let me check my mail." Opening my box, I bundled the stack beneath my arm, and we caught the elevator upstairs.

"I'll put your suitcase in your room."

"Thanks, babe." I sorted through the mail, which consisted mostly of junk and bills. Until I got to a square envelope. Frowning, I opened it and found a card with the letter I on it.

"What's that?"

I looked up at Monty. "I don't know. I got another card like this before we left, but there's nothing really on it. Just a letter."

He took it from me, and his expression turned hard as he examined it. "Where is the other one?"

"Um, maybe in the kitchen. I may have thrown it away."

"Show me."

In the kitchen, I shuffled through the mail from last week and located the card. Monty scowled at them before checking the envelopes.

"No return address, and your name and address are typed on a label." He lifted his eyes to mine. "I'm concerned that these are from Campbell."

I shook my head. "Wesley doesn't know where I live. He has no way of finding that out."

He pushed out a long sigh. "Kass, never underestimate the resourcefulness of a criminal. You're a defense attorney. You know this."

Over the next six weeks, more cards arrived, each with one letter that eventually spelled out:

T-I-C-K-T-O-C-K.

When the second T arrived, Sully and I moved into Monty's apartment.

CHAPTER 55

"Where the fuck is he, Idris?" I growled down the phone line.

"I wish I knew, Monty. You shouldn't have gone to the halfway house," he replied, his tone disapproving.

Idris Peterson was the officer who was handling the case of the mysterious flowers and cards that Kassie had been receiving the past few months.

"I was just going to warn him to back the fuck off. *Someone* needs to be doing something." My frustration made my tone sharp.

"We're doing everything we can, man. There's no evidence."

"There's a shit ton of evidence! You have the cards with the letters on them."

"Monty, you were a cop. You know how this goes. We dusted for prints and found nothing on the cards or the envelopes. I'm sure he wore gloves because he was an attorney for years and knows better. There's nothing tying Wesley Campbell to any of it." When I grunted, he continued. "You and I both know it's him, but we. Can't. Prove. It."

I leaned forward with my hands against my desk at the *Bouvier* building, tension making the muscles in my back and shoulders taut. "I know you're doing everything you can. I'm just venting. And I really was simply going to the halfway house to try and talk some sense into him. Remind him that he would go back to jail if he didn't stop bothering Kass."

And possibly punch him in the face a dozen or so goddamn times.

"He probably saw your big ass hovering across the street and took off when he recognized you."

That could be true. I'd waited in my car for hours, and when it was obvious he'd missed his curfew, I knocked on the door to the house. They wouldn't tell me anything, and I figured I must be at the wrong house—bad intel or something.

"That was last week. He's been AWOL for seven fucking days. Why are we just now finding out about it?"

"There was some kind of incident involving another resident at the house that night, so the director didn't end up reporting it for a couple days. Then, with red tape and all, it was another five days till it hit my desk."

"And you said there's an APB out for him?"

"I put it out the second I learned he was missing. That was a couple hours ago. As soon as we pick him up, he'll go directly back to jail for violating his parole."

"He could be anywhere," I said, hearing the defeat in my voice.

"He's probably on his way to Mexico by now. Most bullies are big cowards down deep."

"Anyone who beats up a woman is a fucking coward," I seethed.

"No argument from me. Do you still have security on Kassie?"

"Yep, I hired one of Cruz's old Marine buddies as a guard and a driver. I take her to work in the mornings, and then he comes on duty. Ferries her back and forth to the courthouse on the days she needs to go there. And he takes her to pick up Sully and then to do whatever else she needs to do after work."

"He working out okay?"

"He's great, built like a fucking grizzly bear. I feel a lot better having him with them when I can't be. Of course Kassie bitched about it at first, but she finally came to terms with it. I can be very stubborn, especially when it comes to hers and Sully's safety."

"Good. I'm glad you have someone you can trust. Kassie is a nice lady."

My shoulders relaxed a bit, and I nodded. "She's amazing."

I hung up the phone and turned to see Devereaux, the head designer at *Bouvier* standing behind me. "Is everything okay?" he asked in his slightly accented voice.

"Just a security issue with Kassie, but Hector is with her, so it'll be all right."

"Okay, good. I wanted to go over these sketches with you." He was holding up the wedding dresses I'd drawn for Kass sixteen years ago.

"It's okay if you tell me they're total crap. I was a teenager when I drew them."

He shook his salt-and-pepper head, gazing down at them. "On the contrary, they're excellent. We'll refine a few details, but the overall designs are perfect. I think we should have samples made of each of them and let your future bride choose."

I grinned at that, my heart entirely full. *Future bride.*

"Sounds great, Dev. Now all I have to do is convince her to marry me."

CHAPTER 56

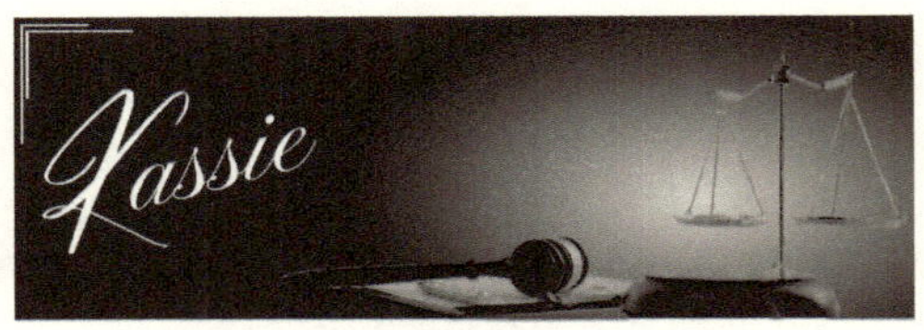

"I'LL SEE YOU LATER, Andrea," I said on my way out the door.

"Sounds good, bosslady. Oh, and Lily said to stop by her office before you leave."

"On it." Walking down the hallway, I pushed open my friend's door. "Hey, woman."

"Hey! Is Sul still staying with us tonight?"

"Yep, but I'm going to take him out for ice cream first since I haven't seen him all day. Hector was going to pick him up from his day camp."

"Did you like that place? I may send Sid next summer."

I nodded. "He loved it. All the counselors have been amazing, and they have so many activities for them."

"Cool. I'll see you after the ice cream party. Have an extra scoop for me."

"With sprinkles," I assured her as I gave her a little finger wave.

Once downstairs, I found the black Mercedes sedan Monty had purchased sitting at the curb. My own personal giant grinned and opened the back door for me. "Hey, Ms. Ramirez."

"Hello, Hector. Can you take us to Scoops? And I've told you a million times, call me Kassie."

"Yes, ma'am." His eyes darted up and down the sidewalk until I was safely in the backseat.

"Mommy! Hector came and got me and took me to the store. Look what I got."

I relaxed back against the seat, reveling in the happy chatter of my son as he showed me the bag full of snacks our sweet driver had purchased for him.

July had been a busy month at the office, and I was stressed to the max. Leaning forward, I informed Hector, "I'm going to my kickboxing class after we drop off Sully."

"Yes ma'am Ms., um, Kassie."

We arrived at the ice cream shop, and Hector found a parking spot and opened the back door for us. "Why don't you join us for some ice cream," I told him.

He rubbed his thick waist. "I don't know. I'm trying to watch my figure."

I poked him in the belly, which didn't have an ounce of fat on it. "Come onnnn, I think I feel an empty spot right here."

Sully poked him in the same spot. "Yeah, Hector. You can't have an empty spot."

The big bear grinned through his full, dark beard and picked up my son. They adored each other. "Alrighty then, little man. Whatever you say."

By the time we'd finished with our treats, it was almost time for my class to start.

"I'm in a hurry and don't have time to go back to Monty's place," I told Hector in the elevator, "so I'll grab workout clothes from my apartment. You drop Sully off at Lily's."

A frown crossed his furry face. "Mr. Bouvier said I'm supposed to stay with you both at all times."

I patted his arm. "Well, you can't be in two places at once. I'll be five minutes, and Lily's apartment is only one floor down from mine."

"You're sure?"

"Five minutes, Hector. It'll be fine."

The elevator opened on the fifth floor, and he exited with my kid hanging on his back. "I'll come to your place and ride back down with you," he said over his shoulder. "Don't leave the apartment without me."

"Aye aye," I said, giving him a snappy salute before pushing the button for the sixth floor.

In my bedroom, I had just thrown on a black sports bra and matching fitted shorts when I heard the front door open. Walking down the hallway, I called out, "That was fast. Let me grab a T-shirt from the laundry room, and—"

I froze.

Instead of the huge, dark-haired teddy bear I'd been expecting to see standing in my living room, I found the last person I wanted to see.

Wesley Campbell.

Fuck.

His blond hair was disheveled, and his shirt was filthy and wrinkled, like he'd lived in the same garment for days.

My heart raced at the sight of him, and not in a good way. Fear took root at the base of my spine, and I used it like Andrea had preached to us in class every week.

Use that fear to make you stronger.

Lifting my chin, I managed to control my voice, keeping it even. "Wesley, I hope you enjoyed jail because you're about to go back for violating the restraining order."

He took a step toward me, and my first inclination was to back away. Again, I heard Andrea's voice in my head.

Never trap yourself. You don't want to help your attacker.

So I stood my ground because the only exit was directly behind my ex-husband. I needed to get to that door.

"It's good to see you again, Kassie. It's been too long."

His eyes dropped to my breasts, and I resisted the urge to cover myself. I needed to keep my hands free.

Be prepared for anything. Always.

"You need to leave. My bodyguard will be here at any moment." I was proud of how firm my voice sounded.

"Is that so? Then I guess I need to make this quick. Where is my little spawn? It's a boy, right?"

The mention of Sully filled me with a strength I didn't know I had. "*My* son is none of your concern." I shifted to the right, taking a small step sideways, but Wesley countered the action.

His grin was pure evil, and I wondered how the hell I'd missed that while we were dating. "Oh come on. Don't you think he'd like to meet his daddy?" he asked, stretching out that last word in a drawling taunt. "Maybe he'd want to come live with me."

"No fucking way in hell," I snapped.

He strolled toward me, his gait slow and confident, like he didn't have a care in the world. Like he didn't have to worry about weak little Kassie.

That pissed me the hell off, and anger burned away every bit of fear inside me. I wasn't afraid of him anymore. In fact, I was spoiling for a fight. How dare he fucking mention my son.

Bring it on, asshole.

Wesley lunged at me, arms outstretched like he was going to grab me around the throat, and my years of training kicked in.

I swept my left arm over the top and knocked his arms away at the same time I punched him in the nose with my right fist.

His face registered surprise as blood sprayed from his nostrils. "What the—"

But I wasn't done with this piece of shit, and I heard Andrea speaking as loudly as if she were in the room with me.

Kick his nuts so hard they fly out the top of his head, ladies.

I did, and as soon as he bent over, I followed up with a knee to the face. My ex-husband flew over the back of the couch and cracked his head on the coffee table, his neck twisting at an unnatural angle as his upper body slipped between the couch and the table.

It's always best to avoid a confrontation, ladies, but if you can't, disable your attacker and then get away. Say it with me.

Disable. Get away.

Disable.

Get the fuck away!

So I did exactly as Andrea always preached. I ran straight for the front door.

As soon as I opened it, I crashed into a wall. No, not a wall. Hector. *Thank god.*

"Kassie, what's wrong? Kassie!" Large hands gripped my shoulders.

"H-he's here. Wesley." I pointed, the adrenaline in my system making my hand shake.

The big man leaped into action, pulling his handgun from its holster as he swung it in the direction I'd indicated. He shifted until his back was to me and herded me until my own back hit the wall.

"Stay. Here. Don't move," he ordered, keeping his eyes on his target. All teddy bear-ness was gone. Hector was now in protective mode. He was a machine.

All I could focus on was my guard's broad back as he crept forward with his gun trained on Wesley. He squatted, and I assumed he was checking for a pulse.

When he stood, holstered his gun, and turned around, I knew. The only reason he'd turn his back on a threat was if they were no longer a threat.

Because Wesley Campbell was dead.

CHAPTER 57

I WASN'T SURE IF my heart would ever beat normally again. When Hector called me, Cruz broke about fifty different traffic laws to get me to Kassie's apartment building. When we hit a traffic jam, I'd hopped out of the car and sprinted the last three blocks.

She was safe. Not a scratch or mark on her except for some swollen knuckles from punching that asshole.

I was so fucking pissed at Hector, I couldn't even look at him, but I was aware of him hovering in the corner. It was hard not to be; he was the size of a goddamn bus.

"Miss Ramirez, we'll be in touch," Idris Peterson said, shaking her hand and then mine. He was a tall Black man with wire-framed glasses that kept sliding down his nose. He pushed them back up and smiled. "I'm so happy you're okay."

"Thank you, Officer," she replied. "I'm glad you were here tonight."

"You have nothing to worry about, ma'am. It was clearly self-defense, and I'm sure the DA won't even look twice at this case."

Kassie puffed out a weak laugh. "Let's hope not. He's not my biggest fan, but he is a fair man."

Idris and the rest of the officers left, and Kassie turned to Lily. "Sorry we invaded your home tonight. They needed to process the scene and remove the... you know... the corpse."

"It's fine. I'll message Praveen and tell him it's okay to bring the boys back in a few minutes. I had him take them to a movie as soon as Monty called and told me you needed legal representation."

Kass wrapped an arm around my waist. "He seems to have forgotten I'm an attorney."

Lily rolled her eyes. "You are but remember what our law school professors always said: A lawyer who defends himself has a fool for a client."

"True, especially when the lawyer has a dead body in their house," she said with a shaky breath.

"I know this isn't Lil's specialty," I explained, "but I wanted someone here to make sure your rights were protected while you were being interviewed."

Lily took the ice pack from Kassie's right hand. "Do you need another one?"

Kass looked down and flexed her fingers. "No, I think it's good. Doesn't even hurt anymore."

"Okay, I'll just take this back to the kitchen."

As soon as she was gone, Kassie wrapped her arms around my neck and kissed my cheek. "Would you please say something to Hector? He looks miserable." Her eyes darted to the dining room where he was standing.

"He's going to be even more miserable when I kill his ass," I grunted.

"No, you're not," she said firmly, her eyes blazing. "It was my fault he wasn't here, not his."

"He shouldn't have left you."

"He did what I asked him to do and stayed with Sully. He's my baby and can't protect himself. I, on the other hand, can."

I couldn't help the upward curl of my lips. "That much is obvious. How are you feeling about everything that happened?"

She inhaled, her eyes rolling up in self-reflection. "Confused. I know I should be upset, but he was attacking me, so I did what I had to do. I didn't mean to kill him, but... I don't know. I'm a little freaked out by what I did, and at the same time, I'm relieved he's gone."

"It's hard taking a life, Kass, no matter the situation. I've had to do it once, in the line of duty. I killed a perp and protected an innocent woman. Once the adrenaline wore off, I felt guilty, even though I had no other choice. The department mandated that we speak with the psychiatrist on staff any time there was a loss of life, and she helped me sort out my feelings. I think that would be a good idea for you too. I'll be with you the entire time, if you want."

"Okay, I'll think about it." She poked my arm. "Now go talk to Hector and *be nice*. He's such a good guy, and he's struggling with this."

I crossed the room, biting back my anger as I approached the huge guard.

"Mr. Bouvier, I want you to know I'm so sorry. I fucked up so bad."

The sorrow and remorse in his eyes were like a splash of cold water to the face, and I patted his arm as I blew out a heavy sigh.

"No, you didn't, Hector. I hired you to protect both of them. Sometimes you have to make choices, and you chose to stay with the most vulnerable person. That was the right call. You didn't know this was going to happen."

His gaze flashed to Kassie, who was watching us. "I hope she's okay. I never wanted anything bad to happen to Miss Ramirez. I really like her." Then his brown eyes popped open wide. "Not like *that*. But like a sister."

I chuckled. "I knew what you meant. Why don't you go on home and get some rest. We'll see you on Monday."

"Y-you mean I'm not fired?"

"Not today," I said, lifting one eyebrow at him. "Go before I change my mind."

He scurried away—as much as a man who was six-foot-seven could scurry—and gave Kass a warm, brotherly hug before leaving.

My woman strolled across the room toward me, still wearing her work-out clothes that hugged her body like a glove. "Thank you," she said, reaching up to stroke her fingers down my cheek.

"When you look at me like that, I'd pretty much do anything you asked, sweetheart."

"What about this?" she asked, standing on her tiptoes and whispering something in my ear.

I jerked my head back as my eyebrows smashed together. "Kass, I'm not sure that's a good idea."

"Please, Monty? I have all this weird energy coursing through my body, and I don't know what to do with it." She waved her hands up and down her body. "I need you to take it away." Her teeth bit into her bottom lip as she looked up at me through her dark lashes. "Please, Sir?"

Fucking hell. How could I resist that?

We were back in room 2-B at Club E, as requested by my gorgeous woman. I'd bought a membership, and we'd been here a handful of times the past couple months. She'd declared this her favorite room.

We'd been fucking for hours. Kass had been tied up, spanked, and thoroughly eaten. I'd been in every hole in her body, except for one. However...

"You sure this is what you want, angel?" I asked as I pulled the anal plug from her ass and watched as the lube seeped out.

"Yes," she breathed, looking over her shoulder at me. "I want you to fill my ass."

Sweet Jesus!

Taking the bottle of lube, I squirted a thick dollop on the head of my cock and stroked myself until I was slick and ready.

My hands parted her ass cheeks, and I bit the inside of my cheek. I could come simply from looking at that pretty little hole. Lining myself up, I gripped her hips and pressed forward, groaning when the head slipped inside.

"I'm claiming this fucking ass as my own, Kass."

"It's yours," she panted, her hands tightening in the sheets beneath her.

I went easy at first, allowing her to acclimate to my size, but when she started rocking back against me, I slipped a hand between her legs.

"You're gonna come with my cock up your sweet ass, baby." My fingers found her clit and circled it as she lowered her chest to the bed, fully submitting to me.

My thrusts were hard and deep, my fingers nimble, as her body began to tremble. "Yessss. Monty, yes!"

"Fuck," I bit out as her back arched up and down while I rode her like a beast. "Fuck, you take me so well, Kass."

Twisting her hands in the sheets, she cried my name as her clit pulsed against my fingers. Her orgasm seemed to go on for a lifetime, and I slowed my pace as her hands relaxed against the mattress.

"I never thought that would feel so good," she moaned, and I leaned down to kiss the sweaty skin on the back of her neck.

"You okay?"

She nodded and twisted her head until I could see her eyes. "I want you to put your hand on my throat."

I stilled. "Kassie, no." Pulling slowly out of her back entrance, I turned her over. "I can't do that."

Her brown eyes held no fear, but still... hell no.

"I'm not scared of you, Monty. I trust you."

"Kassie, it's been an emotional night. We can talk about this later."

She picked up my palm and kissed it before placing it around her neck. "Don't squeeze. Just hold me like you own me. Also, if you could put your big dick back in my ass, that would be great."

I couldn't help but laugh. Releasing her neck, I pushed up until I was kneeling. "Roll your hips back for me."

She did, and I guided myself back into her tight hole. "You sure about this?" I asked, gliding one hand up her body and letting it rest at the top of her chest, just shy of where she'd asked me to hold her.

"Positive. I want this."

Slowly—*very slowly*—I allowed my hand to lightly grip her throat. Then I lifted her hand and kissed her palm before wrapping it around my own neck.

"What are you doing?" she asked, her brow creasing in confusion as she tried to pull her hand away. I kept it there with a firm grip on her slender wrist.

Leaning down to kiss her lips, my cock tunneled deeper inside her as I began to fuck her with long, measured strokes.

"I want you to know you own me too, Kass."

CHAPTER 58

"You'll see," Monty said, stopping in front of a storefront on a balmy summer night. It was light blue now instead of rose, but I recognized it immediately.

"Mont?" My voice was high and breathy. "This is where we got our wedding rings when we were teenagers."

He grinned and pulled me toward the door by my hand. When he opened the door and let me precede him into the jewelry store, my jaw dropped. The place looked like a smaller version of the bridal convention I'd gone to with Lily before she got married.

To my left, there were two bakers set up with a selection of wedding cakes. Next to them was a florist with every flower imaginable in large metal containers and then a table full of food and wine.

To the right, there was a rainbow of bridesmaid dresses on a rack, a freaking string trio playing soft classical music, and a woman with a display of wedding photos.

And directly in front of me were three wedding gowns on mannequins.

"Oh my god! Wh-what is this?"

When I turned back around, Monty Bouvier was down on one knee with a grin the size of Texas on his face.

"Kassie, this has been a long time coming, but it seems like just yesterday I was down on my knee in my bathroom—not exactly the most romantic place for a proposal, I'll admit, but I was seventeen."

I covered my giggling mouth with my hand as he continued. "I decided to up my game this time. I asked you to be my wife once, and you said yes. I'm hoping I'll get the same result this time." He took a deep breath, his chest rising and falling before he asked, "Kassie Ramirez, will you please do me the honor of marrying me?"

"Yes!" I yelled as soon as the words left his perfect mouth, and he swept a hand dramatically across his brow as everyone clapped.

That's when I realized that the clapping was awfully loud and turned to find our families and friends streaming in from the back room.

Sully waved happily from Regina's hip. "We're getting married, Mommy!" he yelled, and everyone laughed as Monty stood and took my hands.

"I want to give you a very raunchy kiss right now," he whispered, cupping my face, "but I'm gonna keep it low key because there are children present."

"Good plan," I whispered back. The kiss was sweet and tender and perfect before he pulled back.

"Go say hi to everyone, and then we need to pick out your ring."

"We are in a jewelry store, after all," I said, looking around and waving my hand. "Or I thought we were. What is all this?"

"It's your very own bridal extravaganza. I know you're a busy lady, so I was trying to make things easier on you by putting all the vendors under one roof."

"How many wedding gown designers are here?" I teased, and he leveled me with a playful glare.

"One. I will be designing my bride's dress." He gestured toward the three gorgeous gowns. "These are just samples, so you can change anything you don't like, or I could start from scratch."

"I already have my eye on that middle one."

He wrapped his arms around me and kissed my lips once more. "That's my favorite too. Let's go greet everyone, and then we can look at rings."

Twenty minutes later, everyone was milling around the room, looking at flowers and tasting small samples of cake, food, and wine, while Monty and I stood in front of a glass jewelry case.

"I've been waiting a long time for you two to come back," a frail voice said, and I looked down to see an elderly lady in a wheelchair. It took me a second, but I finally recognized her as the lady who had helped us so many years ago.

"Mrs. James, you're still here!"

"Hello, dear." Her smile was radiant, and I rounded the counter to give her a hug before returning to my fiancé's side. "I'm just here for today. My daughter runs the shop now."

She patted the arm of a young woman in a lavender blouse who gave us a little wave. "I'm Doreen. I was only a preteen when my mother came home raving about the most precious young couple she'd met that day. She's spoken of you two from time to time over the years, wondering whatever happened to you."

"I was wondering where the hell you were," the old lady grumped. "This fella told me he was coming back to buy a diamond." She pointed an accusing finger at Monty.

He chuckled and rocked back on his heels. "It took me longer than expected, but I made it. Thank you both so much for letting us take over your store for the evening."

"It's our pleasure. Now, let me show you the rings."

CHAPTER 59

"YOU LOOK SO HANDSOME, baby," I told my son, lightly brushing my fingers through the hair over his right ear. It was a tad crunchy, but at least it wasn't wild.

"Dad put some stuff in my hair so it would look nice for the wedding."

My heart swelled every time I heard Sully call Monty *Dad*. The adoption wasn't final yet, but it would be soon.

Five months had passed since Wesley Campbell died that night at my apartment. By my hand, or my knee, if you wanted to get technical. Yes, it had been inadvertent, and yes, he had tortured me from afar for years, but Monty had been correct. Taking a person's life brought up all kinds of foreign feelings.

I'd been working through it though, with the help of a wonderful counselor. Monty went with me to every session and held my hand, and I was in a good place now.

"Have you decided whether you want to stand up at the front or sit with the grandparents?"

He sighed like the weariest six-year-old in the world. "I just want to sit down. These shoes are killing me."

I stifled a laugh. "Okay, honey." When a knock sounded at the door, Sully rushed over to answer it. "Hey, Poppy G!" he said when Lily's dad entered.

"Hello, Sully. You look so nice." His brown eyes shifted to me, and his face softened. "And you look beautiful, dear. Are you ready to go?"

"Can you give me a moment, please?"

"Of course. I'll just take this little guy to the front of the church. We'll meet you there."

I kissed both of them, and once they were gone, I turned to stare at my reflection in the mirror. The ivory dress Monty had designed years ago fit me like a glove. It was absolutely stunning.

I smiled as I stared down at the custom-made marquise-cut diamond in a platinum setting that we'd picked out at my very own bridal extravaganza a few months ago. To our mutual surprise, Monty and I had both admitted that we'd kept our wedding bands from all those years ago. Well, I had his tucked away, and he had mine.

We'd truly come full circle.

"Today is my wedding day," I called aloud to the room, and I wiggled on the spot, the excitement taking over. "It's about damn time."

I made my way around to the front of the church and found Mr. Ganjam and Sully waiting for me in their black tuxedos.

"You look like a princess, Mommy," my son said. "So sparkly."

"I feel like a princess," I told him. "Are you ready to walk me down the aisle?"

He nodded vigorously, and I was impressed that his hair didn't move at all.

"The bridesmaids just walked down, so I'll go sit," Lily's dad said, kissing my cheek before bending to Sully. "After you get to the front, you come sit with us, okay, buddy?"

He gave the man a thumbs up. "I got this, bruh."

Good lord, I had no idea where he picked that up, but he called everyone *bruh* these days.

I stared at the back of Mr. Ganjam's balding head as he slipped through the giant wooden doors, and I ran a hand over the rhinestones covering the bodice of my trumpet-style dress.

These rhinestones had turned my fiancé into a full-blown groomzilla, and I giggled when I thought of the phone call I'd witnessed a couple months ago.

These rhinestones are total crap, you understand me? No, I know what Swarovski stones look like, and these are not them... These are for my wife, and sub-par rhinestones are completely unacceptable... Well, I suggest you get me eighteen gross of GENUINE Swarovskis tomorrow!

I had almost squealed in delight when he'd called me his wife. Other than Mommy, that was my favorite name ever.

The music inside the church changed, and the wedding coordinator appeared behind me, fluffing out my train. I liked her. She was unobtrusive and detail-oriented without being a micromanager.

"It's time," she said quietly, and two men in suits opened the double doors.

The sanctuary took my breath away. Dark purple and white roses were everywhere, interspersed with lavender buds that were so pale, they were almost silver.

As I took my first step, I glanced down at my handsome little Sully, and he met my eyes and hissed, "Remember to walk slow, Mom," in that little kid whisper that's not a whisper at all.

Low laughter rippled around the room. The pews were filled with those we loved and those who loved us. Monty and I were done letting anyone else influence our relationship. Now we surrounded ourselves with people that rooted for us every step of the way.

I avoided looking at the end of the aisle because I knew I would probably cry as soon as I saw my groom. My eyes fell on my brother, who had been able to come home for the weekend from where he was stationed in California. He gave me a hearty thumbs up.

I smiled at him and turned my head to see Monty's cousins from Texas. Blaire and Axel Broxton were there with their five kids, and Charli and Beau Atwood had brought their little boy and their ten-month-old.

Our immediate families were in the second pew, the first being left empty except for two white roses—one for Evie and one for Willow—and a white boutonniere for my father. Monty and I had decided together that we would honor our lost loved ones in this simple way.

As Sully and I passed that row, I finally lifted my eyes to the stage and found my gorgeous groom watching me with damp eyes.

He was wearing black pants and an ivory tuxedo jacket that perfectly matched my dress. His shirt and bowtie were in the same shade, and my heart did a crazy little gymnastics move when he dashed a tear away from his left eye.

Jogging down the steps, he bent and kissed our son's head. "You did a great job, Sul, but I can take it from here."

I bent and pressed my lips to his cheek. "Thank you, baby. I love you."

"I love you too, bruh," he said—again, quite loudly—before skipping to sit between my mother and Mrs. Ganjam.

Monty's eyes met mine, and he hooked my hand in the crook of his elbow. "I'm probably going to trip going up these steps because I can't stop looking at the most beautiful bride I've ever seen."

My cheeks flushed at his compliment, and I held on tighter to his arm. "Please don't fall or you'll take me down with you, and then we might get blood on our clothes."

He chuckled and pulled his eyes away long enough for us to mount the three steps. "The church looks amazing," I said quietly. "It's absolutely perfect."

As we turned to face each other, Monty held my face tenderly in his hands and whispered the words that were inscribed on the insides of the wedding bands we would exchange in a few short minutes.

"If I'm with you, it's perfect."

EPILOGUE

"WELL, THAT WAS A wonderful honeymoon," Mrs. Ganjam said.

"Agreed," Lorna Ramirez said as she relaxed in the seat beside the other woman on our family's jet. "Thank you for inviting us, Monty."

Yes, we'd taken Mrs. G and my mother-in-law on our honeymoon—we had our reasons.

I hitched the boy I considered my son up my chest as he slept. We'd only lifted off ten minutes ago, and Sully was already snoozing.

"You could put him on the bed," Kassie Bouvier said, rubbing her hand up and down his back.

"Nah, I want to hold him. I haven't seen him in a week."

"You could put *me* on the bed," she said, wiggling her eyebrows at me.

"I plan on it, wife, after those two go to sleep." I nodded at the two giggling ladies who were already halfway through a bottle of wine.

"Look at them. They look so relaxed. Thank you for bringing them."

"Well, we were gone for a month, and neither of us wanted to leave Sully for that long, especially since we would be honeymooning during Christmas."

"Grandma patrol to the rescue," Kass said, tilting her head over onto my shoulder.

"It was nice having them along. We could spend time with Sully and then hand him over to the spoilers-in-chief so we could have time for ourselves."

"And so we could go on our private cruise this past week."

I winked at her. "I enjoyed rocking your boat all day and all night for seven days, Mrs. Bouvier."

"And I enjoyed being rocked," she said, nipping at my earlobe. "I feel thoroughly used."

"So do I," I said, sighing dramatically. "You're insatiable, woman."

"That's why you married me."

"I married you because I love you to my very soul, Kassie Bouvier."

"I love you too, baby."

Another round of laughter from the grandmothers brought both our heads around. "This trip was good for them too, I think."

My wife—I loved how that sounded—nodded. "Neither of them have ever traveled outside the U.S. They both really seemed to enjoy France."

"And did my wife enjoy France?"

"Oui, oui, Monsieur Bouvier," she replied, sliding the backs of her fingers down my face. "It was so sweet of you to invite Mrs. G to go too."

My eyes slid back to the two lovely women who were staring at a phone and laughing hysterically at whatever they were watching.

"Now that she's finished her chemo and is in remission, I thought she deserved a nice vacation." I brought my gaze back to Kassie's. "I love how she's always treated you and Sully as her family. So now she's my family too."

My wife—see how awesome that sounds?—snuggled closer, and I wrapped one arm around her shoulders, using the other to hold our boy.

"I love our little family," Kass said.

"Including that baby I put in you on our honeymoon?"

Her pretty lips tilted up into a smile. "You don't know that. I just got off my birth control a couple months ago."

"Babe, if the sheer volume of cum I put inside you in the last month doesn't get you knocked up, I'm not sure what will."

She giggled. "That's true."

Less than an hour later, the grandma patrol was asleep, and I laid Sully in the reclined chair beside me and buckled him safely in. After giving one of the flight attendants a signal to keep an eye on him, I took my wife's hand and led her toward the bedroom at the back of the plane.

"Time for us to join the mile high club," I murmured.

"We already joined that," she retorted.

"Oh yeah. Well, I think we need to renew our membership."

Peeling my eyes open, I rolled over and checked the time on my phone. We'd been home for around twenty-four hours, and Kassie and Sully were still passed out next to me in the bed.

Jet lag was a bitch.

Noticing a text from Auburn asking me to call him, I rolled from the bed and carried my phone down the hallway. I took care of my business in one of the spare bathrooms before trudging into the kitchen to make a cup of coffee.

I put one of the little pods in the machine and turned it on before dialing my brother. "Hey," I said. My voice sounded like I'd been asleep for an entire day, scratchy and unused.

"Hey, bro. How was your trip?"

"Absolutely fantastic. How did everything go while I was away?"

"Work was good, but I need to tell you something."

"You're firing me already?" I joked.

"No, it's about Dad."

My fuzzy mind was on the work track, so I asked, "Oh, is he wanting to come back to the office part time?"

"No. Look, first of all, he's okay."

His tone had me concerned, and I paused as I reached for the coffee cup filled with hot brew. "What do you mean he's okay? Why wouldn't he be okay?"

"He's in the hospital. They think he had a mild heart attack."

Panic swept through me, fully awakening my sluggish brain.

"Fuck, which hospital? I'm on the way."

Auburn met me beside the elevators on the cardiac floor and instantly began talking as we walked with swift feet. "I just got here a couple minutes ago, and the nurse filled me in. It was a heart attack, but he's okay. They're going to put a stent in later today."

"Have you seen him yet? Is he conscious?"

"No, I was about to go in when you texted that you were here, so I decided to wait for you. The nurse said he's been awake, and there's someone with him."

As we approached a door on the right, a nurse in dark-blue scrubs nodded politely and indicated that we could enter.

Paul Bouvier was sitting up on the hospital bed, and I was relieved that he looked pretty damn good for a man who'd suffered a cardiac arrest. Maybe a little pale but otherwise like normal.

He smiled when we entered—in that way parents do when they see their children. Full of love and happiness that they are in the presence of their offspring.

I waved to the person sitting in the chair beside him, and they returned my gesture with a small smile.

"Boys! I'm glad to see you. I'm sorry to have interrupted your Saturday," Dad said.

"Hush up, young man," I said because he didn't look like an old man. He looked like... *Dad*. Leaning over him, I pressed a kiss against his forehead, and he gripped the back of my neck and held me there for a long moment.

"Did you have a nice honeymoon?"

"It was perfect, Dad. What's going on with you?"

Auburn had rounded the bed and sat on the edge of it, resting a hand on our father's shin. "The nurse said you're having some heart issues."

"It's fine. Just a minor incident."

"A heart attack," Auburn corrected, and our father waved a dismissive hand.

"That's what they're calling it."

"Because that's what it was," my brother replied gently. "Don't downplay it. You've never had heart problems before. At least not that you've shared with me."

Dad shook his head. "No, this is the first time. Surprised me as much as anyone, but the doc said he's going to do a minor surgery on me today and get me back into fighting shape."

"That's good. We'll be here the whole time," I said, resting a hand on his shoulder.

He glanced around at each of us, and I saw the barest hint of fear in his blue eyes. "I wanted to talk to you about something before they put me under. I was going to tell you the day after Chloe's funeral, but I thought I'd dropped enough on you for one afternoon."

That's the damn truth.

Dad smiled weakly before continuing. "And then it never seemed to be quite the right time. Monty, you moved back, there was all the wedding planning, and then our sweet Janie started walking. I didn't want to overshadow all that."

Little Jane had indeed learned to walk again, after being in that wheelchair since she was two. The entire family had taken a trip to the beach and all the theme parks in Florida for six fun days to celebrate.

"Well, now we're focused on you, Dad," Auburn said. "What do you need to talk to us about?"

"I'm just going to say it." He paused and we nodded. His eyes darted between the three people sitting around his hospital bed. Three sets of blue eyes. Something poked at the back of my brain.

"Auburn, Monty..." Dad took a deep breath, and the person beside his chair reached out and gripped his hand. Dad gave him a grateful look before turning back to us.

After the longest pause in the world, he spoke the words I never could have imagined.

"Cruz is your brother."

THE END... for now.

Well, alrighty then!

Ladies and gents, start your engines. A new Bouvier brother has entered the chat. You know what that means... Cruz gets his own book! Are you excited? I know I am.

You'll see more of the current cast of characters—as well as some new ones—in Book Three of the Bouvier Family Saga.

You may be asking yourself, "What the hell, Jade?" Or maybe you've already worked it out in your pretty little heads. But don't you worry. I'll lay out the entire story for you and answer all your questions.

How did this happen?

What is Cruz's kink that he's too embarrassed to share with Monty?

And the most important question: Is sweet, spunky Lehra into it?

You'll get it all in ***Love Without Demands***, so go check it out! Available on Amazon, or you can order signed paperbacks from my website: www.jadedollston.com

ALSO BY JADE

The Rest of the Bouvier Family Saga

IF YOU HAVEN'T READ Auburn and Gianna's book, you need to check out **Love Without Numbers**. Their age gap story is so beautiful! And steamy AF. Daddy vibes, anyone? It's available to read for free on Amazon Kindle Unlimited, or you can purchase the ebook or paperback.

And I have BIG, BIG news... LWN is now available on audiobook, exclusively on Audible and Amazon! Narrators JF Harding and Emma Wilder bring this one to life, and I hope you'll give it a listen. Get your fire extinguishers ready because if you thought Daddy Auburn was hot on paper, just wait till you can actually HEAR him call ~~Gianna~~ me a good girl.

Love Without Demands, Book 3
Love Without Control Book 4 (series complete)

The Fierce Protectors Series features six super-hot, possessive, growly former Navy SEALs who live to love and protect their women. They're all available on Amazon.

Dauntless Protector- Beau and Charli's Story
Devoted Protector – Tank and Bristol's Story

Deadly Protector – Cam and Shiloh's Story
Young Protector – Cam and Shiloh's Prequel Novella
Disgruntled Protector – Woody and Taz's Story
Determined Protector – Bode and Landree's story
Damaged Protector – Hawk and Mallori's Story

Standalones

The (Kinda) Secret Pineapple Island Swingers' Resort *If you love laugh-out-loud rom-coms, vacation flings gone rogue, and a hero who definitely knows how to handle his (hockey) stick, The "Kinda" Secret Pineapple Island Swingers' Resort is your next must-read.*
Rating the Book Boyfriend – Hilarious Holiday Rom-Com
Delay of Game – Angsty, funny sports romance
I Dream of Johnny – Genie Rom-Com

Highway to Hale Series
Coming in 2025

Follow the Hale Family, owners of Hale Cosmetics, in their amusing and dramatic search for love.

Book 1: Hale Yes
Book 2: Hale No
Book 3: Hale Damage
Book 4: All Hale the Queen

(Titles and order of books subject to change.)

Did you enjoy reading about Arizona Abbott and Layton Lancaster, the softball and baseball stars that Sully and Kassie met in the park? Well, they have their very own book – written by my best friend, the amazingly talented **AK Landow!** The name of the book is **Double Play**, and this author really knocked it out of the park on this one! (See what I did there?) Go check it out and thank me later.

For a good time, hit me up on my socials (Facebook, Instagram, and TikTok). You can also order signed paperbacks on my website, jadedollston.com

ACKNOWLEDGEMENTS

FIRST OF ALL, THANK you so much to my **readers**. It means so much that you took a chance on an indie author, and I appreciate the time you took to read **Love Without Influence.** I love when readers reach out to me while they're reading, so feel free to do so on my social media platforms that are listed on the "Also by Jade" page.

To the fabulous TL Swan: Thank you so much for your encouragement, advice, and humor. If it weren't for you, my stories would still be collecting virtual cobwebs on my computer.

To my beta readers: You chickies are amazing! Lakshmi, Mindy and Thorunn, my days would not be complete without seeing you three argue in the comments. I'll keep writing just for this reason. Also, thanks for the "inspirational" Instagram reels you send me. I adore each of you. AK, LA, and Neena – thank you so much for always keeping me on my toes. Your insights are invaluable, and I couldn't do this without you.

AK Landow: You're my sister from another mister. My book signing roomie. My book bestie. You're an amazing author, and you inspire me every day with your brilliance. Thanks for hashing out every single detail that goes into publishing a book with me. (But seriously, do you REALLY like the L in this font, or should I switch to another one?)

Carolina Jax, and LA Ferro: Thank you all for being such wonderful and supportive friends. It's so awesome to have people who will tell you like it is while always having your back.

Chrisandra: You are the most amazing editor in the history of ever. Thank you for the REAL TALK and for your confidence in me and my writing. I'm also so happy to be your fave – but don't worry... I won't tell the others!

Chanel, Becca, and Kalie of Good Girls PA services: Wow! I am so freaking lucky I've found you ladies. Thank you for handling business like boss bitches so that I can spend more time writing. Your support means everything to me.

To my ARC and Street Teams: I honestly couldn't do this without you! I love getting to know all of you in the groups, and I just want you to know that I think you're the most amazing, beautiful, fun, book-pimping people on Earth. So keep pimping! Mama's got hot pics to buy for her covers.

About the Author

Jade Dollston is a Texas author who loves reading, Doritos, and rum. She is married to her high school sweetheart, and they have one amazing daughter.

Her love of reading all things smutty has turned into a love of writing all things smutty. She enjoys a diverse selection of romance, and this is reflected in her writing style. Be prepared to laugh, cry, cringe, and fan your face, possibly all in a single chapter.

Jade is so excited to share her work with the world and hopes that you enjoy reading the words from her heart.